The Price of Love

The Price of Love

The Legacy Series – Book Three

by

Vicki Hopkins

To order additional copies of this book contact:

Holland Legacy Publishing
www.hollandlegacypub.com

Dedication

To my wonderful readers who found this series worth following. Thank you for allowing me to entertain you with a story of innocence, deception, and love. Remember that everything carries a price.

TABLE OF CONTENTS

Prologue

Confession is Good for the Soul

Lillian Goddard stood at the foot of the bed watching the doctor as he listened to her sister's labored breathing. He rose from his hovered position and shook his head.

"I'm afraid she is no better. Her lungs are filled with fluid, and the fever has not broken." He spoke compassionately. "Madame, you must prepare yourself for the inevitable. Your sister is at death's door."

Lillian's lower lip quivered as she watched Dorcas labor for each breath. "She's been delirious, doctor, mumbling on and on about a baby."

"What baby?"

"I'm not sure," she answered, wringing her hands together. "It's been very strange."

The doctor returned his medical instruments to his black leather case and snapped it shut. "A high fever will make the gravely ill delirious. Try to give her enough fluids to drink and make her comfortable. I'll check back in the morning."

Lillian escorted the physician to the door, giving him a parting word of thanks before returning to her sister's bedside. Each laborious breath broke her heart. She sat on the edge of the bed and looked lovingly into Dorcas' pale and sweaty face. "Dorcas, I'm here," she whispered.

Her hand brushed a matted strand of wet hair from her sister's brow. Then to her surprise, Dorcas reached up and clutched her wrist. Her eyelids fluttered, and she gasped.

"I must tell him."

"Tell who, dear?" Lillian clutched her sister's hand and squeezed it tight.

"Monsieur Moreau."

"I don't understand." She leaned forward in order to hear her muffled voice. "Who is Monsieur Moreau?"

"Write...write this down...before I die. I must confess," she exclaimed in desperation.

Her voice rose to near hysteria. A fitful attack of coughing silenced her sister's voice. After it passed, she lifted her index finger and pointed to the other side of the room.

"Over there...open the drawer," she said, looking at the dresser.

Lillian rose and stood before the furniture piece. "Which drawer, Dorcas?" she asked, looking at the four closed drawers.

"The top..."

Dorcas gasped for a breath again. Lillian halted, stunned to hear her sister's lungs gurgling in her chest.

"Please hurry," Dorcas implored.

She pulled open the drawer and rifled through its contents. At the bottom, a tattered, leather booklet lay hidden beneath her undergarments.

"Is this what you're talking about?" She pulled the book out and held it up.

"Yes. Bring it here."

Lillian returned to the bedside and sat down. Dorcas placed her hand on the cover over the embossed word *Diary*. Tears filled her sister's swollen eyelids.

"Angelique...her name is Angelique Jolene von Lamberg."

Still confused, Lillian cocked her head as she listened. "Who is Angelique?"

"The daughter of my mistress," she began. "But...but she is not her daughter."

Even more confused, Lillian thought the fever that racked her sister's body had taken over her senses. "I don't understand what you mean, Dorcas. You are ill, and your mind is playing tricks on you."

"No, no tricks," she began to weep. Dorcas' face contorted into a mixture of sorrow and fear. "Kidnapped— she took the child from her rightful mother and father."

"Who took her?"

"The duchess—I mean the countess."

"Duchess—countess—who are you talking about, Dorcas? You are making no sense whatsoever." Lillian raised her voice in frustration exasperated about her sister's babbling.

"The Duchess of Surrey, Jacquelyn Holland."

"But wasn't your last mistress Countess von Lamberg?"

"No." Dorcas' voice choked. "She was the same lady I served for many years, the duchess."

A coughing spree silenced her sister again. Lillian set the diary on the nightstand and took Dorcas' hand to give her strength. Distraught over the painful and violent heaving of the congestion that threatened to drown her life, she closed her eyes and prayed. *Dearest Lord, have mercy upon her in this hour of suffering.*

Lillian took a damp washcloth and wiped her sister's fevered brow one more time. None of her comments made sense. Surely, she had been confused over her former mistress.

"Now, calm yourself, Dorcas. You are making yourself worse bringing up memories of the past. No more talk of kidnapping."

"I must ask forgiveness and tell Monsieur Moreau and..."

"And who else?"

"His wife..." A desperate look filled her eyes. "A priest...I need a priest, Lillian, please," she begged. "I must confess my sins."

Lillian didn't know whether to believe or scoff at her sister's ranting. None of it made sense. "Why didn't you say something before, Dorcas?"

"Afraid...I was afraid of prison because I helped." Her eyes fluttered. Dorcas opened her lips once more. "Read my diary. All is revealed within." She heaved a gurgling sigh and closed her eyes exhausted.

Lillian picked up the diary that she had set on the nightstand and looked closely at the tattered book. A fragile binding held a collection of wrinkled and torn pages. She flipped to the first and noted the date *July 7, 1876 - Diary of Dorcas Kirby*. The entry spoke of her new position as lady's maid to Jacquelyn Spencer. Upon a quick glance of the remaining contents, it appeared that Dorcas had recorded years of service.

Her attention had been taken away from her sister for a few minutes until she realized she no longer heard raspy breaths. "Dorcas!"

Lillian dropped the diary to the floor and embraced her sister. There had been no time to fetch a priest for confession. "Dear God have mercy on her soul," she cried, weeping over her body.

After a few minutes of intense tears, Lillian rose from the bed and lifted the sheet over her sister's face unable to bear the sight. "Be at peace, Dorcas." Her lip quivered. As she stared at the shroud, Lillian knew in her heart that no rest would come to her sister's purgatorial soul until she discovered the secrets hidden in the tattered diary.

Lillian picked up the book from the floor and traced the embossed, fading word *Diary* with her index finger. As she flipped through the pages, an envelope dropped to her feet. Lillian recognized her sister's penmanship. She picked it up and saw that it had been addressed to Lady Angelique Jolene von Lamberg in Vienna. The unsealed envelope beckoned her to read its secrets. After unfolding the paper, she noted the date. It had been penned a week ago, about the time she fell ill. Unable to leave its contents a private matter between her and the addressee, she read the letter.

Angelique,

I doubt that you will remember me. You were only three years old when your mother passed away, and I left her employment. My conscience is burdened, and I am compelled to write this letter. You may not believe my words, but at least I will know that I have confessed my complicity in a grievous and sinful act.

The woman you knew as Jacquelyn Bennett, your supposed mother, had not been whom she claimed to be. Her identity and marriage to your stepfather had been perpetrated in deceit and lies. You see, I served your mother as her lady's maid for many years and had been well acquainted with her true identity—she was the Duchess of Surrey, Jacquelyn Spencer-Holland. In a moment of deep hurt, she kidnapped you from your father and mother and fled to Austria. I helped her to accomplish that awful deed. We boarded a train never to be heard from or found again. Her broken heart drove her to desperation.

Years earlier, my mistress had wed Lord Robert Holland of Surrey, England. For years, she bore the shame and heartache of being barren. I shared her sorrow every month. During this time, unbeknownst to her, his lordship had a Parisian mistress. His lover was your mother, Suzette Rousseau.

When she became pregnant with his son, she returned to Paris and married a man by the name of Philippe Moreau. Five years later, you were born of that union, and they named you Angelique. Jacquelyn gave you the name of Jolene.

It is during this time that much happened between all involved. Another adulterous affair ensued between your mother and Robert Holland. My mistress had been terribly hurt when she discovered her husband's unfaithfulness. An opportunity presented itself to ease her pain by bringing about her revenge upon all involved.

At the age of three months, your father entrusted your care into her hands for a short period. Her promise was to keep you for a day, but instead she kidnapped you from your mother and father. To my disgrace, I helped her because of my loyalty to my mistress.

I have no doubt, even though she committed a horrible wrong, that she loved you very much. She married your stepfather and finally experienced a happy marriage to replace the sorrows of the past.

I tell you this now to clear my conscience because I fear death and judgment. Perhaps I should have spoken the truth after your mother died, but I was a coward running from lawful punishment for my participation. Now, I fear the judgment of God and beg for His mercy and your forgiveness.

In closing, I encourage you to seek out those who grieve over your loss. They have every right to know of the outcome of that terrible act and that you are alive and well.

Your humble servant, Dorcas Kirby

When she had reached her closing lines, the tears upon Lillian's face dropped onto the envelope. She brushed them off, careful not to smear the inked address. With a sorrowful face, she looked at her sister's motionless body underneath the sheet. Loyalty had been a strong trait in Dorcas, which apparently held resilient regardless of her employer's actions.

Carefully, she folded the letter and inserted it back into the envelope. She would seal and post it after her sister's funeral, in hopes that the person to whom it was addressed would read its contents. It would fulfill Dorcas' last wishes. Her confession would be spoken. Whether the young woman would believe or forgive, Lillian had to leave in the hands of the Almighty.

As far as the diary, it held too many secrets of Dorcas' life to ignore. Lillian wanted to know them all, and she determined to read every word. When finished with its story, she would hide it away for safekeeping should it be needed in the future.

Chapter 1

Vienna 1905 - A Buried Past

Angelique Jolene von Lamberg tightened the black, wool scarf about her neck. The interior of the coach on a late snowy March day chilled her to the bone. Only a few days ago the temperatures had risen above freezing, melting the remaining winter snow. As if teased by Mother Nature that spring had arrived, she brusquely plunged Vienna into another wintery blast.

The carriage rolled slowly along the snow-covered streets while motorcars passed on their left. Jolene smiled in fascination at the new mode of transportation she had not had the opportunity to enjoy. Secretly, she wished her stepfather would have wanted the modern invention and purchased a new brass carriage, but he never felt inclined to do so.

"It would snow today." Her companion complained through chattering teeth. "Could the day be more miserable than this?"

Her poor elderly aunt sat huddled in the corner, wrapped in a blanket about her legs for warmth. "I am as disappointed as you, Auntie," Jolene replied. She tucked the woven cloth close to her aunt's body.

"We should have had the solicitor come to the estate, Jolene. I'll catch my death from this cold."

"I'm so sorry for insisting that we go out. It's so dreary and lonely in that huge house without father." Her brow furrowed over the thought of his death. "I thought the fresh air would do us good."

"Good? We shall be frozen by the time we reach the solicitor's office." Geraldine continued to whine.

"Now, now, Auntie, it's not that bad," Jolene said soothingly. She reached over and patted her aunt's arm. "We'll be there before we know it."

Her grumpy aunt peered out the window, and Jolene turned her head away to glance out the other. It had been a difficult few months. Lung cancer swiftly took her stepfather's life. The strong man that she once knew withered into a weak frame of skin and bones. As a loving daughter, she attended to his needs, spoke of her love and devotion, and then finally buried him a week ago.

To add to the stressful situation, a letter had arrived in the post only weeks before that had turned her life upside down. Anger and confusion over such a ludicrous message had morphed into confusion and speculation about her identity. It could not have come at a worse time in her life. Instead of taking regard to its contents, she had shoved the letter into a drawer and overlooked it until today. Frankly, she had neither time nor spirit to give it much thought.

After arriving from Berlin for the funeral, her aunt had insisted on remaining until all matters regarding her brother's estate had closed. Even though her aunt lived in Berlin with her husband, Geraldine had been the matriarch of the von Lamberg family. She cared for her brother's welfare when he became a widower. When he adopted Jolene as his daughter, her aunt wholeheartedly received her as a von Lamberg. In fact, her aunt had been the only female influence in her life since the death of her mother. Jolene relied upon her for wisdom and guidance.

As she grew into a young girl, she dispensed with the name of Angelique, complaining that it sounded too French. With a strong surname of von Lamberg, Jolene exuded the essence of her character. When she turned thirteen, her stepfather and aunt indulged her choice and ceased calling her Angelique. Though it remained her given legal name, no one spoke it for the past five years.

"We are almost there, and the driver is slowing," Jolene announced, pointing out the window at the beige building approaching in the distance.

"Well, it's about time," her aunt sputtered with blue lips. "I'm frozen to the bone."

The driver opened the carriage door and helped her aunt out onto the snowy sidewalk. Jolene followed close behind. The icy pavement made it difficult for their shoes to grip the walkway underneath. Afraid that her frail aunt would tumble, she grabbed her sleeve.

"Give me your arm, Auntie," Jolene insisted. She glanced at the driver. "Please wait here, this shouldn't take long."

He nodded at her request and then huddled underneath the overhang of the front entrance to escape the frozen wonderland of fluffy flakes.

Jolene stomped her feet on the carpet inside the doorway of the solicitor's office, and her aunt followed suit.

"Horrible weather. Just dreadful," her aunt grumbled, brushing the snowflakes off her coat.

"Here, let me help you." Jolene flicked off the residue from her red fox collar.

"Komtesse, welcome. May I take your coats?" The clerk greeted them with a friendly but professional smile.

"Not mine," Geraldine barked.

"No, that's fine," Jolene said. "I'll keep mine on as well."

"Very well, then. Please come in and take a seat, and I will let Herr Wilhelm know that you have arrived."

"Thank you." Jolene escorted her aunt over to a nearby seat. "Sit down, Auntie," she instructed, helping her into a wingback chair. She stood by her side and thought about the strangeness of her new position.

"It sounds so peculiar when I am addressed as komtesse," she mused aloud.

The eyes of her aunt twinkled. "You should get used to it, my dear, for you now hold the title passed onto you from the count. Until you are married, of course, you are komtesse. Once you wed, you shall be a countess and whatever married name you acquire. It is an honor that your father wished you would carry with pride."

Jolene pondered the responsibilities she had unexpectedly inherited, as well as the wealth and prestige that now belonged to her at the young age of eighteen. There were moments in which she felt well prepared due to her stepfather's instruction. On the other hand, she also entertained periods of doubt when her confidence waned. She felt like an inadequate orphan entrusted with a task that had far exceeded her capabilities.

"Herr Wilhelm will see you now."

"Let me help you," Jolene said, reaching out and taking her aunt's hand. Jolene gave her a little pull to her feet aware of her arthritic knees. She held her aunt's arm to give her stability as they entered the office.

"Komtesse, you should have let me come to the estate." Herr Wilhelm stepped forward to greet their arrival.

Jolene glanced through the tall window overlooking the street. The snow continued to fall in steady streams of white fluff. "It's no bother, Herr Wilhelm," Jolene said, smiling demurely at him. "I desired a bit of fresh air. But who would have known the storm would be so severe?"

"I told her you should have come," her aunt grumbled. She scurried over to the chair by the fireplace. "At least it is warm here," she said, turning her face into the heat of the flames.

"Warm yourselves," he encouraged. "Would you like a cup of tea or coffee before the reading?"

"Hot tea sounds appealing," Jolene replied. "Auntie, would you like a cup as well?"

"Yes, tea, please," she replied, rubbing her gloved hands together.

"Very well then, my clerk shall have that for you momentarily." Herr Wilhelm called to his assistant giving him orders to make a hot brew. Afterward, he sat down behind his desk.

Jolene positioned herself in front of him upon an empty leather chair. She noted the look in his downturned eyes expressing empathy for her current state of affairs. Nonetheless, she wished to assure him that regardless of her situation she had handled her grief with a mature inner strength.

After all, she had braced herself well before her stepfather's death. In their last days together, they had intimate and candid conversations regarding their love for one another. The count expressed his pride in her as a young woman and confidence that she would continue with honor the von Lamberg family name in his absence.

"I am coping, Herr Wilhelm," she said, sensing his hesitancy to inquire. "The funeral is over, and we buried father with the honor he deserved." Jolene lowered her eyes to the papers on the desk. "I am only anxious about my future."

"Well, you should not be," he said. The solicitor placed the palm of his hand on top of the folded document lying on the center of his desk.

"But I am adopted," Jolene added with a crease of her brow. After all, she was not a blood relative of the von Lamberg family, and it sowed seeds of insecurity about her position.

"Your father did everything legally, I can assure you."

"Are you certain?"

"Absolutely. Since he had no living heir, the count petitioned the Emperor to adopt you into the von Lamberg family." Herr Wilhelm clasped his hands together and leaned forward. "You, young lady, have the Sovereign's approval to inherit not only your father's estate and wealth but his title as well."

The clerk entered with two cups of steaming tea upon a wooden tray, offering each of them the hot brew.

"Oh thank you, kind sir." Geraldine replied. She took the cup and saucer and lifted the hot liquid to her lips. "Oh, just what I needed," she moaned.

"Well then, shall we proceed with the reading?" Herr Wilhelm looked at Jolene for confirmation.

"Yes, by all means," Jolene replied. Her focus remained on the papers beneath his hands.

Herr Wilhelm placed his reading glasses on the bridge of his nose. "This is the Last Will and Testament of Count Eduard Karl von Lamberg of Vienna, Austria," he began. He cleared his throat and lifted his eyes to Jolene.

"I'm listening," she told him as if he needed reassurance.

"I, Eduard Karl von Lamberg, hereby bequeath to my daughter, Angelique Jolene von Lamberg, my estate in its entirety. If I should die before my daughter attains the age of twenty-one, I request that one-fourth of my estate be given to her forthright, managed by my appointed executor. The remaining three-fourths shall be held in trust until her twenty-first birthday, with the exception of my lands, residences, and her mother's jewels, which I immediately bequeath to her in their entirety for her use and benefit."

Herr Wilhelm stopped and raised his eyes to look at Jolene. He had left everything to her. She turned her head and glanced warily at her Aunt Geraldine, who displayed a satisfied smile.

"I'm sorry," Jolene said, feeling the need to apologize. Her father had left nothing of his fortune to his sister.

"You have nothing to be sorry for, my dear. I knew of the contents of your father's will before his death. We had discussed his wishes in considerable detail. Besides, I am a rich old lady as it is. I do not need my late brother's fortune."

"But you are his sister." Jolene felt the need to protest once more.

"This is your heritage, not mine." Her aunt replied with conviction.

Jolene felt as if she should weep over his generosity, but she did not. Instead, she carried an undeserving guilt. After all, she was not the natural blood daughter of Eduard von Lamberg. Yes, he had been the only father she knew. Vague memories remained of her mother, when at the age of three, she tossed a rose upon her coffin.

"You are one of the richest women in Vienna," her solicitor spoke. "But I would give you a word of caution as the executor of your father's estate." Herr Wilhelm cleared his throat once more and leaned forward.

"And what would that be?" She cocked her head to the right waiting for his cautionary words.

"You should be careful with potential suitors, who may look to you as a means for riches."

Instantly, her aunt agreed. "Herr Wilhelm is absolutely right. Jolene, you must use caution. Men can have ulterior motives."

Jolene smiled, thinking the advice overly vigilant. Had they thought she possessed some weakness in this area of her character? In her mind, no one could ever deceive her heart. "I doubt very much that any man will trick me into marrying me for my money. Nevertheless, I thank you for the advice." Jolene did not want to sound impolite.

Herr Wilhelm appeared satisfied with her response and leaned back in his chair. "Good then," he began in a businesslike prose. "I need your signature upon these papers to open an account at the bank where I will deposit your inheritance. Since you are eighteen years of age, I shall release one-fourth of your father's funds and place the remaining three-fourths in trust until you have obtained the age of twenty-one."

He handed her a pen and Jolene perused the documents.

"Where do I sign?" Jolene asked, leaning toward the solicitor's desk.

"Here on this line," he pointed.

Jolene penned her name boldly. A broad smile spread across her face at the thought of the future.

"I shall draw up the necessary deeds to have the residence and property immediately transferred into your name," he added.

Jolene's thoughts were elsewhere as she finished signing her name. "I am going to travel," she announced. "I have never left Austria, and it is time to see the world."

"Alone?" Her aunt sounded like a parrot squawking.

"Yes alone. I'll bring my attendant with me, of course."

Herr Wilhelm scowled. "I agree with your aunt that a woman traveling alone, especially at your age, is unwise."

"Where will you go?" Her aunt demanded in an abrupt voice.

"I've always wanted to visit Paris and London," she responded nonchalantly.

"I don't think your father would approve," Geraldine replied.

Jolene set the pen on the solicitor's desk and turned toward her aunt. "Father protected me far too much, Auntie. After mother's death, he sheltered me for fear of losing another family member. He would never let me go anywhere unescorted or barely leave the city. I have spent the majority of my life schooled and housed behind closed doors."

"I agree he was an attentive and protective father. Nevertheless, he had his reasons," her aunt said, defending her brother's actions.

"Well, I no longer need protection," she said. Agitated she rose to her feet in protest. "I'd like to leave within a week, Herr Wilhelm. Will you please obtain cheques from the bank that I may use for my travel and a fair amount of crowns for my purse?"

"Yes, of course. As you wish, Lady von Lamberg," he relented with a disagreeable tone.

The time had come to discuss the other topic that lay buried in the bottom of her purse. "Auntie, I need a private consultation with Herr Wilhelm. Would you excuse us for a moment?"

Her request sounded strange as both of them glanced at her wide-eyed. Her aunt flashed a look at the solicitor and back at Jolene. She rose to her feet grimacing over the pain in her knees.

"Of course," she said, shuffling her way to the door. "I'll wait in the lobby."

Jolene paused until the door closed and then sat back down in front of Herr Wilhelm. The irritation over the letter that threatened to turn her world upside down loomed to the forefront of her mind.

"Herr Wilhelm, I need your assurance that my inheritance and title can never be taken from me." She paused, clutching her hands together. "Am I truly adopted in the eyes of the law as the daughter of Count von Lamberg?"

Herr Wilhelm leaned back in his chair and looked at Jolene with a befuddled expression. "Yes, you may be assured. In fact, I have your adoption papers here in my safekeeping, signed by Franz Joseph himself. Do you wish to see them?"

"That will not be necessary," she said. "I would, however, like the papers delivered into my hand upon my twenty-first birthday."

"That can be arranged, after the disbursement of the remainder of the inheritance."

"Thank you," she said, creasing her brow and still struggling with doubt.

"Why, might I ask, do you inquire of me in private regarding this matter?"

Jolene bit her lower lip. She opened the clasp to her purse and pulled out the letter. "What I am about to show you, Herr Wilhelm, shall not leave this office." She held the letter up for him to see. "Swear to me on your honor before I hand this over," she sternly implored.

"You have my word, of course," he replied, clearly concerned over the appeal.

"Then I shall tell you why, and I would sincerely appreciate your advice."

Jolene leaned forward and laid the letter before him. "I received this in the post about a month before father passed away." She stared at the paper, sanctioning her own distrust in the contents. "It shocked me, and I purposely kept it from father for fear that it would upset him."

He reached across the desk and took the envelope. Without examining the address, he pulled out the correspondence. After adjusting his spectacles on the bridge of his nose, he read the contents. A minute later, his eyes bulged, and his nostrils flared.

"Good Lord in heaven above," his voice boomed like a clap of thunder. "Who is this woman that pens these accusations? Do you know her?"

Almost jumping out of her chair over his reaction, she answered. "No, I do not. I have no recollection of the lady's maid who attended my mother. She claims to have been with her since her youth. Truthfully, I don't know what to believe." She inhaled a deep breath to calm her jitters.

"Rubbish," the solicitor grumbled. He haphazardly folded the letter, shoved it back in the envelope, and then slid it across the desk as if to rid himself of its contents. "Posted from London, I see," he said scowling at the stamp.

Jolene cast a suspicious glance at the envelope while the solicitor studied her intently. For a moment, the absurd notion that he may have known all along prompted her outburst. "Did you know of this?"

He gruffly rebuked her comment. "Heavens no." His bony index finger pointed and wiggled at the envelope. "My advice to you is to forget about this matter entirely. There is absolutely no evidence to substantiate her claim that you were—I can barely speak the words aloud," he groaned. "That you were kidnapped as a baby by the countess."

The dismal fact remained. Someone penned the letter claiming to know her mother. "Regardless," Jolene answered, "I find it disturbing. Why would a person write such a horrid confession to someone she does not know?" Jolene's thoughts ran rife with potential answers to her own question. "If she had not been my mother's maid as she claims, then how does this letter now come into my possession?"

Herr Wilhelm somberly replied. "There are ruthless people in the world that would deceive others in order to take advantage of a person's situation. It is possible that she read of his impending death, learned of your position to inherit his fortune, and then planned to extort money."

"I can't believe that anyone would be so cruel." Jolene scowled over his conjecture. "The letter is clearly a confession and not one of extortion."

"You are an innocent and sheltered young woman. Did you not admit to me only a few minutes ago?"

"Sheltered perhaps," she scoffed. "But certainly not ignorant." She sat up straight in defiance of his inference.

He pulled his gaze away from her in embarrassment. "I apologize if I've offended you, Lady von Lamberg. Nonetheless, if you are worried that these false statements will rob you of your wealth and title, I can assure you they will not. It does not invalidate your adoption or inheritance."

She narrowed her eyes over the possibility. "And what if they are true?"

"It makes no difference," he calmly assured. "You are still the legally adopted daughter of your departed stepfather, Count Eduard von Lamberg."

A sigh of relief left her lungs. Her hand reached toward the desk and retrieved the envelope. The scrawled return address on the back flap held the key. She felt powerless to resist its appeal to meet the author.

The contents could be all lies. The lady's maid may have departed after her mother's death disenchanted and wrote it as some sort of retribution. On the other hand, what if it were true? Had the woman she knew as her mother been a fraud? And if so, did she have parents somewhere in the world she knew nothing about?

The possibilities were haunting. With the loss of her stepfather, she faced a lonely existence. All that remained was her elderly aunt who would one day pass away. She lowered her head and grimaced. The entire matter troubled her deeply.

"It's terrible to think, Herr Wilhelm, that if these allegations are true, my father may have married a woman who had been legally married to another." She shoved the nauseating letter back into the bottom of her purse and fastened it shut.

"You see why I could not tell father about the letter, or even my aunt for that matter. It would have upset him and undoubtedly hastened his death in his already weakened condition."

"Well, it's yet to be proven true, so my advice is not to take it to heart unless you have tangible proof. Frankly, I think it's simply a ploy to obtain money from you."

"Perhaps," she sighed.

"What do you intend to do about it? I sense that you will not leave this matter unresolved."

"I intend to travel," Jolene announced lifting her chin. "First to London and afterward to Paris. I will seek answers along the way and see if there is truth to this confession."

Herr Wilhelm rose from the chair. "Be careful," he said, giving her a cautionary look. "You are young, impressionable, and vulnerable."

His words grated against her pride. Did the man have no confidence in her as a woman? Jolene narrowed her eyes reminding herself that Herr Wilhelm had come from a generation far different from her own. He probably held the misguided belief that women were inadequate creatures unable to make rational decisions without a man's input.

"Perhaps in your eyes, but I assure you that I am not." Jolene rose hastily from the chair. "Please have my cheques and crowns ready per my earlier request."

"Of course," he said. He paused lowering his eyes apparently realizing that he had overstepped his position. "I apologize once more if I have offended you in any way by my advice of restraint regarding the letter. Your father was not only one of my clients but also a man of integrity, who I admired immensely."

Jolene softened her tone and accepted his plea. "Be assured, Herr Wilhelm, that I shall use wisdom and caution."

A sigh of relief puffed from her lips, and she reached up and buttoned her coat in anticipation of the cold outdoors. She bid her solicitor goodbye, hiding the tension inside her heart. "Good day, Herr Wilhelm."

As she entered the waiting area, she approached her aunt and extended her hand to help her from her seat. "Come, Auntie, I have concluded my business here."

The wind brushed across Jolene's face when they stepped outside and cooled her flushed cheeks. She escorted her aunt over the slippery walkway and held her hand as she climbed inside. The driver gave her a supportive hand, and Jolene settled in covering them both with the blanket.

As the carriage made its way through the snowy landscape back to her residence, she felt compelled to ask her aunt a question about the past. "Auntie, I have something to ask you," she began. "Do you remember much about my mother?"

Her aunt glanced her way obviously confused about the reason behind her inquiry. "What do you mean, dear?"

"Oh, I don't know. Father never hesitated in telling me what he knew about mother, how they met, and showing me her portraits and photographs."

"Well, you know the story that they met at the theatre." She smiled. "He admitted to me that she had quickly captured his heart."

"And father married her without a second thought even though she had a child."

"Why yes. He loved you and your mother very much."

"Did mother come alone?" Jolene held her breath worried that she had asked one too many questions.

"I don't understand. What did you mean did she come alone?"

"Did she bring any of her staff, such as her lady's maid?"

"Yes, her lady's maid served your mother until her death and then abruptly left after her funeral. I think her name was Dorothea or Dorcas or something of that nature."

Jolene's breath hitched at the confirmation of her name.

"I know it started with a D, but my poor memory fails me," her aunt sighed.

"My memory fails even me," she replied lightheartedly. There were more questions to ask, but Jolene did not want to raise any suspicions over her sudden interest in a lady's maid who once served her mother.

She glanced at Geraldine, whose head lowered until her chin touched her chest. Apparently, the rocking had lulled her to sleep as they journeyed home.

In the quiet moments, Jolene mulled over the facts she knew to be truth. Jacquelyn Bennett, her alleged mother's maiden name, had been born in England. Angelique, her birth name, sounded strange for a baby with English heritage.

When Jolene's curiosity piqued at an early age, she began asking questions about the whereabouts of her real father. The count explained that he had died in a tragic accident. The story had been a recital of her mother's explanation. If her stepfather knew anything else about her lineage, he never spoke of it.

Though he had legally adopted her immediately after her mother's death, the gaps in her past bothered Jolene. The mystery about her real father had remained a black hole of unanswered questions. What fleeting memories she possessed of her mother brought no comfort. She loved her stepfather deeply, and there had never been any doubt in their mutual affection. Nevertheless, their relationship did not diminish her sense of being a broken branch from an unidentified family tree that her stepfather grafted into another. It was akin to wearing a mix-matched piece of clothing, such as a striped blouse with a checkered skirt. Nothing blended.

In addition, it had been difficult growing up in a household with no women close to her side. After her mother's death, the count retained the governess that her mother had hired when she had been a toddler. They were never close, and the only female companionship she had were the infrequent visits of her aunt from Berlin.

Her hand patted the purse in her lap. The letter buried inside, if true, had the power to redefine her identity. With all that had happened, how could she ignore it?

As they pulled into the drive of their estate, Jolene concluded without a doubt she would seek the truth. And if it turned out to be nothing more than a cruel ruse, she would brush it aside and continue with her life as komtesse of the von Lamberg estate and wealth. However, if it were true, she had no idea how in the world she would be able to handle the shock of it all.

Chapter 2

Patience and Dèjá Vu

When they returned and walked indoors, Jolene swallowed hard finding it difficult to return home. The welcoming of the staff and the beauty of her surroundings did nothing to calm her anxious heart. Ever since her stepfather had died, a spirit of profound loneliness followed her from room to room. The interior of the estate had turned as cold as the wintery day outside.

She glanced at the magnificent grand staircase, which undoubtedly impressed everyone who entered the von Lamberg residence. Carpeted in a deep red with a polished mahogany railing, the first eighteen steps led to a landing beneath an impressive two-story wall. In the center, a large portrait of the count in his full military regalia hung in the center. He stood proudly greeting his guests with his hand upon the handle of a sword of the Austro-Hungarian Empire.

Continuing from the landing, the staircase curled to the right and left, leading up another eighteen stairs to the second story consisting of two wings. An overwhelming sixteen bedrooms and eight bath chambers lined the halls. On the first floor, a massive parlor, music room, library, study, and dining room had been designed by the count to impress. He showcased his wealth in every meter of the mansion with plaster decorative embellishments, fresco painted ceilings, and rich furnishings.

Jolene had no idea how she would survive in a massive residence as one single person. Of course, to maintain the household she relied upon the butler, housekeeper, maids, cooks, groundskeepers, and grooms for the horses. She took for granted the palatial home in which she grew up, until the responsibility for its care had been thrust upon her after her stepfather's death.

The maid took their hats and coats. Geraldine grabbed Jolene by the hand. "Come with me into the parlor, and let us talk for a few moments. I have something to say to you."

Without complaint, Jolene followed her aunt expecting to receive a formal lecture regarding her resolve to travel.

"Before I leave for Berlin, I wish to make a proposition to you regarding your impending journey." Asserting a matriarchal pose, she sat on the divan gazing at her niece.

"Oh, Auntie, don't worry about me," Jolene implored in an exasperated voice. "I'm perfectly capable of taking care of myself."

"Humor me, dear, for a moment. I beg you." She pursed her lips together.

"Fine then," Jolene said. She heaved a sigh and leaned back.

"Our family is not without connections throughout Europe in both Paris and London. If you insist on traveling alone, at least let me write letters of introduction to a few of our acquaintances and procure safe housing for your stay."

"And your motive, I assume, is to see that I'm properly chaperoned."

"No, that is not my intent," she replied, shaking her head. "It will provide accommodations with well-known aristocratic families who have connections."

All of a sudden, Jolene became an attentive audience.

"The families will not only care for your needs, but they will introduce you into society as their honored guest."

"Well, you do have a point," Jolene reluctantly agreed.

"And it will afford some level of safety, rather than traipsing across Europe and staying in strange hotels surrounded by questionable guests."

Intrigued by her aunt's suggestion, Jolene felt inclined to agree. "All right," she replied with a smile. "If it brings you a sense of comfort and relief that I will be safe, then I accept. Who exactly are you thinking about?"

"My husband is well acquainted with the Sauvageau family in Paris through his business dealings. I'm sure they would more than welcome you as my niece into their household."

"But it is my plan to travel to England first," she announced, "What of London? Do you know any families there?"

"I'm not familiar with anyone in England, but let me inquire of my husband after my return to Berlin. He may be aware of a suitable family."

Upon hearing that she had to wait, Jolene's excitement soured. "But that will take time, and I do not wish to postpone my trip," she whined. "It could be weeks before you find a suitable household." She glanced disagreeably toward her aunt. "Certainly, there must be a safe hotel where I can stay in London."

"Please, Jolene, your trip can be put off for a few weeks. Do this for your elderly, dear old auntie, so that I can sleep at ease while you are gone. Your father would have wished that you use caution. If not for me, do it for his memory."

Her aunt had become proficient pricking her conscience and sowing seeds of guilt. Jolene wanted to leave as soon as possible. After all, she had a mission to accomplish. On the other hand, she saw the unmistakable fear in her Aunt Geraldine's eyes as if her beloved stepfather were making a plea through her voice.

"All right then, if it will bring you peace. Far be it from me to give you sleepless nights." Jolene flashed a warm smile. "As long as you don't delay in writing the letters, then I shall be happy."

"Then I will pack, my dearest, and return to Berlin to do just as I've promised. As soon as I receive the invitations for your arrival, you may make your train reservation."

Of course, as the weeks passed, Jolene realized that patience had not been a virtue she possessed. Her aunt remained adamant on her remaining in Austria, until the arrangements for lodging were finalized.

Jolene, on the other hand, continued to feel little concern in traveling alone. After all, she would have her lady's maid with her on the trip. Maria had attended her needs since Jolene's sixteenth birthday. The beginning of their relationship remained formal and aloof, but after two years together, they had grown closer.

Having her own loyal lady's maid, made her think of Dorcas and the bond with her mother. If it were true that she participated in the kidnapping of a baby, her loyalty must have run deep. Would Maria also serve her in whatever she required her to do? As the anticipated trip loomed before her, she wondered if that would be the case. One thing remained certain—Jolene would never ask her to participate in anything illegal.

--·❉·--

Finally, after weeks of anxious waiting, the letter of introduction to the Sauvageau family arrived. They had extended a formal invitation and provided a recommendation to a family in London. As a result, Lord and Lady Whitefield graciously agreed to let her stay in their residence during the height of London's social season. Her course had been set. England, not France, would be her first destination.

When Maria began the daunting task of packing her numerous dresses and undergarments for the months ahead, Jolene turned her attention elsewhere. She headed for the study that her stepfather often frequented. After weeks of the room being vacant, it smelled stale when she entered. The staff had kept it clean, of course, but it gave her a chill as if his presence watched her walk toward the hidden riches.

A brooding portrait of Count von Wilhelm's father hung on the wall behind the desk. She carefully removed the painting, which revealed a safe inserted into the wall. After turning the tumblers to the precise combination, she pulled the handle to the right and opened the door to reveal its treasures.

Her hands retrieved a metal case, which she set upon her stepfather's desk and opened. Inside an assortment of velvet sachets containing jewelry brought a smile to her face. She released the contents of the first and gazed blissfully at the magnificent ruby and diamond necklace that belonged to her mother. For years, she had admired it, when her stepfather retrieved it for her to gaze at the sparkling stones. The time had come when she could not only see it but also wear the jewels around her neck. Jolene turned over the piece and observed the "H" engraved with a small crest, assuming it was the jeweler's mark.

One at a time, she retrieved the remaining pieces of jewelry that were her inheritance. Some of the items were extremely old, while others had been purchased by the count as gifts for her mother. She eyed her mother's dazzling diamond wedding ring, which Jolene had hoped to wear when she wed. Now, with the suspicion that surrounded her mother, it had dampened her appreciation of the stone.

Jolene selected the jewelry she wanted to take on the trip. Satisfied over her choice, she closed the metal case, placed it in the safe, and locked it securely. The eyes of the count's father followed her as she rehung the picture to conceal the location.

After returning to her room, a chill of anticipation ran down her spine. Tomorrow she would board a train with Maria to make her way toward Calais, France. They would cross the English Channel and head to London to begin her adventure. She felt exhilarated over the possibilities that awaited her arrival in England. Hopefully, Lord and Lady Whitefield would be agreeable hosts and new friendships would form.

In spite of her balking over her aunt's suggestion, the exposure she would receive amongst society would be a godsend. Well educated in both English and French, language would be no barrier. In European society, young aristocratic ladies were required to learn the tongues of other countries.

Maria, for the most part, spoke German every day, as did Jolene. Frankly, it would be a welcome reprieve when Jolene needed to retreat to her roots and speak in private. However, she worried about Maria's ability to mingle with the household staff that she would be required to live amongst in foreign countries. Hopefully, they would be welcoming and patient.

When she entered the room, she saw that Maria had organized her clothing for the trip. "How is the packing going?" she asked, glancing at the numerous dresses, undergarments, coats, and hats covering her bed.

"Everything is going well, my lady. I should have your garments packed and ready for the footmen to take the trunks downstairs first thing in the morning."

"Thank you for taking care of my finer garments, Maria. I appreciate your skills and careful attention."

"You do not wish for me to pack your black mourning dress?"

"Absolutely not. Most people I meet will not even know that I am in mourning, and if they do...well, they can gossip all they wish. I shall not be shrouded in black on what is hopefully the most joyous journey of my life."

Before his passing, her stepfather demanded that she dispense with the shroud of mourning quickly. Jolene knew quite well some might take offense to her practice. She, however, considered mourning a delicate and personal matter of her own choice.

"Yes, my lady," she said, pushing the black dress out of sight.

"Are you as excited as I am?" Jolene barely contained her enthusiasm.

"Oh, very much."

"Now before we leave, do you have everything you need in the way of clothes, shoes and hats? Speak up now. If we need to go shopping this afternoon, we will do just that. I don't mind at all purchasing a few new items for you to take."

"Oh would you? My shoes are so old," she said, sticking her toe out from underneath the hem of her dress showing her worn heels.

"Well, I want you to be well dressed, Maria, as you'll be housed with the staff of these fine estates we will be visiting."

"I won't be able to understand except for a few words in English. I do not know French. Will they know German?"

Jolene smiled over Maria's flushed face. "I'm sure someone on staff will be helpful. Besides, you will be too busy caring for my needs to worry about gossiping with the staff."

While Maria continued to pack, Jolene retrieved a small crocodile-skinned box with a lock. She took each of the pieces of jewelry she had retrieved from the safe and arranged them neatly inside. Afterward she secured the lock, and placed it in the bottom of a carry-on piece of luggage she would hang onto during the trip.

"We must keep watch over this case at all times, Maria. They can take the trunks into the luggage car, and we will bring small suitcases with a few changes of clothes for the trip. This one, however, shall never leave our sight. It contains the most valuable of some of my mother's jewels."

"Of course, my lady, I will take great care with it."

"I know you will."

"Well, then, the train leaves in the morning and I think we are about ready to explore the world together," she announced. "Are you ready?"

"Oh, yes," Maria answered with a giggle.

Jolene's face beamed with excitement.

They boarded the Orient Express on the morning of April 18, 1905. Jolene held her right hand over her stomach, nauseated from nervous excitement as they walked the platform to board the train. The air smelled of steam, oil, and steel, which added to her queasiness.

While looking for their correct car, she glanced over her shoulder insuring the trunks and bags were right behind her. An attendant wheeled the heavy load upon a flat, wooden dolly. The narrow walkway between the tracks bustled with travelers.

It was the first time she had ever ridden on a train. The count had only taken her occasionally on trips, and they were always by carriage. The long journey ahead would be a thrilling adventure.

"This is your car," Maria said, holding the ticket in her hand and checking the number. Her maid turned to the porter and gave instructions to take the komtesse's luggage to the correct location for loading. Jolene looked at the steps leading inside the train.

"You'll be all right, won't you?" Jolene worried about leaving her behind.

"Of course, the standard class is toward the end of the train. I will be fine. Here is your ticket."

Jolene grasped it in her left hand, and she clung to a small suitcase in her right that contained her few items and jewelry. She blew out a puff of air from her lungs, suppressing the urge to cry. "Give me a few hours to relax and get settled, then come to me at my cabin, Maria. Be well, and don't hesitate to find me if you need anything."

"Yes, my lady."

Maria gave a quick curtsy and continued down the platform. Jolene watched until she had been swallowed into the multitude of travelers. At the door, an attendant dressed in a dark blue, doubled breasted uniform with golden buttons and blue hat, held out his hand to help her up the steps.

"Do you need to see my ticket?"

He glanced at the number of her sleeping quarters. "Not yet," he replied. "The conductor will make rounds and check your ticket after we get underway."

Unfamiliar with the experience and awestruck, Jolene nodded.

"This way, if you'll follow me, madam, I'll show you to your quarters." He took her suitcase from her hand. "Let me carry that for you."

When they rounded the corner, a broad smile spread across her face. Off to the left a long, carpeted hallway stretched as far as she could see. To the right, private sleeping cabins lined the length of the car. The interior paneling appeared to be oak that had been polished to a high sheen. To the left, spotlessly clean windows gave light to the interior, along with a row of lights at the top of the car's ceiling.

About halfway down the hallway, the porter stopped and opened a door on the right. "Your quarters," he announced, allowing her to enter first. He set her case down and tipped his blue hat.

"The dining car is two cars to your left. If you need anything, please do not hesitate to call."

"Thank you," she said, pressing a crown into his outstretched hand.

The door closed, and Jolene stood in the middle of the comfortable quarters that would take her to Paris. The trip would take two days and one night. They would arrive in Paris, change trains to Calais and take a ship for their trip across the English Channel.

She organized her few items, slipped off her outer coat, and hung it inside a small closet. As she stood thinking of what lie ahead, the train jerked forward catching her off guard. She stumbled back and landed on the plush, wide seat. The sensation of the train with its rolling wheels reminded her of ice-skating. It glided effortlessly as it left the station and then increased in speed causing a slight swaying motion inside the cabin. It took her a minute to adjust. The windows afforded an excellent view of the scenery.

Jolene sensed her heart flutter. It felt as if a thousand butterflies spread their wings underneath her breastbone. Frightened over the sensation, she brought her hand to her chest and inhaled a deep breath. The moment had arrived, and the world lay before her to explore. A knock came at the door, and she rose to answer it. When she slid the door back, a tall man in uniform stood before her. She read the tag on his chest—Conductor.

"May I see your ticket, madam?"

"Yes, of course," she said, spinning around trying to remember what in the world she had done with it. After rifling through her purse and not finding it, she brought her hand to her head and held it there for a moment.

"Forgive me," she said, "But I can't seem to remember what I did with it."

He frowned.

Her eyes glanced at the closet. Finally, she remembered she had shoved it in her coat pocket. "Oh, I remember," she announced, opening the door and retrieving the ticket. "Here you go."

The conductor examined the document, punched a hole in it, and gave it back. "Enjoy your trip to Paris," he said, tipping his hat. He continued down to the next door and knocked on it.

Jolene retreated inside. She placed the ticket back in her purse, reminding herself where to find it when they boarded the train for Calais. Obviously, the trip had already affected her ability to think straight, but it didn't matter. She knew nothing would be the same again.

$$-\cdot \maltese \cdot-$$

After a leisurely dinner alone in the opulent dining car, Maria joined her at her cabin to ready her for bed. Her maid expressed the warm décor and flavorsome food in the standard coach.

"Oh, my lady, thank you for bringing me on this trip. Did you see the beautiful scenery of the mountains and valleys? It was breathtaking."

"Indeed I did and think of the wonders that await us in the months ahead."

Maria had finished her tasks and returned to her own car but not before making her bed and fluffing her pillow. They bid each other goodnight, and Jolene dimmed the lights and crawled under the covers. After pulling them underneath her chin, she lay upon her back and looked at the ceiling above.

She listened to the *click-click* rhythmic sound of the train underneath her body. It sounded oddly comforting lulling her to sleep. She closed her eyes and an odd sensation of having lived this moment before filled her heart. Had this been what people referred to as déjà vu?

Distressed by the emotions that she didn't understand, she turned on her side and eventually fell asleep. Rather than a peaceful rest, she had been ushered amongst ghostly figures hovering above her face. A young woman with blonde hair stroked the side of her head softly. Jolene tossed in bed struggling with the vision of drinking warm milk to fill her belly. A rocking motion and soft voices tried to comfort her discontent. Then the screeching of a baby's voice woke her out of a sound sleep.

The mournful wail startled her, and Jolene flung herself upward into a sitting position. She brought her hand to her chest and felt the pounding of her heart through her nightshirt. The sound of a crying baby had awakened her from sleep. Perhaps a child resided in the cabin next to her, she thought. Jolene kept still, waiting to hear the cry again but only the constant *click-click* of the train taking her to France remained.

Afraid of the dark, as if ghosts lingered in the shadowy corners of her cabin, she reached over and turned on the small lamp by her bedside. Her eyes anxiously glanced about, but no one was there. She exhaled a sigh, closed her eyes, and ran her hand through her damp hair. The action stirred up the memory of the letter that lay in the bottom of her purse.

"We boarded a train. . ."

"Dear God," Jolene moaned holding her head. "It must be my overactive mind playing tricks on me," she tried to convince herself. But a troubled tear welled in her eye instead. For a few minutes, she sat quietly in bed pondering the sensation of having lived this moment before.

Frustrated and hesitant to return to the dark memories of dreams, she opened the curtain of her window. Picking up her watch by her nightstand, she noted the time. It was four o'clock in the morning, and she had no desire to return to the mysterious dreams that might reoccur. In a few hours, the dawn would break over the horizon, and a long day of travel lay ahead.

Her exciting trip had been tainted with foreboding of what she would find in London. Would she meet the woman who penned the letter? Would she confirm the allegations that threatened to destroy her identity? Jolene wrung her cold hands together and stared out the window contemplating her future.

Chapter 3

Like Father - Like Son

The whip cracked hard on the hindquarters of the horse. It snorted and lurched forward into a full run, pounding its hooves into the grassy, wet plain.

"Come on, Moon Shadow," yelled its rider. He kicked the stallion with his heels to urge him onward.

The black, English thoroughbred thundered across the ground. The mile competition to the finish line would be a test of speed and endurance. The young rider was determined to win at all costs, confident he owned the best horse in the district. It wasn't long before he passed three riders vying for the finish line.

"Damn you, Holland!" A competitor screamed as he sped by the last one.

Robert let out a husky laugh. He turned around and waved at the rider, baring his white teeth in jest. "Come on, boy." He held the reins tightly in his hands. "Let's win that prize at the end."

Another kick and his horse obeyed the command. Robert could see the finish line in the distance and the parasols of pretty women with bonny hats all lined up to watch who would win the bet.

He flew like the wind across the finish line and called his horse to a halt. "Whoa boy!" Moon Shadow obeyed his command when he pulled back on the reigns. "I knew you could do it," he said. Robert leaned over and pet the sweaty neck of his horse, who snorted and stomped his foot in reply.

Finally, the losers behind him crossed the finish line. "Damn you, Holland," shrieked the rider. "You and that blasted horse of yours."

"Oh, you're just jealous, Alastair, get over it," he roared in amusement. "It's your own fault for riding that old mount of yours. It's time to put him out to pasture."

Alastair jumped off his horse and walked over to his friend. "I say chap, that's the last time I challenge you to anything when it comes to that horse. Poker next time, that's for damn sure."

"I'll lose for sure," Robert grimaced. "Lady Luck only visits me during horse races, not card games."

Robert eyed the ladies, who giggled like a bunch of school girls huddled together. He sported a wicked smile of victory. "Time to pick my prize," he announced. He strode over to the three beauties and eyed them up and down with delight.

"Now, which one of you fine young women would like to have lunch with me?"

Felicity Wade sputtered with a broad smile. "Me, Robert, choose me."

"And why should I choose you Lady Wade above these two other fine girls?" He stepped closer to her beautiful figure in a yellow dress that shimmered in the noonday sun.

"Whatever she says, Robert, don't listen to her. She's just a flirt." Tiffany Bain, a sassy looking young redhead, tugged on his sleeve pouting with her plump ruby lips.

Felicity threw Tiffany a smug look and brashly reached over and grabbed Robert's hand. "Because you are a bad boy, and I am a bad girl."

Robert couldn't suppress the roar that burst from his throat. Her two competitors glared at their rival with such disdain it was sheer entertainment.

"Bad boy and bad girl it is, then." Robert pulled Felicity off to the side. "Sorry ladies, I like the brash ones." Tiffany stomped her foot like a spoiled brat and flashed a disapproving glare.

"Alastair," Robert shouted. "There are two ladies left for the picking. I've chosen my prize." He leaned over and gave Felicity a soft kiss on her cheek. She giggled over his brazenness. Robert walked back to the Holland estate with two possessions in tow—his beloved horse and his prized lady friend.

"I dare say, Robert," she said, tightly clinging to his hand. "You are looking quite chipper having won the race. I don't think the other boys are too pleased they have lost again."

"Well, you would think by now they would have enough sense not to challenge me, wouldn't you? Moon Shadow is unbeatable. There will never be another to beat this beauty," he said, gloating with pride.

"Do you think I'm a beauty?" Felicity asked with a coy grin.

Robert smirked at her forthrightness. "Indeed, a beauty," he replied. "And I damn well intend on stealing a kiss from you Felicity Wade after I have a bite of lunch."

"Oh, Robert, why wait for lunch? Steal one now."

Robert halted his step and looked at the silly, auburn-haired girl. She would be a good pick for an afternoon of fun, but there wasn't an ounce of sense in her empty head. Felicity's desperation to catch him in matrimony stood out like her shiny nose in the sun. Nevertheless, her perfume enticed him to pull her into his arms and give to her what she wanted.

"Bad girl, indeed," he said. He gawked at her lower than respectable neckline for an afternoon dress. "I'd love to smother those pink lips of yours, Felicity, but not here. If you look up to the west wing, you'll see my father staring down at the two of us from his perch above."

Robert turned his head and looked up at his father watching the two of them as they stood upon the manicured lawn.

"Now be a good girl and wave your hand with me." Robert lifted his arm and waved back at his father. Felicity peeked from under the rim of her hat and lifted her eyes to the window. She gritted her teeth, grinned, and waved her white gloved hand in the duke's direction.

"Now I am nervous," Felicity said. "He probably thinks I have a reputation," she said. A moment later, his father retreated from view.

"Come on, sweetheart. Let us get a bite to eat with my stuffy parents. Then we'll go hide somewhere, and I'll give you that kiss," he said. He winked at her with an air of mischievous intent.

Robert returned his horse to the stables and ordered the groom to give Moon Shadow an apple and sugar cube in reward for winning him the treat of the day.

"Don't allow my father intimidate you or my mother, for that matter," he advised her as they strode toward the entrance to the Holland country manor.

"Okay," she said, sheepishly.

As they neared the door, Felicity slowed behind him. Robert flashed a smile and grabbed her hand pulling her reluctant, cute frame through the door. A maid met them and offered to take Felicity's hat. She unpinned it and handed it over. Afterward she fiddled with a loose strand from her hairdo.

"You look fine." Robert grasped her hand once more and led her to the dining room. Felicity eyes darted from left to right, and her mouth dropped open. The usual Holland ancestral eyes from the hanging portraits followed them down the hallway. Robert pulled his mouth to one side and ignored the ghosts of propriety frowning at his carefree afternoon.

They stepped into the formal dining room and were greeted by his parents. His father stood to his feet upon seeing Felicity enter the room. His mother lifted her eyes in his direction flashing a surprised look.

"Mother, Father," he said, nodding in his parent's direction. "I would like to introduce you to Lady Wade."

"Lady Wade," his father said, nodding in return. "Welcome."

"Thank you, Your Grace," she answered, giving a quick curtsy that looked off balance. Robert grabbed her arm to prevent her from falling over from nerves. He lowered his eyes and shook his head with a silly grin upon his face. *The girl is such a simpleton*, he thought to himself, *but probably a decent kisser.*

"I hope you don't mind. I invited Felicity to lunch because she's the prize I won at the race."

"Prize?" His mother repeated. She watched the couple as he pulled out a chair for Felicity.

"The boys' race, Suzette," his father replied. "You know, the lads and their friendly competitions, though I think Robert knows no one can beat his horse."

"I do," he said, puffing out his chest. "They should know by now I'll always win."

"And you are the prize, Felicity?" His mother raised a brow of disapproval.

"Oh, yes," she replied with a broad smile.

"The prize was lunch with me," Robert clarified. He glanced at Felicity whose swan-like neck had filled with red blotches of embarrassment. "She is not the prize if you get my meaning," he said. He gave Felicity a wink, and then flashed a smile at both of his parents trying to make light of the situation.

His mother frowned. She had become the proper duchess throughout the years, he mused, pulling his mouth to one side and ignoring her gaze. The fun-loving woman he knew as a young boy in France had been transformed by the house of propriety and duty.

"Oh, I see. Well, that doesn't sound quite as improper as winning *her* for your pleasure," his father announced glibly.

"Don't embarrass her any more than needed," he retorted, irked by the inference. Robert glanced at Felicity, who now looked as red as the roses on the table centerpiece. His father cleared his throat and expressed his usual impatience. Robert's exuberant countenance faded as if a cloud drizzled over his head.

The footmen served the meal. It wasn't long after he had taken a few bites when his father began his usual interrogation.

"Have you made a decision about what we discussed earlier?" The duke kept his eyes upon his plate while waiting for a reply.

Truth be told, he hadn't made a decision. After university, he still hadn't decided what he wanted to do with his life. Frankly, he wondered why he had to do anything. He had a generous allowance and the free time to pursue his interests. After years of studying at Oxford, he needed to rest his cluttered mind.

However, his father kept reminding him that the Holland fortune had dwindled in years past. If he expected to keep the Holland manor after the duke's demise, he had better think about how he would support his lavish lifestyle.

Of course, Robert thought marrying a rich woman might do the trick. He had heard rumors that a few young men in society had courted and married wealthy ladies from America who were looking to wed aristocrats. Being a twenty-three-year-old available male sounded more appealing than practicing law in London.

He finally responded to his father. "Perhaps, but I'd rather not speak of it here in front of our guest." As soon as he declared his intent, the usual tension between father and son filled the room. It didn't take but a moment's time for his mother to come to the rescue, as usual.

"Lady Wade, why don't you tell us a little something about yourself and your family?"

Thank you, mother, Robert thought to himself as he glanced over at the stately duke poking at his food in irritation. At one time, Robert had been especially close to his father. At seven years of age when he learned the truth about his parentage, he accepted him with the simplicity of a child's mind. As he grew older, both of their bullheaded notions began to clash. Each incident drove them farther apart. The man, who once wooed him with a pony to buy his affections at five years of age, had no more tricks up his sleeve to control him any longer.

In retrospect, occasionally he would think of Philippe Moreau, who had been his stepfather for the first five years of his life. The last vivid memory he had of his stepfather had been the whipping he got for pushing over his sister's crib. Robert always chuckled at the thought of his jealous and mischievous act. However, the thrill quickly diminished when he remembered the black belt that repeatedly met his bare bottom.

He often pondered whether his mother knew of her ex-husband's whereabouts. She never mentioned him or talked about her history with his stepfather. In some respects, his mother remained a mystery. She had carefully given him only small glimpses into her French background and kept secrets of her youth locked away.

Then, of course, there was the unspeakable matter of his lost sister, who had been kidnapped at the age of three months. No one dared to approach that subject. It had been banned from discussion. Whenever mentioned by his own lips, Robert would be told not to upset his mother. You would think after eighteen years she would have healed from the tragedy, but it appeared she never would.

Robert's mind became aware that Felicity still chatted on and on like an annoying bird about her boring family. When the droll became unbearable, he decided to move things along. Robert finished lunch, refused any dessert from the footman, and took advantage of the opportunity to spirit his prize off elsewhere.

"Fine lunch," he remarked. He rose to his feet and offered his hand to Felicity. "Let us take that afternoon walk we talked about." He flashed a sly smile clutching her hand tightly.

"Oh, okay," she obediently replied. She turned toward his parents before departure. "It was a pleasure meeting Your Graces." Felicity smiled, dipped in another curtsy, and Robert pulled her out the door before the "Graces" could give a proper goodbye.

"Now, you are all mine little lady," he teased. He placed his arm brashly around her waist. She giggled in anticipation while Robert led her out the door to a secluded spot on the estate. He fully planned to lay her beneath a tree and kiss her until her lips swelled.

"You better be a gentleman, Robert Holland," she warned him. He knew she didn't mean it. A roguish chuckle escaped his lips.

"Oh, I am a gentleman in whatever I do."

Chapter 4

A Blessing or Thorn

Robert watched his son leave the dining room with the young lady. His choice in women left much to be desired. He glanced over at Suzette, who had quickly noticed his morose mood. She reached for his hand and gave it a tight squeeze.

"What's that for?" He looked into her eyes that attempted to comfort him.

"A show of affection for my troubled husband."

Her playful look melted his stone facial expression, and a small smile replaced it. "I can clearly envision my father laughing at my predicament from across the expanse of eternity," he announced, shaking his head. "No doubt, he is immensely enjoying my interactions with our son as my punishment."

He squeezed his wife's hand once more and pulled it away. "I now understand my father's frustration with my own youth," he confessed. He threw his napkin down on his plate and rose to his feet. "Surely, I must have been a thorn in his side as much as our son is to mine."

The duke spoke the words in haste and with immediate regret. His wife's empathetic countenance turned into a disapproving frown. Suzette followed suit, threw her napkin down, and rose from her chair.

"A thorn," she said, glaring at him in disdain. "I thought children were a blessing from God." She stomped out of the room unmistakably annoyed.

He glanced at the expressionless footman, who stood ready to clear the table. *No doubt watching the Holland family theatrics infused the gossip downstairs amongst the staff,* he thought to himself in embarrassment.

The duke discounted the blank stare of the young man standing at attention. He left the dining hall to pursue his wife and apologize. After all, he did love his son, but his love had been laced with profound disappointment over his character. Surely, Suzette felt the same way.

Robert had turned out to be a self-centered, pleasure-seeking young man with no ambition or desire to succeed. At the age of twenty-three, he should have settled into an advantageous career pursuit. Instead, he acted like an unbroken stallion. His pride in his son had waned, and he struggled with profound embarrassment among his peers and family. Of course, his sister's son had turned out no better and had obviously been a bad influence in Robert's life.

As he embarked on a search for Suzette, the duke pondered the price he had paid for marrying his mistress. Young Robert had dealt with his share of snide remarks and teasing from his fellow friends, which didn't help matters. Perhaps, he felt ashamed of his father, though he never expressed it to his face. Undoubtedly, the years past had been difficult socially, but the duke harbored no regrets for making Suzette his wife.

After wandering from room to room, he finally found her tucked away in the corner of a small parlor, sitting by a bay window. In her lap lay the latest attempt to embroider another piece of cloth into some pleasant rural scene. She enjoyed the hobby, but Robert often thought the finished product left much to be desired.

Suzette lifted her eyes upon his entrance, scowled, and then returned her attention to the needlepoint. He walked over to her and knelt down on one knee like a repentant sinner.

"I apologize for calling our son a thorn, Suzette. It left my lips in frustration." Purposely, he used a gloomy and somber voice to make his point. "Please forgive me."

For the next few moments, she continued to thread in and out of her creation as if she were silently stabbing him with each thrust of the needle. Finally, she set the fabric down and looked up into his sorrowful eyes.

"I know you are frustrated with him, Robert. There are times that I am too. It's your attitude toward the matter that grieves me."

"Point taken," he swiftly responded. She had been forthright and frankly correct. "I shall reign in my discord and keep my thoughts to myself from now on." He looked at her with a smirk on his face as if the apology had already been accepted. "Is all well?"

"Oh, get up." She flashed a forgiving smile.

He rose to his feet and glanced out the window. In the distance, he could see Robert with his prize standing underneath a large oak tree. A moment later, he began kissing her ardently.

"There he is, even now, out where the entire world can see him, making advances toward the young lady."

Suzette jumped to her feet. She grabbed his arm and peered out the window looking. "Where?"

"Under the large oak to your left," he pointed with his finger.

It didn't take long for her own frustration to fly through her lips as she cursed angrily in French. Robert chuckled at her hypocrisy. Whenever she swore, she did so in her native tongue in case she shocked the staff by her unladylike language.

"Frustrated are we?" He smirked.

"Why must he be so brazen?" Suzette grimaced at his behavior.

The duke glanced back at Robert. "What shall we do with the lad? Lock him in his room? Send him away? Leave him to his own devices?" The duke patted her hand and smiled.

"What did your father do with you?" Suzette looked at him with an inquisitive gaze.

She knew damn well what his father did to him. "He married me off to a woman I didn't love," he said.

"No, Robert, I mean before your marriage," she clarified.

His eyebrows rose. He had never spoken of his father's advice and warnings that he received as a young man. Even when he gallivanted about the countryside and in Paris doing as he damn well pleased.

"He gave me a few stern lectures regarding my responsibilities. For the most part, I did not wish to hear what he had to say. It wasn't until he told me that he was dying that I finally faced my inescapable duties."

"Hmm," she pondered with a slight giggle in her throat. "It doesn't seem that our son is much different. My only hope is that he doesn't wait until you are at death's door to come around."

"Well, you're quite humorous." The duke smiled, feeling a slight relief from his gloomy mood. "I know what you're trying to do—shame and remind me of my former rebellious ways."

"You eventually accepted your duties, Robert. Don't you have enough faith in our own son that one day he will do the same?"

"I only wish the best for him. You know I do."

"Of course, and so do I." She reached over to his forearm and touched him tenderly. "He needs to find his way as you found yours. There may be poor decisions he makes and heartache for us, but I know in my heart that beneath his immature conduct our son possesses the wise and honorable character of his father." She paused for a moment and thoughtfully continued. "I think he needs a good influence in his life, which I'm afraid lacks among his friends."

The duke looked at her lovingly. No matter what he had done in the years they had been married, Suzette never spoke ill of him. Her love remained true and supportive like a bulwark beneath him. As his mother predicted, they had suffered for their scandalous union. To spare his wife from hurt, they often remained in the country rather than traveling to London during the social season. Most of his peers had shunned him, though a few had stayed by his side. Thankfully, they remained close to his sister and her family, which helped somewhat to relieve the situation. The thought of which brought him to the next thing on his mind.

"My sister has invited us to London for their annual affair." Immediately, he could see the reservation in her eyes. "It's been some time, Suzette. I think we should attend this year."

"You know how I feel about it, Robert. I love your sister but am uncomfortable in social settings with proud women with who I have nothing in common. They still think of me as your mistress and not a duchess that deserves any respect in their aristocratic circles."

Robert's hand rose to the side of her face. Gently he stroked her smooth cheek with his fingertips. She had remained as beautiful as the innocent mademoiselle he had fallen in love with twenty years ago. There had not been a day when his adoration for his wife failed to grow stronger.

"I can see in your eyes you wish me to agree," she said, raising her brow.

"We will make it a family affair. I am sure our son will be more than willing to come with us. Who knows, perhaps one of my peers will offer him a job or introduce him to a decent woman. One never knows what the season will bring, do they?"

"You English and your season filled with parties, balls, the theater, and endless social gatherings," Suzette toyed. "The French need no season to find love and companionship. The entire English affair is a matrimonial bazaar. Parents display their children like wares in a market looking for profitable marriages."

Suzette lifted her chin into the air and reached over to Robert's blond hair twirling a short lock in her index finger. With a slight push of her breasts toward her husband, she teased him like a flirtatious young girl.

"The French need no season for love. It is in our blood."

"You are being exceedingly forward this afternoon and should behave. One of the servants might observe us together in this compromising position. Such assertiveness should be shared behind closed doors," he warned her sternly.

Suzette rolled her eyes and dropped her hand to her side. With a step backward, she looked at him disappointed. "Shall I ever be able to express my feelings to you in this house without it being behind a closed door?"

"You know how I feel about displaying our affections before the household servants. It's unbecoming and causes gossip among the staff." Robert lowered his voice and leaned toward his wife. "You know how I feel about you, darling."

"Yes, I know," she conceded.

His wife remained silent pondering the invitation. Having learned never to pressure Suzette, he gave her time to think. He glanced out the window and saw that Robert had disappeared with his prize. He hoped to God they didn't sneak off out of sight to have intercourse.

"All right, Robert. I agree to go to London for the season, what is left of it at any rate. You may send word to your sister that we will arrive before her grand ball."

"Wonderful," he said.

"Will they mind if we stay with them?"

It had been some time since Robert sold their townhome in London due to financial reasons. His sister, however, had been more than welcoming to have them stay. "I'm sure she will accommodate us."

Suzette turned around. A coy smile spread across her face. "I shall require a new ball gown, I'm afraid."

Robert shook his head. "I'm not surprised that I must pay for your less than happy visit. A new ball gown you will have."

"Good then, it's settled." She turned to leave but then halted. "As for later, I shall have more to say to you about this subject behind closed doors."

His wife had been such a tease at the most inopportune moments. Nevertheless, he loved the way she would entice him into their bed.

Chapter 5

Right or Left

They arrived at Euston Station and hired a growler with the capacity to carry the trunk and multiple suitcases. As they began their journey to the Whitefields, Jolene tried to enjoy the scenery during the five-mile trip. The London streets were teaming with motorcars, omnibuses, hackney carriages, and electric trams. To make it even more confusing, they were driving on the left side of the street rather than the right as in Austria. Poor Maria looked as surprised as she did.

"My lady, so many people and the streets are terribly crowded. Why are they all driving the wrong way?"

Jolene giggled at her maid's facial expression of horror. "In England they drive on the left rather than the right side of the road, Maria." She looked out the window and felt disoriented, as well. "It's going to take getting used to, isn't it?"

"Look at the motorcars." Maria studied them with curiosity. "The world is changing around us so fast that sometimes I have trouble keeping up."

"If you think that strange, London has an underground train line beneath the streets."

"What?" She spun her head and looked directly into Jolene's eyes as if she had heard her wrong.

"It's like a tube railway of tunnels underground."

"Heaven help us," she balked. "I would never crawl in the underworld to ride a train."

As the trip progressed further, Jolene absorbed as much of the landscape as she could take in. Vienna and London were different in geography and architecture. However, the country's history had always fascinated her more than the royalty of the Austrian empire.

After some time, Jolene glanced out of the carriage window and noted they had turned on a street named The Boltons where the Whitefields resided. Giving closer attention to the sights, she curiously peered out of the windows at the expanse of impressive white facade buildings that lined the street. She had arrived in the area known as Kensington, which housed some of the richest families in London. She glanced at Maria whose wide-eyed expression looked humorous.

"We should arrive shortly," Jolene announced. As the words left her lips, the carriage slowed and pulled to a stop in front of an impressive home. "Well, apparently that moment has quickly arrived," she giggled in excitement.

A tingle of nervous anticipation sent a shiver down Jolene's spine. Somewhere in the city held the answer to the confessional letter. Jolene could hardly wait to arrive and visit the address on the back of the envelope.

The carriage door opened. She lifted her eyes to see the staff exit the residence and greet their arrival. A serious looking man, who she assumed to be the butler, spoke first.

"Lady von Lamberg, I presume."

After he closely scrutinized her, the housekeeper and maids followed suit. A footman stepped forward and offered his hand to assist her and Maria out of the carriage. Her lady's maid stood behind her eying the staff with whom she would mingle among in the days ahead. Jolene hoped that they would give her a warm welcome in spite of their expressionless faces.

Suddenly, a middle-aged woman burst through the doorway followed by an extremely tall man with salt and pepper, colored hair. Both were impeccably dressed in the latest fashion. When they approached, she knew that she had met the Whitefields. To her surprise, they were both somewhat boisterous over her arrival.

"Your aunt's description of you doesn't do you justice," Lady Whitefield began. "What a beautiful young woman you are."

Jolene smiled demurely, trying not to laugh over Lady Whitefield's gregarious greeting. She didn't expect such an animated personality, since she had been told the British were reserved in social settings. Perhaps, Lady Whitefield was an exception to the norm.

"Thank you. You are extremely kind," she replied, returning a genuine smile.

"Lord Whitefield, at your service. Our condolences on the passing of your father."

The kind tone of his voice touched Jolene. She inhaled a deep breath to suppress her emotions, not wishing to brandish an out-of-control personality. "Actually, he was my stepfather and a wonderful man. I miss him terribly and appreciate your kind words."

As they walked into the foyer of their vast townhome, she was amazed at the décor.

"Our footmen will take your things to your suite," Lady Whitefield announced. She glanced at Maria. "I presume this is your lady's maid?" She raised a brow and gave poor Maria a looking over.

"Yes, this is my faithful servant, Maria Brunn. She's been serving me for a few years now, and I hope that your staff will welcome her."

"Does she speak English?" the butler inquired.

"Yes, enough to get by and understand what is spoken to her. She is not as fluent as I wish her to be, but perhaps our travels will expand her vocabulary. Of course, in private, we speak German to one another."

Lady Whitefield turned to the butler. "Branson, see to it that Maria is shown to her quarters. Let her know where she may find the komtesse and tend to her needs later on."

Maria glanced at the butler, whose expression remained subdued.

"Yes, my lady, I will see to it that she is given proper accommodations and will introduce her to the staff." He barked orders at the footmen to take her luggage up the stairs, and then turned toward Maria giving her an order, as well. "Come along now, and follow me. I'll show you where to put your things."

Jolene watched Maria scurry behind him with a worried look upon her face. It would be an adjustment in a strange household. She was about to say something when she lifted her eyes and noticed a young woman gracefully descend the staircase. Her golden blonde hair, upswept in a low pompadour style, looked perfectly accented with a jeweled hair clip. She wore a pleated, white lace blouse and a dark blue shirt. Her rosy complexion and expressive, blue eyes stood out as her best features.

"Grace, my dear, come here and let me introduce you." Lady Whitefield held out her hand toward the young lady.

She looked kindly at Jolene. A warm, welcoming smile spread across her face. "How young you are to possess such a grand title," she spoke.

Her voice, sweet and sincere, made her feel welcome. Somehow, she knew that they would become friends.

"Grace, what a thing to say," her father scolded her.

"Oh, no, Lord Wakefield, she is right," Jolene agreed. "I am not used to my new title. It's taken me a long time not to feel embarrassed when I hear it spoken."

"Oh, my," Grace blurted enthusiastically. "Your Austrian accent is captivating. Every available male in the city will be lining up to hear you speak."

Jolene didn't know how to respond. The thought of available men pursuing her gave rise to the warnings from her solicitor and aunt. Of course, she had never been pursued by anyone, thanks to her protective stepfather. She often thought that one day he would arrange her marriage since he had come from the old world where the practice had been widely practiced.

"Might I be shown to my room now?" she asked wearily. "I'm feeling a bit tired from the trip."

"I'll escort her," Grace announced.

"By all means," Lady Whitefield agreed. Her husband appeared concerned over her sudden need to retreat.

Grace ascended the stairs, and Jolene followed. When she arrived in her suite of rooms, her luggage had already been deposited by the staff.

"I hope you like your quarters," Grace said, glancing about the room.

Jolene thought it modest compared to the furnishings that lined her own room. Nevertheless, it appeared comfortable. "Yes, they are fine," Jolene replied, walking over to the window. Her eyes scrutinized the gardens below, which immediately brought a smile to her face. "What colorful budding flowers. Your gardens must be ablaze with color when in full bloom."

"Quite, and ablaze with bees, which I detest," Grace quickly replied with a scowl. "For some reason I seem to attract the pesky things. Last year I was stung twice, so now I avoid the gardens completely."

"Oh, what a shame," Jolene replied, feeling sorry for her plight. Maria entered the room and glanced about.

"My lady, shall I unpack your things?"

"Yes, please do. I'm sure everything is terribly wrinkled."

"Our maids can arrange for pressing if needed," Grace offered. Maria opened the trunk, and Grace quickly went over spying a beautiful gown that caught her eye.

"Oh my, what a gorgeous dress," she cooed. "Such beautiful satin and lace."

Jolene smiled. "Thank you. My favorite dress shop carries the latest fashions from Paris, and I must admit that I quickly fell in love with it."

"Perfect for the Chambers ball," Grace announced. "You know, you must go. Our family has been invited. You, of course, as our guest must come with us."

"A ball?" The event sounded intriguing.

"Yes, Lord and Lady Chambers, a friend of the family, holds the most fashionable ball in the spring. All of London's society will attend."

London society, Jolene grinned. "So you think that my accent will attract single men?" she inquired modestly.

"Yes, and I probably should have a long talk with you beforehand to warn you of the men to stay away from. There are a few rascals amongst the lot."

It would be intriguing to meet men, but she feared it might sideline her from her intended purpose for coming to London. "And when is this grand affair to occur, might I ask?"

"Well, I hate to make you feel rushed, but tomorrow evening. I told mother that I was ecstatic over your coming so that I did not have to face the affair by myself."

Jolene cringed at the thought. "So soon?" There would be barely enough time to acclimate to the English way of life.

"Maria, if that's the case, then I'll certainly need you tomorrow to help me groom and prepare," she said, swinging around and feeling a bit panicked.

"Oh, I'd be delighted. A ball, how wonderful," she replied in German.

"I'll have to introduce you to my lady's maid so the two of you can gossip. She's quite the character, and I trust her implicitly to make me look my best."

Maria gave a quick curtsy. "Thank you," she replied, stumbling over her English pronunciation.

"Her name is Francis, and I will send her by later to help you get settled into the servant's quarters. She can fill you in on all the scuttlebutt amongst the staff."

Maria cast a confused look at Jolene. Obviously, she did not understand Grace's pronouncement in English. Jolene repeated it to her in German, which caused her to giggle. Quickly, she returned to her duties of unpacking her mistress' trunks.

"Well then," Grace announced. "I shall leave the two of you alone. We dine at seven-thirty. The usual formal attire is our English way, of course."

Jolene raised her eyebrows over the comment. Did she think Austrians were any different? "We dress for dinner, as well, in our household," she confirmed.

"Very well," Grace quickly responded. Her face flushed with embarrassment, and she quickly left the room.

Jolene wandered over to Maria who snickered. "Does she think we are barbarians in Austria that we need to be told how to dress for dinner?"

"She probably spoke her words before thinking of your position," Maria said.

Jolene allowed the small infraction to pass. The long trip had taken its toll, and she did feel edgy and tired. Perhaps a hot bath and nap would help.

"I think I'll wear my purple evening dress for dinner tonight, but I desperately need a bath and nap first."

"As you wish," Maria answered finishing her tasks.

Jolene wondered what the evening would bring. Conversation always had a way of revealing the personalities of others. Perhaps dinner would be interesting. She had much to learn about her hosts and the British in general. Then, of course, there remained the matter of the letter tucked away in her purse.

She brought her hand to her mouth to suppress a yawn. "Goodness. I do need some rest." Obviously, her fitful night the evening before had robbed her of sleep. Coupled with the long trip and excitement over their arrival, she could barely keep her eyes open.

After lounging in a warm bathtub, Jolene crawled in bed and slept. She rose a few hours later after Maria woke her from a deep slumber. The time had slipped away, and the dinner hour approached.

Maria had taken her gown to have it pressed and brought it back free of wrinkles. After dressing, she arranged her dark hair into an evening coiffure, accenting her dark locks with a sterling silver and diamond hair comb, which her stepfather had given to her on her sixteenth birthday. *"A beautiful hair pin for my beautiful daughter,"* he told her when she opened the gift.

The precious memory remained fresh in her mind, as well as the deep commanding voice of the count. There were moments she felt his spirit as if he stood next to her encouraging her in the days ahead. *"You shall always be my daughter, Jolene,"* he would say to her with kind eyes.

"I know," she whispered, "and you shall always be my father." No matter what the days ahead revealed about her so-called identity, how could she ever change who she had become?

"If you have no more need of me, may I take my leave?" Maria asked, bringing her thoughts back.

"Yes, of course, Maria. Just return to me around ten o'clock to help me prepare for the night."

With a quick curtsy, Maria left her alone to take one last glance in the mirror. After approving of her attire, she departed and made her way downstairs to join the Whitefield family. As soon as she descended the staircase, the butler approached.

"Your ladyship, the family has gathered in the rose parlor. If you will follow me, I'll show you the way."

Branson walked down a long corridor and stopped in front of two tremendously tall white doors. After swinging them open, he announced her arrival. "Lady von Lamberg."

"Oh, my dear," exclaimed Lady Whitefield scurrying to her side. "I do hope that you are settled in and all is well with your accommodations."

"They are extremely comfortable, Lady Whitefield. I'm most pleased."

"Good. If you need anything while you are visiting, please do not hesitate to call upon Branson or Mrs. Hatfield, our housekeeper. They will see to your needs immediately."

Jolene quickly glanced around the room. Grace rose from a chair near the fireplace. Lord Whitefield stood near his daughter with a glass of champagne in his hand, dressed in his formal dinner attire with a white tie. To the left, an unrecognizable young man stood with his hand on the back of Grace's chair. He appeared average in looks, but not uncomely, with light brown hair. Jolene surmised his age to be a few years her senior.

"Lady von Lamberg, this is our son, Alastair. He arrived home from our country estate a few hours ago."

The gentleman took a step toward Jolene displaying a pleased smile on his face. Jolene remained unmoved by his intense examination of her arrival.

"Lady von Lamberg, charmed," he drawled. He reached for her hand, and Jolene offered it. Without making a spectacle of himself, he kissed it.

"It's a pleasure to meet you," she replied, pulling her hand away.

"Don't pay him any mind," Grace said, walking over to her side and giving her brother a disapproving look. "He's just returned from being in the company of some of the biggest philanderers in London. You best prepare yourself for tomorrow evening."

Jolene, about to assure her she could handle herself in the presence of flirts as she called them, halted her words when Branson arrived. "Dinner is served," he announced in his stoic voice.

"May I escort you into the dining room?" Lord Whitefield offered his arm, and Jolene quickly took it noting the disappointed frown on Alastair's face.

"Yes, thank you." She followed his lead as he escorted her into the grand dining hall of their home. He stopped at a chair, left of center, and helped her into her seat. A footman assisted Lord Whitefield, who sat center table. Their backs were to the fireplace warming her comfortably. Jolene felt slightly chilled in her short-sleeved evening gown.

Lady Whitefield, Grace, and Alastair were seated. The table was beautifully decorated with a white linen tablecloth, a bouquet of white roses in the center, and silver candelabras on either side that cast a warm glow on all of the guests. A small card displaying the evening's menu in French lay by her plate.

The table was impressively set with silverware, bone china, and crystal glassware that caught Jolene's attention. They had gone to considerable length to impress their dinner guest. She glanced over at Lady Whitefield and Grace, who keenly watched her from across the table as if they were waiting for her approval.

"Very beautiful table setting, Lady Whitefield," she complimented. A footman poured a glass of white wine, which Jolene looked forward to immensely.

"Tell me, Lady von Lamberg, do the Austrians put as much emphasis upon dining as the British?" Lady Whitefield raised her glass of wine and took a sip waiting for Jolene's response.

"Yes, we are quite the connoisseurs when it comes to fine dining, elaborate meals, and spirits. In our household, though, most evenings only my stepfather and I dined together. He insisted that we dress to keep the tradition."

"Only the two of you?" Grace asked.

"For the most part yes, but the count often entertained government officials at our home. However, such occasions were not a regular evening affair."

"It must have been terribly lonely for you," Lady Whitefield responded sadly.

"Not actually, though it must appear to others with large families. After my mother died when I was three, my stepfather had no desire to remarry. He focused his life upon my upbringing and preparation for the future. I do have a step aunt, who lives in Berlin and occasionally visits."

"You have no other family?" Lady Whitefield inquired raising her brow.

"I'm afraid not. My mother was an only child, and my birth father passed away when I was a baby—the victim of an untimely accident, so I was told."

"Oh, how dreadful," Grace added.

Jolene silently pondered the statement with regret. Perhaps none of what she told them happened to be the truth.

"If your father prepared you to be a countess, then why is your title komtesse? Is that the Austrian pronunciation?" Alastair peered around his father with a curious look on his face.

"Komtesse is the title that denotes an unmarried countess. When I marry, then my title will change."

"Very interesting," he replied.

A footman served the first course of soup, which upon tasting Jolene recognized to be cream of watercress. The next course consisted of fish. They made small talk, until out of curiosity Jolene asked about tomorrow evening's scheduled event.

"Grace told me that tomorrow night is the highlight of social gatherings in London."

"The Chambers' ball," Lord Whitefield muttered.

Jolene turned her head at the surprising response that sounded laced with disapproval.

"Give my husband no mind," Lady Whitefield retorted. "He hates to waltz, needless to say, so he is not looking forward to the affair."

"I can think of better things I would rather be doing," he responded in vexation.

"An evening at your gentlemen's club, no doubt." Lady Whitefield brandished her own frown of displeasure in return.

"Pay them no mind. You'll enjoy it immensely," Grace assured her with a smile.

"I shall enjoy it enormously, if you give me the honor of a waltz before my comrades spirit you away from me."

Jolene looked at Alastair's face, full of anticipation, and decided to agree to his invitation. "I promise you the first dance, Mr. Whitefield, if that is what you wish."

"His comrades," Grace interjected with a smirk. "As I warned you earlier, there will be quite a few compelling personalities in the mix. Take heed and don't say I didn't warn you, in case they fool you with their ploys of sincerity."

"I can think of one in particular," Alastair mused. "He will try his best to gain your attention. The scoundrel wins all the ladies."

"Yes, I'm sure he will do his best." Grace took a bite of fish and glanced at Alastair sporting a smug smile.

"You know, father, Robert beat me again in another mile race. That damn horse of his..."

"Alastair, watch your language. There are ladies present," his father scolded.

"Excuse me, Lady von Lamberg. Let me rephrase my sentence." Alastair wet his tongue with a sip of wine before continuing. "That magnificent horse belonging to Robert Holland. It is impossible to beat that stallion. You know..."

A loud clang echoed in the room as Jolene dropped her fork on her plate. Her hand, upon hearing the Holland name, lost all strength. Immediately, her face flushed in embarrassment. Everyone at the table looked at her in astonishment.

"Oh my," she gasped. "Excuse me for being so clumsy." Jolene went to pick up the fork, but a footman had arrived at her side, plucking it off her plate and setting down a clean one.

"Thank you," she whispered. Her cheeks burned. Jolene took a sip of wine to soothe her nerves.

"As I was saying," Alastair continued, "I'll never be able to beat him unless I get another horse."

"I'm not buying you another horse," his father quickly answered.

"My brother just came back from a weekend in the country visiting with pretty girls and male friends. Take care to remember that name—Holland. Young Robert will no doubt flirt with you, using his striking blue eyes to pull you into his snare."

"You'll have to introduce me to this horseman," Jolene smiled broadly. "In Vienna we do have great pride in our Spanish Riding Academy."

"Lord Chambers' son, Geoffrey, will probably twirl you across the dance floor as well." Grace looked at Jolene and narrowed her eyes. "Beware," she said in a low voice. "The man is the biggest cheat in London."

"Can we speak of something else?" Lady Whitefield interrupted. "The komtesse is going to get the impression that every young, British male she meets tomorrow evening is a villain of some sort."

"Speaking of villains," Lord Wakefield said, "the Chambers do have their dark sheep of the family."

"George, not now," Lady Whitefield snapped, scowling at him.

"Oh, now you have my curiosity stirred." Jolene urged him in a jovial tone.

"Slave traders," he grumbled. "The elder Chambers was a slave trader of the worst sort before the States abolished the practice. Edmund Chambers, his son, kept their sugarcane plantations in the West Indies. It is how the family made their fortune from the sale of human flesh to the sugar on our tables."

"Oh dear, how dreadful," Jolene replied. "Slaves, that is," she clarified. "I do admit that I am partial to sugar, though."

The footman had taken her plate and replaced it with the next course consisting of roasted pork and a variety of vegetables.

"They are related, you know." Alastair added.

"Who?" Jolene glanced in his direction.

"Hollands and Chambers," he replied, shoving a piece of pork into his mouth.

"Not blood relatives," Grace corrected him. "Marguerite Holland married Edmund Chambers. They are only connected through that union and nothing else."

"Who is Marguerite Holland?" Jolene inquired of Grace, trying to keep her demeanor nonchalant.

"She's the duke's sister. Rumor be told, I do not think His Grace has been too fond of the match. Nevertheless, that union happened over twenty years ago, and their son and daughter have grown into maturity. Nora, the younger of the two, married and moved to Belgium with her husband."

"Interesting," Jolene said, cutting her meat and pondering the news. How uncanny that her travels should place her directly into the social center that included the Holland family. Her brow furrowed over the thought. Had fate determined to reveal her identity all along? What if she had never received the letter from her mother's maid? Her visit here would be nothing but ordinary occurrence.

The thought of young Robert Holland making a pass at her suddenly caused her to chuckle aloud. Quickly, she reigned in the levity.

"Is the pork not to your liking, Lady von Lamberg?" Lady Whitefield glanced at her with a raised brow.

Another embarrassing moment caused her face to flush. Between dropping a fork and laughing at the prospects of tomorrow evening, she wished dinner would end.

"No, no, it is very tender, Lady Whitefield. Please, forgive me again." She lowered her eyes. "I am so tired from the trip that I appear to be clumsy and giddy."

"Well, I'm looking forward to tomorrow evening," Grace announced. "I can't wait to waltz the night away."

"And I, as well," Jolene added.

Chapter 6

Convergence of Strangers

Jolene stood in the entranceway of the Chambers' ballroom. Dressed in her finest evening gown with layers of satin cascading to the tips of her shoes, she sparkled like the golden sun. To contrast her attire, she chose a black fan and long white gloves that covered her slender arms just above her elbows.

Rather than wearing a complete upsweep of her dark brown hair, she had Maria pull back the front and sides and fasten her locks at the crown of her head with a diamond-studded hairpin. The remainder cascaded down her back in long curly tendrils meeting the line of satin-covered buttons that held the tight bodice in place. A diamond necklace and teardrop earrings given to her by her stepfather adorned her bare neck and lobes.

"Komtesse von Lamberg of Vienna, Austria."

As soon as her name had been announced, every head in the assembly turned in her direction. A sea of eyes scrutinized her from top to bottom, but she steadfastly maintained her composure refusing to be intimidated. Grace and her parents received their announcement and stood next to her ready to make introductions.

A tall gentleman escorting a beautiful woman approached. The man, impeccably dressed, had a slight round belly, thinning hair, and mustache. The lady, who looked to be in her early forties, wore a blue ball gown with a large sapphire necklace and teardrop earrings. Her blonde hair was upswept in the usual style of the day, adorned by a white ostrich feather and jeweled comb. As Jolene presumed, they were the hosts of the grand affair.

Lady Whitefield enthusiastically made the introductions. "Lord and Lady Chambers, may I introduce to you the komtesse. As you have heard, she is our honored guest from Vienna."

Lord Chambers responded, giving a quick bow at the waist. "Welcome to England," he said in a deep, raspy voice.

He acted humble, but something about his demeanor made her feel uncomfortable. Perhaps Lord Whitefield's statement about his family line of business had tainted her perception more than she realized.

"I understand this is your first visit to our country. Are you enjoying your stay in London?" he asked.

"It is my first upon English soil," Jolene responded. "However, it is a pleasure to have the opportunity to travel abroad and visit the impressive city of London." Oddly enough, he looked unimpressed by her response. Apparently, they had both quickly judged one another.

"May I have the pleasure of introducing my wife, Lady Chambers?"

Jolene shifted her gaze to the elegant woman who studied her closely. After a quick assessment of Lady Chamber's demeanor, she decided the couple shared the same aristocratic airs of importance.

"Lady von Lamberg, welcome to our home," she said in a haughty manner. "I do hope you will allow me to introduce you to some of our guests. I'm sure they are eager to meet your acquaintance and forge new friendships."

Jolene's cheeks burned hot. She flipped open her fan and gave herself a breeze of cool air. Hopefully, her actions did not come across as rude to her ladyship, but every eye in the assembly continued to watch her interactions with the hosts.

Finally, she lowered her fan in time to see the Whitefields take leave and mingle in the crowd. Grace had left her side, as well. A feeling of utter vulnerability swept over her until she reminded herself of her heritage. *You are a komtesse of Austria and a von Lamberg—act like one.* A second later, she straightened her backbone and accepted the invitation with bravery.

"Yes, of course, I would be pleased to make new acquaintances."

It did not take long for Lady Chambers to lead her from couple to couple. After a half an hour of introductions to earls, barons, sirs, and elegant ladies, Jolene had become weary of it all. At last, she escorted her to a couple that stood together seemingly removed from the remainder of the crowd. A cloud of aloofness from the other guests appeared to hang over their heads.

"And last but not least," Lady Chambers spoke, "I would like to introduce you to my brother, His Grace, the Duke of Surrey, and his lovely wife."

Nothing could have prepared Jolene for the moment. She had been told that the Hollands would attend, but had not considered her reaction should she meet them. She had no idea why. Perhaps she did not want to think about it.

Slowly, her eyes shifted to the duchess standing a few feet away. A stunningly gorgeous, middle-aged woman with auburn hair and expressive eyes stood before her. The tone of her complexion, lighter than Jolene's, looked perfect. She possessed a comely, curvaceous figure that fit perfectly into her russet-colored gown, which picked up the tones in her hair.

Jolene looked intently at every aspect of her appearance, trying to find some similarity between them, but no obvious physical characteristics existed. Her thoughts were interrupted when the duchess finally spoke a word of greeting.

"It is a pleasure to meet you. Welcome to London."

Her French accent caught her off guard. Another confirmation of the contents of the letter had occurred. Already, she had memorized every line. *"His Lordship had a Parisian mistress before they wed and kept her afterward as well. His mistress was your mother, Suzette Rousseau."*

"Welcome to England," the duke added. His attentive expression and welcoming voice held nothing in reserve. On the contrary, the duchess appeared far more restrained and cautious in her presence.

"Are you here for the remainder of the season, or will you be returning to Austria before July?"

The duke gained her attention from his wife. Jolene clutched her closed fan in an attempt to channel every rampant emotion that had overtaken her heart beating feverishly against her rib cage. She forced a smile in response to his interest in her travels.

"I'm not quite sure, Your Grace, what my plans are at the moment. However long I do decide to stay, I will not return directly to my homeland. I plan to visit Paris for a month or two as well." Jolene shifted her gaze back to the duchess and spoke softly in French. "Your accent betrays your origin. May I inquire if you have lived in England for long?"

The question brought a blush to the duchess' cheeks. Obviously taken back by the question asked in her native tongue, she witnessed her manner relax somewhat. To her surprise, however, the duchess did not reply as she expected. Instead, she answered in English, no doubt for the benefit of her husband and sister-in-law intensely watching the exchange of conversation.

"I was born in Paris but have lived in England for nearly eighteen years now."

"Has it been that long?" Lady Chambers interjected.

"I'm afraid so," the duke replied. "Nevertheless, let us not dwell on the passage of time. It reminds me of my age."

Everyone chuckled quietly at his comment, but Jolene felt inclined to keep the conversation focused on France. "Do you miss Paris?"

"Oh, dear," she sighed with her brow raised. "You cannot expect me to confess my longing for Paris in a room full of Englishmen." Her voice sounded charming and lighthearted.

"I see your point." Jolene smiled in return, looking about the ballroom. "Then I shall not press the matter further. We would not wish to start another conflict between nations," she teased in a low voice.

"She does miss Paris," the duke responded after a few moments of silence. "In fact, I think it is time that I take her to Paris for a long visit."

He reached over, grasped his wife's hand, and held it. His outward show of affection in a social setting surprised Jolene. Apparently, the couple did not care what others thought of their slight display in public. It seemed a logical explanation to the supercilious reception they received from guests in attendance.

Suddenly, Grace arrived at her side. Jolene sighed desperately needing a moment to clear her jumbled thoughts. "Please excuse me," she said, looking at the duke and duchess. "It seems Miss Whitefield is anxious to give me advice."

"No doubt about the available gentlemen," Lady Chambers replied. "I'm sure Geoffrey, my son, will be most pleased to meet you."

Her eyes shifted to the left upon a young man standing across the room. The tone of her host's voice sounded far too eager, as if she already contemplated a possible match before an introduction. Thinking it was a bit presumptuous on her part, Jolene's attitude toward Lady Chambers declined in favor.

After one last gaze at the duchess, Jolene realized that she had no sense of connection other than curiosity. Not even an inward tug suggested that they might be related. The estranged moment added doubt to the validity of the letter and left a void feeling in the pit of her stomach. Perhaps her expectations had been set too high. On the other hand, perhaps her emotions were numb. Unable to tell which one, she felt relieved to take her leave from the couple.

"Perhaps we shall meet again," she smiled. Jolene turned away and followed Grace close by her side.

Lady Chambers walked toward a small group of musicians and spoke her instructions. Immediately, music began to fill the room. It wasn't long before couples filled the center and began to waltz.

"I hope you don't mind me interrupting," Grace said apologetically. "But the expression on your face looked as if you needed to be rescued."

Jolene brought her hand to her cheek. "How dreadful. I do hope that I have not offended the duke and duchess."

"Oh, I doubt that," she said, leading her over to the other end of the ballroom. "Now, who would you like to meet first, the nobleman, the rascal, or the rogue?"

"Oh, dear, now who among these fine men do you tag with those descriptions?" She flipped her fan open feeling terribly flirtatious as she cooled the blush that warmed her cheeks.

Grace stopped near the refreshment table and leaned into Jolene, intending to tell her about society's eligible bachelors. "Over there by the mirrored wall, see those young gentlemen with champagne glasses in their hands?"

Jolene discreetly shifted her gaze in the direction and observed three young men huddled together periodically glancing her way.

"I'm sure they've already begun making bets who wins your heart," Grace announced, sounding slightly disenchanted. "I told you that you would be the center of attention."

"Well, they may obtain a dance, but my heart, I'm afraid, is mine to keep this evening." Unable to pull her attention away from the assemblage of males, she began questioning their characters. "Who is the rascal, as you call him?" Jolene asked, wondering why such an inference had been given.

"Definitely, Robert Holland, though he does have slight roguish tendencies."

She spoke about him with a tiny note of adoration in her voice. Jolene wondered if Grace had been attracted to him. "Pray tell, why do you call him a rascal?" Jolene angled her head with interest.

"Well, he's twenty-three and shows no sign of responsibility whatsoever. Rumor has it that His Grace is extremely disappointed in his lack of ambition. Robert prefers carousing with the ladies. He comes across as quite the catch, but he never stays with one woman for long, because he plays with their feelings and moves to the next." Grace lowered her voice. "He has a bit of a temper I've heard, too, but I think he is merely afraid to commit to anything that clips his wings."

"That is surprising," she responded in disappointment. "Has he attended university?"

"Of course, he has. He attended boarding school, like all aristocratic heirs, tutored by the best and educated at Oxford. Nevertheless, he flounders like a fish unable to settle into any career or steady relationship. I call him the rascal because he reminds me of an immature little boy."

"So harsh of a judgment," Jolene said, shaking her head. Surely, there had to be more than the lack of character Grace portrayed. If her assessment were true, she already held disappointment in her supposed half brother's character.

"Now the rogue," Grace said in a rather disgusted tone.

Instantly, Jolene knew she spoke of Mr. Chambers, as her brother Alastair certainly did not come across as such during dinner the evening before.

"Geoffrey Chambers?" Jolene clarified, daring to use his first name aloud.

"He's a heart breaker. I've never met a man so despicable in character when it comes to women."

"Is he actually that dreadful?" Jolene examined his tall stature, dark hair, and handsome features. Grace's assessment of his personality left much to be desired. Such be the case, she would have to form her own opinion.

Grace answered her question about his character with another comment that made her gasp. "Well, all I can say is that out of the three, he will try his hardest to woo you into his bed."

"Clearly, you do not like Mr. Chambers to speak of such dark motives," she replied. "Did he break your heart?" Jolene could think of no other reason why she would smear the man's reputation in her presence.

She pulled her mouth to one side as she gazed at him with narrowed eyes. "I had a crush on him when I was sixteen and foolish, but he spurned me. Now that I know more about him, I probably should be thankful that he did."

"I'm sorry, Grace," Jolene replied, reaching out and touching her forearm in sympathy. "Now, tell me about the nobleman, Mr. Whitefield, your brother."

"It's a wonder his character hasn't been tarnished by the likes of Lord Holland and Mr. Chambers, as often as he keeps in their company." Grace paused and looked at her brother with a slight hint of pride in her eyes. "Deep down, Alastair is a man of character. I often hope his good nature will rub off on his friends."

"It is true that a person's character can be influenced for good or bad depending on the company one keeps," she replied.

Jolene glanced back at the threesome and realized that Lord Holland had disappeared. Her eyes darted about the room and caught him walking toward the two of them. Instantly, she noted that Grace perked up like a wilted flower that had been watered. Jolene concluded that her newfound friend liked Lord Holland. By the look of longing in her eyes, she obviously did.

Jolene's nerves tingled through her body as he drew closer. His appearance closely resembled his father—blond hair, piercing blue eyes, and light complexion. Lord Holland carried himself with a self-confident stride. Jolene had an overwhelming urge to burst forth in a huge smile, but she kept her lips tightly shut.

"Lady Grace," he said with a polite voice.

"Lord Holland," she demurely greeted.

He turned toward Jolene. "We have not had the pleasure of being introduced this evening."

Jolene lifted her hand and watched in amusement as he kissed her gloved fingers.

Grace made the introductions. "Lady von Lamberg , may I introduce you to Lord Holland."

"It is a pleasure to meet your acquaintance." He examined her with curiosity, but did so respectfully as a gentleman. "Welcome to London."

"Thank you," Jolene replied feeling slightly tongue-tied. Jolene instantly sensed a kinship draw to Robert, unlike the emptiness over having met the duke and duchess.

Now that he stood near, she took her time to examine him more closely. She estimated his height to be about five feet, ten inches tall, compared to her short height. Unfortunately, she saw no resemblance between each other. Her olive-colored complexion and dark hair were a stark contrast to his light features. Apparently she had gawked far too long as a slight nudge from Grace's elbow brought her around.

"Are you all right?" he suddenly asked. His faced expressed concern.

"Oh, yes, please excuse me. Your appearance reminded me of an old friend, and it caught me off guard." She flipped open her fan and whisked a quick breeze across her face.

"I do hope it is not an old beau," Robert jested.

"Not quite," Jolene smiled broadly. "I am afraid the count, my stepfather, had been extremely protective of my life. There have been no beaus, as you put it that have courted me."

"Such a shame," Robert said, acting as if he were ready and able to take that position should she allow him to do so.

His blue eyes wielded his male charm of interest and then lazily examined her dress from bodice to hem and up again. The courteous manner he had first presented appeared to be weakening. Jolene felt like slapping him but restrained the urge. The thought of such desirability from a man, who might be her half brother, bordered on an unseemly sinful attraction. Then, of course, she reminded herself that he had no idea who stood in front of him, so she forgave his impertinence.

"Lord Holland." Grace spoke his name to gain his attention as if she sensed Jolene's discomfort in the moment.

He looked at Grace apparently understanding her words. Robert precipitously turned into a gentleman, pulling his shoulders back and looking handsome. In his aristocrat inflection, he asked her the question she had expected.

"Might I have the honor of this waltz, Lady von Lamberg?" He held out his hand toward her with a subdued look upon his face.

A spin around the dance floor would allow her a private conversation away from Grace. Her acceptance was immediate and graceful. "I'd be honored, Lord Holland."

She demurely smiled at him as she placed her hand into his white-gloved palm. As they stepped upon the parquet wood floor, she looked into his blue expressive eyes and placed her hand upon his shoulder. Very lightly, he touched her waist and began leading her in a Viennese waltz.

While they spun around on the dance floor, Jolene realized that Lord Holland had attempted to impress her with his dancing abilities. Frankly, she thought him reasonably skilled in the art of waltzing.

As they glided and twirled around in circles, synchronizing with the music, Jolene's stomach churned nervously inside of her. It felt strange touching him as if they possessed a mysterious connection. She pushed the thought aside, not wanting to speculate when the deathbed confession still needed to be verified.

"You waltz divinely," he said in a respectful voice.

"And so do you." She paused a moment and continued with a sly grin. "Except I would not use the word divinely to express a man's skill upon the dance floor."

"True, divinely does not describe me very well," he jested. "What word would you use, Lady von Lamberg, to assess my dancing skills?"

"Oh, now you place me into a difficult position." Jolene's face grew serious as she thought about the proper description for her dance partner. "Proficient, perhaps." He didn't look terribly impressed with her choice of words.

"Well, you can thank my mother, the duchess. She insisted that I be trained in all social graces, including dancing."

"Then she did well giving you that advice." Her dance partner looked thoughtfully at her for a moment, still managing not to run the two of them into another couple.

"You do know," he said with a smirk on his face, "that a hundred years ago waltzing was said to have been the main source of moral weakness in young couples. It corrupted the body and mind of its generation. Did Austrians hold the same opinion?"

"I believe when the waltz became popular, some of the staunch aristocratic families thought the practice scandalous. After all, to be in such close proximity between a male and female in a public assembly was unheard of in the eighteenth century, was it not?"

"Now, look at us. A room filled with modern thinkers enjoying the closeness of male and female on the dance floor."

Lord Holland's hand squeezed her waist. Jolene scowled. "I remind you, sir, that I am a guest in your country." She looked into his blue orbs and gave a stern rebuke. "It is not wise to offend foreigners." His smile faded into a serious frown.

"Of course, as you wish." His hand suddenly went limp upon her waist.

No further words were spoken between them. He continued to twirl her into a dizzy state of mind until the final chord of the musical selection had ended. Slightly out of breath, it felt as if the room still spun while she remained stationary.

"Are you all right?" He reached out to her forearm to steady her stance.

"Yes, please forgive me." She exhaled a breath, glancing over at the refreshment table. "I think a drink might help."

"Please, let me," he said, offering his arm. He escorted her slowly over to a footman holding a silver tray of flutes filled with champagne. Lord Holland retrieved one and handed it to her looking concerned.

"I insist you rest," he said. "I feel dreadful that I may have spun you too often in my attempt to impress you with my footwork." He led her over to a nearby chair.

Jolene chuckled. "Oh dear, don't blame yourself. The evening is proving to be a bit overwhelming with all the introductions and attention anyway."

Lord Holland's facial expression turned sour as another one of his companions approached. "Well, it appears that Mr. Chambers is about to overwhelm you with another spin on the dance floor," he announced. "Shall I send him away?"

"No, let's not be rude," Jolene chided. Robert's lips pressed together in a straight line.

She tilted her head and gazed upon Geoffrey Chambers. He arrived before her, and she glanced upward. When she caught his intensive gaze, Jolene felt like a silly schoolgirl. Her untoward reaction to his presence caught her breath in her throat. Geoffrey's cologne, heady and musky, wafted toward her nostrils. His shoulders were squarely set as he looked down upon her with intrigue.

Jolene rose from the chair, having recovered from her dizzy spell, and presented herself with poise. When she found herself eye to eye, she noticed the perfectly chiseled features upon his face from his brow to his jawline.

"Lady von Lamberg, your beauty fills the room with awe," he spoke with conviction. A moment later, he took her hand before she had the chance to raise it and kissed it firmly planting his lips upon her knuckles. Warmth spread up her arm, and she shuddered over the sensation he elicited from her weak womanhood. The entire moment unnerved her to the core.

"Cousin," Robert droned somberly, "May I introduce Komtesse von Lamberg of Vienna."

Poor Lord Holland sounded rather disenchanted. Grace's caution about Mr. Chambers' character did nothing to dampen her interest. After all, she still needed to form her own opinion, did she not?

"Might I have the pleasure of the next dance?"

"Her ladyship is exhausted, Cousin. I believe that it would be polite to allow her a moment to regain her strength before asking her to dance." Robert's firm voice tried to dissuade his offer.

"I'd be happy to dance with you," Jolene answered. She looked at Lord Holland. "I feel fully recovered," she assured him.

Much to Robert's displeasing glower, she reached out to Mr. Chambers' arm. As he gently led her into the center of the surrounding dance couples, Jolene noticed that a few guests had turned their attention upon them. Off to the right, his parents smiled with obvious approval.

His hand swallowed hers in his palm, and his long fingers firmly grasped her waist. No objection escaped her lips as it did with Robert's squeeze of his fingertips. Jolene glanced quickly over to Robert. He had been joined by Grace at his side, and both displayed an equal frown of displeasure. Jolene looked away and back into Mr. Chambers' eyes.

The charismatic atmosphere that surrounded his person felt unnerving. Jolene had never been exposed to a man with such handsome and charming characteristics. A weakness in her knees caused her to shift on her feet. He calmly, but firmly, held her in his arms as the music began to play.

Chapter 7

Season of Matchmaking

As the music started and the first steps of the waltz began, Geoffrey Chambers kept his gaze upon the stunning beauty from Austria. Determined to make an impression, he began his usual sequence of showing personal interest into a woman's affairs.

"May I offer my condolences, Lady von Lamberg, on the recent death of your stepfather." She pulled her eyes away from him almost as if she were embarrassed by his comment.

"That is very kind of you, Mr. Chambers."

"I think it's unusually bold of you to have done away with the usual black fashion that would have dulled your beauty. I'm afraid our country loves to wallow in black far too long after the death of a loved one."

"I'm not fond of black, and I don't believe my stepfather would have wanted me to wear it for months on end. He was a man who loved life and taught me to love it as well."

Geoffrey noticed that Robert and Grace had suddenly entered the dance floor and were only a few feet away. A bit peeved over Robert's glare and Grace's frown, he decided to put distance between them.

"A wise man, indeed," Geoffrey said, making a rather forceful twirl in the next stanza. He held his hand tighter around her tiny waist should she lose her balance. The movement caught her off guard, but she kept in step with him until he had put a respectable distance between the two people who were intent on eavesdropping.

He returned his gaze into her eyes that appeared captured by his own. Truth be told, he knew it was his best feature. His brown eyes had flecks of gold. Mother Nature had blessed him with dark lashes and perfect eyebrows that were not bushy. Being clean-shaven, with his hair slicked back, put him above his competition.

Geoffrey's handsome demeanor and decent looks had been the successful key to keeping the interest of the ladies. He knew how to place a gentle, but firm touch upon their bodies. A caring demeanor, intriguing look, and gentleman-like behavior usually ended in the same result. There was no better time than to make use of his charms with the komtesse from Austria. The question remained whether she would fall for his disingenuous attempts, or if she would take heed of the warnings some may have given her already about his character.

It is time to find a wife and settle down, he heard his father's stern voice. If he had a wife with such wealth, beauty, and status, he might consider it. Like a rich man looking for the finest in any purchase to own, Geoffrey Chambers was not about to settle for just anyone. He knew his parents expected more. As he saw them in the distance, they smiled and nodded over his present, fortunate position. Slowly moving his eyes back on her flawless complexion, he saw that she continued to look at him with noticeable interest.

"Are you enjoying your stay in London?" He looked directly into her eyes giving his utmost attention in return.

"I've only just arrived," she said. A sweet, but subdued smile curled her lips. "My hope is to see more of London in the weeks ahead."

"Weeks?" He raised one brow over the disappointment of such a short visit. "Will you not stay for the entire height of society?"

"Well, I do hope to remain here long enough to enjoy what the English denote as the *season*."

He lifted the corner of his mouth in a partial grin over her charming accent. "I take it you have no season then in Vienna." He suppressed the twitching smirk on his face.

"Oh, we do of sorts."

After a few more twirls, she tightened her grip upon his hand. He reciprocated ever so slightly in return, but not so much as to be offensive in his actions.

"Well, there is much to see in the way of English history in London. If you would be so inclined, it would be my pleasure to escort you to some of those sites."

A slight rosy blush flamed her cheeks. "I'm sure you have better things to do, Mr. Chambers, than be a tour guide for me."

"On the contrary, I would consider it a great privilege if you will allow me the honor."

It was then the waltz ended and the magical moment faded. The musicians put down their instruments to take a break. Everyone's chatter rose within the ballroom, which had made an untimely intrusion upon his private moment. The komtesse had not yet given her answer to his offer.

While he stood in hope of an affirmative response, to his dismay attendees at the ball suddenly surrounded her in interest. In a moment's time, her attention had been lost. She merely nodded and made her apologies.

"If you'll excuse, Mr. Chambers, while I speak with the guests."

She turned her back toward him and with enthusiasm began interacting with others. Robert Holland strode to his side and pulled him away by his upper arm.

"It's not polite to engage her completely in this setting, Cousin. Step away."

"Fine," he grumbled, jerking loose from his grip. He walked with Robert over to Alastair, who stood by the far wall with an irritating smirk on his face.

"Tell me, what is she like?" He took a speedy step toward him.

"Unlike any woman I've had the privilege of dancing with at a ball." His eyes glanced in her direction. "She is mesmerizing, intoxicating, she's..."

"My goodness, 'ol chap," Robert chided. "Don't tell me you're smitten already."

Geoffrey did not respond. He kept gazing at the golden form on the other side of the room.

"Have you forgotten our earlier discussion that we each get a chance to capture her heart?" Robert reminded him snidely.

"If my senses tell me right, I own her heart already." He sounded superior and smug but didn't give a damn. A footman walked by with a tray of filled champagne flutes, and Geoffrey plucked one off, quickly bringing it to his lips and taking a large gulp.

Robert leaned into him and lowered his voice. "You arrogant son-of-a-bitch."

"Here, here," Alastair chimed in. "Well said, Robert. I have yet to dance with the lady."

Geoffrey laughed at the thought of boring Alastair capturing anything but an elderly spinster. Irritated over Holland's dig, he pulled his mouth back to one side. With a challenging look, he returned the taunt.

"You are just as egotistical as I am and as much a womanizer. Don't lecture me, you bastard."

Bastard.

He had used the word on purpose, keenly aware of the gossip that surrounded Robert's parentage. He had been born as the duke's illegitimate love child. It was only until he married his mistress did Robert inherit an ounce of worth, title, or wealth. The fact that they were related as half cousins through his mother made no difference. He wasn't about to allow his younger relation to get the better of him.

It didn't take long for a frown to spread across Robert's face. He fleetingly thought of raising his fist and punching him in the jaw. Not being a man to back away from a fight, the only thing that constrained his ire was appearing anything but a gentleman in front of the komtesse. A brawl would taint his chances to influence her affections.

"Not here," he growled at Robert. "If you want to save your honor, you can do so later."

After he exchanged his empty glass with a full one from a nearby footman, he stepped away. He strode over to his parents, who were watching the Austrian beauty still surrounded by curious guests wishing to have a word with the foreign aristocratic.

"Did you enjoy your waltz?" His father turned his attention back to his son with a sly smile turning up the corners of his mouth.

"Immensely. The komtesse is quite a woman"

"You won't stop your pursuit after one waltz, will you Geoffrey?" His mother reached over and lightly touched his forearm.

"No, of course not. After a few others have their chance, I shall return to her side."

"Then what are your plans to pursue her further?" His father asked, leaning into him but keeping his voice low.

"I've offered to be her tour guide through London."

"Brilliant idea." He gloated.

"Make sure you bring her over for tea as often as you can," his mother reminded him. "I'm curious about her myself."

Geoffrey took note that the orchestra had returned to their positions and picked up their instruments. With a tap of the wand upon the music stand, the conductor led them in the next waltz. The music quickly drew couples into the center of the room.

He noticed that Alastair had approached, bowed, and asked for her hand. After observing the less than interested facial expression upon the komtesse, he knew that Alastair could not compete with his charm. The only competition he worried about came from Robert, who stood with Grace Whitefield drinking champagne and watching the dancing pair. If his cousin thought he had a chance to win her, he was sadly mistaken. *Sadly,* Geoffrey mused with dark eyes. *I shall not let you win this one Holland.*

Alastair Whitefield approached her as the musicians returned to continue the evening's festivities.

"Lady von Lamberg," he began with an eager expression. He gave a quick bow and then teasingly chided her for having forgotten her agreement.

"I seem to remember that you promised me the first dance this evening. And now look—you have been twirled around the dance floor by two others."

Jolene brought her hand to her mouth in embarrassment. "My goodness. I am so sorry that I forgot." She had never been one to break her word, but her attention toward Robert and Geoffrey had consumed her entirely. "Will you be so kind as to forgive me?"

Alastair flashed a warm smile and extended his gloved hand toward her, which Jolene repentantly grasped. "Forgiven. Now, may I have the next dance?"

His kind demeanor touched her, and she remembered Grace's words of his upstanding character. However, when her hand met his, nothing sparked further interest.

They made their way onto the dance floor, and Alastair gently held her as they waltzed with ease. Jolene mused that every young man of wealth in London must have taken dance classes to be so adept at their footwork. Nevertheless, as Alastair's obvious anxious gaze of interest met her eyes, she felt an inward void. No man had ever incited such a reaction in the pit of her stomach as Geoffrey Chambers. Jolene tried to remain attentive, but intermittently she caught her eyes wandering through the crowd looking for Geoffrey. To her disappointment, only Lord Holland and Grace were visible. Where could he have gone?

As soon as the thought left her mind, he swirled around the two of them with another woman in his arms. A pang of utter disappointment took hold of her, and she stumbled in her step. Geoffrey clutched her hand and waist tightly.

"Are you all right?" He tilted his head with concern.

"Yes, I am." She lifted her eyes and looked at him with warm appreciation. "As you know from my previous embarrassing incident at the dinner table, I tend to have moments of clumsiness."

"Ah, the fork incident," he grinned.

"Yes, the fork incident." She shuddered over her uncomfortable reaction upon hearing the Holland name. At that moment, Robert came back into her thoughts. He joined the dance floor with Grace, looking intently at the two of them. Busybody, Jolene mused.

"What are your plans tomorrow?" Alastair asked, bringing her attention back to him.

"Tomorrow?" She had only one desire for tomorrow. "Do you think your parents would provide a carriage for me?"

"A carriage?"

"Yes, I have someone I wish to visit in the morning."

"Well, of course, I don't see why not. Do you need someone to accompany you? London can be a bit overwhelming."

"No, not really. It's an undertaking I must see to myself."

"What time do you wish to leave?"

Jolene thought for a moment and decided late morning. "Eleven would be convenient."

"Fine. I'll see to it," Alastair announced. "As soon as we return home, I'll instruct Branson to have our motorcar and driver waiting for you out front."

"Motorcar?"

"Why yes," he said a bit surprised. "Don't tell me you've never ridden in a motorcar."

Jolene felt antiquated. "My stepfather held to the old ways, and he resisted modernization at all costs."

"Not our family. My father is always ready for the newest invention. Nevertheless, the motorcar will be your mode of transportation in the morning."

"Thank you so very much for your kindness."

Alastair's smile faded as the music ended. "Thank you for the dance. I am sure that we will have more opportunities to speak in the days ahead."

"Yes, of course," Jolene acknowledged, nodding her head.

"Might I be so bold as to ask for another?"

Geoffrey's confident and smooth-toned voice came from behind. She spun around. "Why yes, I'd be delighted." A moment later, she waltzed across the floor with the charming Mr. Chambers. As she gazed into his brown eyes, speckled with gold, she wondered if it were true that beyond his charming air, a monster lurked underneath.

Chapter 8

Prudent Caution

The lavish affair had ended and the soles of her feet throbbed. She hadn't danced the night away like that in her entire life. When she glanced across the seat at Lord and Lady Whitefield, they looked equally exhausted. However, Grace fidgeted at her side apparently spurred on by boundless energy.

"Did you enjoy the ball?" Lady Whitefield asked with keen interest.

"Immensely. But, I will confess that I am worn out from twirling across the floor."

"As I expected," Lord Whitefield offered somberly, "the attendees were impressed by your presence."

"Let us not forget the young men, too, Father." Grace turned her head and gave Jolene a raised brow as if she wished to scold her rather than congratulate her on the obvious popularity she obtained.

"It bears repeating," Lady Whitefield said, "that a young, rich woman should be careful of insincere men looking to marry for money."

Jolene shook her head. "I've heard the warnings before from my solicitor and aunt before I departed."

"And well advised," Lord Whitefield added, sounding much like her father's voice.

"Alastair, on the other hand, has somewhat of a level head," his wife added. It was obvious that Lady Whitefield had decided to put in a kind word regarding her polite offspring.

"Yes, I find him most agreeable," Jolene replied. There was no reason to insult them regarding the young man. After all, he appeared to be a proper gentleman. Nevertheless, the spark between them failed to ignite.

"Why is he not returning with us?" Jolene looked to Grace for an explanation.

"He's probably with his friends, Robert and Geoffrey, having some evening drink at the men's club to talk about the night."

"Mr. Chambers has offered to be my tour guide through London," Jolene announced. "I thought that a kind gesture, although I have not given him my answer yet." She thought dropping that bit of information would stir the carriage occupants.

"I don't think that is wise, Lady von Lamberg, to have the young man show you London unaccompanied. People will talk." Lady Whitefield appeared disappointed that she even entertained the thought of such a union.

"I could ask Lord Holland to come along, and we'll accompany you. Surely that will not cause such a stir." Grace mischievously smirked.

The thought of their intrusion bothered Jolene. She wanted to reject the suggestion but then realized the advantage of their company. "You danced with Lord Holland quite a few times. Is he interested in courting you?"

"Courting?" Grace cackled. "Oh, God no." She swiftly corrected the assumption, glancing at her father whose face had turned sour as a pickle.

"That might be a good idea," Lady Whitefield commented. "You will not be placed in an uncomfortable situation, should Mr. Chambers decide to be less than a gentleman."

"Your suggestion is wise," she answered with an agreeable voice. "Should he offer again, I will accept with those conditions."

The carriage pulled down The Boltons and halted at the impressive white facade. When Jolene stepped out, the weight upon her feet brought a fleeting grimace of pain. The servants took their wraps, and she climbed the stairs with Grace at her side.

"Can we talk a moment before you retire?" Grace reached over and grabbed her hand.

"Yes, of course." Jolene surmised that more warnings about the men she had danced with that evening were forthcoming. When she opened the door, Maria had been waiting to help her undress and prepare for bed.

"I'm so relieved you are here, Maria. Please help me get out of these clothes." In a matter of seconds, Jolene kicked off her shoes and stood in her sheer stockings wiggling her toes back to life. Her attentive maid came to her side and unbuttoned the long row of fabric buttons down her back. Grace sat down on the edge of the bed quietly watching.

"My instinct tells me that you want to speak to me about Mr. Chambers." Jolene looked hesitantly over at Grace.

After kicking off her own shoes, she puffed a breath of air from her lips. "Your instincts are correct," Grace responded, in a low and apologetic tone. "I know that it is not my place to advise you. After all, we hardly know each other. Nevertheless, if you will forgive my boldness, I hope that we can become friends while you are here."

Jolene's dress pooled at her feet, and she stepped out. Maria picked it up and walked to the closet. "I hope that we can as well," Jolene replied. "I am after all in a strange land, home, and among people I barely know. It is essential that I find trustworthy individuals to help guide me in the weeks ahead."

"Oh, I'm so glad," Grace sighed.

"You have my permission to tell me what's on your mind about Mr. Chambers." Jolene decided that she would give her free reign to speak her mind, although Grace would have done so anyway.

"You like him, don't you." Grace made a matter-of-fact statement rather than a pointed question.

"I won't deny that I found his character and persona quite, shall we say, captivating." Jolene thought for a moment as Maria draped a silk robe over her shoulders. She slipped it on and tied the sash.

"Maria, would you leave me for a few minutes? I wish to speak with my friend alone."

She curtsied. "Of course, my lady."

"I'll ring when I need you to help me prepare for bed." Maria retreated. Jolene sat down on the bed next to Grace.

"Captivating is an apt description," Grace replied. "Alastair says he is relatively harmless, just arrogant and far too sure of himself."

Jolene nodded. "Yes, I agree, but confidence can be a good trait."

"True, but I think my aversion to his personality stems from the dark side of his family. He's apparently inherited the overbearing and controlling nature of his father and ancestors." Grace paused and wrapped her arms around her waist. "I shudder to think of his grandfather's treatment of slaves. It truly has stained the family's legacy."

"It doesn't appear that society has been less than acceptable of the Chambers. If that were the case, why would so many think that the Chambers' ball is so important to attend?" Jolene could not understand Grace's logic. She reached over and grasped her new friend's hand. "I don't think it's fair to penalize Mr. Chambers for the questionable behavior of his ancestors, do you?" To her surprise, Grace burst out in laughter.

"Oh, dear God. You have much to learn about the English." After controlling her giggles, she continued with a smile and sparkle in her eye.

"To the British our ancestry means everything. It is what defines us as individuals. Our family lineage can be traced for centuries, and the conquests or failures of our ancestors follow us throughout our lifetime."

Grace presented her thoughts with such conviction that it shed a light on her own predicament. Heritage sounded odd in her circumstance. All she knew was the inheritance of her stepfather, the count. As much as she loved him, not a drop of blood from his ancestors flowed through her veins.

Looming before her included the doubtful past on her mother's side. If the letter were true that Jacquelyn had not brought her into the world, the prospects of what lay ahead frightened Jolene. The grim frown on her face caught Grace's attention.

"I'm so sorry. How insensitive of me. I forgot about your situation," Grace apologized.

"You are quite right, my friend. I know so little about my own heritage. Only the stories from my stepfather that were passed on by my mother reveal my past. I have no idea who my birth father is or if I'm even..."

Hastily, she inhaled the words back into her mouth that were about to expose her dilemma. She couldn't share such possibilities. Not yet. Not until tomorrow when she would visit whoever lived at the return address on the letter.

"Well, my feet are aching, and you must be tired," Grace said. She rose from the bed and bent down to pick up her shoes.

"Have a good night's sleep. I'll fetch Maria for you."

"Thank you," Jolene said, giving her a kiss on the cheek. "You've been so kind to me, and I appreciate your concern. Truly, I do."

After Grace left, Jolene waited on the edge of the bed until Maria returned.

"Did you have a good time at the ball?" she asked, entering the room.

"Yes, very good, but my feet are pounding."

"Here, let me," she said, kneeling down before Jolene. Maria took one foot into her skillful hands and started to massage Jolene's aching muscles and tendons.

Jolene moaned. "Oh, dear God, that feels wonderful."

"We could soak them for a while if you'd like."

"No, this will do."

After spending a few minutes with one foot, she gently placed it back on the carpet and lifted the other working her magic. "I wish I could tell you something, Maria. My heart is so heavy, and I have no one to confide in."

She wanted to talk to someone about the letter besides her solicitor. Grace might be trustworthy, but she did not know her well enough. Besides, she knew the Holland family and that would be too tempting. She might reveal her purpose of being here long before she would be ready to reveal anything.

"I'm happy to listen."

Maria continued to rub her feet taking much longer with the left than the right. Perhaps she thought if she continued to bring her relief that Jolene would relieve her troubled soul.

"I'll be gone for some time tomorrow morning visiting someone in London."

"I didn't know that you knew anyone here," she said. She put her foot down and picked up the other again. Jolene didn't protest.

"A lady wrote to me a few months ago telling me that she knew my mother. I thought it would be nice to meet her and perhaps learn more about the countess."

"You must be excited. I know you often wonder about your mother."

"I do. As much as I loved the count, there have been times that I feel like an orphan. Without auntie in my life, I would be utterly alone. And I will be alone when she passes," Jolene said with a downcast expression. "Truth be told, that frightens me."

Feeling tired, Jolene pulled her foot from Maria's hand. "Thank you, that helped immensely, but I wish to retire now."

Maria helped her with her evening routine. After she removed the pins from her hair and brushed it thoroughly, she dressed Jolene in her nightgown. Exhausted and anxious for the morning visit, she climbed under the covers and bid her goodnight.

"Come to me about an hour before breakfast is served, Maria. I'd like a bath and will choose my clothes for my outing tomorrow."

"Yes, my lady," she said.

After she left, Jolene sank beneath the covers. The evening had been an emotional one, filled with surprise interactions and new acquaintances. As she relived them in her mind one by one, Jolene examined the reactions she experienced with each person.

Lord Holland gave her a distinct impression of being a rascal when he squeezed her waist. Had circumstances been different, it would be quite possible that her observation of the young man might have differed. She even may have been interested in him as a suitor. Nevertheless, she did enjoy his company but remained cautious to form any additional opinions until she had the chance to know him better.

Her meeting with the duke and duchess has been the most emotional by far. At one point, she thought her hand would snap her closed fan. What could she do, except channel the tension into an innate object? Had she not, there would be no telling what she would have blurted from her mouth, ruining her resolve to remain unknown.

Nevertheless, the longer she stood across from the duchess it became obvious she entertained no feelings of attachment. She was a stranger to her like the hundreds of others she had met in the assembly.

The duke appeared to be a kind and attentive husband. Jolene admitted that his tender and apparent love for his wife had been his most striking characteristic. Though she did not understand the power of love, having never experienced it with the opposite sex, she highly regarded his sentiments.

Then, of course, there had been Mr. Chambers. The alluring male who threatened to take her focus off her intended visit. She toyed with the idea of how much leeway she would allow him to impress her as a prospective beau. Admittedly, the man had an influence upon her womanly desires and could become a distraction. In the days ahead, she would need to decide how much of a distraction she would let him to be.

Jolene closed her eyes. Tomorrow would be a turning point in her search, which both frightened and excited her at the same time.

Chapter 9

What is the Truth?

A tall, thin driver dressed in a black uniform and hat stood by the door of the motorcar waiting for her arrival. The Mercedes touring vehicle parked in front of the house sported its brass trim and leather seats. Every inch of metal had been shined to perfection.

"Where would you like me to drive you?"

She had written the address down on a piece of paper and handed it to him. "Do you know the way to this locality?" He glanced at it for only a moment and shook his head affirmatively.

"I am familiar with the location. It's about a half an hour drive from here across the Thames River."

"If you could take me there, I would be most appreciative."

He helped her into the backseat of the motorcar and closed the door. It felt exhilarating to ride in one. Surely, her stepfather would have enjoyed a car had he given in to the new world of the twentieth century. Once the driver started the engine and pulled away from the curb, she smiled at the sensation of rolling down the road in a horseless carriage.

The streets were a jumbled mass of motorcars, hackney carriages, and other modes of transportation. Every inch of available thoroughfare appeared claimed by travelers in the West End. If traffic were not enough, the sidewalks were swarming with pedestrians. Vienna was a cosmopolitan city in its own rights, but London buzzed with an exciting energy that Jolene could not put into words.

When they crossed the river and drove farther east, she noticed fewer motorcars and more carriages. The poverty-stricken landscape looked different from the pristine, whitewashed buildings of Kensington.

After a few more minutes of travel, the scenery suddenly changed to something a bit more pleasant. The motorcar slowed, and the wheels rolled to a stop in front of a block of modest, redbrick row houses. After he parked, the driver exited and came around to open her door.

"This is the address, Lady von Lamberg."

He offered his hand, and Jolene exited onto an uneven walkway. "Wait for me. I won't be long," she instructed.

Warily, she approached the door. After she grasped a tarnished brass knocker with her fingers, she banged it loudly a few times and stepped back. Her hands nervously clutched her purse, while she inhaled a deep breath in anticipation of meeting the author of the letter.

Just as she exhaled, the door opened revealing an elderly woman standing in the threshold. She looked at Jolene blankly, but her eyes noted her fashionable clothing. By the look on her face, she had no idea why a person of her caliber might be at her door.

"I beg your pardon for the intrusion," Jolene began. "My name is Komtesse Jolene van Lamberg." How utterly foolish to be spouting off her title at a time like this, she thought to herself. It sounded like a rude reminder of their difference in class.

"Are you Dorcas?" she blurted. "I'm looking for a woman by the name of Dorcas Kirby. Does she reside here?" Jolene had not intended to sound so brash in her introduction, but a mixture of distrust and intrigue were difficult to handle under the circumstances.

"No, she is not here," the woman replied sadly. "She passed away a few months ago. Why do you ask?"

Passed away. She had not contemplated such a quick end to her pursuit. Every question she had formed in her mind suddenly evaporated into thin air. Her stomach tightened into a knot. Feeling as if she owed the woman an explanation for standing at her doorstep, she told her why.

"Because I received this letter from Dorcas, and I wished to speak to her about the contents." Jolene pulled it from her purse and held the envelope in her hand. Frankly, she felt like tossing it in the nearby gutter. But to her surprise, the elderly woman brought her hand to her mouth and gasped.

"Oh, dear God in heaven above," she exclaimed. "You are the recipient?"

"Yes. I received it in the post a few months ago." Jolene stepped closer. "Do you know of this letter?"

The woman shook her head affirmatively. "Yes, I do. I am Lillian Kirby, Dorcas' sister. Please, won't you come in?"

Her invitation revived her hope. The door opened widely, and she walked over the threshold quickly glancing about the small household. The air smelled stale and musty, but the modest interior appeared clean and well-ordered. "Thank you."

"Please, your ladyship, come into the parlor. Would you like a cup of tea?"

"No, I'm fine."

"I do hope you'll stay for a while because I have much to tell you and something to give you. Please, have a seat," she offered cordially.

Jolene viewed her choices of a raggedy couch and a single wooden chair with a worn fabric base. Choosing the sturdy chair, she sat down and glanced around the parlor. She had lived in such opulence her entire life that being in a home of modest surroundings made her feel uncomfortable. It served to remind her of the sheltered life she lived, far removed from the world and material struggles of the people who lived in it. She felt ashamed, recognizing her shallow heart of indifference.

"I'm sorry to come here unannounced," she began looking at the elderly woman, who sat across from her on the couch. "But I came to speak with your sister about her correspondence. Did she tell you about it?"

"No, I'm afraid she said nothing about the contents of a letter," she began. "I didn't know it existed until after her death."

"Oh, I see," Jolene said, thinking that she would learn nothing more than the vague accusations written on the paper.

"I did read it, however, before I posted it on her behalf." She hesitated and then added, "I apologize for not recognizing your name. My hearing isn't what it used to be."

Jolene sat forward in the chair. "Then you are aware of what she asserts in her correspondence?"

Lillian Kirby cast a sympathetic glance. "Yes, I do, your ladyship. I know that the woman you believed to be your mother is not who she claimed to be." She spoke with certainty as if she accepted it at face value.

Jolene glanced at the letter in her hand. The confirmation from another person brought an odd sense of grief to her heart. She felt as if she stood at her mother's grave, tossed another flower upon her casket, and said goodbye all over again. A sorrowful sense of finality caused her shoulders to droop. For years, she had ardently retained the memory of Jacquelyn as her mother, but her affection and devotion had been misplaced. It had all been a lie.

Miss Kirby lean forward and then touched Jolene's arm tenderly. "This must be a terrible shock to you."

"What am I to believe?"

"My sister served Jacquelyn as her lady's maid since the day she turned sixteen. She was a loyal servant to her throughout her marriage as duchess. But from what I have read, she became emotionally unsound because of her barrenness and her husband's infidelity."

Miss Kirby's statement confused her even further. "What do you mean from what you have read? I don't understand."

"It is all recorded in my sister's diary. She kept a meticulous account during the years she served her mistress."

"Diary?" Jolene clutched the seat of her chair to steady herself. Her mind whirled in circles at the thought of a written record.

"Yes, a diary," Miss Kirby repeated. "It contains entries about the duchess' life, as well as confidences they shared during her time of service."

Lillian rose from her seat and walked over to a sideboard opening a cupboard. She retrieved a brown, leather-bound book. For a moment, she gazed at it and ran the palm of her hand over the cover as if it were a precious possession.

"You have a right to know what is written in these pages," she began. "However, I do not wish to give it to you unless you are ready to accept the truth." Miss Kirby continued to cling to it, holding the diary against her chest.

What secrets would she learn between the pages of the book? Hungry for answers, she replied. "Yes, I am ready."

Jolene lightly bit her bottom lip. She had yet to be tested. Who knew if she had arrived at the point of true readiness? Old doubts about stories written in the diary remained. What if the words were merely fabricated stories written throughout the years by a lady's maid with an overactive imagination? Could she depend on or believe everything penned on its pages, or were the words mere twaddle?

"If you let me read it," Jolene pleaded, "I promise that I will return it to you when I am finished."

"I've read it from cover to cover and am intimately acquainted with its contents. Actually, the letter that I mailed to you fell out from between the pages after she died." Miss Kirby gave a sorrowful glance at the diary. "I think perhaps she hesitated to post it because of the turmoil it might bring to her life."

"What turmoil?" Jolene didn't understand.

"My sister confessed her participation in your kidnapping on her death bed. She had never told anyone after all these years, afraid that she would be punished by the law."

"Oh, I see." Jolene understood what she must have felt. "But why now? Why after all this time did she tell you?"

"Oh, my dear," Miss Kirby answered. "It was a deathbed confession to rid her soul of sin. She could not go to her grave without setting things right." Miss Kirby's eyes watered in tears. "She helped to kidnap you from your birth parents."

Kidnapped. How could she have loved her mistress to such an extent? Jolene could not understand her blind loyalty. Then again, how could the woman she thought to be her mother fail to admit what she had done before going to her grave? Jacquelyn must have still harbored a vindictive heart not to tell anyone what she had done.

Miss Kirby stepped forward and held out the diary. Without hesitation, Jolene grasped it carefully noting its fragile condition.

"Some of the pages are torn, and the binding is damaged."

"It's on the verge of falling apart," Jolene replied. Though she referred to the book, she expressed her own emotions.

"I pray that you will find it in your heart to forgive my sister once you read the words in this book." Dorcas' sister earnestly pleaded.

"But how do you know this is true? Perhaps she wrote it like a fantasy-filled story for her own amusement."

Miss Kirby smiled rather than feeling insulted that she had accused her sister of another deception. "I doubt that very much. My sister was not one to tell stories. I assure you."

Lillian looked at her with such sincerity of heart that Jolene could not argue her point further.

"You must seek the truth for yourself, your ladyship."

Carefully, Jolene opened the diary and glanced at a page. The paper had yellowed from age, but the ink stain had not faded from the years. "I traveled to England because of the letter. How could I ignore the words she had penned?" Jolene said, looking mournfully at the book in her hand.

"You are now embarking on another journey that will change your life forever. You are not who you think you are," Miss Kirby spoke without wavering.

"I am Komtesse Angelique Jolene von Lamberg," she firmly replied, as if she needed to reaffirm her identity for the sake of her own sanity. "I cannot imagine that I could be anyone else."

"Keep an open heart," she said.

Jolene puffed a breath of air from between her lips. Her emotions heightened and stretched in every direction, begged her to leave. "Thank you," she quickly said, rising to her feet. "Do you wish me to return it after I have read the contents?"

"No, of course not. It is yours to keep."

Jolene accepted the generous offer without complaint. "I shall take my leave." She did not wish to appear ungrateful to Miss Kirby. Aware that her voice sounded short, she softened it in her parting goodbye.

"Thank you for your kindness," she spoke. "And please accept my condolences on the loss of your sister."

"May you find peace in your search." Her compassionate voice touched Jolene.

Peace, she repeated in her mind. The word had become a difficult concept in light of her current situation. "Goodbye," she said, leaving the residence.

The driver stood at attention, opened the door, and she climbed inside. Before he shut it, she asked a question.

"Would you be so kind as to take me to a coffee shop somewhere in Kensington? I would like to get some refreshment and something to eat."

The thought of returning to the Whitefield's residence straightaway added to her anxiousness. She could not face anyone right now or have a civil conversation without losing control of her emotions.

"Of course."

The driver shut the door, and a moment later she sat numbly in her seat looking at the brown diary that contained the pages of one woman's journeys with her deceased, so-called mother. Hesitant to read its contents, she held it in her lap.

After traveling over a bridge that spanned the Thames, the car returned to the Kensington area of London. It slowed and came to a halt in front of a corner café. The driver parked, turned off the car, and opened her door.

"I trust you'll find this establishment to your liking," he said. "Shall I wait for you or return at a prescribed time?"

"Return in two hours, if you don't mind," she said. "I shall meet you here at this location."

He tipped his hat. "Very well."

Jolene entered the quaint establishment. It appeared to be a perfect location to hide away alone. She found an empty table by the window where pedestrians passed back and forth oblivious to her need for privacy. The bright light filtering through the window would help illuminate her reading.

"May I help you, miss?"

A waitress approached, and after a quick look at the short menu of drinks and pastries, she ordered a coffee with milk and a scone. She set the diary face up on the table. Jolene merely stared at it until her order arrived.

A few sips of coffee and a nibble of pastry helped her to procrastinate a few more minutes. Finally, she could ignore it no longer. The first entry dated *July 7, 1876* contained a short account of being hired by the Spencer family as a lady's maid to Jacquelyn.

"My new mistress, Jacquelyn Spencer, is a beautiful young woman with golden blonde hair. She treats me respectfully with a kind tone of voice when she requires my services."

One by one, Jolene flipped the pages devouring descriptions of Jacquelyn. Her mother had turned from being a once familiar memory in her life, to a total stranger that she did not know. Apparently, Jacquelyn had been born into a rich and influential family. As most young ladies, she was well mannered, intelligent, and primed to be the wife of an aristocrat. Dorcas' writings revealed early on how fascinated she had become with the woman that she served. The pages overflowed with compliments as if she worshiped the ground she walked on.

Jolene continued to skim and skip some pages until it brought her to Jacquelyn's engagement to Lord Holland of Surrey. Apparently, the marriage had been one of arrangement and convenience between families. Dorcas relayed that her mistress had shared her excitement over her betrothal to the handsome lord. She had no reservations as they embarked on a short courtship that quickly led to marriage.

"She is so happy. One day she will be a duchess and bear children."

Engrossed in the story, Jolene skipped ahead to read the entries during Jacquelyn's early years of marriage. For an hour and a half, she had not wandered from her table or lifted her head to gaze outside the window. She drank two cups of coffee to keep herself alert. The intimate diary read like a novel of intrigue that she could not put down for one second.

As page after page told the sad tale of her mistress' inability to conceive, the happiness of the marriage began to wane. Jolene found the account so sad that her eyes began to tear. She could feel the pain in Jacquelyn's soul over the continued disappointment recorded each month in the journal entries.

She reached for her purse to search for a hankie to dab her nose. Just as she pulled it out, she halted when a familiar voice spoke her name.

"Lady von Lamberg, what a pleasant surprise to find you here."

Chapter 10

More than Tea and Coffee

Jolene looked up from the diary and gasped as she saw Lord Holland standing by her table. Dressed in a brown sack coat with a vest, dotted necktie, and matching trousers, he looked quite dashing. His hand held the rim of a Homburg hat. In a panic, Jolene shut the book and slipped it onto her lap out of sight.

"Why Lord Holland, what a surprise to see you here," she nervously responded. The corner of her eye twitched objecting to her brazen lie. She hoped he had not noticed her shiny eyes filled with womanly emotion for Jacquelyn.

"I was walking past the shop when I glanced inside the window and saw you alone." He took a step forward and smiled. "It would have been terribly impolite of me not to greet you and offer my company."

Lord Holland glanced at the empty chair at her table, obviously waiting for an invitation to have a seat. It would have been rude to shoo him away because of his untimely intrusion. Nevertheless, it might afford her an opportunity to pry into his life.

"Do you have time to join me for a cup of coffee or tea?" It did not take long before he had pulled out the chair and took his place.

"Thank you for the invitation." He sat down and waved the server to his side. "I'll have a cup of black tea, please."

"I hope I'm not keeping you from anything, Lord Holland." Jolene took a sip of her coffee that had turned cold. She wanted to wrinkle her nose over the stale taste but suppressed the urge. When the server returned with Robert's tea, she asked for another cup.

"No, you're not keeping me from anything," he answered. "However, I insist you drop the lord and address me as Robert." He hesitated for a moment and then daringly asked for the same privilege. "Will you allow me to call you by your Christian name of Jolene?" He took a sip of his tea and kept a steady gaze on her reaction. "Of course, if you prefer that we keep formalities, I'm happy to oblige."

She could tell by the sly look in his eye that he would not be happy should she spurn his request. However, she saw no harm in it and allowed a smile to turn up the corner of her mouth. "No, that's all right, you may call me..."

Jolene caught the name at the tip of her tongue that nearly flew out of her mouth. What was she thinking? Perhaps inwardly she wanted to elicit some type of response by dropping it on the table in front of him. Instead, she chose to remain elusive.

"Jolene."

"For a minute there," Robert replied with a broad grin, "it sounded as if you forgot your name."

She chuckled. *If he only knew,* she thought to herself with a smirk on her face.

"So what are you doing here all alone in a café in Kensington having a cup of coffee? It looks as though I interrupted your reading." He nodded toward her lap indicating he knew where she had quickly hid it from his view.

"Well, I just thought I would explore London on my own, have a bite to eat, and take a moment to read."

"What is the book about?"

His nosiness irked her. "Oh, I guess you could say history," she replied. The server brought her another cup of coffee, and she welcomed a sip of the invigorating stimulant.

"Good lord, how dull," Robert replied. "You appear to me the type of woman who would prefer a book of love poems."

Nearly choking on the brew that slid down her throat, Jolene raised her brow at Robert. "Oh really, and what gives you that impression?"

He shrugged his shoulders and lowered his gaze into his tea. "Just a hunch," he answered.

"I do not like poetry," Jolene admitted. "Often my curiosity lies in other subject matters."

"Such as...?"

She narrowed her eyes over his insistent prying. "Like I said a moment ago, history."

"Hmm," he hummed in this throat, probably realizing she would not elaborate further. "History it is then."

Robert avoided pursuing the conversation after her curt reply. The cue to change the subject presented itself, so Jolene steered it elsewhere. "I understand, Robert, that you are a proficient rider of horses. Have you always enjoyed horsemanship?"

By the twinkle in his eye that sparked forth, she obviously found something that brought him utter joy. No doubt, he would talk her ear off about horsemanship for at least fifteen minutes, if not more. Men always loved to express their prowess in any type of sport in which they excelled.

"I gather you discovered that piece of information from Alastair." Robert shifted in his seat and then leaned forward.

"Yes," she answered, leaning forward herself as if to drop a secret in front of him. "In fact, the first night I dined with the Whitefields, he complained sorely to everyone at the table that you had beaten him at another race." She widened her eyes to feed his obvious ego to hear all about it. "To remedy any future loss, he demanded a new thoroughbred from his father."

"Huh!" Robert laughed aloud with a smug look in his eye. "What did his father say?"

"What do you think he said?"

"Well, if I know the man well enough, he flat-out refused."

"Quite right," she said, leaning back and resuming a relaxed position. "But I would think that if the young Alastair wanted a horse whatever income he would have of his own he could purchase one."

A slow smile spread across Robert's face. His eyes looked at her as if she had no idea what she was saying. It made her feel uncomfortable.

"Alastair couldn't afford to purchase the caliber of horse that it would take to beat my thoroughbred."

His arrogance over the matter surprised Jolene. *Point noted on Robert's character,* she thought to herself. *Can be somewhat smug and arrogant.*

"Well, then no doubt you shall continue to remain victor in every race." She almost wanted to challenge him to knock him off his high horse.

"No doubt," he repeated with surety.

A strained moment of silence came between them. Their eyes locked together while their cups occasionally came to their lips taking intermittent sips. Jolene wondered what he plotted under that blond head of hair. The way he stared at her, he probably entertained thoughts that he should not be contemplating.

Nevertheless, the longer she looked into Robert's eyes, the more nervous she became. As he continued to leer at her, she suddenly saw his hand slowly reach across the table and grip hers. His intentions were clear, when he gently squeezed it and then brought his thumb around in soothing circles upon the back of her hand. He desired her, and the thought so utterly repulsed Jolene that she jerked her hand from his grasp.

"Please, Robert, do not touch me in that manner." Her high-pitched voice brought the attention of other patrons. In response, she pulled away from his intense longing and focused on the coffee in her cup. An overwhelming thought of hiding under the table filled her mind that caused a giggle to escape her throat.

Sheepishly, her gaze lifted to see poor Robert's face looking mortified. She had spurned his slightest show of affection, and it apparently hurt him deeply. Had no woman ever rejected the so-called rascal's advances before? The look of defeat had washed away his handsome countenance, turning it into a miserable scowl.

"I've wounded you, I can see," she said, trying to show him a warm and controlled smile.

"Well, it's obvious had the hand been from Geoffrey Chambers you would have readily accepted his advances." His curt and wounded voice replied.

He had jumped to an unwarranted assumption. "Don't be hurt, Robert. I implore you. I have my reasons."

"And what could those be?" Robert narrowed his eyes.

She wanted to blurt out the truth. *"You could be my half brother."* Each fiber of her being wanted to declare it, but the doubt still raged through her heart. Even though events pointed to the truth, a part of her still wanted to disprove it all. Even so, she had already confirmed many statements in the letter. Fate had brought her face-to-face with the Holland family straightaway, when she had not even started her search.

Nevertheless, so much remained unread in the pages of the diary. Jolene shifted uncomfortably in her chair as she silently mused about what to do next. The movement caused it to slip off her lap onto the floor, face down, opened between two pages. Frozen in horror, her mouth gaped open. Robert quickly came to the rescue. He bent down and picked up the book keeping it open.

"Robert," she called his attention away from the content. "Please give it to me." Her voice demanded his immediate action, but he didn't answer. Instead, he held the diary away from her reach and began reading a portion. Jolene thought she would faint when Robert's face abruptly twisted in anger.

"What is this?" He glared at her and then glowered at the diary. "It has the name of Jacquelyn Holland written in here."

In an attempt to halt further exposure, she reached across the table and grabbed the corner of the diary. "Give it to me." She scrunched her lips together crossly. "It's my property."

Robert retained a strong grip preventing her from retrieving her secrets. His eyes looked back at the words, and she could tell he read a few more lines.

"What the bloody hell is this?" His brow furrowed causing his blue eyes to turn into dark slits of rage.

"Robert, I said give it to me!" She raised her voice so loudly that she caught the attention of the entire café. He scowled.

"How did you come into possession of this? What are you, a busybody reading gossip about my family?"

Jolene trembled. He would not return the book. She needed the book. Once he continued to read, he could refuse to return it into her hand. Like a cornered animal, frightened and defensive over her territory, she inhaled a breath and spewed out the reason.

"My first name is Angelique not...not Jolene." Her voice sputtered. "I believe that you may be my half brother."

Robert's body jerked in his chair. He dropped the book on the tabletop as if it were on fire. Jolene took the opportunity to snatch it from him. Flipping it shut, she shoved it back on her lap and out of reach. When her gaze returned to Robert, a sudden rush of fear struck her heart.

All of a sudden, his hand flew across the table and clutched hers resting by the coffee cup. Angrily, he squeezed her palm until it hurt. "Is this some kind of fucking joke?" His jaw clenched.

His choice of words startled Jolene for she had not expected him to swear at her in such a vulgar manner. Robert continued to channel his anger to her crushed hand between his fingers. She winced in pain. Perhaps too quickly she had opened the door to her identity, and it had been a terrible mistake. Regrettably, she could do nothing about it now.

"Not so tight, Robert," she said in a low voice. "You are hurting me." Her eyes watered. Finally, he released his grip. Jolene brought her hands together rubbing her hurting palm. "I have reason to believe because of what is written in this book that I am indeed your half sister that was kidnapped by Jacquelyn Holland."

There she had said it. Her trip to search out the truth probably would end explosively in a London café. Surely, all of her plans to take time and pursue answers had come to a ruinous end.

"Robert," she pleaded. "I need you to help me to find the truth. Please don't be angry with me." He stared blankly at her, keeping his lips compressed in a straight line. She could not discern whether he believed her or not. Perhaps he thought that she was a charlatan, too, who had come into his life for some ulterior motive of gain. His next movement caught her totally off guard.

Robert threw down his napkin, shoved his chair back, and rose hastily to his feet. "I can't handle this right now," he said. He dismissed their meeting without further comment. Then he turned on his heel and stomped toward the door.

Jolene panicked. The thought of him returning and telling his father and mother of their meeting would ruin everything. It was not time for them to know, or he would destroy all of her plans. In desperation, she jumped to her feet and lurched after him. Like a mad woman, she snatched the arm of his coat and pulled him to a halt. It did not matter who witnessed the slight altercation.

"Robert, please, I beg of you, speak nothing of this to your father and mother. Not until I am sure."

He glowered at her. "You have doubts of your identity, yet you see fit to speak of it to me? What kind of woman are you?" He eyed her with such contempt that it brought tears to her eyes.

"I'm sorry, forgive me," she pleaded. "You have every right to be angry with me." Her plea did nothing to prevent his hasty departure. Robert stormed through the door and disappeared out of sight.

Defeated in heart, Jolene returned to the table and retrieved the diary and her purse. After paying the bill, she noted out the window that the Whitefield's driver had returned and was waiting for her at the curb.

As she exited the café and walked toward the motorcar in dismay, she felt a strong hand grab her by the shoulder halting her steps. She spun around to see who manhandled her with such force.

"I forgot to pay for my tea." Robert said. With an apologetic face, he held out a sovereign in the palm of his hand.

Jolene sighed in relief. "No matter," she replied. "The tea was on me." She looked anxiously at him waiting for him to say something, anything, to tell her he would listen to her story.

"All right, I admit it," he began. He looked at her warily. "You have my attention. I want to know what is in your book of history, as you call it."

Jolene could not help but smile. "I'm happy to share it with you, Robert, but you must promise not to tell anyone else."

He nodded agreeably. "I can do that," he said. "Besides if I told mother, she would no doubt have a heart attack. I do not want to be responsible for her death," he said. A lighthearted grin returned to his face.

Jolene slipped her hand into her purse and retrieved the letter. She held it tightly between her index finger and thumb. Slightly fearful of what she was about to do, she offered it to Robert anyway.

"Take this and read it. It arrived at my home shortly before the death of my stepfather. Let me know what you think. But no one else must read its words," she strongly emphasized.

Robert took the letter and flipped it back and forth. "Posted from London?" He examined the stamp and address.

Jolene shook her head.

"All right, then, it's safe with me." He placed the letter into his inside coat pocket.

"I need your help." Jolene took a step closer in desperation.

Robert glanced at his pocket watch. "I can do nothing further right now. My parents are waiting for me as we speak. May I call upon you at the Whitefield's at noon tomorrow? Perhaps we can get away for a private lunch."

"Yes, that would be fine." She let the enthusiasm in her voice express the urge she felt to hug him, but she refrained from the display of affection.

"I see the Whitefield's driver is waiting for you," he said.

"Yes, I should be going." He looked at her curiously as if he were seeing her in a different light.

"I know it must be hard for you to trust me, but it is hard for me to trust as well." Jolene lowered her eyes ashamed of her own emotions. "I'm afraid, Robert, very afraid that the person I thought I was does not exist." Could he possibly understand her fears?

"We'll talk more of it tomorrow." His voice was kind as he tipped his hat in farewell.

"Goodbye," she replied. Her voice trembled. The driver opened the door. "Would you like to return to the Whitefield residence?"

"Yes, please."

Emotionally exhausted over what had transpired, she clung to the diary during the trip back. The turn of events had altered the course of her search. Hopefully, Robert would keep their confidence. He could ruin everything, but a peaceful calm told her that he would not betray her. She sighed, thinking about the remainder of the day. Her only plans for the next few hours would be to lock herself in her room and do nothing but read.

Chapter 11

Thwarted Plans

The car pulled down The Boltons, and as they approached, she noticed another motorcar parked in front of the home. Apparently, they had become quite the desired mode of transportation for those who could afford such luxury machines. Jolene had to admit, she did enjoy the ride compared to the bumpy transport of a hansom cab.

After parking, the driver turned off the car and came around to open her door.

"Thank you for the transportation today," she said.

"My pleasure," he replied tipping his hat. "Feel free to tell Branson should you need further conveyance about London in the future."

The door to the Whitefield residence swung open, and Branson greeted her arrival. "I see you have returned."

"Yes, and I will be retiring to my room for a few hours," she announced. Jolene walked past him with the intention of climbing the stairs to the second floor.

"I'm afraid that will have to wait, your ladyship. A young man has called and desires to see you. He's waiting in the parlor."

"What young man?" Jolene thought Robert had second thoughts and wanted to talk to her sooner.

"Mr. Chambers."

"Oh." Jolene was shocked over the announcement. "Well, tell him that I will join him in a few minutes. I must return an item to my room and quickly change."

"Very well," he said. He nodded and headed toward the parlor.

Jolene hastened up the stairs a bit miffed that Geoffrey had intruded upon her plans. On the other hand, his arrival had come at a time when a diversion might be helpful.

Upon entering her room, she stopped and tried to decide where to hide her so-called history book. Walking over to the armoire, she opened the double doors and saw a shelf just above her head. It would be a safe place, but she needed to wrap it in something to keep it hidden.

Her eyes wandered over to her bath chamber remembering the numerous towels. Finding a small hand towel, she wrapped the diary and shoved it on the top shelf toward the back, out of sight but not out of reach.

After removing her hat and the jacket to her walking dress, she straightened her white blouse. A quick check in the vanity mirror told her she needed to powder her shiny nose and rearrange a few loose strands of hair. When Jolene felt her appearance looked acceptable, she headed for the parlor.

When she entered, the diary and meeting with Robert swiftly faded the moment Geoffrey's eyes met hers. She felt his magnetic presence ten feet away. The man was insufferably handsome with his dark-brown hair, tall and imposing stature, and a voice that could melt the winter snow.

"I wasn't expecting you," she said, taking a few cautious steps toward him.

"Pardon my unplanned visit, Lady von Lamberg, but I was driving by and thought I'd take the opportunity to speak with you about my offer to show you about London."

He took a giant stride toward her until he was a few feet away. The cologne he wore mingled with the scent of her own perfume threatening to make her sneeze.

"Yes, the tour," she said, stepping aside and walking toward a chair. "Why don't you take a seat, and we can talk about it." Jolene needed distance from his appeal that unnerved her female senses. She chose a single chair and sat down. Geoffrey dismissed her efforts to put distance between them and pulled a chair closer, settling straight in her view.

Another character note, she thought to herself. Geoffrey Chambers is forward.

Looking confident and comfortable, Geoffrey leaned back, placed his elbows on the armrests, and clasped his two hands together. "Now, what would the beautiful and charming young lady like to see in London? Your wish is my command."

In Jolene's mind, only one word described her desires—all. However, she remembered Grace's proposal that maybe she and Robert should join them. It suddenly made perfect sense, because she admitted her weakness to Geoffrey's charm.

"I would love to see everything," she replied, sounding like an overzealous tourist. "Parliament, Westminster Abbey, Buckingham Palace, the Tower of London, St. Paul's, every museum in the city, and whatever else you suggest."

"Well, you cannot leave London without a visit to Hampton Court and Windsor Castle. Those are absolutes for any tour." Geoffrey added like a staunch history teacher.

"But are they not some distance away?"

"Hampton Court is ten miles down the Thames River, and the Castle about fourteen miles beyond that. I would suggest an overnight stay since it would be over a forty-mile trip in one day."

Jolene considered his motives. Did he just advocate that she go away with him on an extended trip? Could he be that presumptuous to think she would agree? For a brief moment, she wanted to slap his confident face. He must have witnessed the fury in her eyes, because he quickly clarified his suggestion.

"Oh, by no means am I suggesting that you risk your reputation by spending the night with me. That was not my intent."

"Then what was your intent?" She coolly replied keeping her gazed fixed and watching him squirm in his chair.

"My parents' manor estate is not far from Windsor. I'm sure they would not mind if you would be their guest for the evening."

The idea sounded appealing but still left much to be desired. "Then who would chaperon, if I am with you at your country manor and your parents are here in London? I don't understand the arrangement."

"The season will practically be over in June anyway, and they will be returning home." His voice sounded apologetic as if he were trying to redeem himself in her eyes.

"My plans are to visit Paris in June. I don't think it would be possible." As much as she wanted to see Windsor Castle, an important task lay ahead of her in Paris. She needed to find Philippe Moreau. Without any clue where to look, it would take time. A private investigator might need to be hired.

"I won't deny I will be disappointed if you leave so soon, but I am more than happy to show you what I can during your stay."

His demeanor shifted to a more courteous approach. Perhaps he realized he had nearly jeopardized his charming impact upon her heart.

"It is such a beautiful day that it is a shame I cannot drive you to Kensington Palace this afternoon. It's only a few miles from here." He dangled another tempting carrot.

She observed another character note. *The man is indomitable.*

"Grace mentioned that she would love to join us, along with Lord Holland, for the sake of appearances. Lord and

Lady Whitefield thought it would be a wise thing to do. After all, I am a stranger to London. It might appear inappropriate for me to be seen alone with you, gallivanting about the city." Jolene fully recognized she needed protection from herself and not necessarily Mr. Chambers.

His facial expression soured over the suggestion, and he began tapping his right forefinger on the armrest. "I should let you know that my cousin possesses ulterior motives," he began. "He is ambitiously trying to pursue you romantically."

Jolene smirked and shook her head over his attempt to warn her about his cousin. Geoffrey appeared self-righteous as he sat there waiting for her response. "It appears to me that you are as well, Mr. Chambers," she countered quickly. "Besides, Lord Holland and I have already come to an agreement regarding the terms of our relationship."

"Oh, really?" he replied. He leaned forward in his seat indicating his interest.

"Yes really. I'm capable of handling my own affairs when it comes to the male race." With her own confident air, she raised an eyebrow at him to put him in his place. He was about to respond when Grace unexpectedly entered the parlor.

"Geoffrey Chambers," she spoke with surprise. She moseyed over and stood in front of him blocking his view of Jolene. "What may I ask are you doing here?"

Jolene tilted her head to the right around Grace's body to see his expression. He rose to his feet in greeting but cast an annoyed glance. "My impromptu visit is in regard to offering her ladyship a proper tour of London." Mr. Chambers sidestepped Grace to regain his view of Jolene.

"Oh, yes," she said. "The tour." Grace slipped to the left, found a nearby chair and sat down. She flashed a glance at Jolene as if she had rescued her from the worst villain in all of London. Geoffrey retreated and sat too.

"I already told Mr. Chambers that you had offered to accompany us with Lord Holland." Since Robert had mentioned nothing earlier, she inquired. "Have you asked him yet?"

"I have not, but I intend to send a note of invitation this afternoon."

"No need to do that, Grace. I have a luncheon date with Lord Holland tomorrow, at which time I will invite him to come with us." After making her announcement, she intended it to generate a comment from Mr. Chambers. To her surprise, Grace spoke up instead.

"Why are you having lunch with Robert?" Her voice sounded curt and offended.

Her show of jealousy betrayed her romantic interest. Mr. Chambers quickly recognized her sentiments and explained.

"Don't worry, Grace. The komtesse has advised me that they have already come to an agreement about their relationship."

"Mr. Chambers." Jolene scolded him. Clearly, he made the comment to tease Grace. "Our agreement is strictly platonic. Pay no attention to Mr. Chambers' inference otherwise." The tense facial expression on Grace's face waned, and a slight grin replaced her worry.

"So tomorrow," Mr. Chambers reiterated for the benefit of all in the room, "Is merely a friendly lunch between the two of you?"

"Strictly," she assured.

She looked kindly at her new friend. The color in Grace's face returned. It appeared clear that she had a smitten heart when it came to Robert Holland. Mr. Chambers had apparently been aware of Grace's sentiments regarding his cousin. She wondered if Robert had any idea of Grace's affections. Jolene thought they would make a handsome couple, but matchmaking had never been her forte.

"Well, then, it seems as if you ladies have it all planned," Geoffrey announced. "When shall we start the tour? Will the day after tomorrow suffice? How about ten o'clock in the morning?"

Grace looked over at Jolene waiting for affirmation. "If Robert has no objections and can attend, that sounds agreeable." She thought for a moment and then with enthusiasm looked at Mr. Chambers. "May we visit the Tower of London first?"

"Ah, milady wishes to be locked up in the tower, does she?" His brow rose and roguish demeanor possessed him. "I shall rescue you as a damsel in distress." In further jest, he stood and bowed at his waist making a grand gesture with one arm.

Jolene laughed at his antics. Grace shook her head and frowned.

"I shall not keep you any longer, Lady von Lamberg. I should be getting back," he said. Geoffrey looked satisfied that he had accomplished what he came to do.

"I'll see you out," Grace offered.

She rose to her feet to keep her from Mr. Chambers' side, no doubt. A minute later, she returned and pressed for more information about Lord Holland. "So Robert is taking you to lunch? How did that come about so soon?"

"We bumped into each other this morning over coffee at a neighborhood café," she nonchalantly replied.

"Tell me, did he flirt with you and then you put him in his place? Is this how your agreement about the relationship came about?"

Poor Grace. Jolene reached over and touched her forearm. "Dearest, I get the distinct impression that you have an interest in him even though he is such a rascal as you say." She patted her arm reassuringly. "After all, I do seem to remember the two of you danced often last evening."

A second later, Grace brought both her hands to her face hiding in embarrassment. "Goodness, I can't help myself," she admitted. "I am hopelessly and irrationally attracted to him."

"Irrationally...excellent choice of words. I totally understand your dilemma," she chuckled.

"You don't like him then?" She pulled her hands away and looked into Jolene's eyes.

"I like him, but certainly not in the way you think. Let us just say we have some things in common. Nonetheless, we both agreed after spending time with each other, there could be no romantic attachment."

"Thank God," Grace sighed. "He seemed so jealous of Geoffrey last night that I was sure he would make a play for your affections."

"I won't deny that he did not try his best to do so," she confessed. "I quickly put him in his place, and with civility he accepted my wishes."

A frustrated puff of air left Grace's lungs. "I wish he would make a pass at me, but it is obvious that I don't exist in his realm of eligible women."

"Perhaps, after spending more time with you while we tour the city, his interest will blossom."

"I doubt that it will, but I will savor each moment that we can be together."

An obvious reason popped into Jolene's head. "It could be that he respects you, because of his friendly relationship with your brother."

"I can assure you that it has nothing to do with it. I am not the type of empty-headed, silly girl he likes for companionship. Alastair tells me he likes them daft and loose, if you get my drift."

Disconcerted over Robert's reputation with women, Jolene scowled. Irritated, she rearranged her skirt as if she were thinking about rearranging his priorities. "Well, perhaps it is about time someone knocked some sense into his blond head. I would shudder to think that he is actually that shallow."

Obviously, the blood that they shared through their mother had incited a sisterly reaction to his behavior. The concept of sibling rivalry and sparring with one another brought a mischievous smile to her face. Without thinking twice, she had apparently thrown her doubt to the wind with regard to Robert being her half brother. They had not even discussed the possibility in private and already she wished it to be true.

"Well, do me a favor then. Send him a note of invitation anyway just in case I forget to mention it during lunch." Jolene wanted to give Grace the opportunity to write.

"Yes, I'll do that straightaway." Her countenance glowed with thankfulness.

"Grace, if you don't mind, I'm going to retire to my room. I'm a bit tired."

"Of course," she said, rising to her feet, appearing surprised over the change in direction.

"We'll talk later, I promise."

After a slow ascension to her room, Jolene closed the door. She retrieved her hidden treasure and sat in a chair by the window. Flipping carefully through the tattered pages, she found the place where she had read the last entry. Another month had passed, along with another note of no pregnancy.

"My mistress cries each time she bleeds. When His Grace hears the news, he grows despondent and withdraws from her bed. I do not understand why God will not answer her prayers."

For another hour, she read of Jacquelyn's frustrations that she had expressed to Dorcas. There were scattered entries about how she loved to decorate the estate with the help of her mother-in-law. Jolene had not realized up until this point that the dowager duchess existed. It pleased her to know that Jacquelyn had support from another woman.

The pages became repetitious in style. Dorcas focused heavily upon her barren mistress, but after years passed a distinct concern rose in her writings. It appeared her respect for the duke waned.

"Today my mistress bled in her bath water. I had never witnessed such a sight in all of my years. She screamed for me like a mad woman. Her fists pounded the water until it splashed upon the walls and floors, tinted pink with the flow of her menstrual blood. I nearly wept as I pulled her from her bath and consoled her distraught state of mind."

Jolene closed the diary and set it down. It had become too heartbreaking and depressing to read any further. With the growing knowledge of Jacquelyn's sad plight, her heart held little respect for the woman who supposedly was her mother. Dorcas' entries told a tale of a brokenhearted duchess, who suspected her husband's infidelity. Why did Suzette become his mistress knowing it could destroy the heart of another woman? As a tangled web of deceit and betrayal unfolded, anger toward the duke and his current duchess grew.

Agitated over the diary, she wrapped it back in the towel and shoved it onto the shelf and out of sight. Tomorrow, when Robert visited, she would retrieve it with reservation.

Chapter 12

The Power of the Tongue

When Jolene woke in the morning, she only had one thing in mind—her luncheon with Robert. It would be a turning point for both of them. Of more importance, she wanted to know his opinion of the letter.

Feeling rather famished for breakfast, after having a less than hearty appetite for dinner, Jolene entered the dining room. The morning meal was an informal occasion. Each member of the family came to dine anywhere between seven and nine o'clock. Silver warmers overflowed with bacon, eggs, and various sausages, along with a section of grilled tomatoes and mushrooms. A plentiful stack of toast with butter and marmalade sat on the table.

Jolene filled her plate and sat down with Lady and Lord Whitefield. Grace and Alastair were either late or had already eaten. Lord Whitefield hid behind an open newspaper barely taking notice of her arrival.

"Lady von Lamberg, do you have anything planned for today?" Lady Whitefield asked while buttering another piece of toast.

"Actually, yes. I will be having lunch with Robert...I mean Lord Holland."

Lord Whitefield lowered his paper and peered over the top. "Alone?"

"Yes, alone. I'll be fine," Jolene dismissed his concern. She needed time with Robert and determined to keep others away.

"Do you think that wise?" He gave her a fatherly look, which in Jolene's opinion had overstepped his boundaries as a host.

"We have formed a friendship, Lord Whitefield, and nothing more. Robert and I have a common interest in horses and other sports." Jolene was not one to lie, but she had stretched the truth to the breaking point. "I believe he has some questions about the Spanish Riding School in Vienna." Maybe she should bring up the school as a subject, so what she spoke would not count as a fib.

"I see." He lifted the newspaper in front of his face.

Glad that interrogation was over, Lady Whitefield interjected with a question.

"What time do you think you will be returning this afternoon?"

"Time?" Jolene thought for a moment. "Well, our lunch is at noon, so I presume no later than two or three o'clock—unless I decide to do some shopping."

"Excellent," she responded with a broad smile. "I do hope you will be here at three, because I have invited a few women over for afternoon tea. Grace will be joining us too."

"Might I ask who?" Jolene braced herself.

"Lady Chambers and her sister-in-law, the duchess, will be joining us."

Jolene clung to her fork tightly so it would not land in the middle of her soggy eggs. "Well, that sounds pleasant." *Not really*, she thought to herself. Obviously, the diary had tainted her opinion regarding Robert's mother. Still, if she could hold her tongue and reign in her emotions, the three o'clock tea might prove useful.

"Well, I'm happy that you will join us. I know that Lady Chambers is dying to ask you questions about Vienna." She took a bite of her toast and chewed it slowly. After swallowing, she added another comment.

"She may also put in a good word for her son. Frankly, I think that is why she is coming to tea so that she can rave about his admirable qualities."

Lord Whitefield lowered his paper and peeked over the top again. "Qualities?"

"Shush," Lady Whitefield scolded him.

"And why is the duchess coming?" Jolene had to pry about her motives.

"Well, she and her husband are staying with the Chambers until June, along with their son Robert. As you know, they are related, so it's a family gathering."

A piece of bacon stuck to the back of Jolene's throat over that revelation. Quickly she washed it down with a sip of tea. Meals at the Whitefields were turning into informative occasions.

"They don't have their own townhome here in London?"

"They sold it," a gruff voice bellowed from behind the paper. "They owned one in Paris as well, which went on the market only a year or two after they wed."

"Why?" Jolene cringed over her own brash nosiness.

"George, let's not gossip." His wife scolded him firmly.

With a huff, he lowered the paper, folded it, and laid it on the corner of the table. "It's not gossip, woman, it is fact." He turned to Jolene and spouted off the reasons. "The Hollands are nearly bankrupt since His Grace returned..."

"George!" Lady Whitefield abruptly cut him off. "I told you no gossip," she growled.

He narrowed his eyes and glared in return. Jolene cringed at the sparks flying between husband and wife. Slowly, his lordship rose to his feet and looked Jolene straight in the eye. It was obvious he wanted to tell her the sordid truth, but instead he played the gentleman and departed.

Jolene's fork poked at the eggs in the midst of the tense atmosphere that hung in the room. She glanced over at Lady

Whitefield, who was red as a beet. "Your husband does not seem too fond of the Chambers or the Hollands."

"Your assumption is correct. There are things about their pasts that are not readily acceptable in London society. People gossip and keep grudges." Lady Whitefield sipped her tea and thoughtfully continued. "Christian conduct is often lacking in the inner circles of the wealthy. As the Good Book says, 'the tongue is an unruly evil with deadly poison.' My husband has yet to learn that verse, I am afraid."

"I think it is the same on the Continent, Lady Whitefield. Society is no different in Vienna."

Jolene finished the remainder of her breakfast in quiet contemplation. Her activities for the day consisted of the Holland family, and it would undoubtedly be a challenge.

--·✳·--

Branson announced the arrival of Robert, and Jolene smiled in relief that he had kept his promise for lunch. She secured her hat on her upswept hairdo and buttoned the jacket of her tailored, beige walking suit. With her diary in one hand and purse in the other, she descended the stairs to see Robert waiting for her at the door. The moment their eyes met, her heart jumped. He believed, or at least she thought he did by the expression on his face.

"Lady von Lamberg, you look nice today," he politely said.

She kept the pleasantries in front of the staff to a minimum. "Thank you, Lord Holland." She smiled demurely as they exited the house. Robert had arrived in a hansom cab, and Jolene was a bit disappointed it was not a motorcar. Nevertheless, if it were true that the Hollands were in financial difficulty she understood.

After they climbed in and started down the street, Robert announced where they were going. "I thought I'd take you to a small, local pub," he said. "I think it will provide us more privacy." He nodded at the diary in Jolene's hand. "I see you've brought the history book."

"And I'm anxious to show it to you, Robert."

Robert remained pensive for a few moments and then confessed. "There are so many questions I want to ask that I don't know where to begin."

Surprised to hear the nervousness in his voice, Jolene glanced at him. Frankly, she felt the same way.

After a short ride, they exited the cab and Robert escorted Jolene into a pub. It took a few moments for her eyes to adjust to the dark surroundings. Rather than bustling with patrons, only a few people sat spread out at various tables. Robert chose one tucked away from the main aisle. They ordered their lunch and drinks, and then sat awkwardly staring at each other. Finally, Robert pulled the letter from his inside coat pocket and slid it across the table at Jolene.

"I read it."

"And what did you think?" Jolene held her breath.

"From what I've been told, the events did occur in that fashion. What is your book about? May I see it again?"

Jolene handed it to him, and he eagerly took it from her hand. He flipped from page to page scrunching his brow.

"Yesterday, when you found me at the coffee shop, I had just returned from the address on the back of the letter."

"Really? Did you confront the lady's maid about the letter?" A tone of anger came from his voice.

"She's dead."

"Oh, that helps," he said. His shoulders slumped.

"Her sister answered the door and gave me the diary. She read it and believed everything to be true."

Robert shook his head. "I don't have the patience to read all this scribbling from the pen of an emotional woman," he complained. "How far have you read?"

"Enough to aggravate me," she confessed.

"Why?"

"You must understand that your father's first wife, Jacquelyn, was the only mother I've known. Dorcas goes into much detail about her heartaches with your father and her inability to bear him a child."

Robert closed the diary as if he didn't want to know what it said and shoved it back across the table.

"Your mother..." Jolene's words trailed off fearing to speak ill of her in front of Robert.

"My mother was his mistress, and I was conceived a bastard."

The expression on his face grieved Jolene. She had not previously thought of his own feelings about his heritage and past. All the secrets revealed were peeling back layers of hurt and pain.

"I've known for some time," he added with annoyance.

Jolene wanted to object to his identification as a bastard, when he had received full rights and title from his father.

Their order was delivered, and thankfully, their thoughts had been momentarily diverted to food and drink. They ate and chatted about everything else but lay aside the other.

"Geoffrey is taking me on a tour of the city, Robert. It has been suggested by the Whitefields, that for the sake of appearance, that you and Grace accompany the two of us."

Robert smirked over her announcement and shook his head. "I suppose if you are my half sister, I am obligated to protect you from lecherous men."

"Protect me from Geoffrey, you mean?"

"It's true that I cannot damn his roguish character when I am no better myself," he said, cocking his head to the side. "If it were any other woman, I would not care." He leaned forward and looked seriously into her eyes. "Seeing that it involves you, I do care."

Jolene brought her hand to her chest in a swooning gesture. "Oh, now you're going to make me cry, brother."

He raised his eyebrows over her antics. As their eyes met, they looked at each other as if they realized their connection. Robert finished his sandwich and set his plate aside.

"Now, it's your turn," he said with a warm smile. "What the hell happened to you when Jacquelyn kidnapped you?"

Jolene mulled over her answer. Frankly, Jacquelyn had played the ruse quite well. How could she separate the admiration for her from the criminality of it all?

"My mother..." Jolene stopped again and squeezed her eyes together because she could not let go of the association. She began again. "Jacquelyn fled to Austria. She met my stepfather within the first year of her arrival. They married soon after they met, but she died when I was three."

"What happened to her?"

"She became pregnant and had complications before the birth."

"You have got to be kidding me?" Robert thrust his hand through his hair in astonishment. "You mean she actually became pregnant after all that time?"

Jolene nodded.

"Well, I'll be damned. Father will shit when he hears that news."

If she could have raised her brow any higher in disapproval over his language, Jolene would have. *Another character note*, she mused, *cannot stop swearing in front of the ladies*. Noticing her disapproving scowl, he quickly apologized.

"God, I'm sorry," he said grimacing. "My language..."

She narrowed her eyes at him, but her words were lighthearted. "So I hear."

"Then what happened?" Robert leaned forward.

"My stepfather legally adopted me. When he passed away a few months ago, I inherited the title and all of his estate." Jolene hesitated to tell Robert the full terms of the disbursement.

"Well, regardless of the circumstances, I'm happy that your life has been blessed," he replied.

"I'm thankful, too, but I have a confession."

"What's that?"

"That I've always had this sense of not belonging. Though my stepfather was a kind and gracious man, I've been haunted as long as I can remember about my heritage." Jolene sighed wondering if Robert could understand. "Jacquelyn always told the story that my real father had died in a tragic accident. Frankly, after she died, in my own mind I was nothing more than an orphan."

A sympathetic gaze met Jolene's eyes. "If you want to know anything about your real father, I can tell you what I know and remember. He saved my mother's disgrace and raised me in love until…"

Robert looked at her in the strangest way. He lowered his eyes, shook his head, and then chuckled. "Until I shoved over your bassinet in a fit of jealousy when you were three months old."

The laughter that spilled out of Jolene's mouth filled the small pub. Every person's head turned in their direction. Embarrassed, she brought her hand to her mouth and held it there until she could control herself. Robert's eyes twinkled in response.

"Grace was right. You *are* a rascal," she said, still chuckling under her breath.

Neither of them could stop laughing over the funny story. It felt as if they had found an oasis of relief from their painful conversation. Jolene's affection for Robert welled in her heart. She saw the same sentiments in his eyes.

"So did you get a whipping?" Jolene figured as much.

Robert put his hand on his backside in jest. "God yes, I can still feel the belt on my behind."

After a few moments of smiling at one another, Jolene turned her thoughts to Philippe. She did want to know about him. In fact, her heart yearned to know more than she cared to know of Suzette.

"I plan to go to Paris after the season ends and search for him, Robert."

"That's probably wise. Frankly, I hope he is still alive so that he can finally see you again. Mother carries a lot of guilt over how your loss nearly destroyed him."

Suzette again. Would she ever think kindly of her?

"Come with me." The words flew out of her mouth. Robert sat straight up in his chair over the invitation. "I mean it, Robert. I'll pay for everything, just come."

"Are you sure that you want me to accompany you?" He reached over and touched her hand lightly.

A broad smile spread across Jolene's face, and a burden that had pressed upon her heart felt lighter. "Very sure," she replied.

They spent the next half an hour chatting. Robert told her what he remembered about Philippe and how he had married their mother to save her reputation. When he came to the duel, Jolene gasped. She had not yet come that far in Dorcas' diary to read anything about a duel, which she omitted from her letter.

"Oh, my God, Philippe tried to kill your father?"

Robert shook his head as if he could not believe it himself. "Yes, father shot him in the shoulder after Philippe missed."

"Unbelievable." Jolene was awestruck over the tale of revenge. She chuckled. "Who would believe such a mess?"

Robert's countenance changed. His voice softened. "I'm glad you have found us after all these years. If it were not for that deathbed confession, we would have never learned of your fate."

"I think fate has returned me for a reason."

"What are your plans to tell my parents? Do you wish me to say anything?"

"No, please say nothing. If all works out, I want to bring all of them together—your father, mother, and Philippe and then tell them at once."

"My goodness," Robert said in astonishment, leaning back in his chair. "You have thoughtfully planned this out, haven't you?"

Jolene shook her head. "Yes, but that depends upon whether I can find Philippe. Hopefully, he is still alive."

Robert thought for a moment. "You know, my father may have kept track of his whereabouts. Let me see if he knows anything."

"Oh, that would be wonderful," she exclaimed. Jolene glanced at her watch. "Oh, dear, I'm supposed to be back at the Whitefields at three o'clock. I'm having tea with your aunt and mother."

"Well, I wouldn't want to keep you from that affair," he smirked. Robert rose from his seat and helped Jolene from her chair.

"Oh, I forgot to tell you that Grace will be contacting you about coming with us to the Tower of London tomorrow." Jolene took his arm as he led her out the door. "Do be kind to the girl, won't you?"

Robert cocked his head to the right as if he misheard her comment. Jolene merely smiled, hoping that perhaps one day he would notice sweet Grace.

Chapter 13

Tea for Five

Jolene arrived at the Whitefields at two-thirty. It was barely enough time to change into a casual day dress and freshen up before tea. As much as she had enjoyed lunch with Robert, she scowled at the thought of seeing his mother. For some reason, it felt more comfortable to refer to her as "his mother" or the duchess. She had not arrived at a point of endearment to think of her as anything else.

When three o'clock arrived, she slowly descended the stairs inhaling a deep breath for fortitude. As she reached the foyer below, she heard voices in the parlor. She straightened her spine, lifted her chin and entered. Everyone had arrived, including Grace, who flashed a forced smile in captivity.

"Oh, you are here." Lady Whitefield greeted her arrival, rising to her feet. "You remember Lady Chambers and the duchess."

"Yes, of course. It's a pleasure to see you again." Marguerite Chambers did not impress her either with her pretentious airs.

Jolene took a seat near Grace where she would feel more at ease, who awkwardly opened up the discussion.

"So how was your lunch with Lord Holland?"

Jolene parted her lips to respond to her question, but the duchess interrupted.

"Oh, Robert didn't tell me that he was having lunch with you."

Slowly turning her head in her direction, Jolene nodded in affirmation. "Yes, he had some questions to ask me about the Spanish Riding School in Vienna." She smiled and gritted her teeth at the same time. Lying had never been easy for Jolene, but she could not tell her the truth.

"I'm not surprised. He loves horses," the duchess replied.

The footman arrived with tea on a silver tray along with a few lemon bars and other delicacies. The conversation momentarily ceased until everyone had their bone china in hand and cups full. Jolene wished it were a strong brew of coffee instead.

"Well, now, isn't this pleasant," Lady Whitefield announced, looking quite pleased with her roomful of ladies. She glanced at each of them with satisfaction.

Lady Chambers took the lead by turning her attention upon Jolene. "It was a pleasure having you attend the ball. Did you enjoy yourself?"

"Yes, I found it most enjoyable. By the time we returned and I climbed into bed, my poor feet were throbbing from having danced so much."

"My son mentioned that you dance divinely," Geoffrey's mother said, leaning forward.

Jolene purposely hesitated before answering by taking a sip of tea. Slowly, she set the cup down in the saucer enjoying her control over the conversation. She glanced at Lady Chambers, who waited for a positive statement regarding her son. Finally, she relented and gave her what she wanted.

"Well, let me say," she began, fluttering her eyelashes, "that I found your son to be marvelous in his footwork. A few times he twirled me around so fast it made me dizzy, but I kept up with his enthusiasm."

Grace chuckled. "I can attest to the fact because Robert and I tried to waltz alongside of them, and it proved to be impossible."

It would have helped the conversation if Grace spoke up more often, but Jolene had the feeling she would not come to her rescue at every turn.

"How long are you staying in London?" Lady Chambers continued to lead the conversation.

Before responding, she glanced at the duchess who appeared unusually quiet. Her body language betrayed her awkwardness amongst a group of women. *Has she always been such a timid creature?* Jolene thought.

"Until June and then I travel to Paris," Jolene finally answered.

As soon as she mentioned Paris, the duchess visually straightened her slumped shoulders. She appeared to have more pride in her background than in her title of a duchess in England.

"Have you visited Paris before?" A gleam in her eyes returned.

"No, this will be my first visit, except for merely changing trains at the station. Truth be told, I have never left Austria. My stepfather, the count, was heavily involved in affairs of state. Opportunities to travel outside the country were set aside."

"Such a shame," the duchess replied. "I'm sure you will love Paris."

"Do you miss your homeland?" She had asked the question once before when they first met. Would she now confess the truth?

Suzette shifted uncomfortably in her seat. After taking a quick sip of tea, she answered. "My parents are buried in France. If I miss anything, it is visiting their graves and paying my respect," she said in a low voice.

Her response took Jolene off guard. Already she had judged the woman as a cruel home breaker. She had not expected her to speak of her dead parents with such sentiment. Then, as if a cool sense of reality washed over her, she angrily wondered if she missed her lost Parisian daughter. She clenched her teeth to keep her mouth shut and closed her eyes for a moment to take her gaze off the duchess. Why did she feel such anger toward the mother she always wanted?

Finally, she opened her eyes. They shifted from Grace, to Lady Whitefield, and Lady Chambers. They appeared baffled over her moment of discomposure. She inhaled a deep breath and cast a curious gaze at the duchess to hide the disappointment in her heart.

"You know, I love stories, and enjoy asking couples how they met." She looked pointedly into the duchess' eyes. "I'm curious how a French lady came about marrying an English duke. You must have a fascinating romance story." Jolene knew she had asked a cruel question. When the blood drained from the duchess' face, her sister-in-law cleared her throat and came to the rescue.

"Our family owned a townhome in Paris. We often spent time there." She glanced at the duchess as much to say that she would handle the question. "My brother met her during one of his frequent visits to Paris, I believe at the horse races. Isn't that right?"

The duchess kept her attention upon her sister-in-law rather than answering directly to Jolene. "Yes, quite right. He loved the races."

Lady Chambers' confident look that she had saved family's reputation, annoyed Jolene. Tea for five had turned into an uncomfortable event, so she reached for a lemon cake and shoved it in her mouth to shut herself up. As she was munching the tasty treat, Grace must have noticed her unease. Finally, she turned the conversation in another direction.

"We're off to the Tower of London tomorrow to take the komtesse on a tour of the city. It should be fun, though the atmosphere at the Tower gives me the chills. All I envision are heads being chopped off." She scrunched her shoulders and shuddered.

"Heads being chopped off?" Jolene knew the barbaric moments of English history but played along.

"So many poor women sent to their death," Lady Whitefield lamented. "Queen Anne Boleyn, Katherine Howard, Lady Jane Grey, and that poor woman, the Countess of Salisbury."

Impressive list of names, Jolene thought, but she had not heard about the countess. Naturally, by her title alone, she wanted to hear the morbid tale. "Why do you say the poor countess?"

Lady Chambers interjected with the gory details. "The executioner missed on the first blow and hit her shoulder instead. The story is that she jumped up from the block and ran away. The executioner went after her with the axe. He hacked at her eleven times before he finally brought her down."

"Oh, dear God," Jolene moaned. "How utterly brutal." She looked at the tasty treats that remained, including cherry tarts. "I think I'll pass on the cherry pastries after that story." The levity helped, and the women laughed.

"Well, tomorrow Geoffrey, the komtesse, Robert, and I shall be climbing in and out of the towers. I for one shall spare myself from entering the torture chamber."

Jolene glanced at her mother, who remained silent with an uncomfortable look upon her face. A fleeting thought of making a statement about the French and their guillotines might prove jovial, but she decided to forgo placing her under further scrutiny. Though she wrestled with her emotions regarding the duchess, she would try her best to give her the respect she deserved...if she could.

"Geoffrey did mention to me that he thought it would be nice if you could visit our country manor so that he might take you to Windsor Castle." Lady Chambers pulled her attention back toward her son. "I was disappointed to hear that you will not be able to join us."

"As much as I appreciate the invitation, I do have pressing business I must attend to in Paris. I cannot put it off any longer."

"Such a shame," she responded, lowering her head in disappointment.

The thought of spending time at their manor estate felt disconcerting. Not because of the company she would keep, but the likelihood that Geoffrey Chambers could ruin her reputation. She had never felt the attraction of a man before. It would be so easy to lose her good sense in his arms. Moreover, if he ever kissed her—well, if that happened there would be no hope for her redemption.

Chatter continued between the ladies over trivial subjects. As she continued to interact with the duchess, her heart remained unmoved by her personality and close proximity. Would she ever feel an ounce of affection for the woman who supposedly gave her life? She certainly could not force affection from her heart, but maybe in time it would grow.

-·✳·-

After the guests departed, Jolene retired to her room to relax before dinner at eight o'clock. The time spent in the duchess' presence spurred her to pick up the diary and start reading again. After moving through five years of sadness, Dorcas mentioned a trip to Paris with her husband.

My mistress sat quietly while I brushed her hair this evening. I asked her if she enjoyed her walk with the duke today in the park. She told me of a man and little boy they had met along the way. The child was five years old with blond hair and blue eyes. She thought nothing of it until the boy's father told the duke that the boy's mother had died. The young lad's name was Robert, and the duchess expressed how uncanny his features were like those of her husband's.

Jolene stopped reading and thought for a moment. Her family history had turned into an epic puzzle with pieces scattered everywhere. Why had Philippe told the duke that Suzette had died? Obviously, in spite of the boy's appearance, the duke had been kept in the dark regarding Robert's existence.

"Oh, this is frustrating," Jolene spat. She slammed the book down on the bed and rose to walk over to the window. How long would it take to complete the picture of the past? There were still large unread portions of Dorcas' entries. Perhaps a private detective could read it and summarize it for her. She chuckled at her foolish idea to soothe her momentary frustration.

Regardless of the lack of patience over not having the full story, today she had made progress. A smile replaced her disgruntled frown when she thought of Robert. It felt right to have a half brother, even if he did push her bassinet over in a fit of jealousy. *The rascal*, she thought.

One problem remained, though. How could she get him to Paris without their appearance together looking suspicious? There were still weeks ahead to figure out that dilemma, so she dismissed the worry.

Chapter 14

Off With Your Head!

The foursome arrived at the Tower midmorning. Grace was delighted to see that Robert strode by her side. Geoffrey insisted on offering his arm in escort, which Jolene accepted. The cobblestone pathways were uneven and the stairs up and through some of the towers narrow. She tried her best not to allow his magnetism take precedence over the infamous Tower of London.

As they walked through the gate, Yeoman Warders in Tudor State Dress greeted them. Outfitted in impressive uniforms of dark blue, red and gold trim, with hats, Jolene had no idea why they were nicknamed beefeaters. "What do the Yeoman do, just eat beef?" She shot a confused look at Geoffrey.

"Spoken like a true foreigner," Robert said, giving her a playful look.

"Well, I am," Jolene protested. "Stop teasing me and tell me if they just eat beef."

Geoffrey and Robert burst out in a hearty laugh, while Grace at least had the decency to save her from her ignorant assumptions.

"They are not eaters of beef; it means *beaufetiers* who were royal servants that waited at the buffet while monarchy dined. It is a French term, but it has somehow been converted by the English over the centuries to beefeaters because they could not pronounce the word."

Jolene understood as soon as she heard the French pronunciation. "Thank you Grace," she said, giving Geoffrey and Robert a sneer.

"So, Lady von Lamberg, would you prefer the official tour by the *beaufetiers* amongst a crowd of tourists, or would you rather have a more private and intimate tour guide?"

Before she could answer, Robert interjected.

"If it's private, Grace and I will be attending. Remember, 'ol chap, that we are together for the sake of appearances, not so you can spirit the lady away into some dark hallway and kiss her."

Jolene pondered the choices looking into Geoffrey's hopeful eyes and then announced her decision. "Well, I would like the group tour, but I would also enjoy time alone with the three of you. Mr. Chambers, lead the way."

Like a true Englishman proud of his heritage, he suddenly looked like a puffed-up peacock strutting about the courtyard. "I suggest you take a pamphlet and follow along," he said, offering her one. "You two already know the story." He bypassed Grace and Robert who did not seem to mind.

"The tower we are standing before now is the Bell Tower, built in 1190. It is here where Sir Thomas Moore was kept prisoner before Henry VIII had him beheaded."

Jolene followed along with great interest as Geoffrey played the private Yeoman of the group. From tower to tower, he spewed his intelligent rhetoric. They stopped at the traitor's gate, and he made a particular point to tell the gruesome stories of heads mounted on stakes. They climbed up stairs, walked upon the wall from tower to tower, and up and down winding staircases. They even had a roaring laugh at Grace running through the room past the rack that had been used for torture.

"I swear," she complained vehemently, "that room is haunted with the poor souls stretched to their death."

"Not as bad as the wandering ghosts upon the Tower green where heads rolled," teased Robert. He gently made a slashing movement across her neck with his index finger, provoking a scream from Grace. Jolene gave him an approving nod, but he acted as if he did it to make her happy rather than his companion.

As they meandered along, the group came to a narrow, spiral staircase. Geoffrey let Robert and Grace climb the steps ahead of them, since the stairs were only wide enough for one person to ascend at a time. Jolene went ahead of Geoffrey. About halfway, she felt both of his hands slide around her waist pulling her to a halt.

"Turn around," he demanded, in an enticing voice.

The temptation was too hard to resist in the dark spiral staircase. Jolene obeyed. They faced each other eye-to-eye as Jolene stood a step above and Geoffrey on the step below.

"Let me kiss you," he entreated, staring at her lips in anticipation.

Jolene trembled in his grasp. "Someone will see us," she weakly protested.

"No one will see us. No one is behind us. I checked. And Robert and Grace are far ahead by now."

"They'll wonder what is keeping us," Jolene reasoned. Why, she had no idea. She wanted the kiss and felt as tortured as the souls they had walked past in the last tower.

No verbal assent left her lips but she lean forward. He took advantage and pulled her close slamming her into his hard body. His warm lips wrapped around her mouth with a fervent kiss. Shivers of pleasure sped through her veins like fire. She lost her balance when her knees weakened, but he held her up in his arms like a strong warrior in armor.

The fairytale moment in the tower suddenly broke when she felt a strong hand squeeze her shoulder. Robert's voice echoed in the confined space of stoned walls. "Would you please behave and get on with the tour. It looks as if it's going to rain."

Jolene jerked away from Geoffrey. Flushed from embarrassment and hot from his touch, she spun around. Robert offered his hand to help pull her up the stairs. He acted as if he were rescuing her from a dark knight.

She hesitated until he cocked his head and gave her a brotherly, scolding look of *shame on you.* He was right. She scrunched her face acknowledging her indiscretion. Robert responded by clasping her hand and jerking her forward up the stairs and away from Geoffrey. She was afraid to turn around and see the look upon his face.

When they reached the top of the stairs and exited upon the path that led to another tower, Jolene finally turned around. Geoffrey's eyes sparkled with desire. It only incited her to quicken her step and keep pace with Robert and Grace. It did not take long for her knight to reach her side and offer his arm again.

Grace knew if she touched him, she would be back under his spell. "No, I'm all right, Geoffrey. I can manage on my own."

He pouted but stayed close to her side.

–·✳·–

After traipsing through every corner of the Tower, the foursome decided to leave as the sky threatened rain. As they departed, a few drops had already started to fall, so they hastened to Geoffrey's parked motorcar. Everyone climbed inside, and the group headed for a late lunch as they had planned beforehand.

Geoffrey remained silent as he drove through the London streets back to the heart of the West End. Jolene turned around to see Robert chatting with Grace but could not make out what they were saying. She wondered if Grace made an impression upon her brother. In spite of Grace's infatuation with Robert, she had not decided whether they were a suitable match personality wise. Their appearance together did make them look like a handsome couple.

Her eyes shifted to Geoffrey, who apparently had not recovered from their interrupted kiss. Jolene hoped it would not lead to some kind of altercation between him and Robert over the matter. She was not surprised that Robert had returned to see why they had delayed.

"Thank you for the wonderful tour of the Tower, Geoffrey. You obviously know your history. I am extremely impressed." She smiled trying to break his silence.

"You are welcome. And yes, my English history is quite extensive."

His cool response gave her a chill. He had been so cordial during their last few hours together, and now his demeanor had changed drastically. "I hope you're not mad at me," she whispered. "Public displays of affection are frowned upon in Austria."

"It's not you," he clarified, rolling his eyes toward Robert in the back seat. If Robert had heard his comment, he had decided not to respond.

A few minutes later, they arrived at a restaurant. Jolene was thoroughly confused as to where they were in London. In the distance, she could see Big Ben.

They entered a pleasant-looking restaurant where Geoffrey had apparently made reservations. Led to a large table, Jolene sat next to Robert, and Geoffrey and Grace across from each of them respectively. They perused their menus and placed their orders.

"Do you have a preference as to what you would like to see next?" Geoffrey softened his voice a bit, as he asked the question.

"Oh, dear, I don't know. Is it too late in the day to drive by Parliament, Big Ben, or Westminster Abbey?"

"Robert and Grace, do you mind if we take another hour or two?" Geoffrey looked at them for an answer.

"No, it's fine with me. It will take an hour or so to walk through the Abbey." He turned to Grace. "Is that all right with you?"

"Oh, yes, the Abbey is so quiet. There are only dead monarchs and friendly ghosts."

Jolene laughed until Geoffrey turned to Robert and made a snide comment. His voice was clearly agitated. "Don't worry, Robert, it's hard to steal kisses in the Abbey under the scrutiny of the clergy."

Robert challenged Geoffrey's remark directly. "Taking advantage of a woman in a dark location is not stealing in my opinion, but a direct attempt to use a secluded location to your advantage."

Jolene tensed. Though the two were cousins, it became obvious there existed tension between them she did not understand. She glanced at Grace whose face mirrored her own concern.

"It's all right, Robert," Jolene commented. "I am as much to blame, because I leaned into the kiss before he stole anything."

Perhaps confessing her own indiscretion would help to calm them down. Thankfully, the food arrived halting any further verbal darts flying across the table. Instead, everyone grew quiet and focused on their meal.

"Well, I'm looking forward to the Abbey," Jolene finally announced. "All those dead monarchs buried there and seeing where coronations have taken place, I'm excited."

Everyone looked at her with a dull expression. Perhaps it would be a good place to say a prayer.

--·❋·--

It had been an exciting day seeing only a fraction of the sites in London. When Geoffrey told her of the hours they could fill in museums alone, she tired at the thought. Nevertheless, after finishing lunch, the four planned the week ahead visiting other highlights.

Geoffrey returned her and Grace to the Whitefield's residence. She took a moment and smoothed his ruffled peacock feathers. Robert bid goodbye to Grace, who smiled at him as if she wished he would kiss her. Jolene took Geoffrey's hand and gave him a heartfelt thank you for the time he spent spouting off English history.

"For my sake, please do not be harsh with Robert about interrupting us," she implored. She fluttered her eyelashes using her womanly powers to persuade him. "We have become friends, and there is nothing between us other than common interests that we share. He seems to have taken the role of being my overseer."

Geoffrey raised his eyebrow in surprise. "I find that hard to believe," he confessed. "But if that is what you say, then I will not pursue my irritation with him further."

"Please don't. Between the two of us, I did enjoy the kiss." She smiled at him and suddenly his eyes returned an affectionate gaze. "I'll see you in the morning," she said, wanting to give him a peck on the cheek. However, Robert stood at her side staring at the two of them. He had quickly taken his role of brother quite seriously. It was gratifying to have someone care for her welfare.

The men left, and Grace and Jolene climbed upstairs to their rooms. "How did you and Robert get along?" It appeared to Jolene they were, but she wanted to know directly from Grace. "It looked as if he behaved politely while in your presence."

"Yes, he was polite. Not one kiss stolen. And here I thought he was such a rascal always trying to take advantage of the ladies."

"Well, that can be a good sign. He is being respectable to you as a lady."

They stopped at the landing for a moment. "Well, he could very well be treating me that way because I am Alastair's sister." Grace frowned. "That's it. He treats me like a sister."

Jolene giggled.

"What's so funny?" she asked in irritation.

"Believe me, Grace, he treats you nothing like a sister." Jolene gave Grace a hug. "If it's meant to be, he will come around. Do not give up hope."

They parted and went to their separate suites. Jolene wanted to relax before dinner, but a knock came at the door. "Come in?"

Maria entered. "My lady, is there anything that you need?"

"Not right now. I am a bit tired, so I am going to rest. Come back to help me prepare for dinner."

"Yes, my lady."

After removing her jacket, she retrieved the diary from the upper shelf of the armoire and began reading. Maybe she could put together a few more pieces of the puzzle before the evening meal.

Chapter 15

An Invitation

After a week of tours, Jolene had seen enough of London to last a lifetime. From palaces to museums, Geoffrey continued to impress her with his knowledge. Beyond the obvious charismatic personality, he had proven himself intelligent, well informed, engaging, and driven in his pursuits. Though Robert contained some of those qualities, she had noticed when spending further time with him that his ambitions left much to be desired.

Geoffrey had taken on a different approach altogether by not making any further passes in dark corridors. Perhaps he feared that advances would turn her away, though she did admit she enjoyed the kiss. She felt both slighted and relieved, since her continued reading of the diary produced an urgent need to visit Paris. A male suitor would only distract her from her pursuit, although she admitted it would be an appealing distraction.

The month passed with afternoon teas, a trip to the opera, visits to museums, and time with Grace, Robert, and Geoffrey. As the season came to a close, she received one last invitation to dine at the Chambers. She accepted without hesitation looking forward to spending more time with the duke, duchess, and Robert.

On the day of the dinner, Jolene spent the afternoon reading from the infamous diary. She read a note where Jacquelyn had become impatient with her absent husband, who had taken a trip to Paris. As his excursion lengthened, she decided to surprise the duke by arriving at their townhome and joining him in his pursuits. Little did she know that his pursuits were directed toward another woman—her mother.

Dorcas had written a rather scathing portrayal of having walked in upon them the night they arrived. They found His Grace in a scandalous situation.

When we arrived in Paris, we went directly to the townhome. To my mistress' horror, she found her husband in the parlor with another woman. I saw it with my own eyes. One hand was up her skirt, the other fondling an exposed breast while he ardently kissed her.

My poor mistress swore at him and screamed that he was an unfaithful bastard. I have never seen her so angry. Then to my utter shock, she walked over to the woman and slapped her across the face calling her a whore. I am sure she would have struck her again with greater force had it not been for the duke grabbing her wrist.

The entire account struck a chord of disillusionment in Jolene's heart. Adultery of the worse sort had been committed with no thought of others. Both were guilty of disloyalty to their spouses. What madness had driven them to do such a thing?

Love, Jolene answered herself. Did love make two rational people irrational? Their professed affection received no accolades from her heart. Though she knew without any doubt that some men strayed from their marriage beds and took mistresses, the reality of such behavior appalled every fiber of her being.

As a faithful Catholic, who believed strongly in the sanctity of marriage, Jolene found it impossible to condone what the duke and her mother had done in his own townhome. Three months after her birth, her mother committed adultery. Where had her father been when all of this had gone on behind his back?

Even though she had read the account, hundreds of unanswered questions remained. There were too many pieces of the puzzle scattered across her mind. Frustrated, Jolene slammed the diary shut and threw it toward the end of the bed to rid herself of the sordid tale. In a few hours, she would be the guest of the Chambers and in their presence. Clearly, she needed to calm down.

Reclining on her back, she focused her eyes upon the ceiling. *Inhale, exhale*, she repeated, drawing breaths in and out to compose herself. She had only a few hours before dinner to recuperate from the risqué picture burned into her mind of her mother fondled by her lover. Thank God, Robert would be there. Even if he said nothing, his presence alone would make her behave. On the other hand, she could focus her attention on Geoffrey instead.

"No, that will only get me into more trouble," she said aloud, shaking her head. "It would be best to channel my emotions elsewhere."

Jolene picked up her pillow and gave it a strong punch.

-·❉·-

The Whitefields and their family members had not received an invitation to dine with the Chambers. The dinner party had been arranged as a family affair. If they only knew how much of a family affair it would be, they might never get around to dinner.

When Jolene arrived, Geoffrey dismissed the butler and insisted on greeting her at the door. Dressed in a pressed shirt with a high starched collar and white tie, he looked dashing. His black dinner jacket with tails, impeccably tailored and well fitting, enhanced his tall frame and broad shoulders.

As usual, the moment she saw him, a sense of energy tingled under her skin. No doubt he felt the same, because a sly smile spread across his face knowing exactly how his presence affected her state of mind. *Keep focused,* she reminded herself.

"You take my breath away." He leaned forward and kissed her briefly on her cheek then drew back a respectable distance. "Welcome to our home."

Jolene did not flinch at his touch, nor did she object to his behavior. She merely smiled demurely and took his arm as he escorted her down the hall.

They entered the large sitting parlor. Lord Chambers and the duke quickly rose to their feet, as well as Robert, who flashed an edgy look. No doubt, he didn't approve of her clinging to the arm of his cousin.

Lord Chambers took a step forward and greeted her. "Welcome to our home, Lady von Lamberg. Please, make yourself comfortable."

As if planned ahead of time, all the seats were taken except for a settee for two people. The expression on his mother's face beamed with approval. Perhaps the sole purpose of the event had been geared toward matchmaking.

Jolene lowered herself slowly on the seat and scooted over an inch as Geoffrey joined her. She reached over and gathered her skirt that had touched his pant leg. With a quick rearrangement of fabric, she sat totally disconnected to the man who had already weakened her resolve. Her mind wanted to focus on the duke and duchess, while Geoffrey continued to draw her attention to the warmth radiating from his body.

"It's good to see you again," the duke said. He returned to his seat next to her mother.

Finally, Jolene regained her wits about her and glanced around at everyone. Robert appeared unusually quiet, and she could not help but wonder if he and Geoffrey had a disagreement earlier.

Her mother sat as she normally did, close to her husband. Poised, but remaining silent, Jolene smiled at her warmly. It surprised her that it came naturally, rather than being forced.

"My son tells me your touring of London has come to an end." Lady Chambers captured her attention away from the duchess.

"Yes, we have ended our tour." She looked at Geoffrey and smiled. "I must say he is quite the historian when it comes to English history and especially the sites of London." Jolene saw him soak up her compliment like a dry sponge. His mother proudly agreed.

"Yes, he's an intelligent, young man."

"Of course, there is much more to see of England besides London." The haughty Lord Chambers spoke in a deep voice. "You have not visited Windsor Castle."

Again, they presented the invitation to visit like a tempting piece of cake. Clearly, they could care less about her visiting the castle. They were intent on bringing her into their home to be near Geoffrey. It would provide him intimate opportunities to draw closer to her.

"Frankly, I would like to remain in England and tour more of your country. Actually, I would love to see Canterbury Cathedral, Stonehenge, and visit Bath." Her mind swirled with possibilities. "But alas, I am called to Paris on business."

Finally, Robert, who had been silent as the footman behind him, spoke up. "I'm sure that the komtesse will one day return. She ardently expressed her interest to me in touring more of England."

Jolene flashed a grateful smile in his direction for saving her from the pressure to visit the Chambers country manor. Suddenly, out of the blue, her mother entered the conversation.

"What type of business takes you to Paris? I hope that it will not consume too much of your time, for surely you will want to tour all that la ville lumière has to offer."

How uncanny that she should be the one to inquire about the purpose of her visit. Deliberately, she avoided looking at Robert for fear they would wonder why they exchanged glances over the subject. Jolene froze. The answer caught in her throat. Instead of being able to respond, she looked blankly at her mother taking far too long to compose her thoughts.

The duke interjected with a smile saving her the embarrassment. "My wife occasionally forgets that she speaks in French without a second thought. She meant to say all that the city of light has to offer."

"Oh, forgive me," she burst forth with a giggle. "Your wife caught me off guard. For some reason, my poor brain jumped from German to English to French before I realized what she had said."

"That's quite all right," he replied. The duke looked at his wife with a loving gaze. "I think she wanted to say la ville de l'amour."

Once again, he expressed his uninhibited love for her mother. Though Jolene struggled earlier in the day over their shameless adultery years ago, she acknowledged they were an extraordinary couple. His Grace possessed the uncanny ability of articulating his sentiments through the tone of his voice and the twinkle in his eye when he addressed the duchess. He did not need to make an overtly public display of affection to make his point. *He's a romantic*, Jolene thought, admiring him for that quality. In return, her mother responded with a silent gaze of respect and admiration.

"The city of love," Jolene sighed. "I do remember those words." She glanced at Lord and Lady Chambers, who remained straight-faced and unimpressed. By their own body language, it appeared to Jolene that they did not share the same sentiments of romantic love toward one another. Jolene's judgment of her hosts vanished as the butler intruded upon her thoughts.

"Dinner is served."

Lord Chambers rose from his chair and offered Jolene his right arm as was customary in such a situation. Geoffrey escorted his mother. The duke and duchess walked together while Robert woefully followed behind. Jolene could not help but wonder if he missed the company of Grace. She made a mental note to tell her later in the evening how he appeared so miserable without her by his side.

After being led to her seat, Geoffrey insisted on helping her sit down. He then took his place next to her on the right. Robert sat across the table from Geoffrey, next to his parents.

The footmen went into action and placed the first course in front of the hungry guests. Jolene picked up her spoon and made a mental note not to drop her utensils during dinner.

"Marguerite, when do you and Edmund plan on returning to your country manor?" The duke glanced at his sister and spoke with informality. Rather than giving her an opportunity to respond, her husband interjected.

"As soon as the season ends or close to it, I must take another trip to the West Indies for the last time."

"Oh, why's that?" The duke sounded keenly interested.

Lord Chambers procrastinated in his answer by taking a sip of soup. After he dabbed his lips with his linen napkin, he lifted his head and looked straight into the duke's eyes.

"I'm selling the plantation."

The entire Holland family looked at him in disbelief. The duke appeared extremely shocked as his mouth gaped open and his head jerked back.

"But it's been in your family for centuries. What precipitated this decision?"

Stirring the soup in his bowl, Lord Chambers replied. "Monetary reasons." As he lifted a spoon-full of broth, he spoke in a low voice. "I'm sure you understand."

The duke nodded his head as if it were perfectly understandable. Jolene noticed Robert and Geoffrey staring across the table at one another. Robert's eyes darted toward her and then back at Geoffrey. His non-verbal gesture spoke volumes as Robert tried to convey what he perceived to be Geoffrey's motives.

"*Be careful with potential suitors, who may look at you as a means for riches.*" She heard her solicitor's voice in her head warn once more.

Jolene pondered the situation of the aristocratic men sitting at the table with their wives in fashionable clothing and their well-dressed sons. Their homes, décor, multiple staff, and cars all spoke of bank accounts engorged with English pounds. Had it all been for sheer appearances? She knew that the Hollands were struggling financially, but the Chambers too? Perhaps the rumors that had been floating about Vienna that the aristocracy in England teetered on bankruptcy had a ring of truth after all.

Robert, true to his affable personality, interrupted the gloom. "Well, that does it," he said, putting his napkin down. "I'll just have to find an American heiress. I hear a few young men in society have done remarkably well marrying the wealthy daughters of businessmen from the States. Buccaneers with new money."

"What did you call them?" Jolene scrunched her face over his outrageous characterization of wealthy women.

As usual, Robert laughed, throwing his head back enjoying her naive foreign mind. "Buccaneers. The women across the Atlantic seek titles and stately homes. It is becoming quite popular for young aristocratic men to marry them and bring new money into their families."

He looked directly at Geoffrey, as if to shine a light on his insincere motives. Robert continued. "It seems a rational solution to our English financial dilemma, don't you agree Cousin?"

The atmosphere in the room changed. Then, to her utter surprise, her mother entered the conversation. Jolene nearly dropped her spoon.

"I think it is a shame that women lower their standards and marry for titles. And shame on the men who marry them for their money," she added, glowering at Geoffrey. "They are nothing but scavengers of the worse sort."

Her mother's face actually appeared distraught over the thought. Jolene could not help but wonder if she were attempting to protect her in some motherly way.

"Certainly, many of these marriages are not based on love, but selfish motives of gain and convenience," she concluded.

"Ah, the subject of love returns," His Grace said teasingly to his wife.

Her mother rolled her eyes and gave him a discreet nudge with her elbow. Jolene could not help but smile over their affectionate bantering.

"Well, I suppose a buccaneer is an apt description," Lady Chambers added. "After all, they are like pirates raiding England for their choice houses and titles."

"I wouldn't mind being raided," Geoffrey said, finally entering the conversation. Obviously, he decided on expressing his sentiments and motives exactly as they were without shame.

The footman retrieved the soup bowls and set the second course down. In the interim, Jolene rested her hand on her lap. To her shock, Geoffrey inched his way over and placed his hand on top of hers. She turned and looked at him wide-eyed as if to say, *do you mind*? He quickly retreated, picked up his fork, and began attacking the meat on his plate.

Afterward she felt guilty. Ever since he had stolen a kiss, she had avoided his influence upon her life. She was not sure if she could trust her heart with Geoffrey. If she became emotionally involved, her entire focus upon discovering the whole truth about her family would dissolve into thin air. No, she could not risk it, she decided once again.

She glanced over at the duke who had spoken something in her mother's ear that she could not hear. Glancing over at Robert, he looked anxious as if he wanted to say something. She could see in his eyes they needed a moment to talk. It appeared impossible to pull him away from everyone else to get a moment alone.

The dinner progressed, and small, trifling conversation dominated the table. After a few more minutes, Lady Chambers seemed intent on bringing up Windsor for a second time.

"You will tell us should you postpone your trip to Paris." Lady Chambers grinned with a hopeful glint in her eye.

"Yes, I course, but as I said, I have urgent matters in Paris that I must attend to."

Suddenly, Jolene remembered the duke's comment at the Chambers' ball. He had mentioned that he thought it was time to take his wife to Paris. Nearly jumping up from her chair, Jolene experienced a lightning bolt of an idea.

For the last week, she had been agonizing how to bring Robert with her to Paris without making it look terribly indecent or questionable. She needed him to help her find Philippe. Like a writer plotting her next scene, she made a bold decision to twist the plot.

"My aunt provided an introduction to a family in Paris, the Sauvageaus," she announced nonchalantly. "I am supposed to lodge with them." She thoughtfully dabbed her lips with her napkin and turned her attention directly to the duke and her mother.

"I thought that I might look for a rental of my own since I anticipate staying for some time. I'm sure that I could find a residence large enough to accommodate all of us." She smiled and shifted her gaze directly into the duke's eyes. "Did I not hear you distinctly say at the ball that it was time to take your wife to Paris?" Out of the corner of her eye, she saw her mother's shocked expression. Immediately, the duke dismissed the idea.

"No, that's all right, Lady von Lamberg. We would never think of intruding upon your private affairs." He reached over and touched his wife's hand as if to soothe her disappointment.

Unaffected by his refusal, she turned to her brother. With a quick nod of her head, she encouraged him to join the conversation hoping that he realized the reason behind her maneuver.

"Why not, Father?" He leaned forward and looked past his mother at the duke's somber face. "A trip for mother is long overdue. I think it would be rude not to accept Lady von Lamberg's generous offer to our family."

"Well, I don't know," his father replied. He shook his head and fiddled with the fork by his plate.

Stubborn, embarrassed, and proud, Jolene noted in her character account of faults. She addressed her mother.

"And what about you, duchess? You told me that you missed Paris and the opportunity to visit your parents' graves." She softened her voice pleading to her emotions. "Please, I implore you to convince your kind husband to accept my offer."

It did not take long for the duchess to make her heartfelt plea. "Oh, Robert, can we go?"

He remained silent.

"I shall not impose my presence upon you," Jolene added. "I will rent a large townhome where we can all enjoy our time in Paris. While you are there, you may pursue your delights, and I shall pursue my business."

"Why don't you take her offer, Robert?" Lady Chambers gave a surprising affirmative voice of encouragement.

"Well, I shall be in the steaming jungles of the West Indies. Paris is not for me," Lord Chambers said. "I agree go. Give your wife a holiday."

"Well, I shall not go," Marguerite said glumly. "I have no desire to return to the city at this time. All I wish for is my quiet country manor."

"What about me?" Geoffrey made a disgruntled face like an ignored little boy. He glanced around the table. "Has it occurred to anyone here that I might enjoy a trip to Paris?"

"I don't believe you've been invited," his mother replied glibly.

Jolene wanted to roll her eyes over their pathetic whining and cry for attention.

"Then go," his father said, waving his hand. "Take enough money and get yourself a room at the Louvre Hotel and enjoy the pleasure the city offers while you are young, if you know what I mean."

In a movement that Jolene found rather odd, Lord Chambers glanced at the duke. In response, he scowled. Her mother blushed. Clearly, some knowledge between the three of them had been expressed. Their peculiar behavior baffled Jolene.

Heaving a sigh that the conversation had not progressed as she hoped, Jolene turned her attention to her mother. "Duchess, you have yet to answer my question. Shall I prepare a room for you and your husband?"

Her mother squeezed the duke's forearm, and in a sweet and pleading voice spoke. "What harm could there be, my love, in accepting her offer?"

He looked into her eyes that had welled with tears. Surely, he would not deny her request, thought Jolene. If he did, she would start to cry.

"Come on, Father, surrender," Robert balked. "You love her, so take her to la ville de l'amour and have a good time of it. After all, it's where you met your sweet mademoiselle."

Her mother cringed in embarrassment. "Robert, don't tease your father." She winked at him as if to thank him for his help.

The duke, apparently outnumbered at the table, raised his head and looked at Jolene. She flashed him a warm and welcoming smile.

"Fine then, Paris it is."

"Yes," Robert exclaimed.

Elated, Jolene could not contain herself. "Then it is settled," she announced loudly. "I shall seek out a property landlord and find a rental as soon as possible." Then the thought struck her, what if she could not? "Do you think there will be rentals?"

"Oh, yes," Lord Chambers assured her. "The English are selling their property left and right in Paris. It's ripe for the picking."

Jolene leaned back in her chair and relaxed her tense body. Everything would work out as planned. Geoffrey lowered his head and whispered in her ear.

"Shall I stay at a hotel, or shall I expect an invitation to the townhome?"

She had suspected that he would ask. After hearing his father's suggestion to lodge at a hotel, she agreed it did not make much sense. If she found a residence large enough, they all could stay together. With the entire Holland family at her side, she did not feel threatened by Geoffrey's presence. After all, it would be selfish of her not to offer accommodations.

Relenting, she turned and looked into his hopeful gaze. "You may come," she began, "but I have conditions."

"Fair enough," he replied, clearly pleased about her answer.

Jolene replied in a low voice for his ears only. "You must promise me that you shall not attempt to test my weakness, Geoffrey. It is imperative that I stay focused upon my business affairs while in Paris."

He reached over and touched her hand on the table. "I promise, you have my word as a gentleman."

Jolene turned and looked at Lord and Lady Chambers. "Would you have an objection if I extended the invitation to your son so that he might accompany us on the trip?"

"Of course not. I'm sure his uncle will keep a keen eye upon the boy," Lord Chambers replied. His wife's face beamed from ear to ear over the news.

The duke looked slightly surprised but did not object. "Of course, I'll keep the boy in his place and make sure he doesn't wander around and get in trouble."

Lord Chambers smiled. Marguerite Chambers appeared as if she were about to rise to her feet and clap for joy. "My son is most trustworthy," she said.

Robert slumped in his chair, disgruntled over the extra baggage that would accompany them, but kept his mouth shut.

"Marvelous. When I find suitable housing, we shall choose a date to travel and be done with it."

Jolene caught the gaze of her mother. Her eyes brimmed with thankfulness. It caught Jolene off guard. *If she only knew,* she thought to herself.

The meal continued with everyone at the table unaware of her plot. Even Robert had not yet been privy to all of her strategies. Her detailed plan to bring everyone together began to unfold. She would return them to the city where it all began—Paris. There she would make them face the price they had paid for love. The cleverly orchestrated reunion would explode into untold emotions. Whether they would feel shame, grief, regret or joy in that shocking moment of revelation, Jolene could only speculate. All she knew is that she alone held the power to change everyone's life in a blink of an eye. However, the success of her plan hitched on one point.

Dear God, let my father be alive, she prayed. *I need him to complete the circle or else this will all be for naught.*

Chapter 16

Brandy, Cigars and Secrets

After dinner, Lady Chambers made the nod, and the ladies rose from their chairs. His aunt took Jolene by the arm and led her to the sitting room for coffee. His mother followed closely behind, excluded from the conversation. As usual, the lady of the house ignored his mother when more influential people were present. Her lack of respect irked Robert, and he disapprovingly glared at her as she exited.

As he watched Jolene leave, he felt a stir of pride on how well she had done during dinner. She remained calm and reserved in the midst of his parents. There were moments he wanted to blurt out what he knew. But alas, he had sworn a brotherly oath that he intended to keep. His younger sister had succeeded in wrapping him around her little figure early on in their relationship.

Her manipulating and calculating personality served her well. The brilliant idea of inviting the entire family to Paris on the next phase of her journey nearly caused him to choke on his food. Jolene's ingenious scheme, however, still left him in the dark as to what diabolical plan that pretty head of hers had conjured up. He would have to spirit her aside before the evening ended to find out.

The footmen cleared the dirty dishes, and then placed crystal decanters of port and brandy on the table. Lord Chambers had his butler fetch his box of imported Cuban cigars. The four males looked forward to a moment alone without the women.

The door closed, the menfolk lit their cigars, and the footman filled the glasses. Everyone leaned back comfortably and puffed upon a rolled stick of tobacco, filling the dining room with swirls of smoke rising to the ceiling.

"I say," his uncle began. "The komtesse must be fairly well off. She did not inquire about the potential cost of renting a townhome in Paris." He flicked the end of his cigar leaving the ash residue in a tray on the table.

Robert glanced at Geoffrey, who in response tapped his index finger on the tabletop. No doubt, his cousin calculated the crowns in her bank account. After he had tallied the total, he responded.

"She's probably rich as hell," he said, taking a drag on his cigar. He blew the smoke above his head in a circle. "The gossip from the Whitefields is that she inherited everything from the count—his money, large estate, and property interests. She resides in an enormous mansion in Vienna all by herself."

"No other relatives?" His father shifted his attention toward Geoffrey.

Robert leaned back in his chair studying his father's reaction. His face held the familiar look of fatherly concern.

"She has an elderly step aunt in Berlin, I believe." Geoffrey answered smugly as if he knew every intimate detail about her life in Vienna.

A hushed atmosphere circled the table. Everyone puffed on their cigars and pondered the financially advantageous position of his half sister.

"It's a bloody mess, I tell you." Edmund irritably flicked the excess ash from his cigar in the tray. "Our manor homes and townhouses are far too expensive to maintain, our fortunes are dwindling, and aristocrats by the droves in

England are going bankrupt." After gaining everyone's attention, his uncle pointed his glass of port toward his son. "By God, if I were a greedy man, I would encourage Geoffrey over there to romance the komtesse and bring new money into the family."

The statement proved far too amusing to keep Robert quiet any longer. He snickered. There had to be no way in hell his uncle had not already encouraged his cousin's behavior in the matter.

"Well, my cousin did steal a kiss from the lady, but she hasn't reciprocated since. Frankly, I think he is losing his touch." Robert pulled a smug grin to one side of his face and glanced at Geoffrey. Exactly as he expected, he met his cousin's angry glare in return.

"If you would stop protecting her like a brother, perhaps I could get somewhere."

This is bloody hilarious, he thought as he held his tongue. He felt as if his lungs would explode keeping in what he knew.

"I cannot believe you're selling the plantation," his father said. He appeared agitated as he shifted in his seat. "Marguerite mentioned nothing of your financial situation to me."

"Well, I wasn't about to tell her about it either," Edmund replied. He sucked in his cheeks and raised his voice. "Good lord, Robert, you of all people know how high strung she is. The woman would have driven me crazy with worry and questions."

His father held no argument there when it came to his sister's personality. "True," he replied. "I see your point, but I am sorry to hear of it."

Another few moments of silence, drinking, and cigar puffing ensued as the minds of the men wandered to their various private thoughts. The alcohol and fine tobacco had a way of soothing the unspoken emotions they each pondered at the table.

His uncle raised his eyes and glanced over at Geoffrey with a devilish grin. "When you get to Paris, enjoy yourself, son. I will increase your allowance a bit more so that you can have a Parisian night out on the town."

The comment captured Geoffrey's attention immediately. His blasé attitude of giving his father little attention about any matter quickly changed. Surely, the comment about a night out had awakened his cousin's sexual appetite. Robert scoffed at him.

"There's a fine brothel by the name Rue des Moulins," his uncle began. "They will treat you damn well." He lowered his voice a bit, placed his elbows on the table, and leaned forward. "They have some bold beauties that can do things to you with their lips you have only fantasized about."

Geoffrey salivated over the thought. His eyes grew dark, and his finger once again tapped on the tabletop but with more fervency. Obviously, he seriously considered his father's suggestion.

He calls me a bastard and look at him, Robert grumbled. *If he fucks a whore, I will tell Jolene for damn sure.*

He glanced at his father. To his astonishment, he hung his head and slumped in his chair. He gazed blankly at the linen tablecloth. Clearly, the conversation made him uncomfortable. Perhaps the fact that Edmund had suggested his son find a whore shocked him too.

"Robert, you should try one of the beauties too," his uncle interjected.

Robert spun his head toward his uncle. His mouth gaped open. The devilish expression in his eyes made him squirm. He appeared serious that he should enjoy a night out with Geoffrey.

"Perhaps your old man will give you a few pounds while you are there. It was his favorite pastime during his youthful years of rebellion, much to his own father's chagrin." Edmund expelled a hearty laugh and downed the remaining brandy in his glass.

His father sat straight up in the chair and glared at Edmund. "You never learn do you? It's not as if you haven't fucked your own mistresses for the past twenty years." His skin turned red under his collar.

Robert's jaw dropped to his chest. Geoffrey choked on his port, and they exchanged glances. He appeared just as stunned. Robert knew for years that there had never been any respect between brothers-in-law. Perhaps he should not be so surprised that his uncle had dropped such a rotten egg on the dining room table to stir up things. The disgust his father felt toward Edmund frankly equaled in the lack of respect that Robert held for his half cousin.

His father's comment hit its own nerve with his uncle. His nostrils flared, and his knuckles turned white. For a moment, he thought Edmund would rise to his feet and punch his father in the face. *Time to intervene*, Robert swiftly decided.

"Let's not spill our brandy over this," Robert announced lightheartedly. "Leave your youthful exploits unspoken in front of your sons, or we'll get ideas."

His father's morality had not shocked him before. After all, his mother had been his mistress for years. However, the little tidbit about visiting brothels had been an entirely new revelation. It instantly shed a new light on his father's character that he was not sure he liked.

Geoffrey suddenly slapped the palm of his hand on the table. "I expected as much from my father, but not you dear Uncle," he roared.

His father remained silent, scrunching his lips together.

Edmund continued to gloat. "I'm a man, what else can I say. I like the smell of a perfumed bed and a skinny, young ass once in a while." Geoffrey flashed his father an approving look as if he totally understood his father's logic. He could not believe they spoke with such disrespect for Marguerite. *A poor excuse of a man*, thought Robert.

His father remained silent and deep in thought. There had been no doubt in Robert's mind that he had remained faithful to his mother throughout the years. He hoped his assumption to be true. Their happiness had been quite evident, irrespective of society shunning their union.

Finally, his father moved by tapping his finger on the rim of this glass. The footman jumped into action and refilled it halfway. He tapped it once more, indicating that he was not satisfied with the portion. In response, the servant added more. Afterward, his father gulped a large swig down his gullet. Whenever he drank, Robert knew his tongue would loosen.

Robert leaned in toward his father to attract his attention. "Are you looking forward to Paris, Father?"

After another quick sip and subsequent puff on his cigar, he finally answered. "Not necessarily," he sighed. "Each time we go, I feel like I'm looking down the barrel of a gun."

"Damn, you were bloody fortunate he did not blow your head off," Edmund jabbed. "You stole the man's wife. Frankly, I would have shot you too."

His father sneered at Edmund. Robert felt bad for his father. He seemed unable to leave the past behind when it came to his mother. From passing innuendos his father made throughout the years, he hinted at his regret for Philippe's downfall. As he sat there studying his father, he saw the opportunity to move in that direction.

"Do you ever hear from Philippe?" Robert had not considered the effect such a question would have upon his father until after the words flew out of his mouth. Truthfully, he had been curious throughout the years. He simply asked because he promised Jolene that he would see what he could discover about his whereabouts.

His father's head turned in his direction. The look in his eyes spoke of his displeasure over the inquiry. "Philippe?" he grumbled loudly. "Why in the hell do you want to know if I have ever heard from Philippe?"

You've bloody well done it now, Robert scolded himself. To lessen the impact, he put the thought back in his father's lap where it originated.

"You said Paris makes you think of the barrel of a gun. Since it is his barrel, naturally I wondered if you ever hear from him." Swallowing the lump in his throat, he continued. "It is, after all, a perfectly rational question."

His father shrugged his shoulders and remained silent. The evasiveness of his gaze and demeanor tempted Robert to ask another. "Is Philippe still looking for Angelique?"

"Damn if I know," he answered, slightly slurring his words. "We quit looking years ago."

The glass of brandy came to his father's lips, and his mouth allowed the remainder of its contents to course down to his stomach deadening the guilt.

"I probably spent half of my fortune over the affair. I lost every bloody pound I invested into his business years ago. He ran it into the ground to ruin me, no doubt, as payment for my sins." The duke's head wobbled slightly from the alcohol. "The remainder went to private investigators in our futile attempt to find Angelique."

"Did you finally put your foot down and tell Suzette you would spend no more on the useless search?" Edmund asked in a more amiable tone than his last question.

"She finally came to terms with it five years ago. It has been hard. She carries a lot of guilt."

Still ignoring his earlier question, Robert pressed again. "So I assume you have not heard from Philippe. I would have thought had he found her that he would have had the decency to tell mother."

Once again, his father's slumped shoulders rose. He scowled at him with glassy eyes. "I don't understand, Robert, why the hell you have this sudden melancholic interest in your former stepfather?"

"Here, here," Geoffrey interjected with a grin. "Tell us why, Robert. Frankly, I would like to know as well."

Oh, shit, Robert thought to himself. His prying had succeeded in putting him on the spot in front of everyone. He was not sure how he was going to cover his sudden curiosity without raising suspicion. Geoffrey and his uncle gawked in pleasure as they waited for his answer. *Make light of it*, he told himself.

"Oh, no particular interest," he replied nonchalantly, as if it honestly did not matter one way or the other. "I just wondered since we are headed to Paris."

His father raked his hand through his hair. He avoided everyone's eyes and kept focused on the decanter in front of him pondering another drink. Robert shook his head slightly knowing that he would end up on the table passed out if he didn't intervene.

Surprisingly, his uncle leaned forward and jabbed the next question at his father to get a reaction. "You know, don't you? You sly dog."

For a moment, his father ignored the query. Then as if he were in a confessional with a priest, his tongue loosened. "Yes, I know," he said.

Robert's mouth dropped open. His uncle brought his hands together in a clap and bellowed from his lungs. "I knew it!"

Geoffrey slapped the tabletop. "Shit, my uncle the duke has a deceitful side about him. Who would have thought?"

Edmund bellowed a hearty laugh. "Damn right," he said. "I knew that when your uncle asked me to send Philippe away to my plantation. He plotted to remove him from France for a few months while he pursued his wife behind his back."

Robert felt as if his heart stopped beating. The revelation rendered him speechless. He brought his glass to his mouth and downed the rest of his brandy. His father quickly defended himself, snubbing out the smoked cigar in the tray in front of him.

"I'll admit I had my reasons, but it also included the opportunity to see my son. The bastard knew all along he was mine and didn't even tell me."

Robert could not believe what he heard. There were things about his parents he never knew. At a young age, they had carefully chosen to tell him only what they wanted to reveal. Like any other child who trusted implicitly, he accepted it as truth.

Through the years, society had branded him a bastard of the duke. It had been hard to swallow, even though his father had acknowledged him as his rightful heir. People in society who had remembered and adored Jacquelyn taunted him about his mother being the duke's mistress. She had usurped Jacquelyn's rightful place as duchess, which of course she paid for dearly. At that moment, he began to wonder what else he didn't know or what secrets Jolene might unearth.

His father hung his head and then slowly lifted his eyes toward Robert. "If you want to see him, I know where you can find him. I suppose you have every right, since he brought you up for the first five years of your life."

The duke's dejected countenance grieved Robert. "Father, it's not—"

"I do not care if you do," he briskly cut him off. "He once loved you as a son. Who knows, he might enjoy seeing you as a grown man." The duke shook his head. "I never could bring back his daughter, that's for damn sure."

Robert found it difficult watching his inebriated father display his remorse. The man had been such a staunch nobleman lecturing him about his life and behavior that it surprised the hell out of him to witness his weakness displayed in front of family.

Then to his utter surprise, his father balled his fist and banged the dining table with a thud, shaking everything in its wake. Everyone glared at his out-of-character behavior.

"Bloody Jacquelyn! She only did it to destroy Suzette. The woman was a crazy bitch."

"Crazy bitch or not," Robert said, "You've had enough to drink." He reached over and put his arm around his father's shoulders. "Mother will lecture you the rest of the night if you don't give up the alcohol and go to bed."

He pondered the empty glass before him. "You're right," he said, rising to his feet with a slight sway. "Well then," he announced, "I shall retire before she discovers her husband in this rather uncouth state of mind."

"Give my apologies to Lady von Lamberg, will you son?" he asked Robert sadly. "Tell her that your father retired early because he did not feel well."

With a slight stagger, the duke exited the dining room and closed the door behind him. It had been some time since he had witnessed his father under the influence to such an extent. Since it happened so quickly, he pondered how many drinks he might have had before dinner.

"Hmm," his uncle moaned, downing the remainder of his drink and snuffing out the end of his cigar. "I think the trip to Paris has resurrected some irritants beneath the surface."

Flabbergasted, Geoffrey replied. "That is the first time I have witnessed his stiff upper lip quiver." In a voice that mirrored concern, he looked questioningly at this father. "What the hell was that all about?"

Lord Chambers shook his head. "Take it from me, boys, the decisions you make as youths will follow you the rest of your life. His Grace is a prime example." He pushed back his chair and rose to his feet. "I'll leave you two lads to escort the komtesse back to the Whitefields. Just don't duel over the matter," he said with a smirk as the left the room.

Geoffrey and Robert glanced at each other as if they pondered the possibility.

"You want to flip a coin?" Robert jested.

"Let me take her home," Geoffrey pressed. "I never get a moment with the woman."

"Maybe the woman doesn't want a moment alone with you," he retorted.

Geoffrey swiftly pushed his chair back and rose to his feet. "We'll flip a coin," he announced in arrogance. "You always lose when gambling with money."

Robert knew in his gut tonight he would win. "Fine with me," he announced, rising to his feet. "But I want a third party to flip it."

Geoffrey shoved his hand into his pocket and drew out a gold sovereign. "You there," he bellowed at the footman standing straight-faced by the wall at attention. "Come here."

Like a soldier called to duty, the footman came and stood in front of Geoffrey. "Hold out your hand, man," he said. He slapped the coin in the palm of his white glove. "Toss the coin at my command."

Geoffrey looked at his cousin with a narrowed gaze. "Your call," he offered. "Shall it be Edward VII or Saint George slaying the dragon? Frankly, it doesn't matter," he arrogantly added. "Because you are about to lose the bet."

Robert had a hell of a lot of dragons to slay. It was an easy call. "Saint George."

"Then it's the king for me," Geoffrey claimed. "Flip the damn coin, and you better give me the win."

As if the footman had been an expert in the art of coin flipping, he threw it up in the air. All three watched it fly above their heads twirling the sovereign in every direction. When gravity begun its pull, the coin descended, the footman grabbed it and slapped it upon the back of his left hand. He reached out to the two who stood there waiting for the outcome and privilege to spend time with the komtesse. Slowly, as if teasing the two of them, he raised his hand and revealed Saint George wielding his sword.

"Bloody well yes," Robert shouted.

"You goddamn lucky bastard," Geoffrey growled, snatching the sovereign out of the footman's hand.

Robert saw the servant's disappointment over the disappearing coin, so he shoved his hand into his own pocket and retrieved another. Without hesitation, he gave it to him as a reward. "Well done, chap," he said with a broad smile. "As far as I'm concerned, you deserve to keep it."

The footman smiled. "Thank you, your lordship."

"If you weren't my cousin, I'd strangle you right now." Geoffrey grabbed the remaining port in his glass and brought it to his lips gulping down his disappointment.

"I'm sure you'll have your chance to impress the lady in Paris," Robert reminded him. "I thought that was kind of her allowing you to join us and stay under the same roof." He patted Geoffrey on the back. "You'll get over it."

Robert headed for the door. "I'm off to see whether Lady von Lamberg would like to return home. You won't mind me borrowing the motorcar, will you?"

For once, lady luck had smiled on him, or perhaps it was Saint George. Whatever the reason for the win, he needed the time alone with his sister.

Chapter 17

Winner Take All

Robert strode into the sitting room like a champion. Everyone disappeared, and he remained the victor. He entered the doorway and interrupted the chatter of three women.

"Ladies, I am all that is left from the household of males," he announced. "Might I have the honor of driving Lady von Lamberg to the Whitefields?"

Jolene turned and looked at him in relief from her obvious boredom. He would be bored, too, with the discussions that women entertained. Whatever they spoke about during the past hour, he knew it couldn't have been as lively as the one in the dining room.

"Where is everyone?" his aunt asked.

"Too many cigars and too much brandy, I'm afraid. Father has gone to bed. Uncle went right after him, and Geoffrey—well, let's just say Geoffrey is nursing his loss."

Marguerite rose to her feet. "I don't understand."

His eyes shifted to his mother, who appeared anxious and ready to retire. "Mother, you better take care of father. Go easy on him, because I think he had too much to drink."

She frowned.

"Lady von Lamberg," he said, walking toward her and offering his arm. "May I have the honor of returning you home?"

"Well, home is in Austria," she said teasing him. She stood up and took his arm. "I'll go as far as the Whitefields this evening and Paris very soon."

She turned to Suzette and Marguerite. "Lady Chambers, thank you for dinner this evening. I thoroughly enjoyed myself." She looked at the duchess and spoke. "We shall be spending many more hours together in the next week or two. As soon as I find a suitable rental, I'll notify you about travel arrangements."

"I look forward to it," she replied.

After their final farewells, Robert escorted his sister to the motorcar and opened the door like a gentleman. "I talked them into letting me drive you home."

"You do know how to drive, don't you?" Jolene looked at him a bit worried.

"Well, I do ride a horse much better than driving a motorcar. However, I have been thinking it would be quite the rush to race one of these machines rather than my horse."

"You're teasing me," she complained, glaring at him in fear. "Surely, the driver can take me back to the Whitefields. Where is he?"

"Don't worry, I promise to make sure that you safely arrive at your destination," he consoled. Apparently, she had not come to a place of complete trust wounding his delicate ego.

After starting the engine, Robert pulled out into the street. The avenues were practically empty of traffic. Thankfully, he would not have to dodge carriages and horses. After reaching a reasonable thirty miles per hour, he started a conversation.

"Well, I must say you certainly surprised me this evening with the invitation of my whole family to Paris. What clever thing are you planning, Sister?"

"What I do have planned will not work if we discover Philippe is dead."

Robert could not contain himself. "I have some news for you," he said, grinning broadly and trying to keep his eyes on the road.

"What news?" Jolene turned her head and looked at him.

He wanted to see the expression on her face. It would be far too precious to miss. "Maybe I should pull over so we can talk about this."

"Robert," she protested with a scowl. Jolene poked his leg with her finger. "Don't torture me."

"Just give me a few minutes," he replied, continuing to drive. Finally, after sensing his sister's frustration, he slowed down and stopped alongside the road.

"Look, we're almost at the Whitefields," he announced.

Robert placed the car in a neutral gear. Jolene furrowed her brow. Truth be told, he enjoyed being a tease to his newfound sibling.

"We had a riveting conversation around the dining table over cigars and liquor. My father, thank the Lord above, had one too many. When he drinks, he loosens his tongue and wallows about the past." Robert shifted his body to the side and leaned against the door.

"What did he say?"

Jolene looked as if she were about to poke him again. A spirit of nostalgia whirled around him as he looked at her eager face. She had grown into a beautiful woman he admired and experienced the new emotion of brotherly love. He reached over, grabbed her hand, and held it tight.

"Your father is alive," Jolene. "My father has kept track of him through the years."

"He is?" She glowed with joy even in the dark.

"Not only alive, love, but my father knows where to get in touch with him." Her mouth gaped open but nothing came out. Finally, after crushing his hand, she spoke.

"Oh, my God, he's alive."

"Yes, he is. My father even encouraged me to pay him a visit."

"Why?"

"I'm not sure, but I have my suspicions it's to ease his conscience. He drank a little too much this evening and began wallowing in his brandy." Jolene's eyes watered. "You now officially have a father and mother that are alive."

"I can't believe it." Her voice trembled.

"Have you read much further in the diary? What else did the deceased lady's maid have to say?"

"I have not finished it yet, I'm afraid. I pick it up and read her entries. Most of the time they upset me." She paused and sucked in an anxious breath. "Robert, I feel so many emotions about everyone. For some reason, I'm taking sides in this whole situation that occurred eighteen years ago. I feel miserable after reading what happened to Jacquelyn when she was married to your father. It bothers me that my emotions are indifferent toward our mother."

"And my father?" Robert looked at her knowing she would not reply with anything glowing about his character.

"Well, it is obvious that he deeply loves our mother. Nonetheless, I am angry with him, too, because he destroyed my parents' marriage."

Robert grew pensive remembering his uncle's admonishment. "My uncle made a profound statement this evening," he said. "The decisions you make as youths will follow you the remainder of your life."

"I suppose that is true," Jolene replied. "Hopefully, we'll learn what not to do by their examples."

"You think?" Robert grinned. "But with a rascal like me you never know."

Jolene tilted her head and smirked at his confession. A part of him jested, but he knew that his own rebellious streak certainly could lead to unwise choices in his life. Observing the double-edge sword of his father's existence, he realized that he didn't want to carry one throughout adulthood.

One of Jolene's earlier statements came to mind. "What stories in the diary infuriated you, might I ask?" Jolene paused as if she hesitated to tell him. "Nothing will shock me," he assured.

She inhaled a deep breath. "Well, Jacquelyn traveled to Paris looking for your father. When she arrived at their townhome, she caught them together. Dorcas witnessed the incident herself. They were on the couch..." She stopped and cringed in embarrassment.

"Having intercourse?" Robert wanted to say something a bit gruffer, but for Jolene's sake, he used a more general term. The description appeared to fluster Jolene. In the shadows, he noticed a blush burst upon her cheeks. It seemed his sister had prudish tendencies.

"Close to it," she giggled. "Let's just say one hand was up her dress and the other on her exposed breast."

Robert squirmed in his seat over the thought of it. "God, it must have been something else to watch those two twenty years ago," he said with a smirk on his face. "My stoic father was a rogue." He couldn't help picturing the entire scene in his mind. Jolene drew his attention away from speculating about their sexual exploits.

"Where is father?"

Robert halted his vision of the scandalous encounter. "We didn't get that far in the discussion. I am sure when we arrive in Paris, he will give me the address."

Jolene looked disappointed.

"A lot of things came out tonight, even stories I didn't know about," Robert added.

"Like what?"

He pondered if he should tell her about how his father had acted with such duplicity in regards to Philippe. Would her anger toward him increase knowing how he had sent Philippe away to weasel his way back into his mother's life?

"I'm not sure if we should discuss it here," he said, putting her off. "You've had enough emotion for one night. Let me take you home."

"True," she admitted, yawning. "I am tired. There will be more time to talk in the weeks ahead."

After putting the car back in gear, he proceeded a few blocks until they reached the Whitefields. Jolene held onto his arm as he escorted her to the door. Branson answered.

She leaned forward and whispered in his ear. "I'm so glad you're my brother."

Robert felt her lips touch his cheek with a quick kiss before she entered. Jolene departed, and Branson shut the door in his face.

"Why in the hell did I ever push over the bassinet?" He laughed all the way to the car.

Jolene was right about one thing, though. They did have weeks ahead. Surprisingly he looked forward to seeing Philippe again. The man deserved the homecoming of his lost daughter.

~ ❁ ~

Robert returned to his uncle's house intent on climbing into bed. As he passed the parlor, he glanced inside and found Geoffrey sprawled in the chair that Jolene had been sitting in. Curious as to what he was up to, Robert walked in and stood in front of him.

"What are you doing?" Geoffrey's bloodshot eyes indicated to Robert that his cousin had become inebriated during his absence.

"Smelling the lingering scent of her perfume."

What a bloody fool, Robert thought to himself.

"You enjoy your ride home?" Geoffrey asked, noticeably peeved.

"Yes," Robert replied in a clipped voice.

"You kiss her?"

"I told you that there's nothing between us, Geoffrey. Get the hell over it."

He narrowed his eyes in disbelief. "Something is going on between the two of you," he said, rising to his feet in a wobble. "If I didn't know better, I'd say you're a sneaky son-of-a-bitch like your father."

"You're drunk," Robert said. "And frustrated she's not as receptive of your advances as you hoped."

"I'd like to make her my wife," he slurred. "We could use the money."

"You would marry her for money and probably fuck whores on the side. She deserves far better than the likes of you." Robert's nostrils flared eyeing him up and down.

Geoffrey licked his lips and a mischievous glint sparkled in his glassy eyes. "Well, I'm going to fuck a whore when I get to Paris, whether you like it or not." He pushed Robert on his chest with his index finger. "You wait and see."

"You do, and I'll tell her what an ass you truly are. Then she'll never reciprocate your advances, you reprobate."

"Bastard," he spit back in Robert's face. "You are just a fucking bastard, born of a mistress whore, and you have the gall to lecture me?"

Robert balled his fists. He wanted to punch him in his ruddy face. It wasn't the first time nor would it be the last his cousin would throw the word at him like dirt. The drunken idiot wasn't worth the pain of bruised knuckles, so he relaxed his hand and let it go.

"Go sleep it off, Cousin," he growled at him. Robert turned and retreated to his room.

"So help me," he complained aloud, stomping down the hall to his room. "One of these days, I am going to punch that ass in the mouth."

Chapter 18

The City of Light and Love

It took a few weeks of arrangements, but Jolene found a residence in Paris to rent that would accommodate everyone's needs. It contained eight bedrooms, four on the main floor, four on the second, and five bath chambers. The ground floor had an elegant reception area and a veranda that led to the garden. For male entertainment, it included a study, library, and wine cellar. When she discovered it also had a large garage, she arranged for a motorcar rental to be delivered upon their arrival and a professional driver to transport them about the city.

She funded everyone's transportation to France, though the duke balked in pride. Robert talked him into graciously accepting the gift rather than being so high and mighty. It pleased her to witness the influence her brother had been able to wield on her behalf.

Geoffrey did not travel with their entourage. He made the excuse that he would follow in a few days because of unfinished business in London, due to his father's departure to the West Indies. Robert expressed his delight over the delay. Jolene thought little of it.

When they arrived at the townhome with their piles of luggage, the staff scurried about greeting the new arrivals.

Jolene, based on the floor plan she received from the property administrator, had assigned the rooms for each guest ahead of time.

A butler by the name of Pierre welcomed them at the door, along with the head housekeeper and maids. After introductions concluded, the head housekeeper, Madame Dubois, invited everyone for refreshments in the sitting room.

Jolene handed the butler her list of accommodations and instructions where each traveler's bags should be taken. She had placed the duke and duchess in a suite on the second floor, where she would also occupy a room. Robert and Geoffrey would take the lower bedroom suites.

Maria had already scurried off with the rest of the staff to take her quarters on the lower level. Everything unfolded perfectly according to Jolene's plan. A rush of excitement tingled through her body over what lay ahead.

She entered the sitting room, where Robert and his parents already enjoyed a welcoming cup of tea. "I must say it's a nice townhome, don't you agree?" Jolene looked around at the luxurious furnishings. "It is owned by a Viscount in Aquitaine. He uses the residence sparingly and leases it when not in Paris."

Robert glanced at the French décor scowling at the ostentatious furnishings. "Yes, it is comfortable, but there is no contemporary furniture. It's very...shall we say, Louis XVI."

"Needless to say," his mother intervened, "I like it."

"I'm not getting into this debate," the duke countered with a chuckle. His playful gaze shifted to his wife who ignored his comment.

The glow upon her mother's face lit up the room. Obviously, returning to French soil had infused her with new life. Jolene wondered what memories her mother entertained, reminded once again how little she knew about her. She had no knowledge of her parentage or childhood. So many pieces of the puzzle remained unsolved. Perhaps in one of them, she would find an ounce of motherly affection that still eluded her heart.

Purposely, she pulled her eyes away from her mother and turned to the duke. "You and the duchess had a townhome in Paris at one time, too, so I've been told," she inquired. "It is a shame that you sold it. Do you miss the property?"

Her question dulled the festive atmosphere in the room as if she turned out a light. His Grace's demeanor quickly altered, and her mother's smile faded. After a quick glance at his wife, he answered.

"I sold it for financial reasons a few years after we wed. We decided not to return to Paris often, so there was no need to keep an empty home any longer."

The scene of Suzette and the duke sprawled across the couch partially naked taunted Jolene. Each time she started to see them in a favorable light, another piece of information about their history would sully it.

Pierre, the butler, announced their quarters were ready. "The trunks and luggage have been delivered to the rooms as you requested, Lady von Lamberg. Is there anything else that you require?"

"Would you kindly show Lord Holland his quarters on the first floor, and I shall escort the duke and duchess upstairs to their suites."

Everyone rose to their feet. "What time is dinner served?" Jolene inquired.

"Seven o'clock in the dining room down the hall to your right."

She turned toward Robert. "We will see you again at dinner. Feel free to wander through the study, library, and cellars. You may find something interesting," she teased him.

The impressive central staircase to the second floor loomed before her in white marble. "If you'll follow me, I'll show you to your rooms." As they reached the top and walked down a long corridor, she stopped at the first French doors to her right. "This is your suite. I hope you will be comfortable here. I am across the hall."

Unexpectedly, Suzette reached out and touched her forearm gently. "Thank you for this gift. You have no idea how much it means to me."

Shocked over the physical gesture of her mother's hand, she flinched. It felt strange and uncomfortable, and a lump formed in her throat. The eyes of her mother radiated sincere thankfulness, but Jolene remained indifferent.

"You are welcome," she replied, void of emotion. Slowly, she pulled away from her touch. She trembled as she crossed the hall and entered her room. Overtly displayed emotion in front of the duke and duchess had been something she tried to suppress at all costs. It might give rise to suspicions about her identity, but the act to compose herself had not been an easy one.

"Oh, there you are," Maria greeted her with a smile. "This is a beautiful residence."

Jolene sighed. "Yes, it is grand and comfortable, Maria. It shall do quite well for what I have planned in the weeks ahead."

Maria cocked her head and looked at her strangely.

"When you are finished unpacking my things, I would like a bath drawn. Then I need some time alone to rest and read." It was time to pull out the diary and delve into the story of Jacquelyn's arrival to Paris.

While Maria performed her chores, Jolene thought about how strange it felt to be in Paris. She had been born here, and Parisian blood flowed through her veins. In the past, she saw herself as Austrian. Now that she knew the truth, she frankly felt like a jumbled mess of two competing countries.

"I think the city is beautiful," Maria said.

The statement pulled Jolene's crazed thoughts in another direction.

"It looks so different than London," Maria continued. "It's as if you can sense the excitement in the air and touch it with your fingertips." She giggled like a little girl. "Oh, to be in love in the city of love," Maria sighed wistfully.

To be in love? It was the furthest thought from her chaotic mind. Jolene cringed as she remembered Geoffrey's arrival in the days ahead. Rather than feeling enthralled he would join them, she worried that he would take her aside once more and try to seduce her in some romantic setting. It would be disastrous if she lost all sense of propriety. As it stood right now, she had lost all sense of her identity.

"You are right, Maria. The atmosphere here in the city of light and love is charged with a peculiar atmosphere. I feel it in my heart, even though I do not understand its meaning entirely."

--·�֎·--

Robert, with the help of a footman, unpacked his clothing. His suite looked as luxurious as the rest of the residence. After his clothes and personal items were placed in the closets and drawers, he asked the servant for the whereabouts of the study, library, and the stairs to the cellar.

"As you leave your suite, monsieur, turn to the right back toward the sitting room. You'll find the study down the hall on the left and the library two doors down on the right."

"And the cellar?"

The footman kept a straight face. "You'll need to speak to the housekeeper, Madame Dubois, as she keeps the keys to the cellar in her pocket."

Disappointed he couldn't check the vintage of the wine, he wandered down the hall instead. He reached the study, shoved the door open, and walked into a more masculine décor. The walls were covered in mahogany wood paneling. A large desk sat in the middle of the room with leather chairs on both sides.

Robert strode to the window and surveyed the landscape outside. The residence was located near the left bank of the Seine not far from Notre Dame, though it did not have a view of the river itself. The neighborhood consisted of other expensive homes lining the street.

Satisfied he had examined the room thoroughly, he walked to the library down the hall. After pushing open two French doors, he stood in the threshold astonished and overwhelmed. By far, this room had become his favorite. An impressive collection of books lined the walls from floor to ceiling. The recognizable scent of bound paper volumes filled his nostrils. The room burst with light that filtered through large windows that overlooked the gardens below. Comfortable chairs with tables and lamps were strategically arranged for reading.

Robert wandered over to the bookcase and began looking at the titles. Multiple works written by Victor Hugo lined the shelves. He pulled one out and noted it was an original edition of Les Misérables from 1862. Shaking his head over the collection, he carefully placed it back and wandered down the row. The entire library appeared filled with works from famous French novelists and poets, but it contained little, if any, English literature. The viscount's reading preferences were obviously prejudiced.

"Anything good to read?" He heard his father's voice and spun around to see him standing in the doorway.

"Yes, if you like French authors. We'll need to bring mother in here. She will spend hours reading to her heart's delight."

His father walked over to his side and tilted his head looking at the titles on the spine. "Hugo, I see," he said. "Hmm, any Shakespeare?"

"I haven't found anything yet, but since I've only looked at one-eighth of this massive collection, I'm hoping that I will eventually find a book or two from an English author."

The duke walked over to the tall windows, clasped his hands behind his back, and peered out over the gardens. "This is an impressive townhome. The one we owned years ago was comfortable but not as grand as this residence."

Robert turned around and looked at his father, who appeared to be lost in thought over the past. "I doubt it had been decorated entirely with Louis XVI furniture," he chuckled.

"Hardly," drawled his father. "My wife Jacquelyn had distinct tastes in furnishing and artwork." He turned around and scanned the room more closely. Spying a decanter of brandy on a sideboard, he headed for the alcohol.

"Care for a drink?"

"If mother catches you this early..." Robert warned.

"She's taking a nap. I'm afraid the trip and excitement of being back in Paris has weakened her resolve to keep me away from the spirits strategically placed through the home."

His father pulled the stopper out of the top and poured half a glass. "Here, I'll feel less guilty if you drink with me," he said, offering the liquor. Robert took it from his hand, and his father poured an equal amount for himself. He replaced the stopper, and the duke turned around looking at his choice of seats.

"Sit with me a minute, son." He lowered himself into a comfortable wing-backed chair. As he took a sip, his eyes roamed over the walls of books.

Robert found a chair next to him and settled in for a rare moment of personal attention from his father. The past year they had been estranged on many levels, but now an opportunity presented itself. His father did not act like a pompous, demanding dictator of the Holland realm.

The thought brought him to another recollection. The discussion over dinner a few weeks ago lingered in his mind. It had been nearly impossible for Robert to imagine his father in his youthful years sowing his seeds of rebellion in Paris. Quite aware that Paris afforded pleasures that he hadn't tasted, such as the risqué theatres, casinos, and houses of love, it was hard to imagine his father participating in such acts.

For a brief moment, he felt vindicated for his past carousing. He had to admit that visiting a brothel to try out purchased pleasures would incite most men. Of course, if Jolene found out his participation, there would be no telling what scorn she would rain upon him. *Good lord,* he thought, scrunching his brow. *My sister is altering my moral values. This is disturbing.*

"It is extremely generous of the komtesse to rent this palatial townhome. I'm sure the rent must be emptying her purse a bit," his father said, leaning more comfortably into the chair.

Robert held no surprise that even his father wondered about her financial status. "Well, as Geoffrey mentioned, she did inherit her stepfather's wealth, residence, and lands. I would imagine that she is well off."

Slowly his father raised a brow and curled a smile at the corner of his lips. "Might I inquire if the two of you are becoming romantically involved?"

With a throaty laughter, Robert dismissed his assumption. "Heavens no," he emphatically said, swirling the liquid around in his glass. "We have similar interests, but beyond that we have both expressed no interest in each other romantically."

"Well, that's too bad," he sighed. "I thought the two of you would make a good couple."

"Not every woman sparks my interest," Robert clarified. "I do have my own set of standards in what I'm looking for in a lady. Frankly, I think the komtesse takes too lofty a view of morality for my taste."

His father's brow rose over his statement. Nevertheless, it felt good to expel his preferences from his lips to solidify his true feelings. The thought that his sister had begun to influence his choices, made him shift in his chair.

"Shame," his father replied, looking disappointed. He took a drink and then gazed thoughtfully at Robert. "You know," he began, "I think that she has been a good influence upon you since her arrival." He appeared smug over his astute observation that even Robert had struggled not to acknowledge.

"She is an exceptionally mature woman for eighteen years of age," Robert replied. "As well as being wealthy and stunningly beautiful, she possesses intelligence that makes her wise beyond her years." After pointing out Jolene's virtuous characteristics, he felt lacking in his own.

His father smirked. "Well, whatever it is, I think it's rubbing off on you."

"I doubt that," he defended himself. "You know, I possess those qualities as well, except for the stunningly beautiful characterization. It's just that you rarely see me express them in your presence," he smirked. Apparently, not accepting his self-inflated accolades of his own personality, the smile on his father's face faded.

"And what of Geoffrey? Does he have intentions to win her heart?" He scowled, clearly agitated over the thought. "I wouldn't doubt Edmund encouraging him to marry for money—the vulture."

Robert's brotherly worry for her welfare rose in his own mind. "I feel the same concern. Nevertheless, the komtesse has a good head on her shoulders. Her mind is focused on something other than finding a husband at the moment."

"Well, good for her." His father suddenly shoved his hand into his inside coat pocket and retrieved a piece of paper. "As I promised," he said, handing it to him. "Philippe's whereabouts."

Surprised he had chosen this moment to reveal his stepfather's address, he hesitated before taking it. His father noticed.

"Change your mind?" His hand retreated.

"No, no," Robert urgently replied. He reached forward and grabbed it, noting two addresses penned on the paper.

"This is the last information that I received from my contact in Paris. I hope that Philippe is still at one of these locations. The first is his home, which I believe is across the river. And you will find the second his place of employment at a cigar shop near the Louvre." The duke took a sip of his drink and slumped back in his chair.

"It's been almost eighteen years," Robert said. "How in the world have you been able to keep tabs on him?"

His father focused on a random piece of lint on his pant leg delaying his response. Using the distraction, he brushed it off while keeping his lips sealed in a straight line. Obviously, he felt uncomfortable revealing his conscience concerning the matter. Robert, about to dismiss it altogether and change subjects, halted when his father cleared his throat.

"After I brought you and your mother to England, I felt guilt-ridden over the loss of her daughter. I felt partially responsible. After all, my wife used the situation to her advantage to hurt your mother. Philippe's emotions had been expendable in Jacquelyn's mind. Why should she care?"

He halted for a moment, took a slow sip of alcohol. Robert remained silent allowing him to collect his thoughts.

"When I hired a detective to look for Angelique, I kept him on retainer for years to keep me informed of Philippe's whereabouts."

"For what purpose?" Robert did not understand his father's reasoning.

"Well, for one, the man deplored me and your mother for what happened, especially after he failed to blow off my head."

"Point taken," Robert nodded. "Did you think he would follow you to England and try again?"

A puff of air escaped his father's lungs. "Well, what do you think, son? The man wanted me dead."

"I understand your concern," Robert said.

"In addition, I feared that if he did find Angelique, he would keep that information from Suzette as further punishment." He brushed his pant leg again apparently irritated over another spot on his black suit. "Your mother's sorrow weighed heavily upon my heart. I could not allow him to cause further damage to the woman I loved."

"So all these years, you had your contact in Paris inform you of his movements." Robert leaned forward as if to take closer stock of his father's motives.

"Well, after he drove the business into the ground, and I lost my investment, yes. He hit a pretty rough patch in his life for some time, which only added to my guilt."

His father rose to his feet clearly agitated and strode over to the window. He tilted his head back and emptied the contents of his glass down his throat. After a few moments of silence, he turned around and looked at Robert.

"Finally, after some time, he settled into a mundane employment here and there throughout Paris. Apparently, he never remarried."

Robert sat silently pondering the effect of what had happened over eighteen years ago. Everyone had paid a terrible price. Watching his father during another moment of vulnerability had presented a rare insight into his personality. For a brief moment, with his guard down, Robert asked his father a question that he had pondered for many years.

"Had you not returned to France and broken their marriage apart, things would have turned out much differently." Thinking of Jolene up on the second floor and with the knowledge he possessed of her existence, he couldn't help but ponder the direction their lives had taken. "I would have grown up never knowing you." He paused a moment. "But I can't help but wonder if you regret how it turned out."

"Regret?" His father shook his head. "I have no regrets being married to your mother. She is the sheer essence of my being, and without her my life would not be worth living."

His father strode to the decanter and poured another drink. When he pulled the stopper, Robert witnessed his hand tremble. He had never seen him in such a state. After taking another sip, he returned to the chair and sat down. He gazed into Robert's eyes with remorse.

"You know very little of our past, Robert, as far as your mother and I are concerned. Some of which I shall tell you; some of which I shall not."

The "shall not" irked Robert. He wanted to know it all, if not for himself, for Jolene's sake. "What are you willing to tell me?" he asked.

"When I returned to Paris with Jacquelyn for a respite, we encountered Philippe by chance in a park. I didn't know you were my son."

"I surmised that you did not know," Robert admitted.

"Before your mother became pregnant, I was married to Jacquelyn, but your mother was my mistress." In a nervous move, his father brought his shaky hand to his hair and raked his fingers through his locks. "I did despicable things even to her in my youth," he said, closing his eyes. "I used her for my pleasure and kept her unaware that I had married."

"Had you been courting her with the promise of marriage and then changed your mind?"

"Well, not exactly courting, son. My father would have never approved of the match. By that time in my life, he had made his own marital arrangements. And he damned well expected me to comply."

"So you married and lied to mother." The past few weeks left Robert reeling in revelations. What more could there be? His father had been a womanizer, deceiver, and home breaker. Finally, Robert understood his sister's inability to feel any affection for his parents because of their past actions.

"Well, my deceit got me exactly what I deserved. Philippe came back into her life and told your mother everything about my roguish behavior. He confronted me and convinced her to leave England. Of course, they agreed to keep her pregnancy a well-kept secret." His father heaved a sigh. "My punishment, I suppose."

Things had complicated tenfold. "Now you really have me lost," Robert admitted. "What do you mean Philippe came back into her life?"

"They were engaged before I met her. Long story..." His answered trailed off, and he waved his hand as if to ask not to go down that road.

Robert's head ached. At least his past escapades were a trifle, compared to these sordid affairs.

"When I met Philippe in the park with you in hand, he lied to my face and said that your mother had died. I left that encounter grief stricken but troubled. After all, your name was Robert, and you were a spitting image of me," he huffed.

"I still am," he responded. He raked his fingers through his own blond hair imitating his father's habit.

"As if the man could hide it," he mumbled. "When I returned to England, I started to investigate the truth myself. It was then that I discovered your mother was indeed alive and you were my son. How do you think I felt?"

"Deceived, I would imagine," Robert replied. *Reaping what you sowed,* he thought to himself.

"And ecstatic at the thought of having a son. You have no idea how deep my own disappointment ran in Jacquelyn's barrenness. Of course, I went back to Paris to seek you and your mother. I didn't think twice about it."

"Is that when you asked uncle to send Philippe away? How did that come about?" The story was becoming far too compelling to stop now.

His father snorted a laugh. "I'll admit that I even surprised myself at the lengths I'd go to get him out of the picture."

"Damn, father," Robert encouraged him with a grin. "I am frankly amused at seeing this side of you."

"Amused?" The duke shifted in his chair showing his discomfort in being exposed. He took another sip of his drink and continued. "I had been informed that his business was going bankrupt and arranged to dig him out of the hole by becoming a silent investor."

"That's what you meant about losing your money," Robert pondered.

"So I made a business transaction with your uncle in exchange for sending Philippe off to the West Indies on a ruse to close the deal." The duke snickered and shook his head. "God, I was a deceitful bastard, wasn't I?"

"Then you had mother all to yourself, and one thing led to another." Contentment sparkled in his father's eyes. He retained no hint of regret in winning her heart.

"She didn't love Philippe. I knew when we reunited that I wanted both of you to be my family for the rest of my life." He paused momentarily, hardening his voice. "I didn't steal her from anyone. Her heart had always been mine."

"Had you no affection for Jacquelyn at all?" Robert struggled with the hard-heartedness his father displayed.

"I married out of duty, not love, and fully intended to divorce Jacquelyn. Your mother willingly came back to me, even though she, too, had married another." His cheek twitched as if he wanted to smile but suppressed the urge. "Of course, I encouraged her to do so."

"But..." Robert halted, afraid to point out how it had turned out so terribly painful for everyone involved.

"But what?"

The look in his eye challenged him to continue. Robert couldn't bring himself to do so. As if his father sensed what he wished to know, he answered the question for him.

"I do not regret loving or marrying your mother, nor do I regret you as my son," he answered with conviction. "I do, however, regret the consequences of that love, and how I deceitfully went about getting what I wanted." He scowled. "I destroyed another man both directly and indirectly. Indirectly, I am as much to blame for Angelique's kidnapping as any other." He pulled his eyes away from Robert and looked at the empty glass in his hand. "Love carries a steep price, son. Be forewarned."

After his father's last words, it felt as if he had withdrawn from the room. Robert sensed the conversation had ended. In the last ten minutes, he had learned more about his father than he had known in a lifetime. Often his lectures had fallen on his deaf ears, but now he understood father's motives. What he thought was utter control, had been a bid to save him from his own mistakes. It became clear that the hardened duke merely wanted to prevent the consequences of poor decisions in his life. It confirmed his uncle's comment made only a few weeks ago.

His father rose to his feet and smiled at him. "I better not have another, or your mother will be scolding me for sure."

Robert struggled with an overwhelming urge to embrace his father. He hadn't felt that way since he was ten years old when he sent him off to boarding school. Nevertheless, the stubborn blood of his parent that flood through his veins instilled enough hesitation to forgo the show of affection. Instead, he rose and stood in front of his father, and offered his hand in a gentleman's handshake.

The duke took one look and furrowed his brow. A second later, he clasped his hand and closed the gap between them. With one arm around his shoulder, his father gave him a hearty pat on the back and then withdrew.

"Go see your stepfather," he whispered in a raspy voice.

His father turned to leave, and Robert spoke once more. "Things have turned out as they should," he said, feeling compelled to offer comfort. His father returned a blank look, oblivious to the meaning behind his words.

Robert sat back down in the chair and heaved a troubled sigh. "What a fucking mess," he muttered. "God, Jolene, I hope you know how you are going to bring this to a conclusion without another war ensuing between the wounded."

After a few minutes of reflection, Robert rose to his feet and fingered the paper his father had given him. It was time to find Philippe.

Chapter 19

Family Heirlooms

As they sat around the dinner table their first evening together, Jolene had finally settled down into a peaceful state of mind. The duke, duchess, and Robert appeared to enjoy their accommodations. Her decision had been a wise one, along with her idea to rent for a two-month period. Hopefully, it would be ample time to execute her plans.

"Duchess, you indicated that you wished to visit your parents' graves," Jolene began a conversation. "May I ask where they are laid to rest?"

"Pere Lachaise Cemetery," her mother replied.

"Is that far from where we are located? I am as unfamiliar with Paris as much as London."

"It is about five kilometers from here."

Impressed over her mother's concise answer, she realized that the duchess had not forgotten the Paris landscape.

"It would appear, Lady von Lamberg, that you will need another tour guide," the duke spoke lightheartedly. He glanced at Suzette. "Though I dare not speak for my wife, I'm sure she would be more than happy to accompany you if you desire to see anything in particular."

"Well, I can show her too," Robert interjected. "It's not as if I don't know Paris."

Robert sounded miffed he had not been considered, which made Jolene wonder what he remembered about the city.

"No doubt your cousin Geoffrey, when he arrives, will be vying for the task as well," the duchess remarked.

"Thank you for that vote of confidence," Robert replied.

"I'm not sure what I wish to see," Jolene clarified. She looked directly toward her mother. "You can be assured, though, that if I have any questions about the city, I shall come directly to the source."

"I would be happy to answer anything you would like," she coolly replied.

Their conversation had left the familiar and reverted to the formal. Perhaps Jolene's uneasiness expressed earlier over her mother's touch had caused the deterioration. Jolene attempted to soothe matters between them.

"Whenever you would like to visit the Pere Lachaise Cemetery, let the driver know. The motorcar is for everyone's use." She paused and continued with a sympathetic voice. "Duchess, if you would like someone to accompany you, I'd be pleased to stand by your side. I understand the death of one's parent more than any other, having buried two in the past fifteen years."

Robert glanced at Jolene with a questionable gaze and then looked at his mother waiting for her response. For a few moments, she contemplated the offer, but remained silent sipping her soup. Her obvious delay caused the duke to speak on her behalf.

"Suzette may want to visit alone, as she—"

"No, that's all right, Robert," she interrupted, placing her hand on his forearm. "Frankly, I think that I would like the company of another person. When I visit, I usually return in a morose mood. Perhaps sharing it with you is what I need to return in a better one."

"Tomorrow then?" Jolene did not want to delay.

"Yes, that would be fine."

"I will arrange it with the driver."

The remainder of their dinner encompassed superficial chitchat. When it had ended, Robert set down his napkin and scooted back his chair. Surprised at his action, he held out his hand toward Jolene.

"I would thoroughly enjoy the opportunity of an after-dinner stroll in the garden. Would you accompany me?"

"Do you mind?" She turned toward the duke and duchess.

"No, not at all." The duke replied, rising to his feet as Jolene stood. Her mother failed to comment either way.

--·�֎·--

Robert offered his arm, and Jolene took it as he escorted her out the patio doors to the veranda overlooking the garden. The sun had fallen behind the neighboring buildings and shadows shrouded the foliage and pathway.

"Thank God," Robert exhaled. "I've been waiting to speak with you for hours."

"Why?" She walked over to the rose bed and examined the flora.

"You seem so calm about this entire matter, Jolene. I, on the other hand, have turned into a worrisome sibling."

"Well, I assure you, I had my own rather emotional episode after we arrived," she mentioned.

"What episode?" His sister hesitated for some time with a scrunched brow.

"After our arrival, mother affectionately touched me on the arm. It bothered me."

"Why?" Robert could not understand her reasoning.

"I don't know," she curtly replied. "It just did."

Jolene reached out and felt the petals of a red rose between her thumb and index finger. "Everyone and everything is still a jumbled puzzle in my mind, and I guess

I'm becoming frustrated trying to make pieces fit by shoving them into places they do not belong."

"A puzzle? That's an understatement," Robert replied. "Father, after a few drinks this afternoon, had another confessional episode in the library." Her distraction of playing with the flower abruptly ended. She grabbed his hand and pulled him over to a garden bench.

"Sit down and tell me," she eagerly inquired.

"He expressed regret for the hurt he had caused Philippe."

"Really? I find that surprising," she said, straightening her spine in dispute. "From what I've read, my opinion has formed to the contrary. I doubt he considered the potential damage to Jacquelyn or Philippe. His love for mother blinded his good sense, if he had any."

"Well, that's quite harsh," Robert countered with a scowl. "He didn't even know I existed until by chance he passed Philippe in a park. I was with him that day and distinctly remember the encounter. It is burned into my memory."

"I don't understand what you mean that he didn't know. What are you saying?"

Robert shifted his body in frustration. Being in Paris had resurrected his own ghosts from the past. Jolene appeared edgy. "Let's change the subject," he implored. He reached over and grabbed his sister's hand.

"I have Philippe's address."

"You do?" Her face lit with excitement.

"Yes, father gave it to me." He pulled the paper out of his pocket and held it in his hand. "Once again, he encouraged me to visit."

"Will you?"

Robert held no doubt that he wanted to see Philippe, no matter what had transpired in the past. The fond memories of their relationship together were few. After all, he had been five years old and memories from childhood fade. Nevertheless, he clearly recalled the whipping he received for flipping over the bassinet. In retrospect, perhaps Philippe knew about his mother's infidelity. No doubt, he had directed a lot of his anger toward his rear.

"You know, I think I will—that is if you don't mind if I see him first."

"No, I don't mind, except that I am anxious to see him too. Nevertheless, I've committed to going with your mother to the cemetery tomorrow, so my time is hindered."

A joint trip to the cemetery held no intrigue for Robert. Perhaps Jolene wanted more time alone with her to ask questions. "Well, why don't I go tomorrow and let you know what I find out." Robert opened the paper. "I have his last home and employment address. He apparently works at a cigar shop, of all places." He read the street address. "It's on Rue Saint Honoré, wherever the hell that is," he said.

"I'll have the car tomorrow, though, what shall you do?"

"Let me ask someone on the staff if they know the location. Should it be in walking distance, I could use the exercise. If not, I will hail a cab. Don't worry."

"Oh, Robert, we are so close."

Her enthusiasm felt contagious. "You are carefully planning something to bring this all to a conclusion. How are you going to do it?"

A sly smile slowly spread across her face. "It depends on many factors, but I hope to bring them together and reveal who I am all at once. Then I expect them to behave like adults and allow me to bring our family together."

"Oh, good luck with that," Robert choked, hardly believing her scheme. "I suggest you have the French Legion standing by to maintain the peace," he teased. There would be no way in hell all these sensitive people would come together like rational individuals. Did she envision they would ecstatically share a hug at the moment she announced her name? He shuddered to think of the explosive reactions.

"You jest," she said, standing up. "Come and walk with me through the remainder of the gardens before it gets dark."

"You're going to need some kind of evidence besides a tattered letter and worn diary from a dead lady's maid. I do not think that anyone will accept your word straightaway. They will think you have ulterior motives."

"Well, you did," she said smiling.

"Hmm," he said, rubbing his chin. "I guess I did. But what convinced me were the obvious pieces fitting together in that puzzle of yours as the weeks progressed."

"You need not worry, Robert. I have proof and infallible proof at that." She bent over, plucked a single flower from the floral bed and began twirling it around.

"What proof?" She was teasing him with that damn flower as if she had one up on him.

"Jewelry."

"What jewelry?"

She smirked. "Jacquelyn stole the Holland family jewels when she left your father. Did he not tell you?"

Flabbergasted over another revelation, he halted his step. "I had no idea there were any family jewels. Whatever I saw on mother, I assumed that father purchased for her as gifts."

"No doubt he did, but Jacquelyn came to Austria with a collection of family jewels that dated back centuries. They are Holland heirlooms. A few she sold, Dorcas revealed in her diary, to survive when they first arrived. The remaining pieces my father kept in safekeeping until I had reached an age of responsibility. He gave them all to me."

"Shit," he gasped.

Jolene scowled.

"Oh, sorry, he quickly apologized. "And you have them with you?"

She nodded affirmatively. "I'm sure your father will recognize them. All the pieces bear the letter 'H' and a crest on the back. I assumed they were the jeweler's mark. It wasn't until recently that I realized the 'H' stood for Holland." A brisk breeze blew through the trees like an omen rustling the leaves.

"Jolene, you do realize that you are opening old wounds with everyone. What do you hope to accomplish in the end?"

She had pulled every petal off the bud until nothing remained but a green stem. The palm of her hand opened and it dropped to the grass beneath her feet as if she had accomplished something symbolically.

"When I look at my life, I admit that I have not suffered any wounds from what happened to me. As a baby, I certainly did not notice any difference. When mother died—"

"Jacquelyn," Robert interrupted, correcting her a bit annoyed.

"All right, Jacquelyn," she briskly modified. "My memories are spotty bits of her presence in my life, the coffin, and the rose. Afterward, the count literally grafted me into his family tree."

"You were the victim of a crime, but you profited from it the most. It's almost ironic, when you think about it," Robert said. He slipped his arm around her shoulder in a brotherly fashion attempting to give her comfort.

Jolene nodded. "I know."

"You are intelligent and gorgeous, I might add." Robert smiled endearingly at her. "And you have everything you possibly could need financially for the remainder of your life."

"True," she agreed, gazing off into a nearby bush. "But I am alone."

He drew her closer with his hand on her shoulder. "You don't have to be alone, Jolene. You have a family now."

"By blood but not in heart," she replied, furrowing her brow.

"When all is revealed, what will you do then?" Robert dropped his arm and stepped back anticipating what he did not want to hear.

"My life is in Austria," she quickly responded. "I have no desire to leave everything the count has entrusted to my care. I would feel as if I betrayed his love for me."

"But what about your real father and mother?"

"I want them to know that it all turned out as it should have. The guilt they carry over my loss should cease, the anger and hatred toward one another over what happened should end. Reconciliation should flow between everyone involved. Not until that happens, will I truly open my heart in love to any of them. It's just not in me."

Jolene tilted her head into the evening breeze and closed her eyes. She appeared to be drying tears that threatened her calm demeanor. "You still feel no endearment toward my mother, do you?" Robert dolefully asked.

Her eyes opened sparkling with moisture. "It blows hot and cold. I hope to learn more about her when we visit the gravesites tomorrow. I'm going to see if she tells me about her childhood."

"Well, you'll know a hell of a lot more than me if she opens up." Robert kicked a rock near his foot sending it a few feet into the flowerbed.

"What about the duke?" he asked in a deep voice, emphasizing *duke* jokingly.

"You would ask," she teased. "All I can see is his hand between your mother's legs and the other on her exposed breast."

Robert laughed aloud, and Jolene joined in. Nevertheless, he felt awkward that she continued to harbor ill feelings toward his mother and father. As far as he was concerned, Jolene von Lamberg possessed her own set of faults. She had irrational hopes of righteous intervention into their family affairs, driven by her staunch sense of morality. Obviously, she had never loved a man or experienced the sensation of physical passion that can drive a person to make rash decisions. Because of it, she had become somewhat judgmental of their parents. Robert wondered if she would ever realize those faults.

"I don't mean to say that I have not grown fond of you, dear brother," she offered. "On the contrary, my feelings for you grow each day. Thank you for being by my side through this journey."

"Well, I'll be damned," he grinned. "Even after I shoved you over in your bassinet, I still hold a soft spot in your heart?"

"For the moment," she replied coyly, shaking her index finger at him. "But if you curse or take the Lord's name in vain in front of me one more time, I'm going to shove a bar of soap in your mouth."

Robert shook his head over her threat to discipline his nasty vocabulary. "God, Jolene. Had mother and Philippe stayed together, just think of all the sibling arguments we could have enjoyed. We missed out on some good times."

Jolene's face grew into a broad smile. "Indeed we did."

Dusk had all but turned into nightfall. The wind picked up. Robert thought he caught the smell of rain in the air. "I think we better go in, it's getting chilly out here," he said.

Robert offered his arm and led her back to the veranda. "Tomorrow you'll be at the cemetery, and I'll be purchasing a box of cigars."

"What if he's not there?"

"Then I'll try his home. Don't worry, Jolene, we'll find him."

"Well, if you do see him tomorrow, you must tell me all about it later in the afternoon. Then I'll go on my own the following day."

"Will you tell him who you are when you visit?" Robert thought that perhaps she might change her mind.

"Oh, heavens no," she corrected his assumption. "I'm going to see my father incognito for now. Something in my heart tells me that I may shed a tear in his presence, if I'm not careful."

Robert wondered if he would choke up, too, when he saw him. *No, I'm not that barmy,* he told himself as they returned indoors. If he did, he would blame it on Jolene.

Chapter 20

A Graveyard of Bones

The driver pulled up to the entrance of Pere Lachaise and then turned slowly onto the Avenue Principale. He came to a stop and asked the duchess which one of the many lanes he should follow within the graveyard.

Jolene had heard much about the famous cemetery. After one hundred years since it opened in 1804, it had housed 33,000 gravesites by 1830. How many more since that time had been laid to rest within its gates? Awed by the beautiful trees and landscape of graves, mausoleums, and statues of angels, she waited for Suzette's instructions.

"Do you mind walking to my father's place of rest?" the duchess asked.

"No, of course not," Jolene replied, eager to step out into the sun. "It's a beautiful day, and I'd prefer to walk."

The driver helped them exit onto the cobblestone path. Suzette opened her parasol to shade herself from the sun. The large hat upon Jolene's head sufficiently covered her face.

"Please wait for us," Jolene instructed the driver.

"My father is not far from here." Suzette announced, walking down the avenue.

Jolene strode by her side looking to her right and left at the grounds. The duchess remained quietly contemplative. Jolene respected her need for privacy and reflection and purposely did not initiate a conversation. Fascinated by the beauty of the cemetery, she had more than enough to keep her attention. After a few more minutes, they halted in front of a large monument where the avenue ended.

"This is where my father is buried," her mother said in a somber voice.

Jolene read the location on a nearby sign, *Monument Aux Morts*. The huge structure with its impressive artwork gave her the false impression that Suzette's father must have been immensely rich.

Suzette caught the look in her eye and quickly corrected her misconception. "It's an ossuary. There is nothing there but millions of bones behind the locked doors. The remains of my father have been added to the menagerie of death."

"How sad," Jolene replied, mesmerized by the scene. She looked at the dark doorway containing the sculptures of a naked man and woman, who stood with their backs toward visitors. Other figures stood on either side as if waiting to enter. It gave her the chills.

"My father was buried in a common grave on the outskirts of the graveyard when he passed away over twenty years ago. Later, his body was exhumed, and his bones deposited here."

The sadness on her mother's face intensely touched Jolene. She had not come from a rich family, but rather one of poverty.

"And is your mother here too?" Jolene glimpsed at Suzette staring at the closed door.

"No, my mother has a perpetual grave on the other side of the cemetery. It's about a fifteen-minute walk from where we stand."

"It must be hard for you not having a permanent grave and headstone to commemorate the love of your father." Jolene could not comprehend being unable to stand by her stepfather's grave nor that of Jacquelyn's. Buried next to each other, Jolene had sworn to visit them regularly and leave tokens of flowers.

"Here I am thinking selfishly of my own father," the duchess said with empathy. "Please accept my condolences on the loss of your father. From what I was told that happened only a few months ago."

Jolene looked at her with a blank expression. She had not been thinking of her stepfather. On the contrary, it was Philippe. Without thinking of the consequences of her answer, she pointedly corrected the duchess.

"He was my stepfather, not my birth father."

"Oh," she uttered in surprise. "I didn't realize your situation." The duchess pondered for a moment and then continued. "Might I inquire of your birth father? Do you still see him?"

Jolene's stomach tied into a knot. It would be so easy to look at her straight in the eye and tell her the truth, but she could not reveal herself—not now. She circumvented the question by answering only partially.

"I have not seen my father since infancy. My mother raised me. When she passed, the count adopted me into his family as his daughter."

"I see," she replied thoughtfully. "Well then the count, by all means, is your father in heart."

Jolene pulled her eyes away from her mother. "Yes, he was the only father I knew, and I did love and respect him deeply."

After giving the duchess a few private minutes of silence, she stood by and watched her mother curiously. When she made the sign of the cross, she began to walk away.

"If you'd like to come with me, I'll show you where my mother is laid to rest."

"Of course," Jolene replied, following by her side.

As they wandered through the massive cemetery, Jolene studied the artwork of angelic statues watching over the dead and effigies of souls upon grave tops. The sheer number of entombed bodies and sculptures overwhelmed her emotions, giving her a morbid chill.

A few minutes later, they traversed down a narrow lane and stopped in front of a grave that had been prominently marked with the name of *Rousseau*. At the head, a weeping angel with a bowed head added to the sorrow of the scene. Jolene read the dates and saw that she had passed away many years ago. As she quickly counted the decades, she realized that Suzette had lost her mother when she was a child.

"My mother," the duchess said. "I barely remember her now. She passed away when I was young, and my poor dear father never seemed to recover."

"I see your maiden name is Rousseau," Jolene commented.

"Yes, a French name for a very English duchess," she replied lightheartedly with a smile. "I laugh sometimes that I have the title of an English aristocrat. The fact that I even love an Englishman would turn some of these fine French souls over in their graves."

Jolene chuckled at her statement. "Yes, if I remember my history quite well, your two countries have had their differences."

"Thankfully our barbaric days have ended," her mother commented. "Our two societies have made peace, but..." She paused for a moment. "But old prejudices remain unspoken, I think."

"Do you need a moment with your mother?" Jolene asked. "Just say the word, and I'll wander off and look at all the extraordinary and beautiful graves."

"Not really," she sighed. "I would be talking to an unfamiliar ghost. I simply come out of respect to honor her memory. After all, she is my mother."

Her words wounded Jolene's heart. Respect and honor were not feelings that she felt toward the duchess as they stood side by side.

"What about your mother? I'm sure you have fond memories of her as well."

"My mother?" Her voice was curt. Her throat constricted cutting off her airflow. "I barely remember my own mother," she finally revealed. "She died when I was three years of age."

The momentary pleasure she sensed earlier in her mother's presence died. Instead, it felt as if the devil himself had risen from the graveyard and yanked her heart out of her body. The sensation of abandonment gripped her so tightly that it actually hurt. She brought her hand to her chest as a breath hitched in her throat. There before her, only a few feet away, stood the mother who abandoned her for another.

Unable to look at her while the pain persisted, she lowered her eyes to the ground. She wanted to love her mother, but the anger toward her remained unabated. How could she have left Paris so soon after what happened to her? Had she no sense of decency or sorrow over her loss? The duchess would have abandoned her either way even if she left Philippe to go with the duke.

Jolene wanted to collapse in a pool of bitter tears at her feet. Instead, she shut her eyes tightly, inhaled another deep breath, and buried the pain until it no longer controlled her emotions.

"Are you all right?" her mother asked, showing concern over her demeanor.

"Yes," she quickly replied. "I had a stab of pain in my head and a headache seems to be coming on." She lied.

"Perhaps we should return now," her mother suggested.

As the days grew closer to her revelation, Jolene knew that the woman walking at her side was as much of a stranger as the dead bodies that lay cold in the ground. She tried to remain congenial on their trip back to the townhome, but fell quiet and removed from her surroundings. Her mother remained silent, perhaps falling into her own morose mood, as she called it, after visiting her parents' graves.

When they arrived, Jolene excused herself feigning a headache. The duchess wished her a speedy recovery and left her side. Jolene retreated to her room, unpinned her feathered hat, and set it on the vanity. A quick glance at her reflection in the mirror revealed her emotional turmoil.

Feeling drawn once again to pull the diary from its hiding place, Jolene opened it and began reading the last entries.

"My mistress asked me if I would do anything for her, and I promised that I would. When I assured her of my loyalty, I had no idea that the next day she would test my words.

Today, she returned with an infant in a carriage. When I asked whose baby she had in her care, she stated that Philippe Moreau had entrusted her with his daughter while he took care of business. Then, without warning, she commanded me to pack our things. 'You said you would do anything for me, Dorcas,' she reminded me of my pledge. I nodded in agreement and quickly went about carrying out her orders.

My mistress planned a terrible deed to steal the child. I obeyed and that night we left on a train. How could I refuse? She had suffered much heartache over the years in barrenness and unfaithfulness of her husband. As horribly criminal her action had been, I remained silent and became her accomplice."

Jolene's heart pounded heavily against her rib cage. Philippe, in his own folly to regain his pride and kill the duke, had entrusted her to a stranger. She imagined the entire scene play out before her. Everyone must have felt shock and hysteria when they discovered her gone. They all played a part in her disappearance.

She lowered her head and placed her face in her palms. What had her family done? Every conceivable selfish act played out between them all, shrouded in deception and lies. She wanted to cry, but no tears came. Only numbness flowed through her body.

"Oh, Robert," she whispered. "Tell me that all has gone well in your search for Philippe. Please, bring me no more heartache today."

Chapter 21

A Forgotten Man

Disappointed he didn't find Philippe at work, Robert hailed another cab and gave the driver a second address. The clerk behind the counter had indicated that Mr. Moreau would return upon the morrow. Robert had no desire to wait any longer for Jolene's sake.

The driver traversed the busy streets. They crossed the Seine and entered into a lower income segment of the city. Finally, after a few more minutes, the carriage slowed and stopped along a row house situated on a narrow street. Robert noted the time on his pocket watch thinking of his sister visiting the cemetery. Hopefully, the hour with his mother would go well and bring them closer together.

After he paid the driver, he walked to the door and stood there for a minute contemplating the impending visitation. He hadn't taken the time to formulate his introduction or think about what he would say afterward.

Feeling a bit out of sorts among the lower class neighborhood, Robert glanced about his surroundings. He wondered why Philippe had ended up here of all places. It was a far cry from the expansive and expensive house he had remembered as a young boy. If this had been the outcome of his life, Robert couldn't help but grieve over his situation. His lifestyle had drastically changed from a thriving businessman to that of a mere cigar clerk. A part of him feared what he would discover beyond the door.

Taking a deep breath, he knocked hard and stepped back waiting for an answer. After what seemed like a long minute of no response, he balled his fist and rapped his knuckles harder.

"All right, all right," he heard a faint voice coming from the other side. "I'm coming."

A moment later the door flew open. Immediately, Robert recognized Philippe. He had aged with deep furrows in his brow. The clear complexion he had remembered disappeared behind a scruffy day-old growth. His hair, still dark and thick, looked unkempt and slightly gray at the temples. The muscular and athletic young man in his mid-twenties had turned into a skinny, middle-aged man in his forties with a gaunt face. Philippe looked at him, but he made no indications that he recognized who stood at his door.

"Yes, what is it?"

His curtness and annoyed glower tongue-tied Robert. Memories of his early childhood flooded his mind. The distinct feeling of having once loved him as his father finally gave him the courage to speak.

"It's your stepson, Robert," he replied with a tremor in his voice. "May I come in and visit with you for a while?" He swallowed the lump in his throat and wiped the sweat off the palm of his hand on his pant leg.

At first, Philippe leaned forward and peered at him intensely as if he needed to move closer due to poor vision. The awkward moment passed in silence. He looked at his blond hair and peered into his blue eyes. A slow grin spread across his face when he recognized the boyish lad who had grown into a man.

"Holy Mother of God," he said. His face lit up. "Is that you, Robert?"

Instead of the anger he had rather expected, Robert found his kind voice as a welcomed surprise. "Indeed it is, sir." Robert sighed in relief.

"Well, I'll be damned," Philippe said, opening wide the door. "Come in."

Robert stepped into dingy surroundings void of light and beauty. "I hope you don't mind me showing up on your doorstep like this after all these years," he quickly apologized glancing about the area. "I happened to be in Paris and thought of seeing you."

"Well, I'm glad you did. Have a seat," he offered pointing to a worn-out divan in a small sitting room to the right. "Can I get you anything to drink? I think I have a spot of brandy left in the house."

A drink sounded exactly what he needed to get through the next few minutes. "Yes, if you don't mind."

"No, not at all. Just give me a minute," he replied, scurrying off.

Philippe disappeared to retrieve the spirits, and Robert took a closer look at his residence. *Goddamn shame he's living like this,* he thought to himself. He couldn't help but wonder if his father had been aware of Philippe's financial situation. Though he had been privy to the fact that Philippe had run his shipping company into bankruptcy, he hadn't thought that he would still be living the consequences after all these years.

Robert noted there were no photographs of family anywhere. Nothing of warmth decorated the interior. There were no pictures on the walls, except peeling and faded wallpaper. The threadbare carpet underneath his feet revealed a wood floor. Only one lamp sat on a rickety side table near the divan.

Having heard no other voices since his arrival, he felt sure that his former stepfather lived without companionship. A moment later Philippe returned with two glasses and half a bottle of brandy. He poured him a drink and handed it to him. By the same token, he poured himself one but with less in the glass.

"I think the last time I gave you anything to drink it must have been milk," he said jokingly.

Philippe's welcoming demeanor surprised Robert. However, when he sensed the loneliness within the walls of his meager home, he understood why.

"My God, boy, look how you've grown into a man. How old are you now? Twenty?"

"Twenty-three," Robert answered. He took a sip of brandy to wet his parched lips.

"Twenty-three." Philippe shook his head. "I cannot believe so many years have passed."

"Quite a few," Robert agreed. Philippe studied him for a moment.

"What do they call you now, Lord Holland?" His voice teasingly asked him. "Big man, important father, plentiful bank account..." Philippe hesitated before speaking the remainder. "And beautiful mother, no doubt."

As if someone had blown out the flame of a candle, Philippe's eyes turned as gray as the atmosphere in the room. The pain remained, albeit carefully hidden through years of suppression, Robert thought to himself.

"I hate titles," Robert answered. "And the responsibility that goes along with them."

His stepfather laughed aloud. "Ah, do I sense a slight rebellious streak in the young man?"

"Slight?" Robert resounded. "I can think of many other pursuits I would rather have," he admitted.

Philippe sat on the edge of a worn four-legged chair that looked like it would collapse at any moment. "You've been to university, I image. Did your father send you to some expensive institution like Cambridge or Oxford to study for a vocation?"

Robert sighed at the thought of it. "Law at Oxford," he replied, as if the words stung his lips when they left.

"Well, you should be thankful you had an excellent education. I doubt that I would have ever been able to provide you an opportunity like that."

Philippe's demeanor turned pensive. "How in heaven's name did you find me?" He took a sip of his drink and then glared at him with narrowed eyes as if he somehow knew.

"I..." Robert began but trailed off. He halted considering the consequences of his answer. The hesitation in his voice tipped Philippe toward the truth.

"Twenty fucking years and your father still shoves his goddamn nose in my business, doesn't he?" Philippe's eyes grew dark, and his voice rose in anger. "That's it isn't it? Did he send you here to spy on me?"

The friendly demeanor faded. Robert gulped when he saw Philippe's eyes radiate hate. He looked as if he still held the gun. "Well you can see how I live. Go back and tell the bastard." Philippe brought the remaining alcohol to his lips and gulped it down.

"Philippe," Robert cajoled, "It's not like that—I assure you." A cold stare met his answer. Robert struggled how to respond afraid that he might reveal too much. "I am here because I want to be. You were the only father that I knew for the first five years of my life. Surely, you cannot believe that I harbor any ill will toward you." It took a few moments, but his hardened face eventually softened. Philippe lowered his head and sighed. After staring into his empty glass, he apologized.

"You're right. It's wrong of me to put any blame upon you. You were an innocent bystander in the entire wretched situation." He lifted his head and looked at him with sorrow. "Forgive me for my rude conduct."

"It's understandable," Robert replied in empathy. "And what about you, Philippe? What have you been up to all these years? Did you ever marry again?"

His stepfather leaned back in the chair. "God no," he answered lowering his head. "What woman would marry a man without a penny and a drinking problem to go along with it?"

"I'm so sorry," Robert replied.

Philippe laughed. "Oh, shit, don't be. I lost your father's money he had invested in the shipping business. Truthfully, I enjoyed squandering every penny. Revenge can be sweet with a glass of brandy," he said winking.

At a loss how to respond to Philippe's downtrodden past, he sat there sipping his drink pondering all that had happened.

"Your fucking father sent me a check to help me out about ten years ago. I wrote the bastard back returning it in pieces and told him he could shove it up his ass." Philippe wiped his mouth off with the back of his hand.

His father had tried to financially help Philippe? Of course, he didn't mention it to him. "I certainly don't blame you, Philippe. But I must say I am disappointed in your living conditions. You deserve much more."

Philippe narrowed his eyes and looked at Robert. "What do you expect? Had that bitch never stolen my baby girl, I could have found happiness. Even though your mother left me, at least I would have had a reason to go on living. We could have had a home together."

Robert saw his eyes water, and his heart broke. How in the hell was Jolene going to redeem him from the misery of his past? Just thinking about the emotional turmoil her revelation would bring, made his stomach churn. It was time to leave. All this bloody emotion had taken its toll even on him.

"I'll be here for at least two months," he said, leaning forward toward Philippe. "I'd like to invite you to dinner one night if you'll accept."

"Me? Come to dinner?" He shook his head disagreeing.

"I'm staying at a townhome near Notre Dame with a lady friend." Robert smiled at him mischievously and raised a brow. "She's pretty."

Philippe chuckled. "What the hell am I supposed to wear? I have no formal dinner clothes. Do you want me to show up in my tweed work suit?"

"Hmm, that might pose a problem," he mused, wondering if he would accept anything from him in the way of charity. "I'll rent you the evening wear if you will come and dine with me."

"Shit," he answered annoyed. "I don't know."

"Will you think about it at least?"

Philippe brought his empty glass to his lips, searching for one more drop. "On one condition," he said. "I couldn't give a damn about your father. Nevertheless, seeing you makes me think of..." His voice choked.

"Mother?" Robert answered for him. Philippe nodded. "She's well, Philippe. And as beautiful as you remember her, but a little more fuller in the face. She's kept her figure though," he added proudly.

"Does that bastard treat her good?" He narrowed his eyes.

Robert wanted to tell him that they were still in love, but he knew those words would open wounds. "Yes, he treats her like a gentleman."

Philippe sat quietly saying nothing more. He looked at the bottle of brandy. "You want another drink?"

"No, thank you."

After inhaling a raspy breath, Philippe ruminated over the past. "You probably don't remember our last words before you left with your mother."

He shook his head no.

"'Forgive me,' she pleaded." Philippe stared at the wall behind him as if he were watching the scene all over again. "She wouldn't leave until she received my forgiveness saying she never meant to hurt me." He raked his hand through his hair as if to push the memories away. "There have been times in years past where I've relived that scene over and over in my dreams. Each time, I hear myself say to her what I said then. 'I will never forgive you.'"

Robert didn't know what to say. The memories of that day when his father took the two of them away still lingered fresh in his stepfather's mind, haunting him like a ghost. He had to ask. "Have you forgiven her?"

Swiftly, Philippe raised his head and looked at him. A deep sigh left his lungs. "Hell, if I know."

Robert rose to his feet. "I'm serious about dinner," he reminded him. "What days do you work at the shop?"

Philippe placed his empty glass on the wobbly side table and stood. "I'll be working for the next five days," he answered. "If you want a decent smoke, come on by. I'll hook you up with a good Cuban," he said with a sly grin.

Extending his hand to Philippe, he hoped he would shake it in return. "You can be assured, I'll come by. Think about the dinner, will you?"

Philippe clasped his hand in return and gave it a hearty shake. "Still the same stubborn boy I once knew."

"You're probably right about that," he admitted. "My anger issues, strong will, and lack of responsibility annoys the hell out of father." Robert gave him a wink. "I'm a bit of a rogue with the ladies too."

Philippe roared and patted Robert on the back. "Good for you! Keep it up, boy."

They said their goodbyes at the door, and Robert walked out onto the street looking for a cab to hail back to the townhome. It had been an enjoyable, but emotionally draining visit, which he couldn't wait to share with Jolene.

Chapter 22

A Smoke Screen

As the driver traversed the busy streets toward her destination, Jolene pondered all that Robert had told her the evening before. He expressed relief over Philippe's favorable reception and conveyed to her in detail their conversation. From the words exchanged, it appeared old grudges remained against the duke, but Philippe retained an interest in Suzette's welfare. As far as forgiveness had been concerned regarding her unfaithfulness, it sounded as if wounds remained.

Robert expressed his desire to accompany her and wait in the motorcar, but she declined the offer. It would the first time to meet her father. Unlike the introduction to her mother, she felt this would be different. She wanted to keep it that way, without feeling pressured afterward to express her emotional state of mind.

When they approached the location, she ordered the driver to park one block away and to wait there for her return. He slowed, finding a parking spot near the curb, and stopped the car. She exited with his help and glanced both ways down the crowded avenue.

"Is the address to the right or left?"

"That would be one block to your right, Lady von Lamberg."

Nodding her thanks, she turned and began a leisurely stroll toward the shop. Jolene glanced once more at the address she had scribbled down on a piece of paper. For some reason, she couldn't keep the numbers memorized and referred to it every few minutes. Her eyes darted back and forth at the addresses on the buildings and above doors.

The sidewalks, not far from the Louvre museum, were packed with pedestrians. People hustled back and forth. A few couples walked together, and others passed by with shopping bags or hatboxes. One woman walked a Poodle on a leash, who barked at anything moving. To add to the confusion, motorcars, omnibuses, and carriages filled the avenue creating loud noises. The over-active atmosphere made her edgy.

To make matters worse, it turned out to be an unseasonably warm day. She chose a fashionable walking dress, but the thickness of the fabric overheated her body. Unwelcomed beads of sweat formed on her forehead where the rim of her hat pressed against her hairline. She had forgotten to take a fan and felt as if she would melt by the time she arrived.

As the numbers dwindled to her destination, her eyes spotted a striped, green and white canopy belonging to the cigar shop. It hung over the large picture window with its name and date of its establishment—"Fonde en 1716." Robert mentioned the store had a reputation of being the finest in Paris, carrying a large selection of imported tobacco.

At last, she had arrived. In the window sat a presentation of pipes, cigar boxes, cigarettes, cases, and other smoking paraphernalia that had been set out on display. It made her think of her dear stepfather. The count had a fondness for cigarettes. A pang of sorrow swept across her heart, but she quickly contained it by reminding herself she had come to meet her real father.

Jolene glanced inside and noted two men behind the counters waiting on male customers. She did not want to compete for Philippe's attention, so she waited for the patrons to leave. No doubt, a woman walking into a cigar shop would turn heads anyway.

After a few minutes, the two patrons exited with their purchases. She blew out a puff of air from her lungs and realized she still clutched the paper with the address. Quickly, she shoved it in her purse and retrieved a handkerchief to wipe her brow before entering. When she saw her reflection in the glass picture window, she looked like a scared rabbit. With a quick pull back of her shoulders and a straightening of her spine, her hand reached for the doorknob.

She heard the jingle of the bell above her head announcing the arrival of a customer. A moment later, she found herself standing in the middle of male indulgence. Her nostrils filled with the smell of tobacco, and she wrinkled her nose in protest.

"Might I be of service, mademoiselle?"

A tall man with dark brown hair and gray temples greeted her arrival. She glanced about the shop and saw that the other clerk had apparently retreated to the back room of the store. Jolene returned her gaze to him. His eyes were somber, slightly downturned at the edges with crows-feet wrinkles that made him look sad. His jaw jutted forward square and strong on his clean-shaven face. His stature towered over her small frame, and immediately her mind spoke what her heart wished to know. *Are you my father?* Robert had described his appearance, which left her no doubt that who stood before her was indeed Philippe Moreau.

She quickly drew her eyes away to regain her emotions. A slight smile curled the corner of her lips, and she lifted her head once again. To keep from getting lost in his eyes, she glanced at the large humidor shelves and glass cases filled with cigarettes and pipes. Her nostrils inhaled the awful aroma, but nothing could be done about it.

"I've come to purchase a gift for a gentleman, monsieur," she announced. He didn't appear to be surprised.

"Very well, I can help you with that selection." His kind and helpful demeanor allowed her to relax. "Do you have an idea what you'd like to purchase?"

Jolene looked at him with a blank gaze. She bluntly told him the truth of the matter. "Honestly, I know nothing about cigars."

"Do you know what brand the gentleman prefers? Does he smoke Cuban cigars? If not, we do carry brands from all over the world where tobacco is grown in South America and in the Pacific regions." He paused, but she remained silent. "There are many types of cigars, mademoiselle, that come in all size and shapes."

Jolene felt as if she stood in the tropical regions of South America, because of the heat and smell. She had no idea what to say. In an effort to clear her thoughts, she walked away from him and began to peruse the items in a nearby case. Perhaps she should focus on a pipe instead. Yes, a pipe might do. Certainly, that would make it easier to speak intelligently. Cigars were too confusing with all their foreign names.

"I see you carry pipes, as well. Does a man who smokes a cigar enjoy an occasional puff on a pipe?" Philippe snickered and then quickly drew his face back into a subdued pose. *He's laughing at me*, she thought. She glanced at him in disapproval.

"Well, that depends," he said with a straight face. His tone remained lighthearted.

Obviously, her ignorance of male smoking habits tickled his funny bone. "All right," Jolene swiftly responded. "I'll be honest with you." She looked into his piercing brown eyes. "I know absolutely nothing about this ghastly habit of smoking." Jolene tilted her head. "I assume you smoke, monsieur...monsieur..." She trailed off waiting for him to fill in the blank.

"Moreau," he responded.

"Monsieur Moreau." Jolene repeated his name, letting it sink into her heart. Then, as if someone had pricked her with a needle, her eyes threatened to well in tears. She turned away, walked over to another counter, and lowered her head to peer inside the glass case.

"So tell me, Monsieur Moreau, does your wife tolerate you smoking a pipe or a cigar after dinner?" To Jolene's surprise, he did not immediately respond to her question. She heard his footsteps approach and stop as he stood a few feet away watching her examining the goods.

"Pipes, I'm afraid, are a matter of preference as well."

Jolene lifted her head and turned to look at him, but his gaze had fallen to the objects in the case. She observed his eyes were the same color as her own. After she noted that point, she recalled that he still hadn't answered her question. *The stubborn man,* she inwardly complained.

"Pipes are made of a variety of different woods that produce distinct flavors, and there are a variety of tobaccos a gentleman may prefer according to his individual tastes."

The smoking habits of the twentieth century male had exhausted her patience. "Well, I see that my decision will not be an easy one. Perhaps you can choose something for me. I'm sure I can trust your expert taste and advice in this matter."

"I would not presume to choose such a preference without knowing the individual for whom you are purchasing, mademoiselle. Is this your fiancé perhaps or husband?"

"No, a friend of mine who has accompanied me to Paris." She averted his gaze.

"Is he an older gentleman or one of your generation?"

"He is five years my senior. I am eighteen."

Jolene looked for a reaction in his eyes but nothing came forth. Why did he not answer about a wife? Why was he not putting the similarities of age together? Perhaps her thick accent laced with German tones gave him no need to speculate beyond their encounter.

"Well, he may prefer these." He walked over to the stack of cigars, quickly chose a box, and presented them to Jolene. She looked at the brand and markings. It could have been written in Greek for all she cared because it made no sense.

"How much?"

"I'm afraid they are a bit expensive, mademoiselle." He looked embarrassed that he had recommended them, which made her wonder if he worked on commission.

"Whatever the cost, I'll pay," she answered. She shoved the cigars back in his direction, and he took it from her hand. Philippe stepped behind the counter. Neatly, he wrapped the box in brown paper, tied a string around it, and knotted a small bow on top. Afterward, he rang up the sale, and Jolene handed him the francs to pay for the purchase. She dreaded each second that passed knowing that their encounter would soon end.

To cherish the moment, she kept her gaze upon him. An aura of grief appeared to surround her father like a veil of melancholy. Regardless of the empathy that she felt for him, she would not allow him to avoid her question.

"You failed to reply to my inquiry about what your wife thinks of your smoking habits, Monsieur Moreau. Does she tolerate the pipe, cigar, or cigarette as one of your vices?" Jolene flashed a warm smile hoping that it would entice a response.

"Mademoiselle..." he began.

"It is Komtesse Jolene von Lamberg," she offered, raising her head. Jolene felt her cheeks flush over her snobbish display of class.

He handed over the change from the purchase and cigars. "I beg your pardon, your ladyship," he spoke respectfully. "But I'm not married, so my smoking habits are my personal vices that harm no one else."

"I see." Jolene had been saddened to hear from Robert that he had not found love after all these years. "I appreciate your time and expert advice. Have a pleasant day." She headed toward the door, the bell jingled above her head, and she halted. Her father had already busied himself with other work. "Excuse me, might I ask one more question?"

He glanced her way. "Yes, your ladyship?"

"If these cigars are not to my friend's liking, may they be returned if the box remains unopened?"

"Yes, by all means. You may return them."

"Very well," she spoke. After exiting the shop, she hesitated a moment outside the door. Jolene glanced through the window and saw Philippe at the cash register as if nothing had happened.

She stepped away and began walking back toward the motorcar. Suddenly she felt flush and weak. Halting her step, she leaned against the building for a moment and closed her eyes. The world kept moving with cars, carriages, and people. But for her, it felt as if time stood still. Not a soul around her realized that she had just experienced a momentous occasion in her life.

After a deep breath, she opened her eyes again and found the composure to walk the remaining distance. The driver stood patiently on the sidewalk waiting for her return.

"Take me back to the townhouse, please."

She settled into her seat, and he pulled away from the curb to drive her home. Jolene closed her eyes and thought of Philippe. Their meeting had sparked something positive in her soul, unlike the wavering feelings she retained for her mother.

It saddened her to think of Philippe's poverty-stricken existence and the lack of companionship in his life. She wanted to help him, but how? Robert told her that he had turned down charity from the duke because of his stubborn sense of pride. Surely, he wouldn't accept it from her hand or would he? Jolene tucked the thought into a corner of her heart to ponder in the future. For now, she needed to plot the next step in her family's reconciliation.

As the driver passed Notre Dame, Jolene wanted to see the interior of the grand cathedral. She looked at the impressive monument and the gargoyles on top looking down on mankind. So much of Paris waited to be discovered, but her focus remained on other matters. No doubt when Geoffrey arrived, he would offer to show her the sites.

I wonder what is keeping him? Probably family matters, she concluded. At least he outwardly appeared more driven to succeed than her brother did. Then the voice of reason came to her in the form of Grace's voice. *"He's a heart breaker. I've never met a man so despicable in character when it comes to women."*

Sweet Grace. Jolene had no idea why she did not invite her to Paris. It had been a rude oversight on her part. Upon her return, she would pen a cordial letter and beg her forgiveness.

Chapter 23

The Pleasures of the Flesh

Geoffrey, not giving a damn about his cousin's threat, had arrived in Paris within hours of the others. Instead of proceeding to the townhome, he took the extra spending money that his father had given him and headed elsewhere. After booking a room at an expensive hotel, he settled in for a few nights of lewd entertainment.

The day before he departed, Geoffrey had a private, father-to-son discussion about the best casinos, risqué theatres, and exclusive brothels that Paris had to offer. The exhibition of his father's knowledge of sinful pleasures surprised the hell out of him. Moreover, the old codger gave him the blessing to taste it all without condemning him one bit.

"I tell you, Geoffrey, go to Rue des Moulins. My suggestion is that you talk to the mistress of the house first. Her name is Nadine. Tell her what you want done to you, and she will see to it that the most uninhibited, gorgeous creature will join your bed."

Geoffrey remembered his father's words over cigars and drinks. *"They have some bold beauties that can do things to you with their lips that you have only fantasized about."*

He spent his first evening savoring the theatre and casino, even winning a sizeable amount at the roulette wheel. Leaving the best for last, on the second night, he ordered a carriage to take him to the brothel. His father told him that it had a reputation of only servicing wealthy men. The taste of flesh there would cost, but he had given him more than enough to purchase any whore he wanted.

When he arrived, he was greeted by a slender hostess whose breasts spilled over the top of her bodice. Her curly, red hair had been pinned high on her head and it smelled of sweet perfume. He salivated looking at her, quite aware that he had arrived at the den of seduction and pleasure.

"I've been advised to talk to the mistress of the house first," he said, eyeing her plump bosom.

"You wish for something special?" She batted her eyelashes at him.

"You could say that," he responded. Just the thought of it aroused his male senses.

"Follow me, and I'll take you to Madame Channeau."

She escorted him down a long hallway to a closed door. The tart knocked once and waited for permission to enter.

"Yes, what is it?" An enticing voice answered.

The escort spoke in French. Geoffrey snickered at her description of him wanting to buy something *spécial*.

"Entrée," she said. The door opened into a spacious, dark room, decorated in browns and reds that caught Geoffrey off guard. It took a moment for his eyes to adjust to the dim lighting. Once they did, he saw a velvet, button-tufted chair in front of the desk, alcohol on a side table, and pictures of naked women hanging from the walls. The center of attraction remained on Madame Channeau.

"You wish to speak with me, monsieur?" She rose from her chair and sauntered toward him in a low-cut, red gown that took his breath away. Her fair complexion and golden blonde hair framed her stunningly, beautiful face. Even though she appeared to be in her late thirties or early forties, she radiated sexuality from every pore.

He took her outstretched hand and kissed it. "Might we speak privately," he asked, glancing over at the escort.

The mistress shooed her off with her hand, and in a moment, he found himself alone.

"Now, what can I do for you, monsieur? Pleasure is our specialty."

For the first time in his life, his pride had melted into a puddle at a woman's feet. He felt drained of his arrogance. Eventually, he swallowed the lump in his throat and spoke. "Madame..."

"Please, I insist you call me Nadine." She smiled seductively.

"Well, then," he replied. "Nadine, you may know my father," he announced. "Lord Edmund Chambers from London."

It took a brief moment before she acknowledged. "My goodness," she exclaimed, parting her painted, red lips. "You must be his son. Am I right?"

Geoffrey nodded.

"Ah, I see," she said, smirking at the corner of her mouth. "Your father has given you permission to learn of the ways of French women, oui?"

"Yes, he told me that you had ladies that could..." His voice trailed off in embarrassment.

She chuckled over his stammering. "Women who are proficient with their lips, tongue, and mouth, you mean, do you not?"

It wasn't like Geoffrey had not made it past the bloomers of a few morally loose women. On the contrary, he had done his share. Nevertheless, he could never find one willing enough to go beyond what they considered normal in the bedchamber. "Yes," he finally answered.

"Then, please, have a seat and we shall discuss." She returned behind her desk and sat down looking like the Queen of Sheba.

He nervously plopped on the comfortable chair, but sat up straight, regaining some of his egotistical confidence.

"I do have a few ladies who will be totally submissive to your commands and enjoy being tied up for pleasure. You can even give them a vigorous spanking, and they shall fall at your feet ready to give you as much as you please."

Bloody hell, he thought to himself dropping his mouth open. For a moment, he couldn't breathe.

"Of course," she said, giving him a little wink. "It may cost you a little extra. We have a strict rule here—no bruising on the bodies of my beauties."

"Money is no object," he said, reaching into his jacket and pulling out his checkbook.

"For everything I have mentioned, it will cost you three hundred francs for the evening. We will even provide you with items of entertainment should you wish to bind your purchase," she smirked.

Geoffrey took the pen that she offered and quickly wrote the check. She leaned forward watching his hand write out the numbers. Then, to his utter surprise, she asked a question that froze him in place.

"So, how is your uncle, the duke?"

His pen came to a halt. Geoffrey lifted his head and saw in her eager eyes a familiarity that spoke of one thing. "You've serviced him in the past haven't you?"

"Well, of course, for many years. Until he fell in love with a new hire at the Chabanais, where I once worked. We shared a room together until Robert purchased her freedom."

"He what?" Geoffrey quickly finished penning the check and returned the pen.

"Well, it doesn't matter that I mention it now," she said, reaching out and taking the check from his hand. "Apparently, she died over twenty years ago."

"What was her name?" Geoffrey held his breath as if he already knew the answer.

"Suzette Rousseau."

"Bloody hell, you have got to be kidding me?" His voice bellowed.

She flinched over his reaction and leaned back in her chair. "Well, the last time I served the duke was here in this brothel, long before I purchased it myself." She looked at him confused. "He cried like a baby in my arms that she had passed away."

Geoffrey snickered at the vision.

"Well, maybe not cry," she corrected herself. "However, you could tell he was devastated over having lost his mistress."

"That devious bastard," he said, shaking his head.

Nadine looked offended as if she wanted to defend his uncle. Evidently, by the tone of her voice and look in her eye, she had residual feelings for the man. "She's not dead," he corrected her with a smile. "She is alive and his wife."

Nadine's eyes widened. "Well, now isn't that a surprise," she exclaimed. "The homeless whore became a duchess?"

Geoffrey nodded enjoying the astonishment on her face. *Oh, this is good,* he mused. He had fallen privy to a piece of information that had the power to change everything in his favor.

"Yes, she is the duchess of his grand realm. My uncle discovered he had a bastard son by her that he did not know existed. Years later, he searched Paris and found her alive. She had married, of course, but it didn't stop the two of them from embarking on an adulterous affair. And well, the rest is sordid history."

"Well, good for her," she replied, sounding insincere in her congratulatory remark. "She has become a rich woman and gained a title. Not many prostitutes are so fortunate." She rose to her feet and invited him to begin his night of iniquity. "Let me introduce you to your purchase this evening."

Geoffrey followed alongside as she led him into a reception area where a group of women sat waiting to be chosen by patrons. Shocked that most were topless, his breath hitched in his throat.

Expecting to receive an assignment, the women turned toward their mistress. The ladies of the night gave him the once over, and a few beauties smiled at him boosting his ego to new heights. She approached a prostitute with the largest breasts he had ever seen. Whatever other qualities she possessed faded into obscurity, because he could barely lift his eyes from her chest.

Nadine whispered something in her ear. While doing so, she glanced at Geoffrey and gave him a wink. Madame Channeau presented his purchase.

"May I introduce you to Georgette. She is a tremendously talented lady, who will do anything you desire." Nadine leaned into him and whispered. "Georgette enjoys being bound by a strong man. You may play with her as you wish, but no striking or bruising my beauties, or we shall throw you out on the street stark naked."

Geoffrey believed her warning. Suddenly, desires that he had only fleetingly fantasized about rose to the surface. Power had always been his vice. Now, he had the authority to do as he willed with a submissive whore. To establish the mood, he narrowed his eyes and gave her the first command. "Take me to the room."

"Whatever you wish master." She turned to lead the way, and Nadine nodded in approval. "Enjoy," she said, flashing him a smile.

Damn right, I'll enjoy, he thought to himself. As he climbed the stairs, he thought of Robert's threat to tell Jolene should he darken the door of a brothel. *Fuck you, cousin,* he railed inwardly. Then he laughed watching her swinging ass in front of him. *No, I think I'll fuck her instead.*

She opened the door to an opulent bedroom decorated in gold. Mirrors were on the walls and ceiling. A large, four-poster bed with gold, satin bedding caught his eye. He closed the door behind him and set the lock.

A moment later, his purchase dropped to her knees and began to undo his trousers. He placed both hands on her head, tilted his head back, closed his eyes, and waited for her talented lips to meet his erection.

It would be one hell of a night.

-·✻·-

The next morning, Geoffrey laid in bed stark naked with a sheet draped over his midsection. He had returned to the hotel after the closing hours of the brothel and stumbled into bed thoroughly exhausted and half drunk.

He placed both his hands behind his head and looked up at the ceiling wondering what she felt like being tied to the bed. She couldn't escape his ravenous sexual appetite that she had been responsible for awakening. To his surprise, he enjoyed treating a woman gruffly and letting out his inhibitions. The heated exchange of master and slave to his desires drove him to the brink of insanity. He had never met a woman who wanted it rough for pleasure. Nor did he know how much he would enjoy it himself.

As he thought about the night before, he awakened with more power in his soul than he had ever known. He couldn't help but wonder if his own father had gone down such a dark path of pleasure. However, he remembered the stories of his grandfather and great-grandfather, who had taken female slaves on the plantation for their pleasures. Perhaps the desire flowed in his blood, and last night it had stirred the dormant gene.

Whatever the reason, he was ready to show up at the townhome to spend time with the beautiful komtesse. He wondered how far she would go, if he sexually enticed or coerced her to obey. A wicked smile curled the corner of his lips.

If he continued to feed his active imagination, he would never check out of the hotel on time. He swung his legs around the edge of the bed and sat up. He pushed his fingers through his unruly hair and then stretched his arms above his head. He exhaled a loud yawn wishing he could crawl back in bed and sleep. Geoffrey noted the time on his pocket watch laying open on the nightstand.

"Good God," he moaned. "It's ten o'clock in the morning."

Behind schedule, he proceeded to bathe and dress for the day ahead. It was time to put on his charming persona and mingle with family. Perhaps he would finally win over Jolene.

Chapter 24

A Sibling Tussle

Jolene arrived back at the townhome after visiting Philippe and discovered that the duke and duchess had left for the Louvre. Their absence and lack of invitation to join them on their excursion surprisingly bothered her. Nevertheless, she needed a moment alone with Robert. Informed by the staff that he had wandered into the library, she headed in its direction. When she pushed open the door, she halted at the sight.

Sprawled out on the divan, he had swung one foot over the back, laid the other straight out, and propped his head on a pillow. He hadn't heard her enter, apparently engrossed in his read. She giggled over his lazy position, and set the box of cigars down on a nearby table as she approached.

"Comfortable are we?" She glanced at the book and teased him by snatching it out of his hand. "What are you reading?

Robert shot up from his laid-back spot and sat on the edge of the divan. Reaching out to grab the book, he demanded its return. "Hey, I was reading that," he complained.

Jolene's jaw dropped when she read the title in French—*Justine* by the Marquis de Sade. "Oh, heavens," she squawked. She slammed the book shut, and then reached over and gave him a whack on the head. "How can you read the marquis' trash?

"Ouch!" Robert rubbed the top of his crown and scowled at her. A moment later, he jumped to his feet and lurched forward. Jolene swiftly stepped backward out of his reach. When he tried again to grab the book out of her hand, she ran around to the other side of the room laughing like a little girl. For the next few moments, it seemed both of them had reverted to childhood as they entered into a playful tussle.

Jolene outwitted him at every turn. She thought about tossing the book out the window or into the ashes of the fireplace, but didn't want to ruin another person's property. *Worthless property*, she thought.

Robert's face grew frustrated that he couldn't snatch it away, so he stopped to catch his breath. "I want the book back," Robert heaved. "We are in France, and I should be able to read French literature."

"This is not literature," she railed. "You are a rascal Robert Holland." She scolded him like a mother, shaking the book in his direction.

With narrowed eyes, he surprisingly turned the tables against her. "So how do you know what the book is about, huh? Answer me, if you can, Lady von Lamberg" he teased.

She blushed profusely. "I don't know what it's about, because I have not read it," she replied, shoving her chin in the air. "Nevertheless, I also know Marquis de Sade's reputation regarding his libertine literature."

After a few more moments of glaring at her, he huffed. "Fine, put it back on the shelf." He gave up and plopped on the chair exhausted.

"You promise not to touch it again?" She raised her eyebrow.

"I promise nothing, except that I will not touch it in your presence," he replied, sporting a mischievous grin.

Jolene walked over to the bookshelf and found an open space, then slammed the book as far back as she could out of Robert's vision. "There," she said, brushing her hands off as if to rid herself of dirt.

Robert rose to his feet, walked over to the library door, and locked it. "Come sit with me and tell me of your visit with Philippe." He sat down on the divan and patted the seat. Robert eyed the shelf where Jolene had shoved the book as she sat down next to him. "Did you relent and tell him?"

"Heavens no," she quickly replied, shaking her head. "It's too soon. I just told him that I wanted to buy a box of cigars for a gentleman friend." She reached over to the table and retrieved them. "Here you go," she said. "Take them. They are for you and your father. I'm certainly not going to smoke the foul smelling sticks."

Robert eyed the box. "Impressed," he said, looking at it. "Expensive as well."

"So, what did you think of your father?"

"At first glance, I was awestruck over his height and full head of dark hair."

"I saw a lot of his features in you, Jolene. Did he give any indication of being curious about you?"

She shook her head no. "Not really," Jolene sighed. "He talked about tobacco and pipes, which I found to be a boring subject." She glanced at the box and rolled her eyes. "I asked him a roundabout question if his wife objected to his smoking."

"But I told you he's not married," he replied.

"Yes, but I wanted to see how he would handle the question. I'm sure it brought up memories of mother."

"And did he?"

"No, he purposely avoided answering me until I reminded him he had forgotten. Finally, he admitted that he was unmarried."

"From what I remember when I was young, he had been an impressive and handsome man," Robert said. "Now he reminds me of a lost soul."

"I thought him attractive, but I understand what you're saying. He has this underlying sadness about his eyes as if he aches inside." Jolene felt a lump form in her throat.

"A lot of hurt and anger is still there," Robert admitted. "He still despises my father and wrestles with his forgiveness for mother." He reached over and patted Jolene's arm. "You know, I truly believe you're going to be his salvation once you reveal your identity."

"Perhaps," she mused. "I have this sense he is a proud and stubborn man."

"No worse than my own father," Robert balked. "God, talk about iron sharpens iron."

The reference to Proverbs surprised Jolene. Her brother actually quoted scripture after reading de Sade's tasteless literature. How odd. "A good analogy," she congratulated him. "You do read something besides rubbish."

"Very funny," Robert replied. "It just came to mind. 'As iron sharpens iron, so one man sharpens another.'"

"Yes, let's hope they don't end up stabbing each other with sharpened swords in the days ahead," she said. Perhaps she should take heed to Robert's warning about possible reactions from all involved.

" Jolene, I don't know how you're going to pull this off with everyone together."

He sounded like a skeptic. Not wanting to consider the possibility of defeat, she ignored his doubt. "Well, you did invite Philippe to dinner, which if he accepts will work in bringing them altogether."

"Yes, we can bring everyone together in one place," he clarified, "But the emotions between all involved will be highly charged. It's not enough they will find out that you are Angelique, but being together again—well, frankly, I can't imagine."

Jolene's face turned sorrowful. "I cannot prevent how they will react to the situation. No one is innocent. Everybody played a role in this scandalous tale of love, deceit, and betrayal. And, they are equally responsible for how my life turned out." She lowered her eyes, slightly ashamed. "I cannot complain about my situation in life, though."

"You have been blessed," Robert acknowledged.

She forced herself to maintain eye contact with Robert, even though her emotions teetered on the verge of tears. "Nevertheless, I want them to be together to express my heart and soul to each of them. They need to hear my disillusionment over the discovery about my past, as well as my disappointment in them for their actions." Her heartbeat increased reacting to the edginess she felt.

"I take a hard line between judging them and accepting them. As much as I want a relationship with our mother, I am still not at a place of surrender."

"And Philippe?"

"I believe in time, I shall grow to love him as my father the more we get to know each other."

"Well, then, that leaves me," Robert flashed a boyish grin. "The jealous sibling who pushed you over." He rubbed his eyes with his knuckles. "Sniff, sniff."

"Oh, you," she said, pushing his arm with the palm of her hand. "I don't know what I'd do without you to walk this journey with me." She narrowed her eyes and shook her finger at him. "But if I catch you with the marquis' book again, you're going to fall from my good graces."

The two halted their conversation when they heard someone try the door handle to the library, followed by a hard knock. Robert rose from his seat and opened the door. Jolene saw Geoffrey and jumped up, feeling as if the air had drained from her lungs. She couldn't tell if she felt elated or mortified over seeing him.

"I say, 'ol chap, why the locked door? What's going on in here?"

Before either of them could answer, he gruffly pushed by Robert but quickly halted staring at Jolene. He glanced back and forth at them and jumped to an illogical conclusion.

"Well, I'm glad you are both dressed," he said, looking miffed.

"There is no need to insult the lady." Robert sneered at him.

Obviously, Robert did not look happy over his arrival. She tried to be welcoming, but felt embarrassed feeling a blush on her cheeks. "Geoffrey, what a surprise. We were merely having a private conversation." It perturbed her thinking that she needed to defend her actions.

"Well, thank God I was the one who discovered the locked door and not one of the servants. You would have been eaten alive by gossips in the downstairs quarters this evening." Geoffrey sauntered over toward Jolene attempting to capture her attention with his golden-speckled eyes.

"True," she admitted, lowering her head. "My poor Maria would be embarrassed." She looked over at Robert giving him a glare. "Perhaps it was not a wise move to lock the door, Lord Holland."

Robert changed the subject, barking at his cousin. "What took you so long to get here?"

Geoffrey kept his gaze upon her instead, rather than acknowledging Robert who stood two feet away.

"Business at home," he answered. "Father wanted me to take care of some things for him before he left for the West Indies. After all, I am head of the house in his absence."

"Head of the house and you are in Paris. There is an undeniable disparity in that statement," Robert quipped.

Once more, the sparks flew between them. Jolene had to admit they were another prime example of an iron-sharpens-iron relationship that needed the heat of blacksmith's kiln to melt.

"Well, I'm glad you have safely arrived, Geoffrey. "I am in need of another tour guide. We have the means of transportation, a driver, and plenty of time to see the city."

"A motorcar and driver, eh?" Geoffrey rubbed his chin with his hand as if he were plotting where to spirit her away.

"Palace of Versailles is the place to visit first." He took a step closer, lowered his head, and whispered in her ear. "I know the Queen's bedchamber will be your favorite room."

Jolene pulled away from Geoffrey looking at him in disbelief. "Another libertine rascal," she complained, pulling a face at him to show her displeasure. Geoffrey snickered at her comment, as if he were proud of the name she had called him.

She took a step closer to Robert to put distance between herself and Geoffrey. Then, like an utter fool, she warned Robert not to share his reading selection with his cousin. "You better not tell him about that book." Unaware of the impact of her jest, she gave him a mischievous smile as if she meant to embarrass him for having read it.

"Now you've done it," he responded, sneering. "He will hound me until I confess."

Jolene wanted to pull them both out of the library to save them from corruption. "Well, I'm in need of tea," she announced. "Coming boys?" Hopefully, the book would be forgotten and they would follow.

Geoffrey's head spun toward Robert. "What book?"

Robert raised his brow. "See, I told you," he said.

She would have to sneak back into the library and hide it elsewhere.

Chapter 25

An Emotional Guillotine

She stood next to her brother in bed. He looked a terrible mess with tousled hair, fevered brow, and red nose.

"If you have a fever, Robert, I expect you to remain at home and get well."

Robert moaned. "Well, this is an awful time to get ill. I will not allow you to go off touring Paris alone with my cousin. I do not trust him."

She bunched her lips together and pulled them to one side. "You might as well say that you do not trust me. That's what you mean, isn't it?" She thrust her hands on her hips.

He shook his head, but Jolene couldn't tell if he meant yes or no. Shivering from chills, he grabbed the covers and pulled them underneath his neck. With puppy-dog eyes, he looked up at her and pleaded.

"But I've made a vow to protect you, Jolene, and I intend to keep it."

"Well, I made a vow to see you live a long life. You are staying in bed."

He sneezed, and Jolene brought her own handkerchief to her nose. "Besides, you're going to get everybody else sick. Now stay in bed!"

"All right," he agreed, sinking lower under the covers.

"I'll have one of the maids bring you up a cold glass of orange juice and chicken soup later. It will do you good." Jolene turned to leave, but Robert's weak voice called out after her.

"Be careful."

"I will. Don't worry about me."

Jolene left her sick brother and joined Geoffrey. The duke and duchess had declined to tour the palace, having remarked they had seen it enough to last a lifetime. Since the duke and her mother did not seem too concerned over Geoffrey escorting her around Paris, Jolene felt confident in her decision. She looked forward to perhaps getting to know him a little better. After all, he was family.

As she strolled toward the parlor, she mused to herself. *Does that make him my half cousin? Is there such a thing as half a cousin? Can you marry just half a cousin?* She shook her head over the last silly thought.

"I'm sorry to be so tardy," she said, as she entered the room. She buttoned the jacket to her walking dress. "Robert is ill with a nasty cold. He wanted to join us, but I insisted that he stay in bed."

"Oh, what a shame," he replied.

Geoffrey appeared to suppress a smile, but Jolene instantly recognized the agreeable twinkle in his eye betraying his true feelings. "I told him that you would treat me like a lady, though I don't think he frankly trusts you."

"I promise you, Lady von Lamberg, that I shall be nothing but a gentleman."

She eyed him with a slight suspicion replaying Grace and Robert's voice in her head about Geoffrey's character. His promise sounded sincere without a hint of mischievousness.

"Good," she said. "The driver is waiting for us out front."

Geoffrey offered his arm and escorted her to the car. He sat a discreet distance from her in the back seat as they pulled away down the avenue. Jolene could see Notre Dame in the distance and had yet to see the Eiffel Tower in all of its glory. Feeling somewhat disappointed over everything she had ignored since her arrival, she turned to Geoffrey.

"How many times have you been to Paris?"

He shrugged one shoulder and tilted his head as if he were trying to recall. "A few," he answered.

Jolene thought it sounded evasive, so she pressed further. "Well, the Hollands owned a townhome in Paris for many years, correct? Did your parents own one as well?"

"No, father never purchased one because of his many trips to the West Indies."

"Have you ever traveled with him on business?"

"Heavens no," he lamented. "I refuse to travel across the ocean for an extended period of time, just to go to a hot and humid sugar plantation."

She could understand his aversion, but it surprised her that he lacked so much interest in his father's business. "Well, that will never happen since your father is selling it now. You will not have to worry about inheriting the humidity." She grinned over her amusing comment.

He glanced sideways at her and smirked. "You have a wit about you, Lady von Lamberg, which I find both prickly but entertaining."

"Call me Jolene. You have known me long enough to be on a first-name basis. I don't mind the informality."

A warm smile spread across his face acknowledging his gratitude they had taken a step forward. Jolene looked out the window for a moment at the passing scenery.

"I must admit that I often feel removed from the world, Geoffrey. My stepfather kept me sheltered and protected in Vienna. Most of what I know, I have read in books or been taught in school. Now look," she smiled, seeing the Eiffel Tower off in the distance. "I'm here actually enjoying it with my own eyes."

"I feel honored that I can share it with you," he said, reaching over and touching her hand in her lap.

Slowly, Jolene raised her head and looked into his brown eyes with flecks of gold. "I'm glad you can share it with me."

Her hand remained in the same position without slipping from his tender grasp. Jolene made no objection over the attention received from the handsome man.

-·⁕·-

The opulent palace astounded Jolene. Vienna had its own collection of luxurious, gilded palaces as part of the Austro-Hungarian Empire. Though the French had done away with its aristocracy, Austria still held strong. Her stepfather had told her that there were those that wanted to abolish the nobility in Austria. If that occurred, she would still be well provided for with her inheritance and able to keep her head. She thought of poor Marie Antoinette—born an Archduchess of Austria, married the Dauphin of France, and beheaded in the prime of her life.

After their arrival, they took a leisurely tour. Impressed by the luxury and beauty of the Palace of Versailles, Jolene enjoyed every moment. When they walked through the Queen's bedchamber, Geoffrey had the sense to keep his mouth shut. Instead, he spouted off his knowledge of history, which Jolene had already been privy to from her own studies.

Later, while strolling through the gardens, they enjoyed spirited conversation and shared personal exchanges about likes and dislikes. Nevertheless, by the end of their tour, Jolene discovered that she felt nothing of interest beyond enjoying his company as a friend. The spark she had experienced when they first met failed to ignite with the same intensity. No doubt, her current circumstances and focus had dampened her interest, along with the fact that Geoffrey and Robert did not get along. During their return to the townhome, it became clear that Geoffrey felt differently.

After they climbed into the car, he sat extremely close to her body, making her uncomfortable. She scooted to the right to show her disapproval over his nearness. A brief glance into his eyes revealed his longing. The speckles of gold faded. He looked as if he were stalking her for his next meal.

Since her experience with men had been limited and her virginity intact, she suddenly felt foolish for inviting him to Paris. To make matters worse, she had encouraged him by holding his hand earlier. Scolding herself for doing so, she determined to draw a line that he would understand and respect. Just as she was building her fortitude to put him in his place, he spoke.

"Jolene, you know how I feel about you." His hand moved over to her lap and rested on her thigh giving her a little squeeze. He pulled up the skirt of her dress an inch.

In response, she promptly picked up his hand and pushed it away. "Please behave," she whispered sternly. "The driver will see you."

"You failed to respond to my comment," he said. He tried to put his arm around her shoulder, but Jolene scooted closer to the door and gazed out the window avoiding his eyes.

"I heard your remark," she answered, trying to be nonchalant. After inhaling a deep breath, she turned her head and spoke in a kind but firm voice.

"I know that you have intentions to court me, Geoffrey, but I do not wish to be courted by you or anyone else for that matter. My life is fulfilling, and I have plans. Entering into any kind of relationship or marital arrangement will only impede my personal goals."

Geoffrey expressed her rejection by suddenly inhaling and exhaling rapid breaths. She could not tell if she had hurt or angered him. His strange behavior made her uncomfortable, so she turned her head toward the window. A moment later, his emotions unleashed in a fury she had not anticipated.

"You are too damn high and mighty with your Austrian title of komtesse," he snarled. "You fucking Europeans, who live on the Continent, think that you are superior to the English."

Jolene turned her head and huffed. She nearly slapped him across his face but restrained herself. "How dare you talk to me in that tone of disrespect," she glowered.

Geoffrey burst into a hideous laugh that made her blood run cold. He looked at her with an arrogant grin.

"Very soon, I'm going to push you off that high pedestal of yours. And when I'm through with you, there will be little left of your arrogant pride."

His eyes turned black as coal, and Jolene's breath hitched in her throat.

"Perhaps I'll start right now," he sneered.

The next she knew, his lips pressed hard against her own. His forceful behavior sent her into an angry rage. She hit him hard with her fist on the side of his head. As a result, he pulled away long enough for her to give an order.

"Driver," she screamed. "Pull over immediately!"

He quickly obeyed and slowly the car rolled to a halt alongside the curb.

"Get out, Geoffrey. I don't want to see you again until you apologize for your rude and ungentlemanly behavior."

Without protest, he flung the door open, got out, and leaned down to say his parting words. "I'll apologize when hell freezes over, you bitch." His arm flung the door shut, slamming it so hard it rocked the car. A moment later, he had disappeared down the street.

Jolene's mouth gaped open. Shocked over what had transpired, it took her a moment to regain her wits about her. He transformed into a monster in a matter of seconds. Hopefully, he wouldn't return to the townhome any time soon. At the first opportunity, she would ask him to leave, fearful that he might try to accost her again.

"Please proceed," she instructed the driver with a trembling voice. He turned around and gave her a sympathetic look.

"Yes, your ladyship."

After leaning back in the seat, she felt a foreboding over Geoffrey's remarks. His threat lingered in her mind, "*...when I'm through with you...*" What could he possibly mean?

She tried to dismiss his remark, remembering that Robert had sworn to protect her. Nonetheless, something in her knotted stomach told her that he meant every word snarled from between his pearly-white teeth.

Chapter 26

No Time to Spare

Geoffrey had disappeared and kept away from Jolene for days after their disappointing time together. According to the staff, he would come back late in the evening after everyone retired, and then rise early and disappear during the day. His absence gave her a deep sense of relief that she would not have to face or deal with his immaturity any time soon. Since he had not taken the opportunity to apologize, it became clear that he felt no remorse for his behavior.

Robert struggled with his annoying cold for a few days until finally he began to recover. After rest, soup, and pampering by his mother and the staff, he felt well enough to venture out of his room. Jolene had made regular visits checking on his welfare. The altercation with Geoffrey she kept hidden for fear he would jump out of bed and punch him in the nose.

On the morning when he rejoined his family, he took a seat at the dining room table for breakfast.

"Now don't be too much in a hurry, Robert. Take care of yourself until it has passed entirely."

"I'm feeling much better, Mother," he said, dismissing her coddling.

He filled his plate with scrambled eggs, a large portion of bacon, and a croissant, and then sat down next to Jolene. It felt fitting to have him back in their midst.

"So what did I miss during my days of sniffling?" He shoved a piece of bacon in his mouth and glanced about the table.

"Not much," his father answered. "It's been a bit quiet. We've been waiting for your recovery to take Jolene to see the Eiffel Tower."

Robert glanced about the table. "Where's Geoffrey?"

"He's been avoiding us, I'm afraid," Jolene replied. "We had a bit of a disagreement, and I think I hurt his feelings." Frankly, she doubted the man had any feelings.

Robert raised his eyebrows. Her mother glanced curiously at her, but the duke flashed a knowing glance, seemingly understanding her inference.

"Well, that's interesting," Robert replied. "Not that I'll miss his company or anything."

After they had eaten breakfast, Jolene leaned in toward Robert. "Do you feel well enough to get some sunshine in the garden?" Her eyes conveyed the urgency for a private moment.

"Yes, of course," he quickly replied. "If you'll forgive us," he said to his mother and father.

They appeared apathetic toward their leave from the table. Jolene led the way, and they strode briskly from the veranda into the center of the bushes so as not to be heard.

"God, Robert, I've missed you," Jolene exclaimed.

"Sorry," he answered sheepishly. "I hadn't expected to get sick, but I am glad no one else in the house fell ill."

"We have to move forward quickly. I'm getting extremely eager to bring this to a close."

"Why the urgency?" He looked at her inquisitively.

"My conscience is beginning to get the better of me, I think. This charade has gone on long enough. Everyone is here now, so it's time."

"Well, we still have to get Philippe to the townhouse. I am not sure he is going to agree, without a good reason, to come for dinner."

Jolene had already taken the time to contemplate her next move. Confident her brilliant idea would work, she asked Robert for the prop she needed to continue.

"Do you still have that box of cigars?"

"Yes, why?

"Is it unopened?"

"All these questions," he complained.

"Well are they?" Her impatience enunciated each word.

"Yes, unopened," he sighed. "Again, why?"

Jolene smiled. "Because I'm going to return them for a refund."

"You're what?" Robert frowned.

"Just leave it to me, Robert. I shall have my father here tomorrow evening. I promise you."

"Well, I have absolutely no idea what you have in mind, but I wish you success." A disgruntled look of loss spoke his displeasure. "They are damn good cigars I had planned on enjoying."

"Oh, don't be such a whiner," she teased. "I will buy you another box when this is all over."

"So what is your plan?"

"Men are more persuadable by the presence of a pretty woman." She winked at Robert. "Watch me do my magic," she said confidently. "Philippe will be here for dinner tomorrow evening, I promise."

Robert pondered what plan she had formulated this time.

- · ✳ · -

For a few moments, Jolene stood out of view of the picture window to deal with her nerves over seeing Philippe again. The urgency of revealing her identity gave her the bravery she needed for the minutes ahead. She had become weary of the deception that she had perpetrated to the duke and her mother. In all honestly, she did not have the heart to deceive her father for weeks on end.

After straightening her shoulders and inhaling a deep breath, she walked toward the door and entered. The familiar jingle of the bell above announced her arrival. Philippe lifted his eyes showing surprise over her return. No doubt, the box of cigars in her hand caused him disappointment.

"Your ladyship," he said, walking forward and greeting her. "Is there something that I can help you with?"

An overwhelming desire to hug him and confess everything tempted her will. Her heart pounded, and she could barely speak.

"Are the cigars not to your friend's liking?"

A small smile spread across her face. She looked in his eyes and spoke her startling announcement. "Mr. Moreau, I offered the cigars to my friend but discovered his dislike of the brand." There she was lying again. Her next confession with a priest would be about her deceitful falsehoods, and she shuddered to think how many rounds of the rosary she would have to pray.

"Oh, I'm so sorry." He took the box from her hand. "Please accept my sincere apologies for my poor recommendation."

His disappointment over his failure broke her heart. After all, they were just cigars. "Well, you're never going to believe this," she announced, fluttering her eyelashes nervously. "But when I gave them to my friend, he asked me where I had purchased the box. One thing led to another, and low and behold, he revealed to me that you were his stepfather." Jolene waited for his reaction.

Philippe took a step back and looked at her in confusion. "Oh," he replied, barely showing a trace of emotion. "You must be the lady that Robert mentioned to me." His brow furrowed when he began to look at her more closely with renewed interest.

"Yes, I am his lady friend, as he put it. We met in London at a ball a few months ago. I made a few friends during my stay there. To further our time together, we decided to come to Paris for a holiday before I return home."

"Amazing that the two of you know each other." Philippe sounded cautiously guarded.

"Yes, it is." Jolene saw suspicion in his eyes and feared. Worried that he had doubts about her story, she took her next move. "Now, Robert tells me that he invited you to dinner, but you have not given him an answer."

Philippe moved to the left and set down the box of cigars on the glass countertop. His body language exuded awkwardness. "That's correct. I have decided to turn down the invitation."

His shoulders drooped. Philippe pulled his gaze away as if he were ashamed. The physical act troubled Jolene, because she sensed his unworthiness.

"Well, I'm not going to allow you to turn down the invitation," she sternly replied. Her words caught him off guard. His head lifted, and he looked at her shocked over her spunky reply.

"As much as I would like to see, Robert again," he replied in a harsh tone, "I would not feel comfortable to dine with a lady of your class." He paused for a moment expressing a look of discomfiture. "As I told Robert, I do not possess the white-tie, formal clothing to attend an evening dinner."

"Well, to be frank, I don't care if you do or not," she pressed. "Robert's sentiments are more important to me than what you wear, Mr. Moreau." She eyed him in the clothes that he wore. "You look professionally dressed and tidy as you stand before me now. Surely, you can come to dine with us in this fine suit."

It looked far from acceptable and slightly thread bare at his elbows, but it didn't matter. She had to get him to the townhome. Alarmed that her plan would crumble before her eyes, her hand trembled. His acceptance of the invitation was critical. Otherwise, she would have to blurt it out here and now before she erupted like a volcano. With determination, she again dismissed his refusal.

"I will make you an offer," she continued. "We shall also dress less formal, if that will make you comfortable. There will be no evening gowns or white ties at the table. After all, you are like family to Robert, so there is no need for us to put on airs. Surely, you will not deny us the pleasure of your company."

She hesitantly reached out and touched his forearm. Philippe's eyes looked at her gloved hand. When his gaze rose to examine her sincerity, she saw that he softened his resolve. Once more, using her charms, she tilted her head and pouted her lips slightly.

"Please," she implored in a sweet voice. "Do it for Robert and for me. He is a dear friend of mine, and I want to see him happy. Besides," she continued in sincerity, "I'm interested in getting to know you better."

Philippe shifted in his stance but remained silent. By the look in his eyes, he carefully thought about her plea.

"All right, then. If you are certain that my attire will not offend."

"Oh, for heaven's sake," she said, squeezing his arm slightly. "It will be perfectly fine." With a broad smile, she dropped her hand from Philippe's arm. After touching her father for the first time in eighteen years, she felt an elation that she could not put into words.

"About the cigars," he said, moving around the counter. "Does Robert prefer anything different? I am happy to exchange them or give you a refund."

"I have no idea what he likes to smoke," she admitted. "Why don't you ask him tomorrow evening? Then you can exchange them for something more enjoyable to his male senses," she teased. Finally, the somber look upon Philippe's face faded. With a smile and a glimmer of approval in his eye, he agreed.

"Yes, that will do fine."

"Well then, it's all arranged. Robert can give my driver the address for your residence. I'll have our motorcar pick you up at seven o'clock."

Very well," he acknowledged.

Jolene relaxed. The tension she felt earlier lessened. "Goodbye, Mr. Moreau. We will speak again tomorrow."

"Goodbye, your ladyship."

Philippe directed his attention to replacing the cigar box on the shelf. She exited onto the sidewalk and turned to the left. For a brief moment, a rush of emotion took her breath away. "So much is at stake," she whispered with tears welling in her eyes. "God in heaven, give me the strength to do this."

-·�֍·-

Upon her return to the townhome, Jolene told Robert what had transpired. She had succeeded in using her gift of persuasion to obtain his acceptance of an invitation.

"Well, I'll be damned," he replied with a smile. "How in the hell did you pull that off?"

"The tool of guilt and coercion," she replied.

"Well done."

"Where are your parents?" She glanced around seeing no one.

"They've gone out for a stroll, I believe."

Jolene unpinned her hat, walked over to a chair, and sat down exhausted from emotion. Robert joined her.

"You look troubled," he said, putting his hand on her shoulder.

"I am troubled. What I'm about to do is change all of our lives by one confession." Her voice cracked. "I want my family to reconcile, Robert."

Robert heaved a sigh that caught her attention. "Jolene, listen to me," he said, bending down and gazing into her eyes. "No matter how much you want this, I beg you not to set your expectations too high. People often do not act as we think they should."

"Perhaps after I confess how I feel to each of them, they will come to their senses," she said.

Robert rose and shook his head doubtfully. "I fear tomorrow evening will be one that neither of us will ever forget."

"Probably not." She looked at Robert mournfully. "Will you forgive me, please? I need some time to myself."

"Not until I give you a hug," he said. He leaned forward and gave her a tender squeeze, which she reciprocated in return.

"Would it sound strange, Robert," she whispered, "If I told you that I loved you?" Her cheeks blushed. "You know what I mean, right?"

He chuckled and flashed a boyish grin at her. "I love you, too, Sister," he said, enunciating the sibling notation. "Thank God, I didn't try to kiss you before I found out who you were. Wouldn't that have been strange?"

Jolene brought her hand to her mouth and giggled. "Oh, dear God, just the thought embarrasses the daylights out of me."

"I'll leave you alone to your thoughts," he said, exiting the room.

Robert understood her need for privacy and a moment alone. Underneath that rascally persona there existed a young man with a good heart. Jolene sat back in the chair, looked out the window, and pondered what lay ahead.

Today, she had lied to her father to get him to come to a dinner they would probably never share together. Nevertheless, it had to be done. The significance of bringing the three of them together to announce her identity had been foremost in her mind. She could have easily told them one by one. There had been numerous opportunities to pull her mother aside and the duke to declare everything.

When she first met her father, it would have been glorious to tell him that her name was Angelique Jolene, without spouting off her title as if she were an arrogant aristocrat. Instead, she kept her lips sealed. Even Robert could have brought the news of her return when he visited.

Tomorrow, though, everything would change. She would no longer be the woman she thought. Instead, she would be the daughter of Suzette and Philippe Moreau, who eighteen years ago disappeared. She tried to imagine the emotions they would feel at that moment, but her own clouded the vision.

Obviously, it had been providence that Robert had been the first to discover her identity. He had become her strength, confidant, and invaluable friend through it all. Without him by her side, it would have been a bumbling journey of mishaps.

His earlier warning, not to set her expectations too high resonated in her heart. She wanted it to work together for good, like a miraculous event with heaven's intervention. Yet, a premonition inside her soul told her that it might not go as smoothly as she hoped. Maybe she should call for the French Legion to be on standby. Her heavy thoughts gave way to her brother's sense of humor and she smiled.

Chapter 27

The Day of Reckoning

By the time evening arrived, Jolene had tossed around every emotion the human heart possesses. Sorrow, anger, disillusionment, fear, and even tones of affection for her parents waxed back and forth like a pendulum on a clock.

Earlier in the day, she met with Robert to discuss how the reunion would unfold. They decided he would make sure that his parents were in the sitting parlor no later than six thirty. Robert would open a bottle of wine and offer before dinner drinks to keep everyone occupied. She entrusted him to guide his side of the family while she took care of her father.

Jolene instructed the butler to have Philippe remain in the foyer after his arrival. He would tell her immediately afterward, and she would meet him alone. When her welcoming greeting ended, she would escort him to the parlor to join the others.

The final element in their plan had to do with the evidence she would present to corroborate her story. Jolene had taken Dorcas' diary, along with a piece of Jacquelyn's jewelry, and placed it in the center drawer of the writing desk in the parlor. She chose the ruby and diamond necklace with one large teardrop stone in the middle. On the reverse side of the center ruby, the initial and crest were prominently visible. Jolene would allow the heirloom to tell her story.

As the hour approached, Robert met Jolene in her suite for a few words beforehand. "Are you sure you are ready to do this?"

"Absolutely. I traveled thousands of miles to England and France and am not about to give up on this momentous family reunion."

Robert chuckled under his breath. "Momentous. I would call it suicidal."

"Oh, hush," Jolene rebuked him, in a teasing tone. "I cannot think of any other way to bring this displaced group of souls back together. They all deserve to be told at the same time."

"Shall I stand by your side, or would you prefer that I sit during your speech?"

"Well, you're part of this sibling reveal, so I'd like you to stand by me. I think your knowledge of the situation will bring credibility."

"I can see the anger in my father's eyes that I've known all along. There will be hell for me to pay because of you," he complained with a frown.

With a sly smirk, she reached out and touched Robert's shoulder placing her hand firmly on him. "I'm sorry dear, but you're a necessary sacrifice to make this work." He rolled his eyes.

Jolene glanced at the clock on the fireplace mantel. Soon Philippe would arrive. The duke and duchess would be sipping drinks with Robert.

"I wish you the best," Robert said, leaning forward and giving her a kiss on the cheek. "Be strong."

He left Jolene with last minute thoughts about the time that had passed since she first met the duke and duchess. In the last few days, she had come to her own opinion regarding her mother's behavior. It had been obvious that her love for the duke had clouded her judgment in the choices she had made. Nevertheless, she acknowledged that whatever they shared between the two of them had been genuine and lasting.

Whether she would ever feel heartfelt affection for her remained unanswered. One moment, a sense of emotion weaved through her heart. The next, it blew away as if a strong wind had carried it out of sight. Jolene had no answers to the ever-changing emotions when it came to her mother.

When she pondered what she possessed in the way of character from Suzette and Philippe, she decided very little. Her personality had turned out nothing like her parents. Perhaps, the short influence that Jacquelyn Spencer had in her life imparted boldness. In addition, the considerable influence her stepfather had in the formation of her values had contributed to her strong moral code. He taught her honor, integrity, and morality to prepare her to bear her title and wealth. The life she had been born into had taken a drastic turn at the slight of one person's moment of insanity. Jolene realized that through her kidnapping, she had gained much, while her family had lost.

Finally, a knock came at the door. "Your ladyship, your guest has arrived," the butler announced.

She thanked him and took no hesitation to descend the staircase. Her eyes caught sight of an uneasy Philippe in the foyer. Her heart went out to him, and a lump formed in her throat over what she had planned to do to the poor man. When she stood before him, a pleased smile brightened his face.

"Your ladyship." He gave a curt bow.

She smiled reservedly at him and reached out her hand in greeting. Philippe didn't hesitate to place a quick kiss on her knuckles, and she quickly withdrew.

"Now look at you," she approved. "You are very handsome in your suit and in perfectly acceptable attire."

She felt bad that he probably would get nothing to eat, but she pushed another pang of guilt to the side and regained her strength.

Philippe eyed her in a simple day dress, seemingly happy that she had not chosen an evening gown to make him feel uncomfortable.

"Robert is waiting for us in the parlor with more friends of mine," she announced, leading the way. Not allowing Philippe the opportunity to balk over the additional attendees, she stepped in front of him and stopped at the threshold. She put both her hands on the handles of the French doors and pushed them open in one swift moment. Then she turned and gripped Philippe's hand and led him forward.

"Come meet my friends," she said, leading him through the door. After they entered, Robert moved swiftly behind her and closed the door. She had done it. The moment had arrived. For a second she shut her eyes tight, and then slowly opened them to watch their reactions.

Jolene turned and looked at her father, whose face had paled to the color of the white doors behind him. His eyes grew wide in unmistakable anger as he looked at Robert Holland and his former wife sitting on a divan together. He quickly flashed Jolene a disapproving glare.

"What in God's name is the meaning of this?" His voice bellowed filling the room.

Jolene did not respond. She glanced at Robert, who tilted his head as if to say *I told you*. Then the duke jumped to his feet and demanded answers.

"I might ask the same," he roared. His eyes glared at Philippe in fear and anger. The duke placed his hand upon Suzette's shoulder as if to restate his claim and protect her from her ex-husband towering like Goliath at the other end of the room.

Philippe's heavy breathing sounded like a snarl, and Jolene knew it was time to speak up and take control before fists started to fly. "We are about to have a civil gathering of adults," she calmly announced, standing her ground. "I expect each of you to sit down."

She sounded like a legionnaire barking commands. To her surprise, the duke obeyed and sat next to Suzette. Her mother remained silent, but her face had lost color. Jolene glanced at Philippe, who stood glaring at Suzette communicating his continued lack of forgiveness.

Jolene glanced at Robert, who had taken position by her side a few feet away. The reunion had swiftly ripped open old wounds, and she felt as if she stood in the middle of a pool of blood.

Philippe had not retired to the empty chair as Jolene requested. Instead, his feet planted in one spot and a rebellious grimace etched across his face. He turned and scowled at his stepson. "Robert, are you responsible for this?"

Clearly, wanting to lay the blame with him, Jolene intervened. Robert's mouth opened as if he wanted to defend himself, but Jolene shook her head no. He remained silent and watched instead.

"Monsieur Moreau, I would be most grateful if you would take a seat, please." Jolene reasoned with him in a voice of compassion rather than anger. At that moment, the old saying that honey catches more flies than vinegar seemed an appropriate approach to take. He glowered at her and reluctantly sat in the chair.

"I don't understand why you have brought us together," he barked. "What is the meaning behind this?"

"Patience," Jolene answered. "In due course, you will know the meaning."

She turned to Robert and nodded toward the desk. Robert walked a few feet and retrieved the diary and a small velvet box that contained the jewelry piece that Jolene had decided to present as evidence. He held them in his hands and returned to her side.

"Well, then," Jolene spoke glancing at each person one by one. "Where shall I begin?" She adjusted her stance into an authoritative pose and drew in a deep breath. "As you all know, my given name is Komtesse Jolene von Lamberg. I am the stepdaughter of Count von Lamberg of Vienna, Austria, who passed away a few months ago. I have inherited his title, property, and wealth." She stopped for a moment and studied their faces looking for a hint of recognition as to why she stood before them. They were unmoved.

"I've brought you together this evening because of a diary." Robert handed it over, which she took in her hand and held upright. "It is tattered and old as you can see, but it contains a fascinating story that mentions all of your names." She approached a small table in front of the divan and laid it down before the duke. "It was written by a woman named Dorcas." He gave no reaction except to stare at the tattered volume.

"Well, I'm a bit surprised that name means nothing to Your Grace. Perhaps this will jog your memory." She turned her back toward everyone and glanced at her half brother. "If you would be so kind to help me, Robert."

"My pleasure," he replied. He opened the case and grasped the sparkling, ruby necklace. Walking behind her, he draped it down her neckline, fastened the clasp, and then stepped to the side.

Slowly, Jolene turned around and looked directly at the duke. The identifying reaction she anticipated occurred in an instant. He jumped to his feet and practically lurched at her wide-eyed with a flushed face.

"Where in God's name did you get that piece of jewelry?" He blinked a few times as if he wanted to make sure he wasn't seeing things. "My God," he gasped. Without asking permission, he grasped the large teardrop stone between his thumb and forefinger. Slowly, he turned it over. When he identified the "H" and family crest, he froze like ice.

"Robert, what is it?" Her mother rose to her feet looking concerned over her husband's behavior.

"It's a Holland heirloom. I cannot believe I'm holding one of the jewels that Jacquelyn stole from our estate."

"What?"

Her mother looked as stunned as the duke, who continued to eye the stones. Eventually, his expression changed into one of melancholy as if the memories of years past had suddenly flooded back. He dropped the ruby to her chest and took a step back.

"Lady von Lamberg, how did you come to possess this necklace?"

His eyes filled with suspicion as he stood there eying her wearing the family treasures. Jolene glanced to her left at Philippe, who sat in silent observance on the edge of his chair. The time of her announcement had finally arrived. She literally mourned for everyone in the room and fought back the threat of tears.

"It was my mother's, Your Grace. Her name was Jacquelyn Bennett, at least to the man she married, Count von Lamberg." She picked up the diary and held it out toward him. "The diary was written by her lady's maid, Dorcas. In it, she reveals that her ladyship had two names before she married my stepfather. Her maiden name was Jacquelyn Spencer. Her married name was Jacquelyn Holland, your first duchess.

With her focus on the duke, she had forgotten about her father until he hopped to his feet and screamed her name.

"Angelique?"

Jolene faced him with a sorrowful expression. The duke spun around in time to observe Suzette faint and fall hard into the couch behind her.

"Suzette!" He ran to her side to tend her swoon. Robert came to his father's aid and bent down to help. "Get her some water, son," he asked, holding her up in his arms.

"I'll be right back," he said, passing Jolene and scurrying out the door.

She had not expected her mother to faint upon the revelation and felt concerned for her welfare. Philippe, who had been left alone with his own reaction, pulled her attention away from the commotion. He took a giant stride toward her that caught her off guard.

"You are my daughter?" His eyes pleaded for confirmation.

"Yes, father," she spoke softly. "My given name is Angelique Jolene. The duchess was not too fond of a French-sounding name, so I've always been called by my middle Christian name."

"My God," Philippe whispered. "It cannot be after all these years you have returned." He reached out to pull her into his arms, but Jolene raised her hand and drew back. Robert returned with water in hand, in time to step between them as if to shield her from being crushed by Philippe.

"Yes, father it is. Now sit, please, while I speak of the rest." The astonishment on his face quickly faded to a sorrowful rejection. He stepped aside and did as she requested, keeping his eyes intently upon her.

The duke patted Suzette's cheek and brought her back to consciousness. "Here drink this," he ordered, bringing the glass to her lips.

She took a sip. Robert returned to Jolene's side. Suzette leaned into the duke's arms for support. Jolene watched curiously as her mother kept her eyes averted from her face. It tore her heart that even now she couldn't speak a word of joy over her return.

"Robert, did you know of this?" The duke barked in frustration.

"Yes, I've known since London, but I swore to keep silent. It was not my place to interfere into her affairs."

Jolene's eyes wandered back and forth from her mother and father. Her assessment of their likely reaction had been correct, except for the fainting spell. Her father clamored to hold her, while her mother sat frozen in the arms of her gallant husband. The duchess' face paled to a ghostly white. Finally, she had had enough silence from the woman who birthed her into the world.

"Mother, have you no words for me?" Suzette lifted her guilty eyes when she spoke. "After all, I am the daughter that you abandoned for another man." Her words tasted bitter as they left her lips, but she felt compelled to let her mother know of her sentiments.

"Angelique, I..." Suzette sputtered.

Her tongue-tied mother had nothing to say. "Dorcas, my mother's attendant, happened to be quite thorough in all of her daily notes. Besides the mundane entries of serving the duchess, it is filled with Jacquelyn's disappointments, insecurities, and broken heart. Those entries tell the story of how she kidnapped me as a baby, all to bring vengeance upon you for stealing her husband."

Suzette's mouth shut tight, and she sank lower into the arms of the duke.

"It states that you were his mistress before you married my father. It contains a heartbreaking entry about her the duke's betrayal, especially when she learned that you may have born him a child."

Robert cleared his throat. "That would be me," he said, raising his hand, straining to suppress the grin upon his face. He quickly dropped it and then resumed a somber posture.

"This is not the time or place to discuss such matters," the duke interjected gruffly. Suzette gasped and brought her hand to her mouth apparently stifling a sob.

"Well, let's continue with the scandalous tale." Suzette's flesh turned from ashen to a pink in a matter of seconds. "Mother," she continued curtly, "Philippe, your former fiancé, apparently came to the rescue after his then titled lordship married Jacquelyn Spencer. Dorcas' notes are a little sketchy, because most of what I read was hearsay from the duchess during this time. Am I right though?"

"You are correct," Philippe spoke up. "I wed your mother to spare her the shame. She bore your half brother, Robert, who I raised as my own. Then five years later, you came into the world. My dearest, Angelique," he sighed.

The dearest comment irked her emotional state of mind. "Oh, father, as fond as I am of you, from what I read here, you are not without your own faults. Challenging the duke to a duel? What were you thinking?" Philippe sank into his chair. "Oh, I clearly understand mother's moral fiber was weak when it came to Robert Holland, but still your foolishness led me to the arms of Jacquelyn Holland. From what I read from Dorcas' journal, her mental instability had been evident."

"I trusted her," he defended himself. "She had befriended me, and we both tried to save our marriages and keep these two apart. It was just as much his—"

"Nevertheless," Jolene interrupted, raising her hand to interject his fault slinging comment. "I cannot believe that you felt compelled to have a woman you barely knew watch your three-month-old daughter."

Philippe looked woefully at her as if to admit his own mismanagement of the affair. As far as Jolene had been concerned, he carried as much blame for her kidnapping as anyone else.

"Angelique, forgive me," he implored with desperation in his voice.

She swallowed hard, fighting a wave of nausea. "I need to forgive all of you, I think." She inhaled a deep breath and looked at Suzette. The resentment she felt at that moment after stirring up the past came to a terrible head.

"Mother, I have no respect for you. I am sorry, but your illicit affairs with the duke were quite risqué. You leave my father for him, and after I disappear, you leave for England and forget about me entirely. How could you? What kind of mother does such a thing?" Her harsh words had clearly stung her mother's heart. Suzette wept. Jolene could not discern if shame or remorse motivated her behavior.

"That's enough," the duke rebuked her in return. "How dare you speak to your mother with such disrespect? You have no idea of the heartache she went through after losing you, or how long we both searched for years to find you."

"Nor I!" Philippe rose to his feet in haste. "Do you think she was the only one to suffer? I lost everything in my pursuit of my daughter's whereabouts." The glare of daggers filled his eyes as he screamed at the duke.

Jolene turned toward Philippe and spoke one firm word pointing directly toward her father. "Sit." His eyes darted her way, surprised once more at her fearless demeanor. He immediately complied, and Jolene turned her glare toward the duke to express her displeasure.

"You sir, are a typical old-world aristocrat with no conscience. You purposely destroyed a marriage. Not once since I have been in this room have you even asked what happened to Jacquelyn." Her eyebrows furrowed over his insensitivity. "Do you even care?"

He said nothing in return, as if he were trying to conjure up an ounce of respect for a woman who once had been his wife. Instead, he kept his arm around Suzette showing more concern over his current duchess.

"I don't think he does," Robert interjected clearly peeved over his father's response. "I was more curious than he seems to be at this moment." He turned and looked at Jolene. "Shall I tell him or you?"

Jolene shook her head yes. "Please, do. I don't think I can bear to speak of it in a room filled with people displaying such insensitivity," she huffed.

Robert sighed and then looked at his father. "Your former wife married Count von Lamberg and became pregnant through their union together," he said in a calm tone.

"Pregnant?" His father repeated the word as if he were suddenly interested.

"Yes, you thought she was barren, but apparently the count accomplished the deed. As much as Jacquelyn wanted a child, though, it was not to be. The conception had lodged outside her womb. She ruptured and bled to death."

Finally, Jolene saw the duke express an ounce of sympathy in his eyes. "I was three when my stepfather buried your wife. From what I remember, she had been a tender and nurturing mother. I can still see myself throwing a rose upon her coffin and looking up at my stepfather wondering what would happen to me."

Jolene glanced at the diary untouched upon the table. "You should read Dorcas' accounts about your late wife's state of mind, Your Grace. She had such a sad ending to her life perishing for what she desired most—a child of her own."

She paused wondering whether to express the thoughts of what if's that had tormented her own heart and decided to recite them anyway. "Had you been a faithful husband, perhaps you would have given her a child and none of this would have happened. Perhaps my wandering mother would have stayed with my father. Perhaps all of you wouldn't be sitting here in your regretful state of mourning and guilt."

"I'm assuming then the family jewels were passed to you." The duke eyed her necklace again.

The comment sounded inappropriate for the moment but not unexpected. "Yes, I have your precious family heirlooms. From what I read in Dorcas' diary, some of the pieces were sold when we first arrived in Austria but many remain. Your current duchess may have them," she replied coldly. "They belong to your family, not mine."

Jolene reached behind her neck and unhooked the rubies. She walked toward her mother and handed them to her. Suzette did not respond and kept her gaze down toward the floor. The duke took them in his hand instead, eyeing the lost treasure.

"My great grandmother once wore these," he said. "They meant much to my own mother. She was heartbroken to discover them gone."

At that moment, Jolene staggered in her stance. The weight of the dramatic revelation had taken its toll upon her mind and body. The feeling of estrangement from her true parents weighed heavily upon her heart. Not one sat blameless in the room. They had all participated in how the course of her life had played out.

Her birth identity had changed, but the person she had become remained Komtesse Jolene von Lamberg. How could she set her identity aside for a room of self-centered people who loved, cheated, fought, and abandoned all for the sake of their selfish pursuits? Clearly, she had formed judgments, whether right or wrong, that would not be easy to undo.

"I will leave you now to your thoughts. Please do not attempt to be in my presence or speak with me until I approach you on my own accord." She halted for a moment and placed her hand on her stomach fighting the nausea.

Jolene turned and looked at Robert whose eyes held the empathy of a saint. "Thank you, dearest, for being here."

"My pleasure," he whispered.

Jolene gave him a peck on his right cheek. With that, she left the room leaving behind her own flesh and blood to deal with the disclosure on their own terms.

Chapter 28

The Aftermath of Truth

Robert wandered over to an empty seat, plopped down, and settled in to witness the aftermath of the revelation. "Well, now, that was a pleasant reunion," he announced lightheartedly.

"Why didn't you tell us?" Finally, his mother found her voice. She looked at him clearly peeved that he had kept the secret from her for so long.

"Because it wasn't my place," he quickly responded.

"And I thought you had come to visit me for other reasons." Philippe sneered at him expressing his own discontent over the situation.

His comment opened an assortment of problems. Robert glanced at his mother, who had been unaware of their visit. Instead of asking him about the encounter, she turned her attention to Philippe.

"How did Robert find you?"

"Ask your conniving husband," he spat. "His fucking insatiable need to keep involved in my life never ends."

His mother turned her head, frowning in disapproval over what she had learned. "Robert, is that true?"

"That's not the point," his father quickly dismissed the question.

Saving his ass, Robert thought knowing he probably would pay for it later behind closed doors. Then he turned the attention back to his involvement.

"How did you find out her identity?"

"The day after uncle's ball, I happened upon her sitting in a café. She sat reading the diary over a cup of coffee," he said, pointing to it. "She had tried to hide it from me, but it accidentally fell to the floor. Like a gentleman, I bent over and picked it up. Afterward, I nearly choked on my tea having read Jacquelyn's name inside." Robert snickered and shook his head. "I confronted her about the book. One thing led to another, and eventually she blurted out the truth." Robert smiled remembering his thoughts months ago. "Imagine my shock when a woman I'm attracted to physically, turns out to be my half sister. You have no idea how I felt."

After he thought that he had brought a touch of humor to the situation, Philippe suddenly rose to his feet in a fit of anger.

"Damn all of you," he growled. "Especially you, Suzette. If you hadn't been unfaithful, none of this would have happened."

Robert could hear the lingering hurt in his voice. Suzette shot to her feet responding in a rage. Robert's mouth gaped open at her sudden physical response to his railing about her behavior.

"Blame me, will you? Angelique was right. If you hadn't been so pig-headed and proud demanding retaliation, our daughter would not have been carried off to some godforsaken place by a woman out for revenge."

Robert had never heard his mother raise her voice to such a pitch in his entire life. His father grabbed her hand and pulled her back into her seat. "Sit down, Suzette." She looked angrily at him but complied.

Philippe stood his ground with a blatant unforgiving temper. Robert had to intervene before he said something else to stir up the pot.

"Godforsaken, Mother?" Robert countered the ridiculous statement. "She is one of the richest women in all of Austria. She bears the title of komtesse, as well as being beautiful, intelligent, and well bred." Even his buried emotions had come to a head over his family. Their behavior irked him. "Frankly, I think she did quite well by the former duchess and the count."

"I cannot believe that you would say such a thing in my presence," Philippe said, looking at Robert in disillusionment. "Do you think that I would not have given her a decent life? Some strange man in Vienna lived the years that were owed to me. She was and is by all rights my daughter," he snapped.

"And you would have taken her from me," his mother said, gritting her teeth. "I have no doubt in my mind that you would have denied me the pleasure of watching her grow into womanhood."

"And why shouldn't I have kept her from you? The courts would have granted me custody. You were an unfit mother, an adulterous..."

"Enough!" His father jumped to his feet and took a step toward Philippe.

Oh shit, Robert thought. Swiftly, he rose in response and blocked his father's path, holding him at bay by placing his hand on his chest. Then he turned his head and spoke to his stepfather instead.

"I think you should leave, Philippe. If this turns into another duel to defend your honor, Angelique may not forgive you." Robert sternly urged him.

Philippe's nostrils flared as he eyed his father displaying his regret that he had not succeeded in killing him eighteen years ago.

The gathering turned into the volatile situation just as Robert feared. He knew with one spark an explosive situation would ensue between two men that he would not be able to stop.

"I'll take my leave," Philippe finally relented. "Frankly, I've had enough of all of you."

Philippe headed toward the door, but Robert followed and halted him briefly before he exited. In a low voice, undetectable to his parents, he spoke. "Angelique will contact you directly, Philippe. Give her a few days. My sense is that her heart is softer toward you than it is with my parents. After all, as estranged as the four of us are, we are the only family she has except for an elderly step aunt who lives in Berlin. Vienna holds nothing for her, except an empty house and no companionship."

Robert saw the wrath dissipate in his eyes. His voice softened. "Tell her that I look forward to seeing her again." Philippe glanced at Robert and Suzette once more. After another disapproving scowl, he briskly exited the room.

Robert looked over at his father, who had retreated to his mother's side. The two of them appeared despondent over what had transpired. Nevertheless, as he watched his father caress his mother in comfort, he could not deny their love for one another. He wondered if such love had been truly worth it, or if he would ever experience such devoted passion. With a heavy heart, he walked toward his parents and stood before them.

"You know, I did confess to Angelique my jealous rage of flipping over her bassinet at the age of five," he said, looking at his mother. "She found that easier to forgive, I'm afraid, than the disappointment she holds in her family. Perhaps one day she'll come to love you." He stepped away, distraught over the grief-stricken look upon his mother's face.

"Now, if you'll excuse me, I'm going to tend to my sister."

He left them behind and strode toward the library where Jolene had indicated she would retreat after the revelation. God, he needed a breath of fresh air. The last hour had affected him as well, and he worried how Jolene fared. As he approached the door, it was obvious because he heard her sniffling on the other side.

Robert gave the door a light rap and then opened it. He stuck his head around the corner and found her huddled in a chair.

"May I come in?"

He didn't wait for an answer. Her hands covered her face. Pulling his handkerchief out of his pocket, he offered it to her in the absence of her own.

"Here, take this," he said, holding the white linen. "You have my permission to blow your nose in it."

A second later, she snatched it from his hand and did just that. When she did, her nostrils made a snorting sound and they both laughed.

"You're not getting this back," she said, blowing once more.

"I don't want it back," he grinned, "not after what you've done to it."

After she composed herself, he placed his hand on her shoulder and gave her a gentle squeeze. "I thought you presented yourself remarkably well, with poise and grace. It wasn't easy, though, was it?"

Jolene raised her head. "Robert, I'm so angry at them. Why do I feel such resentment rather than joy that they now know the truth?"

He sat down next to her. "Perhaps it's the shock. After all, for eighteen years of your life, you believed in a different heritage that you proudly bore. Then when it's finally stripped away, it's replaced by a broken family filled with animosity." Robert's lip pulled upward in a knowing smile. "Truthfully, I can understand why you cling to the count as the foundation of your life. You are a product of his upbringing and not of your real parents."

"I wish that I could yell at them all and be done with it," she huffed.

"If it's any consolation," Robert interjected. "You're not the only one who has to deal with this shock. My mother will probably be an emotional wreck filled with remorse for weeks. As far as Philippe, I had to step in between him and my father who were about to have another duel. He finally left without throwing down the gauntlet, thank God."

Robert's levity is what Jolene needed. She giggled and shook her head. "My God, that must have been quite the sight—two grown men dueling over your mother."

"Yes, it would have been something to watch."

"Well, thank God neither of them died." Jolene shook her head in disgust.

"So, what is your plan now?" Robert sat in a chair across from Jolene. "Are you going back to Austria?"

"I don't know what I will do." She took his handkerchief and dried the remaining tears on her cheeks."

"Why don't you stay here in Paris and at least spend time with them? I'm sure my mother would like it, and I dare say Philippe will be overwhelmed with joy."

"Perhaps once my anger subsides." Jolene cast him a look of sisterly love. "I'm glad we have made our peace, Robert."

"I think in time, you'll make peace with all of them. Just give your heart the opportunity to heal and the opportunity for them to adjust."

"I don't understand mother, do you?"

"It's hard to understand either of them, when we actually have no idea about their lives when they were youths. Did you find out much when you went to the cemetery with her?"

"Only that her father died when she was eighteen and her mother when she was much younger."

"Well, I guess it doesn't matter," he concluded, brushing it aside. "They are what they've become, like us."

Jolene's shoulders slumped in exhaustion, and she brought her hand to her chest. "I'm so tired," she confessed. "Too much emotion in one short hour. I'm going to retire."

Robert rose to his feet and offered her his hand. "Let me escort you upstairs to your room." After giving her an affectionate hug, he returned downstairs to check on his parents and have a stiff drink.

Chapter 29

Intentional Harm

Jolene retreated into her suite. The room was stuffy, so she walked over to the balcony and pushed open the double doors to step outside for a breath of fresh air.

The small balcony hung from the side of the townhome, giving her a viewpoint of the city. Darkness had covered the landscape, shrouding the buildings with shadows. Flickering gas streetlights sparkled like fireflies as far as she could see. A warm evening breeze swirled through her hair cooling her heated body. The rustling leaves of the tree below where she stood calmed her anxiety. The moment was quiet and surreal.

Soon there would be nothing to keep her in Paris. She had accomplished her purpose, finished the puzzle, and revealed her identity to those who lost her eighteen years ago. Vienna would beckon her home to assume her responsibilities as komtesse of the von Lamberg family. Everybody's life had changed in a blink of an eye, and at that moment, she felt utterly alone.

Finally, with Maria's help, she prepared for bed. Jolene tossed and turned for hours. She glanced at the clock ticking on the fireplace mantel and noted the time. It was two in the morning, and she barely had stolen a half an hour of sleep.

Her mind whirled from the day and all that happened hours earlier.

In a huff of frustration, she got out of bed and thrust her arms through her robe, tying the sash around her waist. Thinking that a warm glass of milk might help her sleep, she wandered downstairs to the kitchen. The entire household lay quiet behind closed doors. She felt jealous that they apparently had found rest when she could not.

After warming milk in a pan, she poured it into a large mug. The heat of the cup soothed her cold fingers. Not wanting to return to her room, she shuffled down the hallway in her slippers and entered the parlor. To her surprise, Dorcas' diary lay on the table untouched. It bothered her that neither the duke nor her mother cared to read its contents. Perhaps they didn't wish to know the mind of Jacquelyn and all that had happened after she left. Jolene felt far more acquainted with her dead spirit than she did with the live one belonging to her real mother.

She found a chair and settled into it, then started to sip the warm liquid. It traveled to her throat warming her empty stomach. No one ate dinner that evening after she had made her announcement. It destroyed her appetite and probably everyone else in the room.

A few minutes later, she heard the front door open and slam shut with a bang. The sound startled her, and she sat up from her slumped position in a fright. When she heard footsteps approach, Jolene rose to her feet. Geoffrey staggered to the doorframe and leaned against it for support. Even though she felt thankful it wasn't a burglar, she had no words of welcome for the insolent Mr. Chambers.

He took one look at her and smiled crookedly. "Well, if it isn't her ladyship" he slurred like a drunk. He eyed her up and down in her silk robe and grinned at her bare toes poking out from the ends of her slippers. Raising his eyebrow in an approving fashion, he stepped forward and stopped a few feet away.

"And what, might I ask, are you doing up all by yourself at two o'clock in the morning?"

Jolene wrinkled her nose over the foul alcohol and cigar-smoke breath he blew in her face. She turned her head to the right in protest. "I almost forgot all about you, Geoffrey Chambers. Since I haven't seen you in days, I had hoped you left for London."

He snickered over her statement. "Don't you wish," he said. "No, I haven't left. There are too many pleasures to be had in Paris like gambling, cancan dancers raising their skirts, and prostitutes parting their legs."

Jolene shut her eyes envisioning the scenes. He was such a disagreeable man that it turned the milk in her stomach sour. "My goodness, Geoffrey, could you be any more tactless in front of a lady?" She shook her head and blushed.

Suddenly his demeanor softened. "Oh, I apologize. Those were visions no man should speak in front of a lady." He wielded his repentant charm at her and plopped like a drunken fool into a nearby chair.

Jolene relented, giving him the benefit of the doubt since his apology sounded somewhat sincere. The milk cooled, so she took a few sips hoping it wouldn't make her sick.

"You didn't say why you are up at this hour?" He looked at her curiously.

She lowered her eyes and released a puff of air. "I couldn't sleep. It's been a stressful day." Her comment brightened the stupor on his face, and suddenly he became interested.

"Did something happen?"

Jolene looked at Geoffrey and cringed. *Dear God, I'm related to this scoundrel,* she thought. To think that she had fallen for his disingenuous charm made her sorry that she didn't take Grace and Robert's advice to heart. Just the thought of how physically attracted to him she had been when he touched her sent a chill down her spine that no cup of warm milk would cure. Frankly, Geoffrey Chambers had been nothing more than a jagged piece to the puzzle and part of the dysfunctional family she had recently joined.

Taking another sip of milk, she kept her eyes upon him and decided the best way to sober him up would be to tell him the news. "You shouldn't be eyeing your distant cousin in such a sinful fashion, Geoffrey." Jolene sounded smug, and she knew it. "I don't think my half brother, Robert, would appreciate it very much."

"What the hell are you talking about?" He gawked at her with his bloodshot eyes.

It couldn't be helped, but a teasing smile spread across her face. "My real name is Angelique Moreau. I am Robert's half sister, which I think makes you a relation to me as my half cousin or something of that nature—if there is such a thing."

Geoffrey said nothing. He stared at her blankly as if his mind were trying to process the news. Then without warning, he rose to his feet and hovered above her body. His stealthy move stripped away her sense of security. She set her empty cup on the side table and readied herself defensively.

"You are bloody kidding me?" he spat. "Is this a joke or does everyone else know?"

She lifted her eyes and nodded affirmatively. "I told you that it has been a stressful day. I told my mother, father, and the duke. Robert has been privy to that information for quite some time."

"You mean Philippe Moreau is your father?"

"Yes."

Geoffrey suddenly leaned over and placed both hands on the armrest of her chair preventing her from moving. "Please leave me alone," she said, gritting her teeth.

He guffawed. "I don't think so, cousin. I don't take orders—especially from women."

Jolene winced and turned her head away from his hot, stale breath. He didn't appreciate her spurning action.

Cautiously, she looked into his eyes. They had turned black like coal, fading the gold speckles.

"You know your mother is a whore," Geoffrey announced coolly.

She leaned back as far as she could in the chair. "I already know she was the duke's mistress," she answered in agitation. "I'm aware of their relationship."

Geoffrey smirked. He released the armrests and stepped back. "You don't know, do you?"

Jolene looked at him cockeyed. "Know what?"

"You think that you have cleverly put all the pieces into place," he sneered. "But in the end, you've created the wrong picture altogether."

"What do you mean?" She angrily jumped up to confront the pompous ass.

Geoffrey flashed a menacing look in return. Unprepared for his next move, he took a stride toward her and stood flush against her body. His right hand trailed his fingertips down the side of her cheek. She flinched. Irritated over his touch, Jolene tried to sidestep him. She didn't want to fall back in the chair, lest he corner her helplessly.

In response, he grabbed her by the waist, coiling his long arm around her like a snake. Then with a quick jerk, he pulled her against his rock-hard frame. He placed the other hand on the back of her head preventing her movement.

Resisting with all of her strength proved fruitless. She winced in pain. Every squirm she made, he applied more pressure to her neck. Suddenly, he leaned toward her right ear. His hot breath met the side of her face, and he whispered.

"You think your mother met the duke at the horse races," he snarled in a sinister tone that gave her a chill. "But he paid to take her virginity as a common whore and prostitute at a brothel called the Chabanais. Your duchess mother is nothing more than the cheapest of whores, who fucked men for money. That is the true story of how they met."

The words cut deep. As if she wasn't already in enough emotional pain, he had sickened her even more. Geoffrey grabbed a fistful of her hair. Gruffly, he pulled her head backward, and Jolene had no choice but to relent. Their eyes met. She trembled under his power.

"If you would like confirmation, love, I can introduce you to the brothel mistress who knew her twenty years ago. Apparently, my uncle used to fuck her, too, even when he was married to Jacquelyn."

Geoffrey kept her head pulled back in a painful strain. Then what she feared the most happened. His eyes turned wicked, glaring at her with heated desire. She felt his erection press against her body.

"Let me go!" Her voice growled like a cornered animal. It did nothing to stop his advance.

"What would society in London, Paris, or Vienna think if they knew your mother had been a prostitute in a brothel? No man of respectability would dare to marry you no matter how wealthy you are. You would be an outcast, just like the duke and duchess." He paused and snickered. "No doubt, you'll die an old maid because of it."

She narrowed her eyes over his threat. "You wouldn't dare spread such gossip," she countered. "Your own family would be affected, not just me. Think of the reputation of your parents or cousin for that matter."

Geoffrey stared at her with dark intent. "Give me what I want, and I'll keep my mouth shut about your whore of a mother."

He pressed harder against her frame. She squirmed. "No! I demand this instant that you unhand me!"

Wiggling from his grasp proved useless. She was no match for his strength. Swiftly, he released her hair and put his palm on the back of her head again. Then he pushed her toward his mouth. Geoffrey forcefully kissed her and drove his tongue between her pursed lips. She whimpered over the foul taste of his flesh down her throat. When he had finished, he pulled away.

"If you don't give me what I want willingly," he sneered. "I'll have to take it without your permission, Cousin."

She saw darkness in his eyes and opened her mouth to scream. Anticipating her next move, he clasped his hand over her mouth to silence her and then with the other pressed her downward to the floor until she collapsed on her knees in pain. A second later, he had her pinned to the ground and began clawing at her nightgown.

After wrestling against his actions, Jolene had lost the battle. He had placed her in the position he wanted. With his free hand, he unfastened his trousers.

"You know you want it, you slut," he said.

To her utter horror, he put himself in a position to violate her body.

"Like mother, like daughter," he said coldly.

Finally, his hand slipped from her mouth. Jolene screamed. She heard heavy footsteps coming toward them, and Geoffrey lifted his head detecting the intruder.

Jolene could not see who had entered the room, but it didn't stop her from screeching. "He's going to rape me!" In a split second, Robert came into view, took hold of Geoffrey, and pulled him from her body.

"You fucking bastard," Robert cursed. "I'll kill you for touching her."

Giving Robert no chance, Geoffrey defended himself by throwing the first punch. His clench fist landed on Robert's lower jaw, sending him reeling backward. Quickly, he recovered and threw a punch back into Geoffrey's face hitting him in the cheekbone. The two began a vicious brawl.

Jolene clamored from the floor and stood to her feet. Her hand came to her mouth as she watched in horror the two cousins unleash their hatred toward one another. Punches flew left and right. Tables and lamps tipped over breaking and strewing glass across the floor. Helpless to intervene, Jolene spun around and ran up the staircase. She pounded with her fist upon the duke's door until it opened.

She reached out and grabbed his arm, pulling him out the door.

"Robert and Geoffrey are fighting in the sitting room. Someone is going to get killed!" She could hear the struggle continue downstairs. "Geoffrey tried to rape me," she explained, to the duke as they ran down the staircase to the sitting room.

When they reached the door, everything went deadly quiet. Jolene, fearing for Robert's life, flew into the room first. Robert stood over Geoffrey's motionless body sprawled across the floor, rubbing his bruised knuckles.

"I knocked blackguard out," he declared in triumph.

Jolene ran to her brother and flung her arms around his neck. "Oh, Robert, I owe you my life," she cried. She trembled in his arms, and he gave her a hug in return.

"I told you that I would protect you, Jolene, and I meant it."

Geoffrey stirred and moaned. His eyes fluttered open, and the duke strode toward him in anger. He grabbed him by the lapels of his coat and roughly pulled him to his feet. "Get the hell out of here before I kill you myself," he ordered.

After rubbing the blood from his split lower lip with the back of his hand, he flashed a detestable gaze at his uncle. "Fine, I'm glad to leave, you arse," he spat.

He turned and headed for the door. All of the commotion had brought her mother to the scene. When he saw Suzette, he sneered. "Oh look, the prostitute from the Chabanais has arrived." He lifted the corner of his mouth in a sinister smile. "Your old roomy, Nadine, congratulates you on your fortune."

Jolene wanted to throw up. She glanced at her mother, whose eyes widened in not only shock, but also acknowledgement over his comment. The duchess turned toward Robert, blushing scarlet red.

The duke strode toward Geoffrey, grabbed him by the collar, and shoved him out the doorway. "Get the hell out and don't come back."

Jolene heard the front door open, another short scuffle, and the sound of Geoffrey landing hard on the step outside. "I'll tell my father, you fucking bastard!"

The butler appeared, apparently awakened by the ruckus. "Slam the door shut," the duke ordered. "Gather his things and throw them outside."

"With pleasure, Your Grace."

She heard the door close with a thud and the lock set. A moment later, the duke returned and hastened to his wife's side, slipping his arm around her waist.

"Tell them," he encouraged her. "They will understand."

"Understand what?" Jolene asked. How would she understand anything more when she couldn't understand her mother? Suzette looked mournfully in her direction and spoke.

"Just as your brother has apparently saved you from rape, so did my husband, Jolene."

"I don't understand," she swiftly replied. "Is it true that you were a prostitute in a brothel, and that is how you met?"

She shook her head affirmatively. "There is so much you do not know, my daughter." Suzette looked over at Robert grimacing over the well-kept secret.

"Did you know?" Jolene turned and looked at Robert. He shook his head.

"No, this is all news to me as well," he replied.

"Perhaps the two of you should sit down," the duke suggested.

Anxious to hear the story, they both sat side-by-side on the divan. The duke escorted Suzette to a chair, helped her to feel at ease, and then stood behind her in a supportive stance with his hands on both her shoulders.

Her cheeks remained crimson rose, and her voice trembled when she spoke. "What I shared with you at the cemetery about my father dying when I turned eighteen was the truth." Sorrowfully, she frowned. "What I did not tell you is that I had been left destitute and homeless afterward. The Sisters of Charity took care of me and then helped me get a job as a laundress here in Paris. One of their clients was the Chabanais, a well-known brothel that catered to aristocrats. I washed their sheets and delivered them daily to the brothel for several months."

Jolene glanced at Robert whose face mirrored her own surprise.

"The mistress of the brothel coerced and blackmailed me into working for her by having me fired from my job." Suzette reached back and touched the hand of the duke. "Fearful for my life, I succumbed to the temptation rather than having the strength to say no. I agreed to become one of her girls, but I was still a virgin."

"Good God, mother," Robert said. His voice was not judgmental but empathetic.

The duke looked at his son. "The Chabanais was my playground if you will, for many years," he confessed. "I came there often and paid for sexual encounters with beautiful women."

"So Uncle Edmund's comment a few weeks ago was true?" He looked at his father in amazement.

"I'm afraid so. You would have thoroughly enjoyed witnessing the hell I put my own father through, while I procrastinated in taking responsibility for my life."

"So you bought her," Jolene said, hardly able to speak the words.

Her mother answered. "He paid to take my virginity, yes, for a high price."

"I'll be damned," Robert responded.

"Only, I never did—at least, not in the brothel," the duke clarified. "Your mother had fallen on hard times, but she was sweet and innocent. I purchased her for three nights, and led the mistress of the house to think I had done my duty."

The duchess continued the sordid tale. By now her blush had faded, and her voice spoke strongly and unashamed. "But she was a shrewd woman who realized what had happened, so she sold me again to a terrible man without Robert's knowledge. She determined to see me initiated into the brothel and kept in her debt."

"All right," Robert interjected. "Now I am confused." He leaned forward, putting his elbows on his knees and holding his weary, bruised head in his hands. "Did that man take your virginity?"

Suzette tilted her head back and glanced at her husband with a grin. "Robert arrived just as he was about to rape me. He broke the door down, pulled him off my body, and flung him to the floor."

The duke smirked. "I wanted to stick a knife in his fat gut, but thankfully I didn't."

Suzette looked at Jolene, tilting her head as if to plead for her understanding. "The rest is history. Yes, I became his mistress and bore him a son out of wedlock, but he came back for me five years later. He loved me and I him." She patted the duke's hand still resting on her shoulder. "I don't know where I would be today if it weren't for him. No doubt, I would have died a prostitute."

Flabbergasted over the story, Jolene didn't know how to react. She may have found love and happiness with the duke, but her father received nothing but heartache. Didn't he deserve better? Yes, it was a beautiful love story, but the duchess paid a price regardless.

"Father," Robert asked. "Why didn't you marry mother after you brought her to England the first time?"

"Because my father forbade it, of course. He had introduced me to Jacquelyn with the expectation that I would take her as my wife. The arrangements with her parents had already been made. As a rule, especially back then, men never married their mistress. My father was dying, and I wanted to do as he wished."

"But you deceived mother, correct?" Jolene accused him angrily.

"I deceived him, too, Angelique. Don't you see? I became pregnant with Robert, and Philippe offered his hand to me in marriage to keep me from shame."

"So you used him." Still exasperated over her mother's actions, she could not reconcile any of it. Her poor father had been a mere pawn. "Did you ever love father?" she pressed with an angry look.

"Once I did. Philippe and I were engaged to be married long before I met Robert. He had a career as a naval officer. At the time my father passed away, he was at war halfway around the world. Robert came into my life, and I gave him my love and devotion."

Robert interrupted. "It's late," he said. "Let's not continue this tonight. We're all tired, emotionally distraught, and my hand hurts." He looked at his red and bruised knuckles.

"Perhaps my brother is right." She rose to her feet and glanced at her mother. Suzette's eyes pleaded again for leniency. *Not yet*, she thought. "Goodnight."

As they exited the room, she heard the duke say, "Give her time."

Would time help? She had no idea.

Chapter 30

A Fork in the Road

Maria entered the bedroom and pulled aside the drapes letting the daylight filter through the sheer curtains underneath.

"Oh, dear God," Jolene moaned. She covered her eyes with her hand. "What time is it?"

"Almost ten o'clock, my lady," she announced. "Lord Holland gave me instructions to rouse you from your slumber, though I did protest."

"Oh, did he?" Jolene sat up in bed feeling perturb over his instructions. "Why? He knows that I didn't go to sleep until some ungodly hour last night." Her palm held the side of her head, and she scrunched her brow in pain. "Besides, I have a splitting headache."

Maria gave her a sympathetic look, but ignored her protests by drawing her morning bath. By the pulsating pain, it felt as if she had one too many drinks last night, which of course was not the case. In a sense, she did overdo it, by sharing far too many emotions the day before.

Then there was the matter of Geoffrey, who made her blood run cold. Hopefully, he had gathered his things that had been tossed out the door and departed for London. She had been such a fool to be so fond of him in the beginning. On the other hand, she thanked her lucky stars that Robert had promised to take care of her safety. What would she do without him when she returned to Austria?

As she slipped into the hot tub and leaned her head back on the rim, she wondered what the day would bring. A part of her wished she could continue to pretend to be someone else to avoid the new challenges that she faced. On the other hand, she felt a responsibility to become part of the family from which she had been stolen. To achieve that end, she would need to redeem the years away from her parents.

Unable to hide any longer, Maria helped her with her morning routine by doing her hair and choosing her dress. When she had finished, she took a deep breath and opened the door to her suite.

Jolene wandered downstairs to the dining room hoping to get a bite to eat and complain to Robert for waking her up. It would have been enjoyable to sleep all day and hide under the covers. Frankly, she was in no mood for anything except a strong cup of coffee to relieve her headache.

When she arrived, she was surprised to see Suzette sitting alone at the dining table eating a piece of toast. The footman poured a cup of hot tea and set it in front of her. The dark circles under her eyes were signs she did not sleep well either.

"Where is everyone?" Jolene asked, motioning to a footman. "Can you get me some coffee, please?" Her mother lifted her eyes and smiled. Jolene barely reciprocated with a weak grin.

"My husband and Robert have left on an outing," she announced. "I wished them well and sent them on their way."

"An outing where? I thought he was the one who told Maria to awaken me from my slumber, and now he is gone?"

Suzette smiled sensing her morning touchiness. "Yes, they went to see Philippe, I believe."

"They what?" A twinge of pain stabbed her head. Jolene discovered a full cup of hot coffee in front of her, mixing it with milk and sugar, before downing the first sip. Hopefully, it would go straight to her brain and stop the incessant pounding.

"I have my suspicions as to why they went, but they've decided not to fill me in at this juncture. No doubt, they don't want me to have unrealistic expectations of whether they will succeed or not."

After gulping a few sips that nearly burned her tongue, she set her cup down and scowled at her mother. "Well, I hope they won't make matters worse, because I wanted to spend time with Philippe to get to know him better. I don't need them alienating him any further." Her voice sounded rude and abrupt. "I apologize for being so harsh this morning. It's that I have a splitting headache."

"I'm sorry you're not feeling well." A motherly look of concern filled her eyes. "You should spend as much time as you can with Philippe. He is your father who has been robbed of the pleasure of knowing you for eighteen years."

Why did everything that came out of her mother's mouth irritate her so much? Before she could even think if her words might hurt her, she made a snide remark. "Did you feel robbed of my presence all these years, too?" She asked harshly with cynicism. Suzette did not flinch at her comment but appeared to accept it with understanding.

"When I left your father, Angelique, it was during a time when the courts would have never given me custody of you. I knew that no matter what the outcome, the ruling would not be in my favor because I had committed adultery. Your father, I believe, would have been intent on keeping me from you out of anger anyway." She lowered her head thinking for a moment and then continued. "Of course, we will never know what would have happened because Jacquelyn robbed us of the future."

Jolene considered her mother's rationalization. Eighteen years ago, divorce laws even in Austria were much stricter.

What may have happened could only be speculation now. She agreed.

"No, it seems as if Jacquelyn stole that right from both you and father." As she sat there considering the mother she had never known, she pursued questions that still needed answers. "Did you not care to stay and look for me? Why did you leave Paris?"

Her mother exhaled a deep sigh and downturned her gaze sorrowfully. "I don't expect you to understand the decisions that I made eighteen years ago, except to say that Robert promised me he would do everything in his power to find you." Suzette lifted her head and began to reason. "What could I have done? I had no money or means to help."

Jolene thought about her question. "I don't know," she admitted, feeling confused.

"When we returned to England, Robert kept his promise. He hired private detectives who searched years for you, Angelique." Her mother's voice trembled. "Believe me when I tell you there hasn't been a day that has gone by when I did not think about you or your welfare."

Speechless and touched by the sincerity in Suzette's voice, she desperately wanted to believe her words. As she sat there looking at her mother, the stone heart in her chest cracked. Perhaps the basic need for nurturing had finally broken her resolve to remain aloof.

The pleading look in her mother's eyes convinced her that she had been terribly unfair and critical. Now that she knew everything about her past—her childhood struggles of being abandoned and alone— she realized the similarities they shared. Jolene had turned eighteen, the same age that her mother had been when thrown into a situation of destitution and despair. Had it been her, would she have made the same decisions? It must have been terribly frightening for her mother, and yet Jolene had harshly judged her at every turn. Whatever the mistress of the brothel had used to intimidate her to stay, she did not know.

However, it happened and by God's grace, the man who fell in love with her rescued her from a life of prostitution.

Jolene sighed and lowered her head fighting tears. Her hand wrapped around the coffee cup feeling its warmth in her palm. At that moment, she felt a twinge of warmth rise in her heart toward her mother. She glanced up and saw that Suzette had pulled her gaze away from her as if she had given up all hope of reaching her daughter. Finally, the urge she had kept penned up for months released through her lips.

"I want to love you, Mother, honestly I do. I don't know how." Her breath caught in her throat, and her chest felt crushed under the weight of her confession. She waited for her mother to answer. An understanding glow brightened her face.

"In order to love someone, Angelique, it takes time. We hardly know each other, and the years we could have had together have long since passed." Her countenance filled with sorrow. "I doubt we will have much of an opportunity in the future either, once you return to Austria to take your place as komtesse. I shall return to England, and who is to tell if fate will allow the two of us to see each other again?"

Unexpectedly, her mother rose and walked over to the other side of the table, pulling out an empty chair. Jolene stiffened unsure what to expect. She sat down, smiled, and then reached out and took her hand.

"I want you to know," she began with a trembling voice, "that I am sincerely sorry if I have hurt you by my actions. I made the decision to go with Robert, whether you deem it morally right or wrong. I cannot undo the past and, in the end, I accept the consequences of that decision."

Touched by her plea for forgiveness, Jolene nodded. "I understand, Mother. Perhaps if Jacquelyn had not taken me, we would have had some sort of a relationship." She squeezed her mother's hand in return. "It is wrong of me to blame you." She fought back tears as she confessed her own fault. "I have judged you severely, and for that I ask for your forgiveness."

Tears welled in her mother's eyes, and she bent forward giving her a hug. Caught off guard by her actions, it took a few moments before Jolene found the courage to return the embrace. After holding each other in silence for a few moments, Jolene pulled away, wiped a tear off her cheek, and smiled.

"Have you ever been in love with a man, Jolene?" Her mother looked at her endearingly.

It was an odd question. She lowered her eyes. "No, and perhaps that has been my problem. It has been hard for me to understand the passion and love that drove you and the duke to want to be together. Nevertheless, it is not my place to judge, and I feel convicted from heaven above for having done so."

Jolene thought for a few moments and then looked at Suzette. "Perhaps we can write while apart. I would like to confide in you, Mother if you wouldn't mind. One day I will need a woman's advice should I fall in love."

Her mother glowed. "I would love to," she said lightheartedly. "It's not easy being a duchess in a stuffy English household. I often wish for a woman to talk to as well."

"Well then," Jolene replied briskly, "We shall write often and share our joys, worries, and hopes with one another."

Suzette returned to her seat taking a sip of tea. "I wonder how Robert and my husband are progressing."

"What are they up to?" Jolene asked, leaning forward.

"They are making a bid to end the war, I imagine."

"Oh, dear," she said. "Do you think they will succeed?"

"Philippe can be stubborn and prideful," Suzette declared. "Let us hope for your sake, he softens and releases the bitterness of the past."

"I don't want any more strife," Jolene said, shaking her head.

"I know, dear, and God willing it will soon come to an end."

Robert glanced through the glass window and quickly retreated out of sight. He walked a few steps back toward his father.

"Yes, he's working, but there appears to be a patron in the store at the moment."

"Then we'll wait," his father replied.

Robert, unable to remain in one spot, paced a few steps back and forth. He turned and looked at his father, worried over the impending meeting. "Now, you promise this won't turn into some brawl," he joked.

With a sly smile, the duke lifted one corner of his mouth and responded. "As far as I know, but I cannot promise how he will react."

"Dear God, let's hope he keeps a level head and doesn't have a gun behind the counter," Robert said.

His father frowned over his comment. "All will be well, Robert. Trust me."

A few minutes later, the customer left with a cigar box in hand. Robert's father nodded toward the door and led the way. Without an ounce of hesitation, the duke placed his hand on the handle and pushed the door open. The bell rang above his head, catching Philippe's attention. Robert followed close behind his father. After they entered, he closed the door and flipped the sign over to *CLOSED*.

Philippe scowled. "What do you two want?" He ignored their presence and began fiddling with boxes of cigars on the shelf.

The duke approached the counter where Philippe stood. "I'd like to have a word with you, Philippe." He hesitated, sucked in a deep breath, and spoke resolutely. "I've come to make peace between us."

"Peace?" Philippe spun around. His eyebrow rose questioning the words. "And what, might I ask, does that mean?" His mouth pulled to one side in disgust.

"Your daughter wants reconciliation in her family," the duke answered without a waver in his voice. "For her sake, we need to put behind us what happened eighteen years ago."

Philippe stepped back and postured himself showing his height above his old rival. "Don't you think it's a bit late for that?" He appeared unmoved by the offer.

"It's never too late," the duke replied. He stood his ground and continued. "Eighteen years ago I manipulated and deceived you in the vilest possible way in order to steal your wife."

"I haven't forgotten," Philippe replied. His nostrils flared. "If you recall, I tried to kill you because of it."

"No, I haven't forgotten," the duke replied miserably, looking as if he were staring at the barrel of the gun once more. "Perhaps I owe you an apology for the way I went about bringing Suzette and Robert back into my life." He stepped closer. "But I cannot apologize for the years I have enjoyed having them with me."

Philippe looked at him showing no emotion. Robert held his breath hoping that he would be the man he believed lay underneath his hardened exterior. Frankly, Robert thought it sounded like a half-ass apology, but at least his father had admitted his duplicity after all these years. Philippe appeared unmoved and no closer to reconciliation. His father tried once more.

"I apologize."

Philippe stared into the duke's eyes. "Humph," he spouted. The moments ticked by to the tune of the clock on the wall, while Philippe mulled over the duke's words.

"Must I remind you that you were guilty of deception too?"

Philippe picked up a white cloth from below the counter and began wiping the glass countertop back and forth. Silent and not responding, Robert couldn't figure out what the hell he was doing. Was he ceremoniously cleaning the excrement of his father's words or erasing the past once and for all?

"Of course, I deceived you," Philippe said, finally stopping and focusing his attention upon the duke. "We feared you would take Robert, so I lied to protect him." He glanced at Robert with a glint of affection. "I also lied to protect Suzette."

Philippe returned to cleaning the counter. Irritated that nothing had been accomplished, Robert thought they had failed. Apparently, his father bothered by his lack of response also, pressed for an answer.

"You haven't accepted my apology, Philippe." He sighed, clearly showing his frustration. "Are we going to end this once and for all or not?"

Having had enough, Robert spoke up keeping his temper under control. "For heaven's sake, Philippe, this isn't about the two of you and your petty grievances any longer. It's about Angelique and her wishes for the future. Do it for her." Robert reasoned with Philippe's heart. "It's about her—your daughter, who has finally returned to you and mother. Have you no delight in her discovery?"

The frown on Philippe's face dissipated into a somber admission. Offering a gentleman's handshake, the duke stretched forth his hand toward Philippe.

"Robert is right, Philippe. It is for her—not for you or me. Let us bring peace once and for all." He glanced at Robert. "From what my son tells me, we are actually all she has left in this world. Can we at least give her a loving family to make up for the lost years?"

Philippe laid down the white linen cloth on the counter. He looked at the duke's outstretched hand and grimaced. "I'll be damned, you blackguard, if you think I'll ever love you."

Robert swallowed the lump in his throat and prepared to intervene once Philippe threw the first punch. Then to his utter surprise, his stepfather cracked a smile.

"But for Angelique's sake, I will call a truce between us."

Robert released a sigh of relief and lowered his tense shoulders. Philippe reached out, took his father's hand, and shook it. He narrowed his dark eyes to make his last point.

"I do it for her, not for you."

"Fair enough," his father replied. "I do it for her as well."

"Well, it's about time." Robert clapped. The sound of his palms slapping back and forth echoed in the small shop. He felt as if he had watched the ending of a dramatic opera scene. "Well done," he congratulated them both.

The two clasped hands of foes parted. Philippe looked at the sign. "You're hurting our sales, do you mind?" He nodded his head toward the door.

"Now that's over, I'm happy to reopen," Robert replied, walking over and turning the sign over.

Robert and his father looked at each other satisfied over what had transpired. But one thing remained unsolved in Robert's mind, and he determined to bring it up before departing.

"Do you remember the conversation we had the other day and the question I asked you?"

"You're asking a lot," he grumbled.

His father appeared confused over the conversation but didn't pry. "We are having dinner at seven thirty this evening. As I recall, we never fed you last night, and I think that's the least we can do. Why don't you join us tonight and take care of it then?"

"You bloody Englishmen" Philippe complained.

"No white ties," Robert assured him. "Come as you did last evening."

Philippe thought for a moment and smirked. "Well, I did go home hungry, I'll admit that much."

"Will you take care of it when you come?" Robert asked again.

"I will think about it."

Robert shook his head over his stepfather's stubbornness, but something in his voice told him he would relent. "Well, don't think about it too long," he scowled teasingly. "You have had eighteen years to decide whether you would grant it or not."

"Fine, I'll take care of it," he said. "Now stop pressuring me about it."

Robert smiled.

Chapter 31

The Final Pardon

Jolene had spent the majority of the day upstairs in her room. She returned to bed to sleep off the pain. The headache would not go away despite all the coffee she drank or the cold compresses she placed on her forehead.

The only comfort in her pain had been the release of estrangement that she struggled with concerning her mother. Unfortunately, their future relationship would probably consist of nothing more than correspondence between the two of them. It would not be the perfect relationship she envisioned, but nonetheless the thought of having no one would be worse.

As she pondered her days ahead, the thought of Jolene's future began to look dim. Eventually, she would need to return to Austria alone. Everything she had set out to accomplish had been done. Whatever time remained in Paris with the duke, Suzette, Philippe, and Robert, she would try to savor until the day it ended. Responsibilities toward her stepfather's estate awaited. For now, she must attend to the legacy he so graciously gave her to oversee.

Punching her pillow with her fist, she rearranged the feathers to support her aching head. Worrying about what to do next would only make her feel worse, so she closed her eyes and took a nap.

After a few hours of deep sleep, Jolene awakened. Her eyelashes fluttered, almost afraid that the light might pierce her with pain again but it did not. The headache had finally subsided. When she sat up and looked at the time, she couldn't believe the late hour.

She rang for Maria, who swiftly arrived to help her bathe and dress for dinner. Everybody by this time probably wondered why she had kept herself locked in her room all day.

"Will everyone be home for dinner this evening?" she asked Maria. "I've barely exchanged a word with our guests except with the duchess."

"Yes, as far as I know. The duke and duchess, plus his lordship are in the parlor together."

Jolene looked in the mirror feeling awful. Dark circles were underneath her eyes, her hair was in disarray, and her nose hadn't been powdered all day. "Well, you have your work cut out for you, Maria. I look wretched."

"Oh, now, it's not that bad," she comforted her as she brushed the tangles from her hair. "Did something happen to make you ill?"

Poor Maria hadn't a clue as to what had transpired all these months. "Yes, much has happened Maria. When we return to Austria, I shall tell you all about it." For now, Jolene couldn't even bring her mind to think of the next half an hour, let alone rehash the last eighteen years of her life with her lady's maid.

After a few more brush strokes, Maria stopped. "I'll go draw your bath water and put in lavender scent. The aroma will relax you before dinner."

It sounded inviting. Jolene glanced at the clock counting the minutes she had left to bathe, dress, and join the family. *The family*, she thought to herself. A grin spread across her face at the thought that she had a family. But then, as if the joy had been snatched away, she remembered that soon she would be required to leave them all behind.

-·❈·-

Nothing could have prepared her for the sight her eyes beheld when she joined everyone in the parlor before the dinner hour. When she entered the room, she came to an abrupt halt. Philippe sat next to the duke, calmly sharing a before dinner drink. Her mother and Robert looked as peaceful as doves.

All the men stood to their feet upon her arrival. She brought her hand to her chest catching a breath of air. What were they all doing here? "Well, this is a surprise," she said, slowly stepping into the room.

"Hello, Angelique." Her father greeted her with a smile and approached giving her a fatherly kiss on the cheek. At first, she shied away, at his touch. Afterward, she gave him a warm smile of approval.

"I wasn't expecting you," she admitted. Her eyes darted over to the duke and Robert for an answer. Robert flashed a sly smile of victory before answering.

"Well, father and I thought it was rude of us not to feed Philippe last evening, so we invited him over to make up for the oversight."

"And you came," she said, looking at Philippe.

"Yes, I came for you," he replied, giving a quick glance at the duke.

Her mother smiled approvingly at the scene. They were all together, the family that she had been born into. They were acting civil and courteous in one room. Every eye looked at her with love.

What happened next had been entirely unexpected. Suddenly, she heard herself sob. Her arms wrapped around her waist, and she bent over heaving from emotion that came from her soul. A torrent of tears burst forth uninvited and uncontrolled.

Robert came to her side and put his arm around her shoulder as if he understood the reason for her outburst, even though she did not.

"It's all right, Jolene. There is no more need to be angry. Everyone has made peace just as you wished. The animosity is over now."

The words did nothing to stop the tears she could not fight. The next she knew, they all flocked to her side. Her father put his arm around her waist to hold her up, while her mother took her right hand and squeezed it gently. Through her tears, she saw the blurry vision of the duke smiling warmly at her, and Robert's kind eyes imparting his brotherly love and affection.

"We are all so happy to have you back in our lives," her mother said in earnest. "Aren't we Philippe?"

"Indeed," he said, choking up in his own emotion. "I'm so proud of the woman you have become, Angelique. My sorrow has been turned to joy because you have returned to all of us."

After another minute, Jolene stopped sniveling. Robert pressed his handkerchief into her hand again. She quickly wiped her tears and then looked at them. Her heart felt as if it would burst from emotion. Her eyes looked at her father and pleaded.

"Father, may I hug you?" Her voice sounded like a child.

Philippe placed his arms around her and held her close. "You are home now, that's all that matters," he said, stroking her back gently. "We have the rest of our lives ahead of us."

Jolene pulled away and wiped her tears once more. She looked at the duke who stood nearby. His face radiated relief.

"I have a sense, Your Grace, that you are responsible for this reunion. Thank you."

She quickly stepped in his direction and gave him a tight hug. He reciprocated, and whispered in her ear. "It's for you."

Finally, she turned toward her mother. Their words of reconciliation had already been spoken. Without saying anything more, she hugged her as well. Suzette held her for some time before they finally released one another.

Afterward, she noted that Philippe focused his gaze upon Suzette as if he wanted to say something. She stepped out of the way and glanced over at the duke and Robert looking for direction.

"I could use some fresh air," Robert announced. "Anyone wish to join me on the veranda?" Robert nodded at his father to follow, and the three of them departed. Jolene saw that Suzette had turned to leave as well, but Philippe gently took her by the arm.

"Stay," he urged her.

Obviously, something immensely personal would soon transpire between them. Jolene glanced at the two standing face-to-face. They were her parents, and it was a vision she wanted to keep in her heart forever.

Jolene joined Robert and the duke on the veranda. "Is Philippe doing what I hope he is?" she asked Robert in anticipation.

"Yes. Eighteen years is a long time to nurse an unforgiving heart, don't you think?"

Jolene stepped toward her brother. "You did all this, didn't you?"

He smiled at her and reached out taking her hand in his. "Well, His Grace over there helped somewhat," he added, giving his father credit.

"I wonder what he's saying to her," the duke said, staring at the doorway waiting for the two of them to emerge.

"You should leave that between the two of them, Father," Robert encouraged. "It's their business, not ours."

"Perhaps you're right," he acknowledged, sighing. "Your mother deserves what I hope he grants."

After what seemed like an eternity, Suzette walked out on Philippe's arm. He escorted her over to the duke.

"Your wife, I believe," he said, handing her over.

Suzette's face glowed with a rosy tint appearing embarrassed over what had transpired between them. The sparkle in her eye spoke of release, and Jolene knew they, too, had made peace with the past. Before another word could be spoken, the butler appeared on the veranda.

"Dinner is served," he announced.

With that, everyone turned toward the dining room to have a peaceful meal together. Jolene wanted to jump up and down like a little girl having been given a wonderful gift at Christmas. Instead, she merely smiled and controlled the urge. After all, she was still a komtesse.

Chapter 32

Season of Change

A telegram arrived that once again turned Jolene's life upside down. She had only spent two weeks with her reconciled family, barely having enough hours to make up for the lost years. Nevertheless, fate would allow her no more—at least now. Word had arrived from her aunt's husband that Geraldine had been taken gravely ill. Jolene had kept her aunt apprised of her whereabouts by posting letters to Berlin in case something like this happened.

After seeking out Robert, she discovered him in the library. She found him sprawled on the divan in his favorite position with a book in his hand apparently engrossed. As soon as he heard her coming, he slammed the book shut and set it down.

"I have no time for your foolishness," Jolene said, not actually caring at that moment what he read. "I've received bad news."

Robert swung his legs around and sat up straight. "What news?"

My stepfather's sister, Geraldine, is sick. She is calling for me to come to Berlin. It sounds serious as if she might die."

"You intend to go, I take it?" He rose to his feet and stood before her looking as forlorn as she felt inside.

"I have to, Robert. She's been my aunt since childhood. She's loved me like a daughter and been like a mother to me." Jolene brought her hand to her head in despair. She sat down on the couch and grabbed his hand pulling him down by her side. "I don't want to go. I feel horrible admitting it, but the timing is dreadful."

"Yes, quite," he replied. "But you should go. It would not be right for you to disregard her request for your presence, Jolene. I'm sure that you would never forgive yourself if she passed away without being at her side."

"It's not just that, Robert," she moaned. Jolene brought her hands to her face in despair. "I'm afraid that afterward I shall be alone. What am I to do? I don't want to leave you or anyone else behind."

Robert gently pulled her hands away. "Look at me," he pleaded. "You don't need to be alone. Take Philippe with you."

Her brow wrinkled. "Philippe?"

"Yes, your father. His life here is an empty shell. He works in a mundane job and lives on the verge of poverty."

The proposal sounded plausible and well thought out. With Philippe by her side, the trip to Berlin and its sorrows that it may hold would be of immense support. "Do you think he will come?"

Robert sighed. "Well, with Philippe you never know," he jested, "But I cannot think of a reason why he would decline. He has years of your life to catch up on. I am certain that he would appreciate the time together."

"I like the idea, Robert." Jolene relaxed seeing an answer to her dilemma. "After Berlin, I wonder if he would come to Vienna and..."

"Stay?" Robert answered her thought.

Jolene smiled. "I don't want to be alone, Robert. The estate is my responsibility. I owe it to my stepfather to care for his property and accept my title. One day I may sell it, but I cannot right now."

"I think having Philippe by your side will help you to accomplish those responsibilities. He will be a great support and help to you." Robert paused, looking at her sadly. "I'll miss you."

"Then why don't you come?" Excited at the thought, she reached over and took hold of his hand.

"I cannot," Robert quickly responded. "Like you, Jolene, I have responsibilities. My father looks to me to continue the Holland realm, marry, and produce an heir." Robert smirked at Jolene. "He actually told me that he thought you were a good influence on me."

Jolene giggled. "Well, I would like to think so."

"Honestly, I will admit your maturity and feisty spirit did cause me to reflect upon my own character." He shook his head. "We have both learned so much about our parents these past weeks."

"Yes, we have," Jolene agreed.

"I see my father in an entirely new light than I did before. We have grown closer, and I have you to thank for it."

"So, you are no longer a rascal, eh?" Jolene teased him with an endearing smile.

"Well, that's to be seen," Robert laughed. "Who knows, I may even start practicing law in London. God knows, father needs the money to keep the estate going."

"I have more than enough to help, Robert, should your father not be too proud to accept it."

"Nice gesture," he responded with a snicker. "But his pride would not allow such charity."

Jolene's smile faded. She had much to do. The train from Paris to Berlin would be a day's travel. The tickets needed to be purchased, their bags packed, and a visit to Philippe made.

"Well, I should begin preparations," she sighed.

"I will talk to father and mother and will make arrangements to return to England by the end of the week," Robert advised. "I'm sure they will completely understand your dilemma."

They both rose and stood face-to-face holding hands. "I love you," she said affectionately, kissing him on the cheek.

"And I you," he warmly replied. "We shall write one another and perhaps one day meet on holiday."

Jolene nodded struggling with a lump in her throat. Her eyes glanced at the book that Robert had set down. The marquis had apparently lost the bid for his attention as she noted the title, "The Hunchback of Notre Dame." Jolene reached down and picked up the book, thinking about how appropriate it was for the current situation.

"For love is like a tree," she began. "It grows of itself; it sends its roots deep into our being, and often continues to grow green over a heart in ruins."

Robert gazed at her strangely not understanding her recitation.

"Remember those words when you read them," she said, handing him the book. They were poignant for the moment. Her family, who had broken apart eighteen years ago, had come back together through love. One day, as love continued to grow, it would cover their hearts that had once been in ruin. Satisfied that she had accomplished what she set out to do, she prepared to return home.

--·✤·--

Anxious to speak with Philippe, she wasted no time. A few hours later, she instructed the driver to take her to her father's residence. Robert had confirmed that he would be home. She had given Maria instructions to begin packing. After seeing Philippe, she would purchase train tickets for three.

Robert had told her of his living conditions, but when the driver pulled up to the row house where he lived, her heart sank. Her resolve to take him to Berlin grew stronger each passing minute. Philippe deserved restoration in every possible way. Hopefully, he would not spurn her request from pride. If he did, she feared that she would kidnap him to make a point.

After a few sharp taps, he opened the door. As soon as he saw her on his doorstep, he shrank in embarrassment.

"Angelique, what are you doing here?"

"Let me come in, Father, and I'll tell you."

"All right," he said, opening the door wide.

He kept his head lowered and led her into the small parlor. When she witnessed the surroundings in which he lived, she understood how mortified he must feel over her arrival. Nevertheless, she did not come to judge his living conditions. On the contrary, she came to give him something better.

"Father, I have bad news," she began. With an outstretched hand, she grabbed his and held onto it tightly. "I must leave for Berlin immediately. My stepfather's sister is gravely ill and has asked me to be at her side. She is elderly and frail, and I fear she may pass away." Her voice cracked. "I want the opportunity to bid her goodbye."

Her father's shoulders slumped, and he lowered his head. Plainly, her announcement broke his heart.

"I have something to ask you." She glanced at the floor for a brief moment to formulate her words. "I will not be able to bear it if you say no."

"Then ask me," he encouraged her warmly.

"Will you come with me?"

He said nothing in response, but his eyes widened. She continued to persuade him toward a favorable answer. "I want you to be at my side in Berlin to support me." She paused briefly to inhale a breath before continuing. "Then I want you to come to Vienna and stay."

Philippe's face flushed. "Oh, Angelique," he said, shaking his head as if it were a preposterous idea. "I couldn't."

"You have nothing here, Father," she said, glancing at the tattered furniture and bare necessities. "I have more crowns in the bank than I know what to do with. Please, allow me to share my life with you and give you the home you deserve."

With a hard line of his brow, he projected his pride. "But I don't want your money." He sounded offended by her offer.

Stubborn man, she complained inwardly. She raised her voice at him.

"Don't you dare be stubborn and bullheaded with me, Philippe Moreau." Jolene tightened her lips in protest. She wanted to shake him by the shoulders to bring some sense into his head. "Do you expect me to return home like an orphan, alone and without companionship to live my life in Vienna?" Tears stung her eyes over the thought. "I have been denied your presence for eighteen years. Now you want me to turn my back on you? How could you even think I could do such a thing?" Indignant and determined, she waited for him to respond.

Once again, her spunky attitude appeared to catch him off guard. Perhaps he had seen a part of himself in her fiery eyes as she stood there making her prideful demand for restoration. She realized at that moment that her own stubbornness of character must have come from Philippe's genes. Jolene almost laughed at her robust scolding.

"Well, if you put it that way," he answered with a smirk. "I suppose I better come along with you, or I'll be in trouble." He stepped forward, placed both of his hands on her shoulders, and looked affectionately into her eyes. "Are you sure?"

Jolene's spirited attitude melted at this touch. A broad smile spread across her face as she recognized his willingness to be at her side. "Yes, Father, very sure."

"Then, when do we leave?"

Jolene flung her arms around his neck and held him tightly.

Chapter 33

Parting is Such Sweet Sorrow

Jolene stood by the balcony and looked out over the city one last time. She never did get an opportunity to see everything that she wanted, but perhaps one day she would return. With everything packed and ready to go, the time had come to bid her goodbyes. Her heart ached thinking about it. The last few months had given her a family and drastically changed her life and that of others.

"My lady, they are waiting," Maria announced, walking into the suite

"All right," she relented, grabbing her purse. "Just give me a moment alone." Maria curtsied and left.

Jolene knew that one last task needed completion. As bizarre as it might appear to others, she felt compelled to do so before she departed. If it had not been for one woman who found the courage to confess the truth, none of this would have happened. She would have lived her life as someone else. Her father and mother would have continued to grieve, and a wonderful brother would have been lost to her forever. She closed her eyes and spoke in a low voice.

"Dorcas, I don't know if you can hear me, but I cannot leave without thanking you for telling me the truth. May your soul rest in peace."

Jolene had turned to leave, when unexpectedly a tug came at her heart. Everyone involved had come to a place of reconciliation, but one person remained forgotten.

"Jacquelyn," she said, "I forgive you for taking me from my parents. Your actions made me an instrument of reconciliation amongst my family. May you forgive them for your pain, too, and find eternal peace." Jolene pictured her in heaven with her unborn baby happy and loved. A tear trickled down her cheek, and Jolene quickly caught it with her hankie.

She inhaled a deep breath and composed herself before going downstairs. The footmen had finished loading their luggage, and in a few short minutes they would depart. Everyone stood in the foyer waiting for her arrival. She glanced at her father, and he smiled with anticipation etched upon his face. She knew in her heart that their life together would be everything she hoped.

When she glanced at her mother, she saw sorrow. Her eyes sparkled with tears. Jolene stepped forward and gave her a hug. "We will write, Mother, just as we talked about. There is plenty of time to get to know one another."

Suzette squeezed her tightly in return. "I hope someday we can be together again."

Jolene pulled back. "Of course, we will. I will travel back to Paris for holiday, and we can rent a townhome again. You can show me everything in the city that I missed."

She turned toward the duke who stood quietly watching. *Quite the man*, she joyfully mused. Robert stood next to his father, and the two of them looked so much alike it appeared comical.

"Thank you for what you've done to bring us together," she said.

"My pleasure," he responded with a warm smile.

For a moment, she wondered if she should hug him. Her eyes darted toward Robert, who gave a slight nod toward his father. She did as he suggested, and stepped forward putting her arms around him. He reciprocated for a few seconds and then pulled away.

Looking at Robert, she felt like bursting into laughter and then crying like a baby. "You already know how I feel about you, Robert. You have been my friend, support, and wonderful brother. I love you so much."

"Listen," he said, gruffly. "Don't try and make me cry." His own eyes glistened with moisture.

"Rascal," she said, giving him a wink.

"I'm a changed man," he quickly retorted. "And it's your fault."

"Iron sharpens iron, "she smiled.

He leaned into her ear for a private word. "I've been thinking, too, that I might court Grace when I return home and see where it leads."

Her eyes widened in approval. "Well, good for you. Please write and tell me all about it." She smirked and teased in return. "And I shall write Grace to find out if you are behaving."

They hugged each other for the last time. With difficulty, Jolene released him and stepped away. She turned toward Philippe. "Well, Father, it's time."

"Indeed," he said, offering his arm. He looked at the duke, Suzette, and Robert. "I'll take good care of her," he announced. "Perhaps one day soon we will see each other again."

He escorted her out the door to the waiting motorcar. She turned and looked at her family, who stood outside waving goodbye. One more glance would burn them into her memory.

"I love you," she said with tears in her eyes. They climbed inside, and the driver closed the door. Jolene felt as if she were leaving a part of her soul behind.

Her father sensed her struggle, reached over and took her hand. He patted it gently. "It won't be the last time, Angelique, that you'll see them."

"No, I think not," she said.

The car pulled away heading toward the train station. "Though I leave them behind, I have you," she reminded herself. "I won't be alone."

Philippe smiled and settled back into the seat keeping her hand in his. With one last glance, Jolene looked out the window and said goodbye to Paris.

It truly had been the city of light and love.

The End

The Legacy Series

For more information about *The Legacy Series*, updates on Book Four, and interesting historical facts woven into the series, visit http://legacyseriesbooks.blogspot.com. The series will be available on audio in early 2014 at Amazon, Audible, and iTunes.

About the Author

My publications include:

- *The Price of Innocence*
  (Book One – The Legacy Series)

- *The Price of Deception*
  (Book Two – The Legacy Series)

- *The Price of Love*
  (Book Three – The Legacy Series)

- *The Phantom of Valletta*
  (A continuation of Gaston Leroux's Phantom of the Opera)

- *Dark Persuasion*
  (Award-Winning Victorian Romance)

All books will be available on audio in 2014.

Author Links

For more information and updates on forthcoming publications, visit my websites at:

Website   http://vickihopkins.com

Facebook   https://www.facebook.com/Vicki.Hopkins.Author

Twitter   http://twitter.com/VHopkins_Author

Thank you for reading *The Legacy Series*.